Dare To Hold

Dare To Love
Book 1

Amber Nicole

Also by Amber Nicole

To every author and reader walking the hard road of setting one story down so you can pick up the one God is calling you to—I see you. I'm cheering for you. We're in this together.

Dear Reader,

Before you dive in, I want to take a moment to share a few things about the heart behind this story.

Dare to Hold is a clean Christian romance, filled with swoony moments, real struggles, and deep faith themes. It's a love story—but more than that, it's a story about grace. About redemption. About what it means to be loved by a God who meets us right where we are but refuses to leave us there.

You'll meet Ivy, a woman wrestling with shame, doubt, and the fear that she isn't "good enough" for faith—or for love. And Gray, a man who loves Jesus deeply but still struggles with control and temptation. Their story doesn't begin with perfect choices or easy answers. It begins in the mess. In the longing. In the questions.

You'll see flawed characters make mistakes. You'll watch them wrestle with conviction. And—my prayer—you'll watch them grow. Because this story reflects what I believe to be true: that God is patient, that He doesn't wait for us to be

Content Warnings

This story gently touches on the following themes:

- Past substance use and addiction
- Absent/neglectful parents
- Faith struggles and spiritual doubt
- Emotional and spiritual battles
- Mild romantic tension/temptation
- Brief mentions of alcohol

These elements are not graphic in nature, but they are noted here so readers can feel informed and safe before diving in.

Chapter 1
Ivy

"Your turn, Ivy."

Ugh, I hate this part.

It's a rule we made years ago: no skipping, no backing out. Just one simple game. One wild, sometimes embarrassing, always meaningful dare. One by one, we take turns. And unfortunately, I'm up next.

It started back in high school with Harper and me—two painfully shy girls in the small town of Ashen Mills, desperate to push past the edges of our comfort zones. Olivia joined us when we met in college at UNT Dallas. From asking for extra sprinkles in a British accent to serenading the barista with a Disney song—the dares have always been our thing.

They're more than a game now, though. They're a way to remind each other to live. To be bold. To stop waiting around and just go for it.

And sure, now that we're grown and allegedly mature, the stakes feel higher. The dares get bolder. Public, risky, and usually just mortifying enough to make me want to melt into the floor.

Which is why I already know I'm in trouble.

Because Harper is grinning like she's already picked the perfect dare.

And Olivia? She's just sipping her drink with that quiet smirk that always means she's in on the plan.

And me?

It's pretty clear I'm today's entertainment.

My stomach twists as I glance around the bustling city square. We're only in New Orleans for the weekend, a quick spring break girls' trip before reality sucks us back in. But it doesn't matter where we are, when it's my turn, I always feel the same: vulnerable.

I lift my glass of sweet tea and take a slow sip, hoping they'll go easy on me. Last time, they dared me to photobomb a group selfie. The girls thought it was hilarious. The bridal party I interrupted? Not so much.

"Alright, Ivy." Harper leans in, her eyes sparkling with trouble. "You ready?"

I force a weak smile. "Can I just buy someone a coffee? Compliment a stranger's shoes?"

"Nope," Olivia says, popping the p. "It's gotta be harder than that."

They scan the street, whispering as if they're choosing a victim. My pulse thunders in my ears as I watch their expressions light up as if they've spotted something. Or someone.

"There." Harper points across the street. "Go up to that guy and hold his hand."

I follow her gaze and instantly regret it.

He's standing near a street performer, one hand in his pocket, the other hanging loose at his side, as a guitarist strums a slow rock ballad. But it's not the music that grabs me—it's him.

Tall. Really tall. Dark hair, just messy enough to look like he didn't try but still somehow perfect. Light stubble brushes his jawline, sharp but not too much. His black T-shirt clings to a broad chest, sleeves casually pushed up to reveal arms covered in ink; bold lines, intricate patterns that trail down to his wrists. Faded jeans ride low on his hips, and a pair of battered Vans finishes the look. He shifts slightly, relaxed and completely unbothered, like the kind of guy who doesn't second-guess a single thing he does.

And the girls want me to go hold his hand.

"No way," I blurt out, shaking my head. "Pick someone else."

Harper grins. "Come on, Ivy. It's harmless."

"Are you insane?" My voice is half-whisper, half-squeak. "I don't just...walk up to guys like that."

"Exactly," Olivia says, like I just proved her point.

Harper leans in, her tone hushed and coaxing. "He's alone. It's not like he's with someone. Just walk up, take his hand for a few seconds, then walk away. That's it."

I try to swallow, but my mouth is dry. The thought of walking up to a complete stranger, especially this very specific stranger, and touching him makes my skin buzz with nerves. It's not just that he's hot. It's that he looks like someone who lives in a different world. Confident. Edgy. Unreachable. A guy who would never see a girl like me.

But my friends are watching. And worse—they're enjoying this.

"No. Nope. Not doing it," I say, arms crossed.

Harper raises a brow. "You made me sing karaoke stone-cold sober last night, remember?"

"That was different," I argue. "You have stage presence. I have...social anxiety and questionable judgment."

Olivia laughs quietly but doesn't push. She just gives me a look that says you can do this, even without words.

I let out a dramatic sigh. "Remind me again why we still do this?"

Harper reaches over and squeezes my arm. "Because comfort zones are boring and you, Ivy Taylor, are one yes away from something good."

I glance between them, already crumbling. I hate how well they know me.

I push my chair back, muttering under my breath. "If I trip, cry, or burst into flames, I'm blaming both of you."

Harper claps her hands. "That's the spirit!"

My legs feel like Jell-O as I stand. The city hums around me—laughter spilling from café tables, the distant honk of a car, the shimmer of a saxophone, a trumpet calling from somewhere down the block, and the steady heartbeat of drums weaving it all together. And somehow, every note feels like it's carrying me closer to him, like the entire city is in on the dare.

He hasn't noticed me. Not yet.

Good. Maybe I can get this over with before he even registers what's happening.

I reach him just as the song shifts, the melody softer now. My heart slams against my ribs. *Okay, Ivy. Just do it.*

Before I can overthink it, I close my eyes, take a breath...

And grab his hand.

The moment my fingers touch his, it's like flipping a switch. His hand is warm, and for a beat, he doesn't move. Then his fingers tighten around mine, deliberate and sure, which sends a jolt right through me.

I look up, and suddenly, the world spins.

His gaze is intense, unreadable, but not cold. No, it's

worse than that. It's curious. Focused. Like he sees right through me.

He's taller than I expected, towering over me in a way that makes me feel both tiny and completely seen. A ripple of cold works its way down my spine. There's something dangerous in the way he holds himself, all calm and confident, like nothing ever surprises him. And yet, there's a flicker of something softer in his eyes too, as if he is happy to see me.

We stay like that, locked in this odd, pulsing moment. His fingers are still laced with mine. The music in the background feels far away, secondary to the way his thumb brushes lightly against my hand, like he's not ready to let go.

I need to say something. Anything.

"I—uh—your hand is...big."

Oh my gosh. Why am I like this?

His lips twitch into a smirk, a slow amused curve that makes my stomach flip. He says nothing at first, just watches me with those midnight eyes. The silence stretches long enough for me to want to dissolve into the pavement. I try to pull away, but his grip tightens.

My heart stutters. "Um...are you gonna let go?"

He tilts his head, just a little, and there's that flicker again. Interest and a bit of amusement. "Do you want me to?"

I blink, completely thrown. What kind of question is that? And why, why does a tiny part of me whisper no?

He is so not the type of guy I normally go for. I'm a book-before-bed kind of girl—the one who'd rather spend Friday night curled up with a novel than out at some loud party. I like dependable. Quiet evenings with a blanket and tea. I'm the one who sends polite texts and overthinks my punctuation. The girl who feels more at home in a library than in a crowd. I like safe. I like predictable.

This man? He looks like a story with a twist ending. Tattoos and secrets. The type of man who walks straight into the storm because he knows he can handle it.

And I...I hate storms.

I clear my throat, my voice higher than usual. "Well, uh, this was fun. Good handshake. Solid...fingers. Okay. Bye."

I tug my hand free and step back, face flaming. But just as I turn to make my escape, his fingers wrap gently but firmly around my wrist.

I suck in a breath as he pulls me toward him. I nearly stumble into his chest, caught by surprise. He smells like leather and vanilla frosting, which is unfairly good.

"Have coffee with me," he says, like it's not a question at all.

I mean, it doesn't sound like a question. But it's not quite a command either. He acts like he already knows I'm going to say yes.

And the craziest thing? A tiny part of me wants to.

Which is absurd.

I open my mouth, but nothing coherent comes out. I should say no. Step back. Apologize for the weirdness and return to my friends with my dignity intact. But I just stand there, heart racing, caught between curiosity and caution.

"I..." I pause, blinking up at him. "I can't. I mean, thank you, but I'm here with my friends. It's a girls' trip, and we've got plans."

His gaze shifts, just briefly, over my shoulder to where the girls are clearly watching us. Olivia is grinning like a lunatic. Harper has both thumbs up like she's coaching me from the sidelines.

His eyes come back to mine, and there's something playful in his expression now.

"I don't think they'd mind," he says, voice low.

My laugh is a breathy and nervous sound. "I should probably check."

For a second, when I try to step back, he doesn't let go. Not in a controlling way, more like he's trying to decide something. His eyes search mine, and it's like he sees more than I want him to. My hesitation. My curiosity. My heart that is still bruised from the last time I took a chance.

Then, slowly, he lets go.

The absence of his hand is immediate. Sharp. Like stepping into cool air after being out in the scorching sun all day.

I exhale as I turn away, not sure if I'm coming back. But the thought of never seeing him again slams into me like a warning. It's absurd—I don't even know his name—but something in me rebels at the idea of walking away. It feels like I've stumbled into a chapter I was always meant to read, and if I close it now, I'll never find my way back to it.

I weave back through the crowd, my pulse still racing, the heat of his hand lingering against mine. By the time I reach our table, both girls are watching me like they're about to demand every detail, down to the punctuation. Harper narrows her eyes in suspicion, tilting her chin as if she's trying to read every detail on my face. Olivia's fingers drum against her glass, restless energy radiating off her as she leans forward, lips pressed tight to keep from blurting something first.

I stop in front of them, feeling their curiosity wrap around me.

"He wants to take me for coffee." The words feel surreal as they leave my lips.

Harper smacks the table with both hands. "Go!"

Olivia, the ever cautious one, blinks at me. "Wait, seriously? Ivy, we don't even know this guy."

"Shut up, Olivia," Harper says, rolling her eyes.

"Fine," Olivia huffs, crossing her arms. "Coffee is... acceptable. But keep your phone in your hand, not in your purse. And text us every five minutes."

"You don't have to text us," Harper says, her voice softer now. She reaches across the table, placing her hand over mine, which brings out her maternal side. "Just keep your phone close. But mostly? Just...have fun. You deserve it."

I glance between them, my heart fluttering like I'm fifteen again. Part of me wants to retreat into the safety of my comfort zone and lock the door. But another part—restless, unfamiliar, a little reckless—is already standing, ready to see what happens next.

I hesitate for just a beat longer, then glance back toward him.

He's still standing exactly where I left him, hands tucked in his pockets and his eyes locked on mine.

Like he was just waiting for me to walk up and grab his hand all day.

My feet move before my brain catches up, and before I know it, I'm standing beside him again.

He glances down at me with a half-smile. "Your hand's shaking a little."

"Crowds make me nervous," I admit.

His voice is light. "For the sake of public safety, I better hold your hand."

"Ok but just for stability," I echo.

He tilts his head, studying me like he's taking that in. Then his fingers brush mine, warm and sure, and my pulse trips. He catches my hand fully this time, the grip steady, protective.

"You hold on to me, I'll hold on to you," he says, voice low enough that it feels like a secret. "We'll call it stability… but between us, I just like having an excuse."

The air between us shifts. My lips curve, but my chest is too busy forgetting how to breathe to manage anything more than that.

"Come on," he says, and once again it's not a command, not exactly—it's an invitation.

We weave through the crowd, the sound of street music wrapping around us from every direction—brassy trumpet notes, the rhythmic beat of a drum, a saxophone's soulful cry. The air smells faintly of powdered sugar and roasting pecans, sweet and warm and a little dizzying.

I don't look back toward the girls. If I do, I might lose my nerve.

I sneak a glance up at him. He walks like he belongs to the moment. As if the chaos of the world simply parts around him.

Meanwhile, I'm practically vibrating with nerves. Every brush of his arm sends a spark to my fingertips. Every inhale catches halfway in my chest.

What is happening to me?

I don't do things like this. I don't follow strangers down crowded streets. I'm the girl who makes lists. Who plays it safe. Who plans everything down to the minute.

And yet, here I am, walking beside a man who makes my heart race like it already knows him.

"So…" I manage, my voice quieter than I mean it to be. "Do I get to know your name before we get coffee?"

His lips twitch, just barely. "Gray."

Of course. A name like that belongs to a man like him.

Gray.

It suits the way he carries himself with that calm, quiet intensity.

"It's short for Grayson," he adds, then glances at me. "But don't call me that."

I almost smile at how quickly he says it. Not angry just, final. Like it belongs to a different version of him. A chapter he doesn't open often.

"Got it," I say, tucking the information away. "Gray."

He looks at me again, eyes flicking down to meet mine like he's weighing the way I say it. There's something searching in his gaze, like maybe he's not used to people really seeing him.

I should be unnerved by how naturally we fall into step. But I'm not.

We pass a violinist on the corner, and I notice Gray dip his hand into his pocket and quietly drop a few bills into the open case. He says nothing about it. Just keeps walking, like kindness is a habit he doesn't feel the need to advertise.

It sticks with me.

He doesn't just look good. He seems good.

"You got a name," he says suddenly, "or am I just supposed to call you hand-holding stranger forever?"

I laugh, caught off guard. "It's Ivy."

He repeats it slowly, as if trying it on. "Ivy."

My name has never sounded like that before.

We turn the corner, and a coffee shop comes into view— tucked between a narrow bookstore and a flower shop spilling color onto the sidewalk. Twinkle lights drape lazily across the awning, and window boxes overflow with blooms, petals brushing the glass as if they're leaning toward the sunlight.

The air is a heady mix of espresso and roses, warm and sweet—like a memory I'll want to keep.

Even with our hands linked, he walks close enough that I can feel the heat of him, every step syncing with mine. It's ridiculous how a simple touch can make my pulse trip over itself.

I sneak a glance up at him. He's watching the street ahead like he owns it—like the crowd parts because he's here.

"You're quiet," he says suddenly, voice low, certain.

I shrug, pretending his nearness isn't short-circuiting my brain. "I'm just...taking it all in."

One corner of his mouth tips up. "Taking me in, you mean?"

Heat crawls up my neck. "Wow. Modest, aren't you?"

"Not modest," he says, eyes flicking down to mine for half a beat. "Just observant." His gaze drops to our joined hands. "Like the way you haven't let go."

"I told you—stability," I counter, tightening my grip just to prove a point.

"Uh-huh." His tone says he doesn't buy it. "Whatever helps you sleep at night, Ivy."

The way he says my name—it's not casual. It's deliberate. Weighted. My stomach flips.

"What?" I ask, my voice barely above the hum of the saxophone.

His lips twitch as if he's holding something back. "Nothing." He holds my gaze for one breath too long before looking ahead again.

We reach the door, and he steps forward to hold it open. "After you, Ivy."

The way he says it, it feels like a promise.

As I step inside, I can't help but wonder if this moment is the beginning of everything I never saw coming.

Chapter 2
Ivy

The scent of espresso and buttery pastries hits me the second we step inside the coffee shop. It's cozy, all warm wood tones and the low hum of indie music. A chalkboard menu hangs above the counter, and an array of eclectic seating fills the space. It reminds me of my favorite coffee shop back home.

Gray pauses beside me, scanning the room with a thoughtful hum before heading toward a small table in the corner. He pulls out a chair and gives me a quick smile. "Ladies first."

I blink at him. "Chivalry? In the wild?"

He grins, and something in me unwinds a little. "What can I say? I'm full of surprises."

I sit as he takes the seat across from me. Thank goodness. I'm not sure I could handle him sitting next to me, not with how my brain short-circuits every time he moves.

"So," he says, folding his hands on the table, "are you always this nervous around guys who you randomly approach on the sidewalk, or am I just special?"

My jaw drops. "I am not nervous."

He tilts his head, eyes playful. "Really? Because you've already rearranged the sugar packets like...three times."

I look down. Yep. I've made a perfect little lineup of raw sugar, Stevia, and Splenda.

I nudge them aside with a groan. "Okay, maybe a little nervous."

"Don't be," he says, and his tone softens. "This isn't a job interview. There are no wrong answers...unless you order decaf."

That makes me laugh, and just like that, the knot in my chest loosens a little more.

He glances toward the counter. "What's your coffee order?"

"Vanilla oat milk latte," I answer without hesitation.

"Got it." He nods like he's committing it to memory.

As he heads toward the register, I pull out my phone. A quick text to Harper and Olivia.

IVY

Still alive. Still holding hands. Now there's coffee involved

I set my phone back in my bag, unable to resist watching him instead.

He stands there with that unhurried ease, one hand in his pocket, the other gesturing as he talks to the barista. His thumb brushes his jaw, then his chin, like he's working something out in his head. He sways slightly while he waits, shoulders relaxed, head tilted so the light catches in his dark hair.

Then, as if he can feel my gaze on him, he glances over his shoulder. Our eyes meet. A pause. A smirk. And then—a slow, deliberate wink that knocks the breath right out of my lungs.

I quickly look away, pretending I'm not grinning like I've lost all self-control.

A moment later, he's back, setting my latte in front of me before sliding into the seat across from mine, his coffee in hand.

I tilt my head, curious. "What'd you get?"

"Black coffee," he says without hesitation. "It's the only way to go."

I make a face, wrapping my hands around my latte. "Only way for who? Cavemen?"

His mouth quirks into a grin. "Nah. For people with taste."

I lift my cup in mock offense. "This is taste."

He chuckles, the tension easing as our cups clink lightly against each other.

There's something about him. Sure, he's handsome in a sharp, unfair kind of way, but it's more than that. He has this calmness, like nothing rattles him. Like he trusts the moment, even if he doesn't know where it's going. It makes me want to lean in and ask questions.

"So," I say, placing my hands in my lap in an attempt to stop fidgeting, "you from around here?"

He shakes his head. "Nah. I'm just visiting."

I wait for more, but he doesn't offer it, just stares at me like he's got all the time in the world.

"Are you always this mysterious?"

"Only on Fridays," he says without missing a beat.

I snort. "Lucky me."

He leans in slightly, elbow on the table, like we're already old friends. "Okay, your turn. Why New Orleans?"

"My friends and I do a yearly girls' trip," I say. "This year, we picked this beautiful city. Beignets, jazz, good food, what's not to love?"

"Solid choice," he says, nodding. "And I'm guessing I was a...spontaneous addition to the itinerary?"

My cheeks flush. "Yeah, I didn't exactly plan on grabbing a stranger's hand today."

Gray raises a brow, amused. "Really? Because you did it like a pro."

I cover my face with one hand, groaning. "It was just a dare."

Gray leans back in his chair, lips quirking like he's not buying it. "Was it?"

I open my mouth to answer, then close it again. My pulse does this weird skip, and I suddenly forget how words work.

Gray watches me with a quiet curiosity, his elbow propped on the table, fingers brushing his jaw.

"You sure you're not scared?" he asks, voice light, teasing. "Because you're blinking like someone just told you your coffee was decaf."

I let out a breathy laugh. "Okay, maybe I am a little nervous."

He grins. "Good. That makes two of us."

My eyes widen. "You? Nervous?"

He shrugs, like it's no big deal. "Well, not right now. But you should've seen me when you grabbed my hand. I thought maybe I was getting pickpocketed by the world's sweetest-looking criminal."

I laugh, tension melting off my shoulders. "You're hilarious."

"Possibly," he says. "But also charming, right?"

I shake my head, smiling despite myself. "That's still up for debate."

He grins, then glances down at his cup. "You know, I

wasn't sure if you were going to come here with me. You looked like you might bolt."

"I thought about it," I admit.

His eyes meet mine again, warmer now. "I'm glad you didn't."

The words settle somewhere low in my stomach.

I clear my throat. "You're just...a little intimidating."

Gray looks genuinely surprised. "Me?"

I gesture toward him. "You've got that whole 'tall, dark, and probably-rides-a-motorcycle' vibe. And the tattoos? Definitely don't help."

He laughs, a full, easy sound that turns heads in the café. "I'll have you know, I've never even ridden a motorcycle."

"I bet you own a leather jacket though," I tease.

"Guilty." He pauses, then adds with a wink, "Though I'm still missing someone to steal it and never give it back."

I grin. "So, you're only moderately intimidating."

"Moderately attractive too, I assume?"

The question catches me off guard. My cheeks heat instantly, and I look down, smiling into my coffee.

Gray leans in just a little, voice low but still soft. "You don't have to answer. Your face is saying enough."

I peek up at him, trying not to smile, but fail big time.

Then he lifts his hand and gently taps under my chin, coaxing my gaze back to his.

"I like you, Ivy," he says simply. "I wasn't expecting this spontaneous date to happen today, but here we are."

There's no pressure in the way he says it. No intensity, no edge. Just honesty, and maybe a tiny spark of hope.

My heart does that fluttery thing again, but this time, it's not fear. It's curiosity. It's excitement. It's the unmistakable thrill of being seen and liked.

I look at him for a beat longer than I probably should.

And then I smile. "I might like you too."

I lean back; fingers wrapped around my mug. "Okay, wait—you don't have a girlfriend, do you?"

Gray's brows lift, a slow grin tugging at his mouth. "Why? You jealous?"

My face heats. "No! I just...I mean, you grabbed my hand too. Technically."

He chuckles, leaning in slightly, his eyes warm and teasing. "For the record, you grabbed mine first."

"Technicalities," I mumble, swirling my coffee, hoping he can't see how fast my heart's racing.

Gray tips his head. "If I had a girlfriend, do you think I'd be here with you?"

And just like that, the world tilts, the coffee forgotten, and I fall harder than I ever meant to.

We fall into an easy rhythm, and it feels so rare and effortless.

We keep talking, drifting from one topic to the next like we've known each other for more than just a coffee and a dare. The conversation drifts from our favorite snacks to the worst movies we've ever seen, then somehow back to our childhood dreams. Gray listens like no one has ever listened to me, with real focus. He asks questions, not just to fill the air, but because he genuinely wants to know.

"So, what did little Ivy want to be when she grew up?" he asks, leaning back like he's settling in for a good story.

I laugh. "A baker. I had this whole plan to drive a cupcake truck around town, handing out happiness one sprinkle at a time."

"Cupcake truck? That's adorable," he says, grinning. "You'd have been famous."

I nudge his foot under the table. "Okay, your turn. Let me guess...rockstar?"

His smile tilts, a little sheepish but proud. "Bingo." He glances down at his hands for a second before meeting my eyes again. "But I didn't necessarily want the fame. I just loved the way music could say what I never could."

This has me admitting I have a soft spot for early 2000s boy bands, and I give a whole spiel about how they got me through my middle school years.

"You're serious?" he asks, nearly choking on his drink.

"Dead serious," I say, sipping smugly. "Backstreet Boys over NSYNC, obviously."

"I can't believe we're having this conversation."

I lean in, smirking. "Don't act like you didn't have a favorite."

"I absolutely didn't," he insists, though his mouth is twitching.

"Liar."

And just like that, we're both laughing. It's real, honest laughter that fills the space between us. It's easy. Fun. The kind of moment that feels like it could stretch on forever if you let it.

And when I catch my breath, I swear something in Gray's face changes. It softens. Like he's just as surprised by how right this feels as I am.

But eventually, the moment begins to settle. I glance at my empty cup, wishing it wasn't.

I look up and he's already watching me.

My heart gives a small, unexpected tug. I don't want to go.

And judging by the quiet shift in his posture, the way his fingers tap restlessly on the table, I don't think he wants me to either.

The air thickens, not with tension, but with possibility.

Then, my phone rings, shattering the spell.

I jump, fumbling in my bag until Olivia's name glows on the screen.

I glance back at Gray, almost apologetically.

He meets my gaze, then gives a soft, understanding nod —like he already knows I'm about to ruin something we were just beginning.

I answer, slower than necessary. "Hey, Liv."

"Just checking you're still alive," she says dramatically. "Cough twice if the hot stranger has you tied to a chair."

"I'm fine," I say, smiling despite myself, twirling the edge of my sleeve just to give my hands something to do.

"Well, in case you forgot, girls' weekend is still a thing. Dinner in two hours. Harper and I are headed back to the hotel to change."

"Right." I hesitate, eyes drifting back to Gray and staying there a beat too long. "I'll be there soon."

I hang up. But I don't move.

Because if I stand, this moment ends—and some irrational part of me is already terrified of not getting it back.

Gray's gaze holds mine, which isn't making this any easier.

"I should go," I say at last, the words catching somewhere between my chest and my throat.

He offers a small smile, one that doesn't quite reach his eyes. "Yeah. I get it."

We stand, though I'm fairly certain my body is staging a slow-motion protest. I follow him out of the coffee shop into the golden warmth of the New Orleans afternoon. The streets hum with life—tourists meandering past locals, a saxophone wailing from a nearby corner, the sweet scent of beignets mixing with something spicy and rich in the air.

We step out into the warmth, the late afternoon light catching on his hair. He glances down at me, still holding the door open until I'm clear, then falls into step beside me.

"Which way am I walking you?" he asks, like it's a given that he's not letting me go alone.

"The Belle Maison," I say. "It's about three blocks from here."

He nods once, like that settles it, and then his hand slips into mine—like it's the most natural thing in the world. My pulse trips over itself.

And it's completely undoing me.

I don't look at him, I can't. Because if I do, I'm afraid he'll see exactly how much this tiny gesture has knocked the air out of my lungs. Instead, I focus on the rhythm of our steps.

After a few strides, he glances down, a hint of a smirk pulling at his mouth. "Crowds make you nervous," he says casually, "but I'm starting to think you get quiet when you're trying not to smile."

My head snaps toward him. "That's not true."

The corner of his mouth kicks up. "Oh, it's true. You're doing it right now."

I roll my eyes, but I can't fight the smile that edges in anyway.

"See?" he says, giving my hand a little squeeze. "Knew I could get one out of you."

And just like that, we're moving down a narrow side street draped in hanging plants and the soft hum of music spilling from an open doorway. His thumb brushes against mine in an absentminded rhythm that feels anything but accidental.

"So," I say, glancing up at him, "since you're apparently not a local, what do you think of New Orleans?"

He shrugs. "It's alright."

I gasp. "Alright?"

Gray chuckles. "I mean, it's cool. The food's great. The history's wild. But the humidity?" He shudders. "Criminal."

I laugh. "Okay, fair." I glance around at the bright awnings and moss-draped balconies. "It has a certain kind of magic, though, doesn't it? Like, there's something about this place that makes you want to believe in...I don't know, fate?"

He doesn't answer right away. When I look up, he's already watching me.

"Ivy," he says softly, "I think you want to believe in fate."

I start to reply with some quick comeback, but the words vanish.

Because maybe he's right.

Maybe I do.

Before I can untangle the flutter in my chest, we reach the hotel. The tall building rises behind me, its glass doors gleaming. We stop just outside, the noise of the street blurring around us.

Neither of us moves.

We just...linger.

The silence between us is charged with something we're both too aware of.

Then, Gray steps closer.

Before I can think, his arms are around me.

I don't hesitate. I sink into him like I've been waiting for this all day. Maybe longer.

His chest rises beneath my cheek. I breathe him in, that oddly satisfying mix of leather and vanilla. My hands hover at his sides, then curl into the fabric of his shirt, holding on.

His breath brushes my ear, low and teasing. "I'm glad you grabbed my hand today, Ivy."

My pulse stumbles.

"Even if it was a little creepy."

A laugh bursts out of me, warm and unwilling, and I swat his arm. "You're the worst."

That grin—wide, easy—breaks across his face like he just won something. But then it softens, the edges blurring into something quieter. Deeper.

We don't move. The city spills on around us—laughter, music, the clink of glasses—but it feels like we're sealed inside our own moment, suspended in the air between us.

His gaze drops briefly to my hand, and for a second, I swear he almost reaches for it again. My heart hammers in anticipation...but then his fingers flex at his side, like he's decided against it.

Something unspoken passes between us—something that says we could make this more, could close the gap—but neither of us does.

I swallow. "Bye, Gray."

He holds my gaze, eyes catching the sunlight, and his voice dips low. "Bye, Ivy."

I turn toward the hotel, but my steps drag, each one heavier than the last. And when I dare a glance over my shoulder, he's still there, hands in his pockets, watching me go.

It's not until I disappear inside that I let out the breath I'd been holding—because the thought of never seeing him again doesn't feel small. It feels like a door closing that I wasn't even ready to walk through.

Chapter 3
Ivy

The elevator lurches upward, a slow crawl that feels like it's carrying me straight into some kind of heartbreak I didn't see coming.

I lean back against the cool metal wall, palms damp, my pulse still pounding in my ears. Holy moly.

I didn't get his number.

I don't know his last name.

I don't know where he lives.

The realization hits in waves, each one a little sharper, a little more ridiculous. My hands curl into fists at my sides, not because I'm angry—though maybe I should be—but because I feel unsteady. Like I've just been handed a rare book and told I have to give it back before I've even read the first chapter.

What was I thinking? That we'd just...magically cross paths again?

The elevator dings, jolting me back to reality. I step out, moving down the hallway at a snail's pace as I approach the room I share with my two best friends.

I stop in front of the door, key card in hand.

I'm not ready. Not ready to see Harper's raised brows or Olivia's knowing smirk. Not ready to relive every detail while they dissect it like a true crime podcast.

And yet...

I press my forehead to the door for just a second, letting the weight of the day settle in my chest. Because as much as I want to hide, I need them. I need the comfort of their voices, the easy banter, the way they can make even my worst day feel like an inside joke worth telling.

Taking a breath, I swipe the card, the green light flashing, and push the door open.

Two heads snap toward me instantly, like I've just walked into a press conference.

Harper—her long, bright red hair practically glowing under the warm hotel lighting—nearly trips over a half-zipped suitcase as she scrambles off the bed. She's all urgency and momentum, like she's been pacing the walls waiting for me.

Olivia moves slower, more deliberate. Her sleek blonde hair is tucked behind one ear, her expression calm but her eyes...they're searching. Eager. Like she wants every single detail, but she's willing to wait until I'm ready to give it.

Harper gets to me first.

"What happened? Where'd you go? Was it good? Was he nice? Did you talk about anything important? Did you laugh? Did you—"

"Harper." My voice is half-laugh, half-breathless as I lift my hands in surrender. "Slow down."

But I can't keep up with her questions. The words blur together, buzzing in my ears until something slips past my guard—a tear I didn't even feel coming, sliding down my cheek.

That's when Olivia reaches me. She brushes the tear

away gently with her thumb, her touch cool and steady in a way that makes my chest ache.

"Come on," she says softly.

They each grab an arm, steering me toward the bed until I'm collapsing backward with a muted thump. The mattress dips beneath me, their knees pressing into the edge as they lean in, two different energies wrapped around the same unshakable love—Harper's effervescent fire and Olivia's quiet anchor.

And just like that, the dam starts to crack.

The hot water pours over me, streaming down my neck and shoulders in steady rivulets, but it does nothing to wash away the ache in my chest. Steam thickens the air, curling around me until the world beyond the glass feels far away. I brace my palms against the cool tile, head bowed, eyes closed.

And then I'm not in the hotel shower anymore. I'm back in that charged moment when Gray's fingers slid under my chin, tilting my face up. His touch was barely there, yet it pinned me in place, left me nowhere to hide. I can still feel the warmth of his skin, the quiet command in his gaze—like he could see past every defense I've ever built.

And the thought strikes hard, almost enough to steal my breath.

What if that was the only time I'll ever feel it?

I like you, Ivy.

A shiver ripples down my spine despite the heat.

Did that really happen?

I exhale sharply, tilting my head back under the spray, letting the water drown out the frantic rhythm of my thoughts. Maybe I imagined it. Maybe I've finally let these dares from Olivia and Harper get to my head.

Because never in my life has a dare led to something that turned my world upside down.

But this one did.

And the worst part? It's over just as quickly as it began.

I lather shampoo into my hair, working through the tangles as my thoughts churn. Years of silly challenges like singing in a busy room, ordering the weirdest thing on a menu, sneaking notes to boys we crushed on in the past. But none of those moments lingered. None of them carved out space in my chest the way Gray just did.

I rinse the suds away, eyes squeezing shut as regret presses behind my ribs.

We didn't swap numbers. Didn't even follow each other on social media.

He's just...gone.

I press my lips together as I scrub my skin with body wash, like maybe I can wash the ache away too. But the truth won't budge.

Gray shifted something in me, though I couldn't tell you what. All I know is, the girl who woke up this morning isn't the same one standing here now.

Maybe that's the worst part.

Still wrapped in thought, I step out of the shower, dry off and pull on a fluffy hotel robe. Laughter bubbles from the bedroom, the familiar sound grounding me back to reality.

Just outside the door, the energy buzzes.

Olivia stands in front of the mirror, a vision with her blonde hair falling in effortless waves that somehow look both glamorous and low maintenance. She's the kind of natural beauty who turns heads without trying, her serious expression at odds with the bold dresses in her hands—one deep red silk, the other glittering silver with a plunging neckline.

"I can't decide which one," she sighs. "This is our last night. We have to go out with a bang."

On the bed, Harper snorts, her red hair already escaping the messy bun she'd half-heartedly attempted. The fiery strands match the spark in her personality—quick, unapologetic.

"Go with the silver," Harper says without hesitation. "That neckline will stop traffic." She tilts her head, then smirks. "Although, if we're aiming for subtle, you might blind someone under the streetlights."

Olivia laughs, holding the dress up to herself in the mirror. "Subtle is overrated."

Their laughter fades when their eyes drift back to me. For a beat, neither says anything—just this quiet, almost sympathetic pause, like they can still feel the weight of what I told them about Gray.

Harper straightens, breaking the moment with a bright grin. "Okay. Tonight's mission? Fancy dinner first, then we hit Bourbon Street like we actually know how to have fun. No moping allowed."

Olivia sets the silver dress down and turns toward me, her lips curving into something softer. "Who knows? Maybe we'll see him while we're out tonight?"

The thought sends a little spark through me before I can help it, chasing away some of the heaviness in my chest. "Maybe," I say, trying to sound casual, but my voice comes out a touch too hopeful.

Harper pats the space beside her on the bed. "Come on, love-struck, sit before I start dragging you."

I sink down next to her, the mattress dipping under our combined weight, and for the first time since I left the coffee shop, I feel like I can breathe again.

I flop back onto my hands, my voice coming out flatter than I mean it to. "I don't know if I feel like going out tonight."

Harper gasps like I've just suggested canceling Christmas. "Do you have any idea what I'm walking into next week?" She throws her hands up. "Twenty-five kindergartners who forgot how to sit in a circle and think glue sticks are a food group. I need this last night of spring break."

Olivia sets the silver dress down and turns toward me, her lips curving into something softer. "And what about you, Ivy? Are you excited to be free from your boring desk job?"

I shrug, fiddling with the zipper on my cosmetic bag. "I don't know. I mean, freelancing full-time was the plan eventually. I've got a couple of clients lined up, but it still feels surreal. Like I'm either on the verge of something amazing or a total disaster."

"You're brave," Harper says softly, with that same blend of admiration and concern she always uses when I leap without a plan. "But it's going to be good. I can feel it."

I sigh and perch on the edge of the bed.

Olivia perks up. "It's going to be amazing. You're insanely talented. And now you can work in your pajamas and design from cafes in Italy if you want."

"That's the dream," I say softly. "Right now, it's mostly designing real estate brochures and logos for dog grooming salons."

"Hey," Harper says, raising a finger. "Those dogs need solid branding."

Laughter ripples again, and for a second, the ache in my chest dulls.

Olivia plops onto the edge of the bed, both dresses pooled in her lap. "We are all starting new chapters next week."

"Are you ready for your new title?" Harper asks her.

Olivia nods, then lets out a deep breath. "Yeah. No more supervision, no more paperwork hoops. I'm officially full-time at the practice starting Monday morning."

"That's amazing," I say. "You've worked so hard for this."

She shrugs, but her smile is proud. "Thanks. I just hope I'm ready. It's one thing to be the intern. It's another to have people fully trusting you with their mess."

"You've been helping people for years," Harper says, sitting up straighter. "Now you're just getting paid more for it."

Olivia laughs. "Spoken like a true teacher who deserves three times her paycheck."

Harper grins. "Don't I know it."

There's a moment of soft silence, that only happens between friends who've grown up and grown close, where no one feels the need to fill the space.

Then Olivia lifts both dresses again with a dramatic flourish. "Alright. Therapy talk over. Now which one of these says I might be a licensed mental health professional, but I also deserve to turn heads on our last night in New Orleans?"

"That silver one," I say, pointing. "Even though we all know you could make a grown man cry in sweatpants."

Harper stretches out on the bed, looping an arm around my shoulders with a grin.

"Come on. Let's put you in a dress that says, I'm definitely not spiraling over a guy I just met."

"More like, I barely remember his name...even though I've replayed every second of that coffee date in my head." Olivia adds, her lips quirking.

I groan, but I'm smiling now. "You guys are seriously the worst."

Harper lifts a brow. "Says the girl who's been overthinking a five-minute hand-hold like it was a marriage proposal."

I grab a pillow and launch it at her face.

And just like that, the moment shifts. The weight on my chest eases. It's not gone, but it's manageable. Maybe I'll never see Gray again. Maybe that's okay. Or maybe, just maybe...fate isn't done with us yet.

But for tonight, I have my girls.

And that might be enough.

Dinner is a blur of laughter, clinking glasses and plates being passed around the table. For the first time all day, I let myself forget. I forget about the way Gray looked at me. The way his touch lingered just a second too long. The way my heart ached as I walked away.

Instead, I let myself live in this moment with my best friends on our annual trip, before it ends, and we go back to real life.

Harper's leaning halfway across the table, fork in hand,

trying to steal a bite of Olivia's dessert. Olivia smacks her hand away without even looking.

"Get your own, thief," she says, eyes still glued to her phone. "This was the last bread pudding on the menu, and I earned it."

Harper pouts. "You earned it? You've been glued to your client emails all day."

"I've worked too hard to go full-time and not check in," Olivia says, finally putting her phone down. "Next week I'll have no supervision. I'm allowed to panic."

Harper grins. "You'll be amazing. And don't worry I'll send you emotional support texts when my class of tiny gremlins launches full chaos at me."

"I still think you deserve combat pay," Olivia says, raising her glass.

"She's a hero," I agree. "Trying to convince five-year-olds to sit still and not eat glue? Saint-level patience."

Harper laughs. "You're both dramatic. But I will take outfit help for the first day. I need to look calm and collected, even when a kid throws up on my shoes."

"I've got you," Olivia says, smirking. "Something that says, 'warm and approachable' but also 'don't test me.'"

"You've nailed that vibe," I add.

"And you," Harper says, turning to me. "Freelance Ivy. How's it feel knowing you are about to be your own boss?"

I lift a shoulder, smiling. "Terrifying. But also, kind of amazing."

"I still can't believe you quit," Olivia says, eyes softening. "That was a big move."

"It was time," I say, exhaling. "I got tired of designing for people who didn't care. Now I get to pick my projects and avoid meetings that should've been emails. Honestly? Feels like freedom."

By the time we're walking along Bourbon Street, exhaustion starts creeping in. The neon lights blur together, and the pulse of music from every bar vibrates through my body.

"We aren't in our early twenties anymore, are we?" Harper groans.

"Nope," Olivia yawns dramatically. "It's like, the day after I turned twenty-five, my body just gave up on staying awake past ten o'clock."

"Honestly, same," I add. "I only had one drink and now I need a nap and a neck massage."

We all laugh, a little too loud.

Harper gestures toward a bar with a live jazz band playing in the corner. "Let's sit for a bit. I need to rest before I drop dead in the middle of the street."

We all agree, weaving our way through the crowd until we find an open table. I sigh as I sink into the chair, letting the hum of conversation and the smooth sound of the saxophone wash over me.

"I could live here," Olivia says, sipping a daiquiri. "Beignets for breakfast, daiquiris for dinner, jazz on every corner."

"You'd be broke in a week," Harper says.

"Details." Olivia waves her off. "I'd start a TikTok series. Something like Single Girl in New Orleans. It'd go viral."

I laugh. "You'd have local sponsorships by day two."

And for a moment, just a moment, I've completely forgotten about what happened earlier today.

Until a deep, smooth voice from behind me sends a shockwave through my spine.

"Can I buy you a drink?"

My heart stops.

Time slows as I turn, my fingers tightening around my glass. A tall, dark, and devastatingly handsome man towers over me, his presence commanding.

But as my eyes trail up his frame, drinking in broad shoulders, sharp cheekbones, and dark eyes that gleam under the dim lights...

It isn't Gray.

And the realization hits me like a wrecking ball.

"No, thanks," I say, maybe a little too harshly.

The stranger shrugs, giving me a lazy smirk before sauntering off. But when I turn back, I'm met with two pairs of wide, knowing eyes.

"Oh, girl. You have it bad," Harper says, shaking her head.

Olivia raises an eyebrow. "Who turns down free drinks from a guy that hot?"

"Only someone who already has her heart set on someone else," Harper adds, sipping her drink like she's just cracked the biggest mystery of the night.

"I hate all of you," I groan, dropping my head onto the table.

"Sure you do," Olivia sings, tossing a napkin at me. "Drink up, babe. You're in love with a stranger, and we still have leftover beignets to eat before bed."

They just laugh, and I can't help but smile along with them, because we all know the truth.

Gray might be gone.

But he's far from forgotten.

Chapter 4
Gray
3 Months Later

Early mornings in Dallas are my favorite. Before the traffic builds on Elm Street, before the sidewalks buzz with office workers clutching to-go cups, before life feels like it's moving faster than I can keep up with.

My hands are shoved in the pockets of my leather jacket as I walk my usual route to Royal Brew, the coffee shop I've been coming to for years. Routine keeps me grounded. And Lord knows, if I don't keep my routine, that's when the doubt creeps in.

I push open the café door, the scent of fresh coffee wrapping around me like a familiar embrace. The line is longer than usual, the buzz of the room flooding me like a song lyric. Pulling out my phone, I start typing notes.

When the morning breaks, Your mercy's new
You walked the fire just to carry me through
My hearts still bruised, but You hold it whole
You never let go, You never let go.

I'm lost in it, fingers flying over the screen, so deep in thought that the world around me fades.

Until I hear a voice.

"Can I get a vanilla oat milk latte, please?"

My fingers still. My brain blanks.

I know that voice.

My jaw goes slack as I snap my head up, eyes locking on the woman ordering her coffee. She's standing a couple of spots ahead, small in frame but holding herself like she's trying to take up less space. One hand grips the strap of her bag, the other tucks a piece of hair behind her ear even though it's already in place. Her weight shifts from one foot to the other. She's full of nervous energy, but her spine is straight, like she's willing herself to stand tall.

Her hair's just like I remember—dark, loose waves spilling halfway down her back, the ends brushing the curve of her waist. Even from here, I catch the faintest trace of a floral blend when the air moves between us. And I don't need to see her face to know.

Ivy.

I'm frozen.

She pays, slipping a bill into the tip jar, and steps aside to wait for her drink. My heart slams against my ribs, my pulse roaring in my ears.

Is Ivy really here? In Dallas?

What do I do? What do I say?

My fingers twitch at my sides, my mind scrambling for some kind of logical explanation. This can't be real. For three months, all I've thought about is her. That one day in New Orleans, that random moment that somehow altered the entire course of my life. I told myself it was just a fleeting thing, that I'd forget about her eventually. But I never did.

I kept replaying that afternoon like a song stuck on a loop.

The way she grabbed my hand, how a single touch from a stranger managed to shake something loose in me. The way she laughed, wide open and unguarded. The way she looked at me, like I wasn't just some broody, intimidating guy.

People usually make up their minds about me before I even open my mouth. I mean, I get it. The tattoos, my wardrobe consisting of mostly black clothes, the dark hair. I'm used to the assumptions. Used to being misunderstood.

But Ivy, she was different.

Even if she was a little unsure at first, she saw through the rough edges in a matter of minutes. And somehow, that scared me more than anything.

For three months, I've been wondering what would've happened if I had asked for her number. If I had chased after her when she walked away. If I had done something, anything, to keep her in my life.

But I didn't. And now, by some impossible twist of God's timing, she's here.

"Sir?"

I blink, the memory shattering as I snap back to the present. The barista is staring at me expectantly.

Crap.

It's my turn to order.

"Just a black coffee," I say, my voice rougher than I expected.

The barista nods and rings me up, but my mind is elsewhere. My eyes flick to the spot where Ivy had been standing waiting on her drink, only to find it empty.

She's gone.

Panic grips me. Did I just miss my chance?

I grab my coffee as soon as it's placed on the counter, barely hearing the barista call out my name. My head swivels, scanning the café, my heart hammering in my chest.

And then, I see her.

She's tucked into the corner by the window, fingers curled around her cup like she's soaking up the warmth. The light spills across her face, catching on eyes I'd swear are brighter than I remember—soft, searching, impossible to look away from. She's not wearing much makeup, but she doesn't need it. Her skin is clear, her lips full, the kind of natural beauty you can't fake. Her shoulders are relaxed now, the earlier nerves gone, but there's still a quietness about her, like she doesn't realize she's drawing every bit of my focus.

At the same time, she looks up, her gaze locking with mine.

Her lips part in shock.

Everything else falls away. The noise of the café, the clatter of mugs, the buzz of conversation—it all fades into nothing. It's just her and me.

I can hear the song lyrics forming in my head.

Met you in the middle of a moment I didn't see coming
Your hand in mine like a spark in the dark

Something, an invisible force, a magnetic pull, draws me forward.

Three months, and I've thought about her every single day. I'd be mid-song on a Sunday morning and catch myself picturing the way she laughed in New Orleans, the way she tilted her head when she was trying not to smile. I can still see her standing in the middle of that crowded street—confident and shy all at once—and how I couldn't stop staring at her lips, fighting the urge to close the distance right then and there.

I told myself it was just a moment. One of those once-in-a-lifetime encounters you look back on but never get to repeat. But here she is.

And I'm not the kind of man who believes God wastes moments like this.

Before I realize it, I'm standing at her table. Then, without thinking, without asking, I sit down across from her.

Silence stretches between us, thick with something unspoken.

She's real. She's here.

And this time, I'm not letting her go.

I lean forward, resting my forearms on the small café table, still trying to convince myself this moment is real.

Ivy blinks a few times, like she's doing the same. Then, slowly, a smile tugs at the corner of her lips. "Gray?"

"Hey, you." The words slip out softer than I mean them to, like any louder might shatter the moment and send her disappearing.

She exhales a breathy laugh and shakes her head. "I—I can't believe it's you."

"Believe it." My mouth curves into a smirk, my confidence kicking in. "Unless you regularly run into guys you once picked up on a dare?"

She groans, covering her face for a second before peeking at me through her fingers. "Oh boy, you're never gonna let that go, are you?"

"Not a chance."

Her laugh is soft but full of warmth, and something about it makes my chest feel lighter. It's been three months, but sitting across from her now, it's like no time has passed.

Like my world just realigned into the place it was supposed to be all along.

She stirs her coffee absentmindedly, her eyes dancing over my face. "What are you doing here?"

"Getting coffee," I tease, taking a slow sip of mine.

She rolls her eyes. "You know what I mean."

"I live here."

Her eyes widen slightly. "You live...in Dallas?"

"Yeah. Been here a couple years. And you?"

"I live here too." She shakes her head, laughing. "I can't believe this."

She's been here this whole time. Three months of aching, dreaming of a possibly impossible future and she was here.

"You and me both."

She tilts her head, studying me. "You look good."

"So do you," I say, my voice dropping just slightly.

"You are wearing a leather jacket."

"I am." I let out a laugh. "Just for you."

The tension between us is palpable now. The café fades away, and it's just us, like that afternoon in New Orleans.

But this time, I don't have to wonder if I'll ever see her again.

Because now that I've found her again, letting her go isn't an option.

Ivy blinks at me, like she's still trying to process that I'm actually sitting here in front of her. Honestly, I'm trying to process it too. Of all the coffee shops in the city, of all the mornings she could've walked in, she picked this one.

She laughs under her breath, a hint of disbelief in her eyes.

I grip my coffee cup, half expecting this moment to slip

through my fingers like a dream. "So...what have you been up to these past few months?"

Her fingers skim the lid of her cup, tracing the rim. "Work, mostly. Nothing too exciting."

I tilt my head, watching her. "What do you do for work?"

She hesitates for half a second. "I'm a freelance graphic designer."

My brows lift. "Oh yeah? That sounds cool."

She shrugs, smiling softly. "I like it. I get to work in sweatpants and make things look pretty for a living. Logos, websites, random event flyers, whatever pays the bills."

I chuckle. "So, you're the reason every cute coffee shop has aesthetic menus and perfectly filtered Instagram posts."

"Guilty." Her grin widens. She shifts in her seat, her fingers gripping her coffee cup a little tighter. "So...what do you do?"

I smirk, letting the suspense linger. "Take a guess."

Her brows pull together as she eyes me. "Hmm...let's see. Mysterious. A little broody. Smart. Hot."

I choke on my coffee. "Hot?"

Her cheeks flush, but she doesn't back down. "Don't let it go to your head."

"Too late." I lean back, grinning. "But keep going. I like where this is headed."

Ivy squints at me over her coffee cup, lips curving into a mischievous smile. "Fine. My guess is something secretive. Are you like a private investigator or something?"

I chuckle. "Not quite."

She tilts her head, studying me like she's trying to crack a code. "Okay, I give up. What do you do, stranger?"

I lean back in my chair, tapping the side of my cup. "I sing and play guitar on my church's worship team."

She laughs, a short, surprised sound. "Wait, seriously?"

Her eyes widen, searching my face for the punchline.

I raise an eyebrow. "Why do you sound so skeptical?"

"Because..." She gestures vaguely at me, trying not to smile too big. "That was a joke, right?"

I run a hand through my hair, not saying anything yet. Just watching her.

She blinks. "Wait. That wasn't a joke?"

"Nope." I let the word hang there.

She stares for a beat, then bursts out laughing again. "Sorry, it's just...you don't look like you'd sing at a church."

I fold my arms, playing along. "And what exactly does someone who sings at a church look like?"

"Well," she says, waving her hand in front of me, "not like this." Her voice softens, but her eyes are dancing. "Not all tall and broody in black, with tattoos down both arms and that whole 'mysterious musician' vibe going on."

I lean in slightly, grinning. "Says who?"

She opens her mouth, then closes it again like she's not sure how to respond.

I flash a wink. "Jesus loves everybody, Ivy."

This time, she laughs with me.

Then, there's a quiet moment between us. She tucks a strand of hair behind her ear, still smiling.

"So..." I say casually, "since you live here, you should come check it out sometime. My church."

Her brows lift. "Oh, um. I've never really, been to church before."

"Then you're overdue," I say, my tone light.

"I don't know what to expect." Her eyes dip to her coffee.

"You can expect melodies that feel like a hug you didn't

know you needed, a message that just might surprise you, and if you stick around after...lunch with me."

Her cheeks flush, and she looks away again, like she's trying not to smile too hard. "I bet they don't include that last part in the announcements."

"No," I say softly, "that part's just for you."

Her eyes meet mine and the café noise fades into the background.

And I can tell, she's thinking about saying yes.

Chapter 5
Ivy

Gray is sitting across from me. In my coffee shop. The one I go to almost every freaking day. And he lives in the same city I do. All this time, he's been so close.

The past three months have been devastating.

Not in some dramatic, world-ending way. But in a quiet, aching kind of way. Like a piece of me got left behind in that New Orleans coffee shop. Like no matter how hard I tried, I couldn't stop thinking about him. His voice. That slow, amused smile. The way his hand fit perfectly in mine, even if it was just for a dare.

I told myself it was just a moment. But it stuck with me. He stuck with me.

And now, he's here. Real. Solid. Looking at me like he remembers it all too.

His voice cuts through my internal spiral. "What are you thinking, Ivy?"

I blink, snapping back to the present. "That I can't believe this is real."

He smiles gently. "It is."

I hesitate, then ask the question that's been lingering at

the back of my mind since he first sat down. "You're not going to just disappear again, are you?"

He sits back, the smile softening, his thumb brushing along the edge of his coffee cup like he needs something to do with his hands. "I didn't disappear, Ivy. You went back home. I went back home. Turns out, home was the same place."

I press my lips together, absorbing that. "Feels like the universe has a sense of humor."

One corner of his mouth lifts, but his gaze drops to the table for a beat before meeting mine again. "Or maybe God's just a fan of plot twists."

I glance down at my coffee, trying not to grin.

He shifts in his seat, biting his lower lip for the briefest second before leaning forward, forearms resting on his knees. "So, would you ever come to church with me?" His voice is light, but there's something tentative underneath it, like he's testing the waters. "That was a serious offer."

Of course he would say that. I mean, he's on the worship team. It's kind of his thing. Still, the question catches me off guard. Not in a bad way, just...it's unfamiliar territory. Church wasn't something we ever did growing up. It's not that I'm against it. I just don't know how to believe in something I've never been part of.

I raise an eyebrow. "You really want me to come?"

"Yes." His smile is easy, but I catch the way his fingers drum against his leg before he steadies them on the table. "Come for the music. Stay for the message. Have lunch with me after."

I fold my arms. "That's a pretty strategic invite."

He shrugs. "I'm just saying, you won't regret it."

I study him for a moment, then finally nod. "Okay. Sure. I'll come."

"Yeah?"

"Yeah."

He pulls out his phone. "Can I get your number?"

I rattle it off while he types it in, just as a calendar notification pops up on my screen. I glance at the time.

"I've got a Zoom meeting in a few minutes," I say, the words catching in my throat. I don't want this to end, not when we just found each other again.

"I should get going anyway," he says, though his eyes linger on mine. "Rehearsal."

"Guess this is goodbye again."

"Not goodbye," he says, standing up. His voice is lower now—smooth, warm, like honey poured slow. "Just 'see you soon.' I'm holding you to that lunch after church."

The corner of my mouth lifts. "You're confident."

He hovers over the table, close enough that I catch the faint scent of his cologne. His voice dips just for me. "Only about the things that matter."

It's ridiculous, the way those simple words can set my pulse racing. Heat blooms low in my chest, curling into my stomach until I'm shifting in my seat, suddenly aware of every inch of space—or lack of it—between us. My fingers grip my coffee cup like it's the only thing tethering me to reality.

Because this isn't just playful banter. There's weight in his tone, something steady and unshakable that makes me want to believe him...about everything.

And I hate that part of me already does.

The bell above the door jingles as he steps out, tugging at the collar of his black leather jacket like it's second nature. Broad shoulders, easy strides. Every step is deliberate, like he owns the ground under his boots. In the dim morning light, he looks dark and untouchable, almost dangerous.

Almost.

Because I know better.

The man who just walked out isn't some brooding stranger with a secret past—though, judging by the way he wears that jacket, he could pull it off. He's a worship pastor. The guy who sings about grace and love and a God I've never known. That still throws me. I wouldn't have guessed it in a million years when I met him in New Orleans.

But now? Now I can't unsee the contradiction—leather and light, mystery and ministry.

My eyes track him through the café window as he crosses the street, my pulse tripping over itself like a lovesick fool. He pushes a hand through his hair, glances over his shoulder once, and I'm gone—completely lost in a daydream that's one breath away from embarrassing.

And then—ding.

My laptop springs to life with a notification, snapping me out of the fantasy. My Zoom meeting is starting.

Reluctantly, I drag my gaze away from the window, slip on my headphones, and try to remember how to function like a normal human being. But it's useless.

The Zoom meeting takes entirely too long.

Normally, I wouldn't mind helping a small business fine-tune the graphics for their upcoming event. But this particular client was...passionate. And by passionate, I mean she changed her mind about the font choice six times.

After an hour of painstakingly adjusting colors, repositioning elements, and watching her circle right back to the original layout I presented at the beginning, I'm absolutely drained.

Before I even push back from the table inside the coffee shop, I grab my phone and fire off a desperate message to the group chat with Harper and Olivia.

IVY

SOS. When can y'all video chat?

As I step out into the crisp fall air, my phone immediately starts buzzing with responses.

OLIVIA

I'm free in 15.

HARPER

If you're headed to jail, I call dibs on bailing you out.

I laugh, actually laugh, as I type back.

IVY

Meet in 15. You're not ready for this.

My heart is still buzzing from coffee, from Gray, from the fact that he wants to see me again.

I'm barely through the door of my apartment when my phone starts ringing with the video call.

I kick off my shoes, toss my bag on the couch, and plop down in the middle of the living room floor like I'm about to deliver national news.

Two familiar faces light up my screen: Olivia curled up on her bed in full gossip mode and Harper already munching on popcorn like she knows this is gonna be good.

Harper leans in first. "Okay. Spill. You're glowing, which either means you met a man or finally found the perfect throw pillows for your apartment."

"Definitely not pillows," I say, biting my lip.

Olivia gasps and claps her hands. "Girl, don't make us drag it out of you."

"Okay, okay!" I say, holding up my hands in surrender. "You remember that guy from the dare? The hand-holding guy in New Orleans?"

Harper nearly chokes on her popcorn. "THE dare guy?! Tattooed mystery man?! He's back?!"

"He's not just back," I say slowly, enjoying the suspense. "He's here. As in, lives in this city. I ran into him today. At Royal Brew."

They both scream. I have to pull the phone away from my face.

"No. Freaking. Way," Harper says. "What are the odds?"

"I know, right?" I say, flopping back onto the rug. "Apparently he's been living here this whole time. And get this, he asked me to come watch him sing."

"Oh my gosh, he's in a band?" Olivia asks.

"Technically, he is a worship leader at his church."

Dead silence.

Then...

"You're going to church now?!" Harper shouts. "How fun! I used to go all the time growing up, but that's beside the point."

"I mean, maybe?" I say, my voice going way higher than normal. "He made it sound like a free concert. With lunch after."

Harper grins. "Lunch with him after, I assume?"

"Obviously," I mutter, hiding my face behind a pillow.

Olivia raises a brow. "This seems too good to be true."

"Tall, dark, handsome, tattooed and he sings about Jesus?" Harper nearly squeals, "It may seem too good to be true, but this is perfect for you Ivy!"

I can't help but laugh. "I still can't believe I ran into him."

Harper leans closer to the screen. "This Sunday, right?"

"Yeah" I say, the nerves beginning to well up inside me again. "I mean, I've never even been to church. What if I have no idea what I'm doing?"

Olivia shrugs. "You'll be fine. Just nod when everyone else nods. And maybe don't yell 'Amen' unless you're super sure."

Harper adds, "Wear something cute but holy. In both senses."

I roll my eyes and laugh, but my heart is still jumping like it's on a trampoline. "I don't know what this is, but it feels like something."

They all go quiet for a second.

Then Harper smiles. "Ivy, this is definitely fate."

After hanging up with the girls, I toss my phone onto the couch and let out a long, dramatic sigh. My apartment is quiet. Too quiet after the chaos of group chat laughter and teasing.

Sunlight filters through the sheer curtains, casting warm patterns on the hardwood floors. My place is small, just a one-bedroom with a kitchen that's way too tiny for anyone who actually cooks, which I don't, but it's mine. With thrifted wall art, mismatched furniture and a candle on the coffee table that smells like cinnamon and nostalgia. It's cozy and safe.

I curl up on the couch, pulling my favorite blanket over my lap, and stare up at the ceiling.

Church.

He asked me to church.

It's not that I'm against it or anything. I just, don't know anything about it. What if I stand when I'm supposed to sit? Or sing the wrong words? Or everyone there can tell I don't belong?

What if it's weird?

Worse, what if I don't like it?

My phone buzzes next to me.

UNKNOWN NUMBER

You looked really pretty today. I can't wait
to see you again this weekend.

My heart does this ridiculous skip-jump like it's auditioning for a rom-com.

It's him.

Gray.

Before I can even process how to respond, another message comes through.

GRAY

I promise I'm not stalking you. But I did
pray we'd run into each other again, so
technically this is God's fault.

I actually squeal. Out loud.

Then immediately slap a pillow over my face.

I can't. I literally cannot with him.

He's flirty and sweet and sarcastic and somehow, has managed to leave me speechless more than once.

I stare at the screen, cheeks burning, grinning like a fool while I read his text messages over and over again.

Chapter 6
Gray

The morning sun cuts through the blinds, spilling golden light across the living room floor. I nudge the apartment door shut with my shoulder, my black Vans whispering across the floor as I head for the counter. My keys land with a soft clink in the ceramic dish, right beside a stack of unopened mail I keep pretending I'll get to.

It's not messy in here, but it's no showroom either. A hoodie's slung over the couch arm, my Bible sits open on the coffee table, and the dining tables buried under loose sheets of lyrics. Some are half-finished, some are just single lines I can't shake—pieces of prayers I keep trying to turn into songs.

A loud, throaty yowl comes from the kitchen.

"I'm coming, Goliath," I call.

The big white cat rounds the corner, tail high like he owns the place—which, to be fair, he kinda does. I crouch down, scooping him into my arms before he can get to his food dish. He's heavier than he looks, solid muscle and attitude, but he melts into me like we've been best friends forever.

"Remember when I found you?" I murmur, scratching behind his ears until he leans into my hand with that low, rumbling purr. "Hiding under that dumpster behind that venue in Austin, all skin and bones and ready to claw the world to pieces." I smile faintly at the memory—him hissing at me for twenty minutes straight before finally letting me wrap him in my sweatshirt. "Guess we were both a little lost that night."

He blinks at me. Slow. Judgmental.

"You'll never guess who I ran into this morning," I tell him. "Remember that girl I told you about? The one from New Orleans—the one I couldn't stop thinking about?"

Another slow blink.

"Yeah. Her." My grin tugs tight. "Turns out she's here. In Dallas. Just...sitting in my coffee shop like it's the most normal thing in the world."

He flicks his tail like he's still not impressed.

"I know," I say, dropping my voice. "She's even prettier than I remembered. And yeah, I invited her to church. Don't give me that look—you'll see. She's worth it."

I set him down, fill his bowl, and watch him dig in like food's the only thing worth living for. My gaze shifts to the corner where my favorite guitar waits. Sunlight cuts across the strings, making them glint like they're itching for me. I pick it up, sink into the chair by the window, and let my fingers find a slow, familiar chord progression—something that's been stuck in my head since New Orleans.

But even with music filling the air, my head's not here. It's back at that coffee shop. Back to the way Ivy looked when she saw me, like she'd been thinking about me too all this time.

Three months. Every single day, she's crossed my mind. Sometimes in flashes—her laugh, the way she tucked her hair behind her ear. Other times it's been heavier, like a weight I carry without meaning to. And now she's here. Close enough to reach again.

I strum the last chord and let it hang, the low hum fading into the quiet.

The next couple of hours blur together in the best way —finishing the song I've been working on since before Christmas, starting another one that's been buzzing in my head all morning, and pulling together the final set list for this weekend's services. I play through each song once, making sure it feels right. When it clicks, I jot quick notes on the chord charts and slide them into my folder, ready for rehearsal.

I glance at the clock and sigh. "Alright, Goliath, I'll be back before dinner," I tell him, standing to stretch. "Don't have too much fun without me." He blinks like he's already plotting something.

I grab my leather jacket from the back of the chair, sling my guitar case over my shoulder, and lock up behind me. The late morning air is warm, the kind that sticks to your skin, and I let it wake me up as I head for New Chapter Church.

By the time I pull into the church lot, the sun's climbing higher, painting the brick building in gold. A few scattered cars sit near the front entrance, the quiet hum of a weekday morning settling over the place.

Inside, the sanctuary is a different story. Cables snake across the stage, Caleb's already behind the drum kit, tapping out a lazy beat on the hi-hat, and Jess is at the keys, warming up with a run of chords that sound like they belong in a movie soundtrack.

"Hey, Gray," Jess calls without looking up. "Thought you were too cool to show up early."

"Just trying to keep you guessing," I shoot back, setting my guitar case down by my spot.

From the sound booth, Gabe leans over the railing. "Man, you're practically whistling. Did you get good news or something?"

I shake my head with a smirk. "Just a good morning."

That earns me a few raised brows. Across the stage, Molly and Luke—two of our vocalists—share a look before going back to flipping through their sheet music. Caleb keeps up the soft drumbeat like he's scoring the moment, and I'm not about to give them anything more to speculate about.

I take my guitar out, checking the tuning, and the familiar weight settles in my hands. This—these people, this stage—it's the one place outside my apartment that feels like home.

We run through the first couple of songs, finding our rhythm without much effort. Between takes, Caleb cracks a joke about Jess's "overly dramatic intro," Molly teases Luke about missing his harmony, and Gabe calls for "one more run" even though we all know it's solid. It's the kind of banter that's stitched into every practice—effortless, comfortable, making you lean on without realizing it.

We run the last song twice just to nail the transitions, and Jess finally calls it. "Alright, I'm declaring us officially good enough for Sunday."

Caleb stretches his arms over his head. "Good enough? We're amazing."

I'm winding my cables when the sanctuary doors swing open and Micah—my best friend and the children's ministry leader here at New Chapter Church—strolls in, a travel mug in hand. "Look at you guys, actually wrapping up on time for once."

He comes up the aisle, giving me one of those knowing looks. "Why are you smiling so much?"

Before I can answer, Caleb smirks from behind the kit. "Yeah, something's up with this guy today. He's practically glowing."

Molly laughs. "Maybe he finally wrote that love song he's been pretending isn't a love song."

I shake my head, heat crawling up the back of my neck. "You're all ridiculous."

Gabe leans over the booth railing. "Sure, man. Keep your secrets."

I close my guitar case a little harder than necessary, more to hide my grin than anything else.

"Hey, Micah—you got time to chat?"

"Always."

We leave the team to their teardown and head out of the sanctuary. The halls are alive with the quiet hum of midweek ministry—nursery volunteers wiping down toys in the kids' wing, the faint smell of glue sticks and goldfish crackers drifting from behind the bright double doors. We pass the row of classrooms where small groups meet. Down another hallway, the café is still open—student-run, the espresso machine hissing as a young woman in a mission's T-shirt hands off a latte to a smiling woman in scrubs. Every dollar raised goes to send those students across the globe each summer.

The space smells faintly of fresh paint from the last renovation, a reminder of how much this place has grown in the last few years. New Chapter Church isn't quite a mega church, but it's big enough to feel full every Sunday. Still, it's the kind of place where people remember your name—and for me, it's the place that changed everything.

If I hadn't stumbled in here one-night years ago—tired, hungover, looking for nothing but a quiet corner to sit in—I'm not sure where I'd be now. The thought makes my chest tighten. This place gave me a reason to keep going. Gave me Jesus. Gave me a family.

We step into the lobby, the tall windows spilling sunlight across polished floors. A bold navy accent wall anchors the space, the church's logo stretched across it in crisp white lettering. Leather couches in rich brown line the wall, structured but still soft enough to sink into. I drop into one, letting the cushion ease me back, but my mind is already somewhere else—six days from now, wondering if she'll actually walk through those doors.

I rub the back of my neck, trying to figure out where to start.

"Okay, so... remember that girl I met in New Orleans?"

Micah smirks. "The one you wouldn't shut up about for three months? Yeah, I remember."

"Right. Well, I ran into her this morning. At Royal Brew." I lean back, my foot tapping against the floor. "She still drinks vanilla lattes with oat milk...and she still does that thing where she tucks her hair behind her ear when she's thinking."

Micah lets out a low laugh. "Bro, you're already gone. You remember what she did with her hair?"

I shoot him a look, but I can't stop the corner of my mouth from lifting. "I'm just saying... it's not every day you see someone you thought you'd never see again."

Micah leans back, eyebrows lifting. "And the problem is?"

I shrug, trying to play it off, but my voice gives me away. "I don't know, man. She's just—" I shake my head, a half-laugh slipping out. "It's like I blinked and there she was. The same girl I've thought about every day since New Orleans."

"That's not a problem, Gray."

I let the silence stretch, my gaze dropping to the church logo on the wall like it might give me courage.

"Yeah... maybe. Except—" I take a breath; the words heavier than I want them to be. "I don't think she's a Christian."

Micah's smirk fades. He sits forward, elbows on his knees, eyes locking on mine. "Ah. Okay. That's different."

I nod, the unease settling deeper. "Yeah. I mean, I didn't ask outright, but... I can tell. She didn't grow up around it, never went to church. I invited her this Sunday, but..."

"But you're already halfway in," he finishes, his voice low but steady. "And you've been down that road before, you know it's not easy."

"I know."

He leans back, exhaling through his nose. "Look, I'm not telling you to write her off. I'm saying you need to date intentionally. You know what happens when you get wrapped up in someone who isn't walking the same road you are. You've lived it."

I stare at my hands, jaw tight. "I know."

Micah's tone softens, though the weight of his words stays. "You've got a good thing going right now. God's been doing work in you. Don't compromise that—not even for someone who makes you smile like you've been smiling all morning."

I huff out a laugh, more of a release than anything. "That obvious, huh?"

"Everyone noticed," he says, cracking the faintest grin. Then, more seriously, "Just... guard your heart. And hers."

He leans back against the leather. "And hey—this could be a good thing. You might be the one who helps lead her to Christ. That's worth praying over."

I nod slowly, but he's not done.

"Also... don't fall too hard too fast," Micah adds, his tone gentler now. "I've seen guys get so wrapped up in the possibility that they miss the reality. Give God space to work. And give her space to figure out what she believes—without the pressure of it being about you."

Before I can answer, a voice calls from down the hall, asking for Micah. He pats my shoulder as he stands. "I've gotta get back to prepping for youth night. You good?"

"Yeah," I say, leaning back as he heads off.

The lobby feels quieter without him, and I just sit there for a minute, staring at the wall.

I want to fall. Hard. Everything in me wants to lean into whatever this is with Ivy. But Micah's words stick. Guard your heart. Give God space.

I close my eyes and bow my head.

Lord... if this isn't from You, shut the door before I walk through it. But if it is, if Ivy is meant to be part of my life, let her be open when I share the Good News. Prepare her heart for worship and the message on Sunday. And give me the wisdom not to get in the way of what You're doing.

When I open my eyes, the prayer lingers like a steady hum in my chest. Somewhere down the hall, the band's still playing—slow and steady, voices weaving together. They never did pack up. The melody slips under my skin, guiding my thoughts back to her.

I picture Ivy stepping into this place for the first time. The way the lobby light will hit her hair. The way the sound will roll through the hall and find her, the same way it found me all those years ago when I stumbled in by accident. I pray she'll feel that same pull—that same holy weight in her chest that won't let her leave the same as she came in.

Eventually, I stand, sliding on my worn leather jacket and grabbing my bag. Out in the parking lot, the late afternoon sun's warm on my face. I'm halfway to my truck when a few lines tumble into my head, uninvited.

I stop dead, fishing my phone from my pocket before the words vanish. Thumb tapping furiously, I get them down, just enough to remember later, before slipping the phone away.

Didn't know then what You were starting
But You wrote it on my heart

The engine rumbles to life, and I can't help the grin that creeps in. Goliath's in for a treat tonight. Can't wait to sing him this new part of the song.

Chapter 7
Ivy

The sun's warm but not suffocating, the kind of perfect late-summer afternoon that makes the park's walking path feel more like a runway for strollers, joggers, and overly enthusiastic dog owners. Harper and I claimed a picnic table under a maple tree, sandwiches from the deli spread between us, shopping bags tucked by our feet.

I tear into my turkey club, the knot in my stomach has nothing to do with hunger. "So... tomorrow." I keep my voice casual, but it still comes out a little tighter than I mean. "I'm nervous."

Harper glances up from unwrapping her sandwich. "About church?"

I nod. "I have no idea what to expect. I mean, I've seen church in movies, but that's probably not the same thing."

She smiles like she's been waiting for me to ask. "It's not as scary as you think. They'll probably have someone greet you at the door, maybe give you a bulletin or program. The music will be... well, different than a concert, but still really good. And people might introduce themselves after. Or not. It depends on the church."

I tilt my head. "And you know all this... how? You said earlier you've been before?"

Her smile quirks a little. "Oh, yeah. I grew up going to church. Every Sunday morning, every Wednesday night—pretty much my whole childhood."

I freeze mid-bite. "Wait. How did I not know this? I've known you since kindergarten."

She laughs lightly, but there's a flicker of something quieter in her eyes. "You know how my parents are. Not exactly the warm and fuzzy type."

I do know. They've always been polite to me, but there's a strictness to them that makes me feel like I'm on some sort of invisible grading scale.

"Our church was really small," she goes on. "Just outside Ashen Mills. And honestly... I didn't really want to bring friends. Not because it was bad, it just...wasn't my favorite place back then."

I nod, letting her keep it surface-level.

"But since then, I've tried other churches. Sometimes I'll watch online. And..." She pauses, picking at the crust of her bread. "You know what? I kind of miss it. I can't go tomorrow, but maybe I'll tag along with you next time. I miss the community part of church the most. Serving in the kids' area was always my favorite."

A faint shadow passes through her expression before she shakes it off. "I guess I've been meaning to go back for a while. Just... haven't found my place yet."

I grin. "Of course you ended up a teacher."

She laughs, shaking her head. "Some things are just built in."

We linger over the last bites of our sandwiches, drifting into talk about work deadlines and weekend errands. By the time we toss our trash and gather our shopping bags, the afternoon sun has shifted, casting long shadows across the grass.

We hug goodbye in the parking lot, and I head home, the weight of tomorrow sitting quietly in the back of my mind.

That night, I stretch out in bed, but sleep doesn't come easy. My mind runs through a hundred what-ifs—what the music will sound like, how the people will act, whether I'll fit in at all.

And most of all...what it'll be like to see Gray again.

This clearly matters to him. And if this thing between us goes anywhere, I know it'll have to matter to me too. The thought is equal parts exciting and terrifying.

Somewhere between nervous and hopeful, I finally drift off, tomorrow already pulling at me.

The hum of my coffee maker fills the quiet of my kitchen, the scent of vanilla drifting through the air as I lean against the counter, staring at my phone like it might tell me what to wear.

Church.

I'm going to church this morning.

With Gray.

Well, not with him technically. He'll be on stage. I'll be somewhere in the crowd, pretending not to fall apart at the seams.

I wrap my hands around my mug, trying to steady myself.

This week has been better than I expected. Freelance

life still feels like walking a tightrope without a safety net, but somehow, miraculously, I landed two new clients. Real ones. Who were excited about my designs, who didn't treat me like I am replaceable.

And somewhere between it all, I texted Gray.

We'd been texting off and on all week. Little things here and there, nothing too deep.

How's your day?

What are you working on?

Drinking coffee and thinking of you.

Simple. Easy. Sweet in a way that left me smiling at my phone like an idiot more times than I cared to admit.

Now, my phone sits on the counter next to me, the screen still lit up from the last message he sent just a few minutes ago:

GRAY

I can't wait to see you today, Ivy.

I trace my thumb lightly over the screen, feeling my heart flutter in a way I haven't let myself feel in a long time.

I blow out a breath and turn back to my closet, glaring at the rack of clothes like they personally offended me.

"What does one even wear to church when they're not trying to look like they have it all together but also don't want to appear that they are falling apart?" I mumble to myself.

Not too casual.

Not too polished.

Something in between.

Because the truth is, I don't. But for some reason, that doesn't scare me as much as it used to.

Maybe it's him.

Maybe it's something bigger.

Either way, I know one thing for sure: I'm not the same girl I was a few months ago.

And somehow, I have a feeling today is going to change me even more.

I pulled into the lot a full forty-five minutes early. New Chapter's only a ten-minute drive from my place, but with Dallas traffic, you never really know—and I'd rather be the awkwardly early girl than the one slipping in late.

The lot was still mostly empty, the morning sun just starting to warm the crisp June air. I could've gone in right away, but nerves pinned me to my seat. I didn't want to be the first one. Didn't want to stand there awkwardly, not knowing where to go or what to do.

So, I sat.

I scrolled through my phone, checked my lip gloss in the mirror, tapped my fingers against the steering wheel. Anything to pass the time without completely talking myself out of walking inside.

A few more cars trickled in.

Then a small white sedan pulls into the spot next to mine, and I watched as a woman about my age slipped out. She smooths down her skirt, adjusts her purse strap, and heads toward the entrance alone.

Without letting myself overthink it, I grab my bag, climb out of my car, and follow her. Not too close, just enough to mimic her movements like a shadow.

As I approach the main doors, a man with a kind smile

and a lanyard around his neck catches sight of us and pulls one open.

"Good morning!" he greets, his voice warm and genuine.

I murmur a soft "Thank you," and step inside.

The bright scent of citrus and a trace of clean floors lingers in the air, as if the whole place was scrubbed and polished just for today. Light streams in through huge windows, and soft background piano music plays overhead. People mill around, chatting and laughing in small groups, their smiles easy and unforced.

Well, most of them.

A family of five rushes in behind me, looking every bit like they'd just finished a full-blown argument in the car.

The dad's shirt is partly untucked.

The mom gives him a look that could curdle milk.

One kid yawns so big it looked like his jaw might unhinge, another is crying and tugging on his mom's arm, and the oldest took off at a sprint toward a group of friends without so much as a backward glance.

I bite back a laugh, feeling a tiny piece of the tension inside me loosen.

Maybe I'm not the only one who doesn't have it all together this morning.

The woman I'd been trailing rounds a corner, and I quicken my steps to follow.

Then I see them—the big double doors leading into the main area where I am assuming the service takes place.

There are several people holding the doors open, and from where I stand, I can see a glimpse of the edge of a stage, the soft glow of lights illuminating it.

My heart picks up speed.

This is it.

No turning back now.

I wipe my palms on the sides of my jeans and draw in a steadying breath before slipping through the doors, hoping that somehow, this morning will be exactly what I need.

Even if I'm not exactly sure what that is.

I step through the double doors and freeze.

The sanctuary is bigger than I expected. With high ceilings, rows upon rows of chairs, a stage framed by soft, warm lights.

But somehow, despite the size, it still feels cozy. Welcoming.

Not cold or intimidating like I feared.

The woman I've been trailing moves with quiet confidence, and I follow her, keeping a little distance. She slips into a row about a third of the way up, joining a small group already gathered there.

I hesitate, then slide into a seat a few rows behind them.

Not too close to the front, where I might stand out.

Not too far back, where it might seem like I don't really want to be here.

The middle feels safe—visible enough to belong but still tucked into the background.

I tuck my purse under my chair and take a slow breath, letting my eyes wander.

A woman about my age walks past, then pauses like she recognizes me—even though we've never met.

"Hey! I don't think I've seen you here before," she says, her smile bright and easy.

I shake my head. "First time."

"Well, welcome to New Chapter! I'm Jenna." She gestures toward the stage. "If you need anything, just wave me down, okay?"

She squeezes my arm before heading toward a group by the far wall, leaving a little warmth in her wake.

The room buzzes with life—people laughing, hugging, catching up like old friends. The low hum of conversation wraps around me like a blanket.

Then the first notes of live music float through the air—low, steady, and brushed with a peace I can't remember ever feeling. Like someone's whispering my name without a sound.

People start moving toward their seats.

The music grows louder, deeper, and the energy in the room shifts.

A guitar strums softly. A bass thrums low. A drum taps out a rhythm that feels like a heartbeat.

And then I hear it, a voice I know, one that has been living in the corners of my mind all week.

"Good morning, everyone. It's a great day to praise the Lord. Let's stand and worship together."

Gray.

I look up, and there he is standing on stage, guitar strapped across his chest, a small smile tugging at his mouth.

Gray starts singing an upbeat tune. The others on stage stand to his sides, but he's right in the middle, clearly leading the singing. Is he the lead singer? I wonder, watching him with quiet awe.

I've only seen him in person twice, but now I watch as he sings with everything he has. His voice is raw and full of soul, pouring out a melody that sends shivers down my spine.

The first song is lively and seems to make the whole room move. The woman I followed sways gently from side to side, eyes closed, hand raised, lost in the music.

Then the tune shifts. The next song is softer, more inti-mate. I lean in, listening closely to the lyrics that seem to fill the space around me and fill something inside me, too.

A few people nearby raise their hands, eyes lifted toward the ceiling. I feel an unfamiliar warmth rise in my chest, a swelling emotion I can't quite name.

The words wrap around me like a whispered promise. I blink back tears, overwhelmed by the feeling of being seen, heard, and maybe even understood.

Here in Your light, I'm found, not lost,
More than I knew, worth every cost.
You see me whole, beyond my pain,
In Your love, I'll never be the same.

As the last note lingers and fades, a hush settles over the room. The lyrics echo in my mind, strange and personal, like someone reached inside me and put words to feelings I've barely admitted to myself. It's like they saw the parts I keep hidden and suddenly I'm not so alone. My chest tight-ens, a bittersweet warmth spreading through me, and it takes all of me to hold back the tears I didn't expect.

Then another man steps onto the stage as the band quietly slips away.

"Good morning New Chapter Church family! Turn and say hi to those around you," he says warmly, inviting connection.

A wave of panic crashes over me. My heart hammers against my ribs as I freeze, the vulnerable openness I felt moments ago retreating fast like a tide pulling away from shore.

But then, faces turn toward me, smiles full of kindness

and welcome. A woman nods with genuine warmth; a man offers a soft wave. Slowly, almost without thinking, I return their greetings. The genuine friendliness surprises me, softening the tight coil of nerves in my chest.

"Alright, alright," he says, motioning for everyone to sit. "If you've got your Bibles, open up to Matthew chapter six..."

I freeze for a second. I don't have a Bible. Was I supposed to bring one? My gaze darts around—some people are flipping pages; others just watch the pastor like they've heard this voice a hundred times. I'm not the only one empty-handed, so I let out a small breath.

The pastor's voice is steady. "Today we're talking about worth and grace. About finding light... even when life feels heavy." He pauses, then reads, "Look at the birds of the air; they do not sow or reap or store away in barns, and yet your heavenly Father feeds them. Are you not much more valuable than they?"

I sink into my seat, my fingers curling loosely in my lap.

"Jesus tells us here," the pastor continues, "that your worth is not tied to how much you achieve, or how perfectly you perform. If He cares for the sparrows, if He clothes the lilies of the field in beauty beyond kings, how much more does He care for you? Grace means you don't have to earn it. Light means you're not walking through the weight alone."

And just like that, it's as if every sentence is somehow aimed at me, slipping into places I didn't even know needed healing. Just like that first song.

Did he know I'd be here today? The thought is absurd, but it sticks. How else could he speak so directly to my heart?

Tears prick at the corners of my eyes, but I blink them away. I'm not here to cry in front of strangers. Still, something in me softens.

When the message ends, heads bow in a simple, unhurried prayer. A piano hums softly beneath the words, each note settling over the room like falling snow. I close my eyes and let the stillness wash through me. The quiet feels like more than silence—it feels alive.

"Amen," the room echoes, and the music swells again, lifting the moment into something I can't quite name.

Opening my eyes, I catch sight of Gray on stage, guitar in hand, leading worship with that same intensity I saw earlier. My lips curve into a smile. I get to see him again at lunch, just us.

With the final note, Gray's voice rings out, warm and familiar, "Go out and love the world today, y'all!"

The band fades away as people begin to stand and exit. I gather my things, following the crowd toward the lobby. But as soon as I step out into the open space, a creeping realization hits me. We never decided where to meet after service.

Scanning the room, I spot a cozy couch tucked away in the corner and sink down, pulling out my phone. I check my messages. Nothing. My thumb hovers, tapping the screen anxiously. The lobby empties around me, but my phone stays stubbornly silent.

A nervous knot twists in my stomach. What if he forgot?

Just as I rise to leave, my phone rings. Gray's name flashes across the screen.

I answer immediately, heart pounding when I hear his voice. "Where are you?"

I glance around, searching for the right words. "I'm by the couches near the entrance."

Then I see him, rushing toward me, that big, bright smile lighting up his face. Without hesitation, he wraps me in a hug so warm and real, I almost forget where we are.

"Hey you," he murmurs against my hair.

Chapter 8
Gray

God, I don't want to mess this up. I don't want to get in the way of whatever You're doing in her life—or in mine. But I can't lie...I want this. I want her to be part of the story You're writing for me. Help me trust You with it.

I don't want to let go. There's a soft floral note to her that I remember from New Orleans, like wildflowers and sunshine, and I'm not sure I'll ever stop craving it. Holding her here, in my church, feels surreal. Like some quiet miracle.

I slowly pull back just enough to look down at her. Her eyes meet mine, wide and a little vulnerable, and my heart tightens.

"You're here," I say, voice low, almost a whisper. "I still can't believe you're actually here."

She looks up at me and smiles. For a moment, everything else falls away. No worries, no past mistakes, just this.

I shift, trying to act casual but feeling like I'm barely holding it together. "So, what'd you think about the service?"

She playfully slaps my arm. "You didn't tell me you were the lead singer."

I shrug, brushing off the compliment like it's nothing. "Eh, we all take turns."

Inside, I'm proud, but I don't want to hype myself up. Not yet at least. Right now, I just want to focus on her.

"I did like it. I was surprised, but yeah, I really did."

I smile, if only she knew how much that means to me.

"Your voice, it's... something else. And you have this presence on stage. Like you own it."

I shrug again, trying to play it cool. "We all do our part. Nothing special."

She chuckles, but it feels lighter than before. Like she's letting her guard down just a little.

We stand there in silence all while her eyes hold mine. I can feel the air thicken between us.

"Come here, you." I pull her back into another hug, tighter this time.

I want to press a kiss to her hair, to tell her she's safe here with me, but I don't want to scare her off. So, I just breathe her in and pull away gently.

"Let's get some food," I say, voice a little rough. "I know I've set myself up being all chivalrous and should ask the lady where she wants to go, but there's this killer Mexican restaurant that just opened up. I'd love to take you there if that's okay."

She smiles. really smiles, and nods. "I'd like that."

As we turn to leave, I'm fighting the urge not to grab her hand. It's like a magnet pulling me toward her, and man if it doesn't make my heart race. I just don't want to make her hesitant by moving too fast.

But then I remember, she was the one who grabbed my hand first.

So, I reach out slowly, my fingertips brushing hers, silently asking for permission.

She looks up at me, a playful smirk tugging at her lips. "Are you asking if you can hold my hand Gray?" she teases.

I grin. "Well, it's polite to ask first...though some people don't."

"Hey," she laughs softly, slipping her hand into mine. Our fingers intertwine, and the same electric spark pulses through me like that very first time.

"You don't really need to ask," she whispers. "After all, this is how it all started, right?"

Si Señor smells like sizzling fajitas and warm tortillas the second we step inside. The place still has that "new in town" feel—sunbaked terracotta walls, hand-painted tiles climbing halfway up, strings lights above fluttering in the AC breeze. Every table is alive with chatter, the clink of silverware, and the hum of Spanish guitar drifting from overhead speakers.

We grab a booth by the window, sunlight pooling over the polished wood.

Ivy leans forward, elbows on the table, totally focused on conquering the tacos in front of her. She tries to take a bite, laughing when half the filling threatens to spill out.

"These are incredible," she says, setting the taco down and swiping salsa from the corner of her mouth.

I smile, not just because she looks effortlessly beautiful, but because an hour ago she was sitting in the middle row at New Chapter Church. My church. She didn't just show up

—she leaned in, listened, and stayed through the last note. I keep replaying the moment I spotted her walking in from backstage, a mix of surprise and gratitude settling in my chest.

"You like it here?" I ask.

She nods. "Might be my new favorite."

I hope she's talking about more than the tacos.

I lean back, eyes on her. "I get it, I've already eaten here twice this week."

Ivy looks down for a second, then meets my eyes. "Can I tell you something weird?"

I glance up from my plate, giving her my full attention. "Always."

She lets out a breath, not quite a sigh, more like a release of something she's been holding onto. "I've always wondered about God. Not in a deep way, not really. I think I just never had the space, or the people, to ask questions."

I nod, silently urging her on.

"It's like..." she pauses, searching for the words. "Like I've been walking around with this low-level ache I couldn't name. And now that I'm here, now that I'm seeing all of this, it's not that I suddenly get it. I don't. But something in me, I don't know, something kind of wants to."

I let her words settle, the weight of them both familiar and sacred.

"That's not weird," I say quietly. "That sounds honest."

She looks up, seeming surprised by the lack of judgment in my voice.

I lean forward, resting my arms on the table. "I used to think faith was about having all the right answers. But it's not. It's about asking the right questions and being brave enough to sit in the in-between."

Her brows pull together slightly. "Did you ever feel like you didn't belong? Like, maybe this wasn't for you?"

"All the time," I admit with a soft chuckle. "Especially at the beginning. I'd show up, hear all these words I didn't understand, watch people raise their hands in worship like they were fluent in something I hadn't learned yet. I felt like an outsider."

Her shoulders relax a little, like hearing that untangles something tight in her chest.

She blinks at me like she's trying to decide whether I'm for real. Then she exhales, a dry sort of laugh slipping out. "Okay, but what if you're not brave? What if you're just confused and googling weird things at midnight and hoping for a lightning bolt?"

My lips tug into a smile. I know that kind of desperation where you are grasping for something you can't name, hoping it reaches back.

"Then you're human," I say, my tone soft.

She leans back, arms crossing. "Good. Because I've watched like six videos on the book of John in an attempt to at least know something before I walked into a church. And honestly, I still don't even know who John is."

I chuckle, causing her to laugh as well, and it's probably the best sound I've heard all week. All my life, really.

She doesn't even know it, but she's already seeking Him. Pursuing, searching, leaning in. It's messy, yeah. But real.

"You'll figure it out," I tell her. "Don't rush it. Let God meet you where you are."

She goes quiet, fingers twisting the corner of her napkin. Then, barely above a whisper, "What if where I am isn't good enough?"

Oh Ivy. If only she could see what I see. If only I could spill my whole life story right now, she would see that I was, and still am, the farthest thing from 'good enough'.

"No-one is good enough, Ivy." I say without hesitation, reaching for her hand and slowly brushing my thumb along her knuckles. "Because God's grace doesn't wait for us to get it right. It just shows up."

"I know the pastor talked about grace in church today, but I am getting stuck on the difference between grace and mercy." She says, dunking a chip into the salsa.

"Think of it like this—if you were speeding and a cop pulled you over, mercy would be him saying, 'I'm not giving you the ticket you deserve.' Grace goes even further. It's him handing you a lollipop or a hundred bucks and saying, 'Here, lunch on me.'"

Her eyes lift to mine, curious.

"That's what Jesus does for us," I continue, my voice low. "We don't deserve grace. We mess up, ignore Him, run the other way. But He doesn't just withhold punishment—He gives us more than we could ever earn. He gave His life for us, knowing we'd never be able to pay Him back. That's grace."

I let the words hang there, praying they land in her heart the way they still shake mine.

I watch her as she sips her Diet Coke, her fingers fidgeting like she's trying to act normal, but I know better. I saw the way her voice trembled when she wondered if she wasn't good enough.

That question...man, I've asked it too many times myself.

She thinks she's not enough, and I wish I could reach across the table and pull that lie right out of her chest. Replace it with truth. With grace.

Instead, I just sit here, heart aching in the best kind of way, because this beautiful woman is letting me see her heart. And I don't take that lightly.

She doesn't know it, but this moment has changed something in me.

I thought I was already falling just from one chance encounter in New Orleans. Turns out, I haven't even scratched the surface.

It's not just the way she looks at me or the spark in her voice when she teases me, it's this. Her honesty. Her hunger for truth. Her willingness to wrestle with it.

But there's something I have to tell her. And I hope it doesn't scare her away.

I shift in my seat, fingers drumming lightly against the table before I finally meet her eyes. "I need you to know...I don't date casually. If I'm going to be with someone, it's because I'm building toward something real. And for me, that has to mean being on the same page spiritually—knowing Jesus, loving Him, following Him. That's not just important to me, Ivy. It's everything."

Her gaze holds mine and it makes my chest ache.

I take a breath. "I know we technically just met, but...there's something here. I feel it. And I think you do too."

Her cheeks flush, and for a second, I almost lose my nerve. Still, I reach across the table, threading my fingers through hers.

"I know today was your first time in church," I continue, my voice low. "And I know faith doesn't happen overnight. I'm not expecting you to suddenly have it all figured out. But..." My words falter, and I run my free hand over my jaw, feeling awkward in a way I hate. "Would you be willing to try? To explore it? So that...we can move forward in this, together?"

I'm holding my breath without meaning to, my head lowering slightly, bracing for the polite letdown. Then her other hand comes across the table, gently cupping my cheek.

"I do feel it," she says softly, and the way she looks at me —like she's seeing straight through the walls I've built— makes my heart kick hard. "And I want to see where this goes. I want to try."

I can't move. Can't speak. All I can do is take in the warmth of her touch, the sincerity in her voice.

She could've put on a show. Tried to act like she had it all figured out. But instead, she let me see the questions.

And that's what wrecks me most.

Because this searching—it isn't for me. She's not doing this to impress me.

She's doing it for herself.

And in that moment, I know—I'd wait as long as it takes. I'd walk beside her at whatever pace she needs. Because the last thing I ever want to do is rush what God is gently unfolding in her heart.

Her smile is small but genuine, lingering there like it's holding onto the last thread of the moment we just shared. I want to stay in it, to keep holding her hand, but the air between us feels so weighted with meaning that I know we both need a breath.

I clear my throat and lean back slightly, still letting my thumb brush over her knuckles before releasing her hand. "So," I say, a faint grin tugging at my mouth, "tell me about you. What's a day in the life of Ivy look like?"

Her brows lift just a little, like she wasn't expecting the question.

"I mean," I add, still watching her, "when you're not

bravely walking into church for the first time or letting some guy ramble on about grace and mercy over lunch."

She laughs, that easy, real kind of laugh that makes my chest tighten. "Honestly? Pretty boring. Freelance work keeps me busy. I'm still figuring out how to balance work and life without burning out. And weekends? Usually low-key. My perfect weekend would be staying in with some takeout and way too many Netflix episodes."

"Sounds perfect," I say, grinning. "Sometimes I think I should do that more. Although my idea of low-key usually involves a guitar and late-night thinking."

She leans forward, interested. "What do you think about when you're up late with your guitar?"

I shrug, pretending to be casual, but inside, I want to tell her everything. The doubts, the hopes, the parts of me I barely admit to myself. "I guess, just life. The usual stuff. Sometimes music just makes sense when nothing else does."

She nods, like she understands more than she lets on. "I get that."

There's a pause, then she asks, "What's something no one knows about you?"

I smirk. "Well, I have this ridiculous guilty pleasure for cheesy romantic movies. Don't tell anyone, but I could probably quote half of them."

She laughs, clearly surprised. "You? Watching sappy movies?"

"Hey, don't judge. We all have our secrets." I lean in. "What's something no one knows about you Miss Ivy?"

She bites her lip, glancing down at the table like she's debating whether to say it. "Okay...I still sleep with the same stuffed animal I've had since I was a kid. His name's Moose, and yes—he's a moose."

I chuckle, imagining it. "A moose, huh? That's adorable."

She blushes, but she's smiling now. "Don't make fun. He's been through everything with me."

"I'm not making fun. I think it's cute. Everyone needs something that reminds them they're safe."

Her eyes lift to mine, soft, vulnerable, and I feel it again—that pull to know every piece of her.

I eat the rest of my burrito, watching her as she talks about her favorite books and what she's binge-watching lately. It's easy, way easier than I expected. Like the walls I usually keep up start to come down without me even trying.

Then I catch myself, this feeling of wanting more time with her. Wanting to keep this going.

"So," I say, trying to sound casual but failing a little, "you think you'll be back next Sunday?"

She looks up, eyes curious, maybe a little hopeful. "I think so."

I lean in just a bit, lowering my voice. "I'll be honest, I don't know if I can wait a whole week to see you again."

Her smile gets softer, more real. "Well, maybe you won't have to."

That hits me in the chest.

We sit there for a beat, both knowing this is just the beginning.

We pull into the church parking lot after lunch, and I kill the engine, not quite ready for this moment to end. The afternoon light streams through the windows, casting a warm glow over everything.

"What about tomorrow afternoon?" I ask, trying to lock in our next date.

"Tomorrow's a no, I have back-to-back meetings with clients."

"How about Thursday evening?"

"Family thing," she says, shaking her head.

We go back and forth, every day and time I suggest she has something. I'm starting to think she's a master of busy schedules.

Finally, I say, "Okay, breakfast Friday morning?"

Her eyes light up. "I can do that."

"Same coffee shop where you just happened to crash into my life?"

She laughs softly. "I'm in."

When it's time to say goodbye, I open her car door, feeling that familiar tug at my chest.

"You know, I'm not really fond of these goodbyes," I admit, my voice low, "but at least I know I get to see you twice this next week."

She looks up at me, her smile soft but her eyes flicker with a hint of sadness.

"You can always text or call," she says, trying to sound casual.

"Definitely will," I promise.

I watch her slide behind the wheel, the sunlight catching the edges of her hair. She takes a deep breath, and I see her face filled with hope. "Bye Gray,"

"Bye Ivy," I say before closing the door.

As she pulls away, I'm already counting the moments until I see her again.

I'm back at my place. The quiet presses in around me, heavy and thick. I drop my keys on the counter and lean against the wall, letting out a slow breath.

My mind keeps drifting back to Ivy—her smile when she complimented my worship songs. She didn't just say it to be nice. There was something real in the way she talked about the music, like it touched something deep inside her.

It's unexpected, this feeling stirring in me.

A sudden weight lands against my shin. I glance down to see Goliath winding himself around my leg, tail flicking like he's got opinions about how long I was gone.

"Hey, buddy," I murmur, crouching to scratch behind his ears. He purrs like an engine, loud enough to fill the room. When I pull back, he just sits there staring at me—slow blink, head tilted, like he's silently asking if I'm seriously going to stand here daydreaming about a girl instead of feeding him.

"Yeah, yeah," I mutter with a smirk, heading toward the kitchen.

Just as I start to let my thoughts settle, my phone buzzes on the table. Mark from the worship team.

"Hey, have you finalized the lyrics yet? We need to lock them in for the sound check this week."

A knot tightens in my chest. The deadline's looming, and honestly, I'm not sure I'm ready. Between this new thing with Ivy and work responsibilities, my mind feels stretched too thin.

I glance down at Goliath, who's now lounging on the

counter like a furry judge, tail flicking in quiet disapproval. I wish I had his level of calm.

I let out a shaky breath. "Almost there. I'll send them tonight."

The pressure's on. Good thing I've got some new inspiration...and one very patient cat.

Chapter 9
Ivy

I don't like not being prepared.

Sunday at church, when everyone around me opened their Bibles, I just...sat there. Hands empty. Heart pounding.

It wasn't like anyone pointed or whispered, but I felt it —like I'd shown up to a test without even knowing there was one. And I hated that feeling.

Besides, if I really am going to try this whole Jesus thing...shouldn't I take it seriously? Isn't this book like super, important?

What could go wrong? I don't like it, and I lose out on the man of my dreams? The man who consumes my thoughts every time I close my eyes? The one whose voice still echoes in my head from yesterday?

Gray, leaning forward, hand warm against mine, his tone so steady it made my chest ache: *I'm not expecting you to suddenly have it all figured out. But would you be willing to try?*

It was the way he said try. Like he wasn't asking me to perform or prove something. Just...take a step.

And after the way he helped me finally understand grace and mercy, how could I not?

Grace—God giving me something I don't deserve. Mercy—not giving me what I do deserve. Both, wrapped up in love so deep I can't begin to measure it.

I grip the steering wheel tighter, staring through my windshield at the bookstore.

Okay, Ivy. Step one.

I pop the door open, cool air brushing against my legs as I climb out. The faint smell of coffee drifts from the little café tucked in the corner of the store, mixing with the warm scent of paper and ink that greets me the second I step inside.

Somewhere in here, there's a Bible with my name on it.

Easier said than done.

I weave past the fiction shelves, glancing at bright covers and bold titles, my usual comfort zone. I've never needed help in a bookstore before—this is my natural habitat. But the Christian section? Apparently, it's hiding.

I slow my steps, scanning the aisle signs. Cookbooks. Travel. Self-help. Where in the world are they keeping Jesus?

I must look as lost as I feel because a voice pipes up beside me. "Can I help you find something?"

I instantly wave him off. "Oh, no. I'm good."

Except...I'm not. Not even a little.

Two more steps and I stop, pivoting awkwardly back toward the poor bookseller who's halfway down the aisle now. "Wait! Actually...yes." My voice comes out sheepish. "I'm looking for...uh...Bibles."

He smiles like it's the most normal request in the world. "Right this way."

And just like that, I'm trailing behind a stranger to the one place in this store I've somehow never set foot in.

When we turn the corner, I stop short.

There they are—rows and rows of Bibles, stacked and lined up like they've been waiting for me. Suddenly I feel that same strange, warm ache I did on Sunday during the music.

Maybe this won't just be about being prepared.

Maybe it's about being found.

I pick up the first one that catches my eye—soft pink leather with delicate gold lettering. Pretty. The kind of book you'd want to leave out on a coffee table, even if you never opened it.

Then I notice a navy one with a zipper closure and a cream one with tiny, embossed flowers curling along the spine.

But then I freeze.

Each one has a little set of letters under the word "Bible." NIV. ESV. KJV.

Wait...what?

I grab my phone and type, "What does KJV mean?" Articles pop up with words like "translation," "literal," "thought-for-thought," and "paraphrase."

I read through a few until I get the gist. They are all versions of the Bible—saying the same thing, just in slightly different ways—but how am I supposed to know which one is right for me? This feels less like picking a book and more like picking a side.

I sigh, setting the pink one back.

That's when something colorful on the next shelf catches my eye. A whole display of pastel highlighters, gel pens, and the cutest little Bible verse stickers I've ever seen.

There are tabs with gold-foil lettering, too, like tiny jewelry for your pages.

I glance back at the Bibles, then at the pens.

If I'm going to study this thing...I feel like I need these. Not want. Need.

Because apparently, buying a Bible is now a full-blown experience.

I'm still staring at the rainbow pack of highlighters when my phone buzzes.

GRAY

How's your day going?

I glance between the pens in my hand and the row of Bibles in front of me, suddenly tempted to ask him for help. But instead of thinking it through, my thumbs just type:

IVY

I need help.

Not even two seconds later, my phone starts ringing.

I answer, startled. "Hello?"

"Ivy—are you okay? Where are you? What happened?" His voice is tight, urgent, like he's already halfway to his truck.

My eyes widen. "Oh—oh my gosh, no! Sorry! I'm fine. I'm literally in a bookstore. I just...worded that really badly."

There's a pause, then a long exhale. "You cannot text me 'I need help' with no context. My heart just shaved five years off my life."

I bite my lip, feeling a little sheepish. "Noted. For future reference, 'I need help picking a Bible' would've been the better route?"

"Much better," he says, though I can hear the smile in his voice now. "Alright, tell me what's going on."

I lean my hip against the shelf, cradling the phone between my ear and shoulder while I glance at the row of Bibles again.

"So, here's the thing," I say. "I picked up a few that looked pretty—like, really pretty. But then I noticed all these little labels—ESV, NIV, KJV—and now I feel like I'm trying to order at a restaurant where the menu is in another language."

Gray chuckles softly, the sound low and warm. "Okay, so those are just different translations. The Bible was originally written in Hebrew and Greek, so what you're seeing is basically the English version someone translated it into. Each one has a slightly different style of wording. Same truth—just different ways of saying it."

"Right...so...how do I know which one is my way?"

"Well," he says, "I personally use KJV—King James Version. It's beautiful and poetic, but it's also written in old English. Lots of 'thee' and 'thou' and words we don't really use anymore. Honestly? I wouldn't start there."

I huff out a little laugh. "Good to know."

"For you, I'd recommend NIV—the New International Version," he continues. "It's easy to read but still accurate. Flows more like the way we talk now, which makes it a lot less intimidating when you're just starting out."

I glance down at the Bible in my hand, then at another one that says NIV on the spine. "So basically...KJV is the gorgeous antique bookshelf piece, but NIV is the one I'll actually understand?"

"Exactly."

My gaze drifts back to the display of pastel highlighters

and Bible tabs. "Okay...so I also got pens, sticky notes, stickers, highlighters...anything else you think I need?"

Gray's laugh rumbles through the phone. "You're turning Bible shopping into a full-blown Target run, aren't you?"

"Don't judge. If I'm committing to reading the most important book in the world, it deserves accessories."

"Oh, I'm not judging," he teases. "I'm just making a mental note that if you ever join a Bible study group, you're gonna be the most prepared person in the room. Color-coded and all."

"Obviously," I say, grinning at the highlighters like they've just been promoted to VIP status. "I'm nothing if not thorough."

His chuckle softens into something warmer, and before I can stop myself, I ask, "So...how's your day going?"

He exhales slowly, like my voice just unraveled whatever knot he'd been carrying. "Better than it started," he says. "A lot better now that I'm talking to you."

The way he says it makes my pulse skip. "Smooth," I tease, but my voice is softer than I mean it to be.

"Not trying to be," he says. "It's just the truth."

I glance at the shelf in front of me, not even registering the rows of Bibles anymore. "Careful, Gray. Keep talking like that and you're gonna make me blush in public."

His laugh is low, warm. "I'm good with that. I'd love to see it."

I shake my head, grinning despite myself. "You're trouble."

"Probably," he admits. "But I also hold doors open and pray for you, so I'm hoping that balances things out."

My heart does an embarrassing little flip. "That's...not the worst kind of trouble."

There's a beat of silence, the kind that feels comfortable instead of awkward, and I realize my arms are aching from everything I'm holding. "Well, I better go check out before my hands give out on me."

He chuckles. "Go on, Sunshine. But just know—you've already made my day."

We hang up, and I lean against the shelf for a second, grinning like an idiot. My arms are full of books and pens, but my heart? Full of something I'm not quite ready to name.

By the time I get home, I'm actually excited. Which feels weird. I never thought I'd be excited about buying a Bible.

I drop my bag on the couch and head straight for my desk. The shopping bag hits the surface with a satisfying thud, and I pull everything out like it's Christmas morning —pens in every pastel shade imaginable, sticky notes in the shape of little speech bubbles, tabs that shimmer in the light, and highlighters so pretty they might just deserve their own display shelf.

I peel the plastic off each one, lining them up neatly, because if I'm going to do this, I'm going to all in.

The Bible sits in the center, still in its box. I slide it out carefully, like it might break if I move too fast. It's heavier than I expected, the leather smooth and cool under my fingertips. I flip it open at random—Matthew. I skim the words, feeling...lost. Do I just start from page one like any other book? Or jump around? Is there a "Beginner's Guide to Reading the Bible" section I somehow missed?

I bite my lip, tapping the page with the tip of my pen. And then it hits me—the verse from Sunday. The one Pastor Jack read when he talked about worth and grace.

"Look at the birds of the air; they do not sow or reap or store away in barns, and yet your heavenly Father feeds them. Are you not much more valuable than they? Can any one of you by worrying add a single hour to your life?"
Matthew 6:26-27

Something about that moment flashes back—Gray, sitting across from me at lunch, his voice low when he explained mercy and grace over tacos. The way he looked at me like he saw something worth waiting for.

I grab my phone, wanting to dive in more, and quickly search: bible verses explaining grace. Ephesians 2:8-9. My fingers tremble just a little as I flip to the page, the thin paper whispering with each turn. Finally, I spot the words.

"For it is by grace you have been saved, through faith—and this is not from yourselves, it is the gift of God— not by works, so that no one can boast." Ephesians 2:8-9

My chest tightens in the best possible way.

I uncap a highlighter, the mint green one, because why not start with my favorite color, and drag it slowly across the lines.

These two verses are the first things I've ever marked in a Bible.

And somehow, it feels like the first step toward something bigger.

Chapter 10
Gray

Goliath is out cold, a warm, snoring weight sprawled across my lap. I absently run a hand over his fur, my other hand hovering over the notebook balanced on the arm of the couch. There's a fresh page open—supposed to be filled with lyrics for a new song or at least the set list for Sunday— but all I've managed so far is a few half-formed lines that don't go anywhere.

Because my head's not here. It's two miles away, in a coffee shop where I saw Ivy last week.

It's almost Friday. Almost time to see her again for our scheduled breakfast date.

But I don't know if I can wait that long.

All week, I've lived for her name lighting up my phone.

A text in the morning, usually something random like her latest coffee order or a blurry photo of the sunrise.

A string of messages by lunch full of banter, thoughts about a verse she read, or a meme she knew would make me laugh.

And somewhere between dinner and midnight, a call that lasts way too long and ends way too soon.

It's become our rhythm.

Easy and constant, like breathing.

And I can't get enough of it.

Every ping of my phone is a rush of dopamine. Every message feels like a thread pulling her closer. But somewhere in the back of my mind, the worry whispers—Am I overwhelming her?

Am I trying to hold something that needs space to breathe?

She hasn't said anything. In fact, she meets me there. Text for text, call for call.

Still, part of me panics when I haven't heard from her in a few hours. Not because I don't trust her. But because I'm scared she doesn't want this as much as I do.

I shake my head, pocket my phone, and reach for the song sheets on my desk. Work. Focus. I know how to do that.

I make it about three minutes before I'm pulling my phone back out.

I stare at the screen. Tell myself it's not a big deal. It's not pushing if I'm just checking in. Just making sure she's good.

I'm still holding the phone when it buzzes.

A text, not from her. But a reminder from the group thread about Sunday's setlist.

I groan, tossing the phone onto the couch cushion. *This is ridiculous, Gray.*

Just wait. Control yourself. You don't need to be the one always reaching out.

But what if she's waiting for me?

I sigh, raking my hands through my hair. I'm halfway back to the song sheets before I finally break.

Screw it.

I snatch my phone off the cushion and type two words.

GRAY

You busy?

I stare at the screen. Regret it. Then don't. Then regret it again.

Until she texts back.

IVY

Not too busy for you.

I blink and exhale as I feel something warm spread across my chest that I wasn't prepared for.

Before I can second-guess myself, I reply.

GRAY

Good answer. Wanna go for a drive?

Three dots pop up immediately. I hold my breath.

IVY

I can be ready in fifteen.

I can't help but grin. She sends me her address and I slide my phone back into my pocket and reach for my keys. I glance over my shoulder at the setlist I still need to complete, but it can wait.

Because I get to see Ivy tonight.

Because no song, no setlist, nothing compares to being with her.

"I'll be back Goliath!"

Fifteen minutes later, she slides into the passenger seat of my truck, still smelling faintly of that floral perfume she wears. Her hair is up in a loose knot with a few strands falling around her face, and she's wearing an oversized cream sweater with soft, wide sleeves and a slouchy neckline that looks like it was made for cold nights and lingering conversations.

"Hey, you." I rest one hand on the steering wheel, the other draped over the center console.

"Hey." She smiles as she buckles her seatbelt. "So... where are we going?"

I tap the steering wheel with my thumb, leaning just a little closer. "It's a surprise."

Her eyes narrow in playful suspicion. "A good surprise?"

"The best," I promise, my mouth curving. "There's this place just outside of town I've been wanting to take you. It's...hard to explain. You'll see when we get there."

She tilts her head, curiosity written all over her face. "Mysterious."

I grin, shifting the truck into drive. "Exactly."

We drive for a while—long enough for the city lights to fall behind us and the narrow backroads to stretch out. Ivy's window is cracked just slightly, the cool evening air slipping in and brushing against her hair.

We don't talk much at first. She watches the trees blur past, fingers tracing invisible patterns on the window. I glance over sometimes, quick glances that don't last long enough.

The quiet isn't heavy. It's comfortable. Like neither of us needs to fill it. But still, I want to do something—something that will make her smile again.

So, when I spot a patch of wildflowers along the side of the road, I ease the truck onto the shoulder.

Ivy turns to me, brows lifted. "What are you doing?"

I throw it in park and grin. "Stay here."

Before she can argue, I'm out of the truck, crossing the ditch toward the little cluster of flowers growing wild and unbothered. I crouch down, picking the best ones I can find —yellow, purple, white—nothing fancy, just simple and real.

When I come back, she's leaning out the window, chin resting on her folded arms, watching me with that curious, amused look that makes my heart race.

I hold out the small, messy bouquet, and she takes them slowly, like she's afraid they might fall apart in her hands. She lifts them to her nose, closing her eyes as she inhales. The tiniest smile curves her lips, and it feels like she's not just smelling wildflowers—she's breathing in this whole moment.

When her eyes open again, they're warmer, softer. "You're something else, Gray."

"I'll take that as a compliment."

I slide back into the driver's seat, her flowers now resting in her lap, her thumb tracing one of the petals like it's the most delicate thing in the world. It's not long until we pass a faded sign for the old overlook. I almost drive by, almost. But then, without thinking, I turn the wheel, and gravel crunches under the tires as we pull off the main road and onto the winding path.

She glances over, eyes sparkling with curiosity. "So where is this mysterious place you're taking me?"

"You'll see."

She laughs, a little skeptical, but she settles back against the seat.

The overlook is empty. It always is. It's a spot I found

years ago when I needed somewhere quiet, somewhere I could breathe and not have to be everything for everyone.

I back my truck up near the edge and kill the engine. Beyond the guardrail, the sun sets behind downtown Dallas, which looks like a thousand tiny lights spilled across a blanket.

Without a word, I hop out, dropping the tailgate with a soft thud. Ivy slides out after me, curiosity in her eyes as she climbs up to sit beside me. The evening air wraps around us, it's cooler up here, quiet except for the hum of the city far below.

Ivy leans forward, elbows on her knees. "How did you find this place?"

"Just one of those nights when I needed somewhere to go," I say, shrugging.

She glances over; her face soft in the glow of the city lights. "You come here often?"

I nod. "When I need to think. Or not think." I watch her take it all in, her eyes reflecting the view like tiny sparks. "Figured you might like it."

Her smile is slow and real. "You figured right."

We sit there for a moment, our legs swinging off the edge of the tailgate, the silence settling between us and it is so comfortable. I almost leave it there. Almost. But then I lean back on my palms, eyes on the city.

"I have a serious question."

She angles toward me, raising an eyebrow. "Serious?"

"Very," I say, keeping my expression flat.

She laughs, pulling her knees up to her chest. "Alright, hit me."

"What's your favorite color?"

Her head drops back, and she laughs—a deep laugh, the

sound carrying into the night. "That's your serious question?"

I shrug. "Look, it says a lot about a person."

"Does it now?" she teases.

"It does," I say, fighting a grin. "I read it somewhere. Very scientific."

She rolls her eyes. "Fine. It's green."

"Green?" I pause, pretending to consider. "Good choice. Very reliable color."

She squints at me. "Reliable? What does that even mean?"

"You know...dependable, grounded, a little stubborn."

Her eyes narrow. "Are you just making this up as you go?"

"Absolutely."

We both laugh, and it's easy. Effortless. Like I'm not carefully choosing each word, like I'm not fighting the instinct to keep her at arm's length.

She leans back on her hands, looking over at me. "Alright, your turn."

"For what?"

Her eyes glimmer with challenge. "Favorite color."

"Easy, black."

Her nose scrunches a little, like she's thinking too hard about it. "Yeah... I figured."

I raise an eyebrow. "What's that supposed to mean?"

"It's just...you," she says, shrugging.

I nod. "I'll take it."

She swings her legs as we sit on the tailgate, the quiet night settling around us. Her hand rests casually beside mine, fingers so close they're almost touching. I don't think she realizes it, but the edge of her pinky brushes against mine, light as a breath.

I don't move. I just let it stay like that, the warmth of her skin grounding me.

The breeze we've had all evening fades into stillness, and the air feels heavier somehow—like the whole world has leaned in a little closer. She shifts, just enough that her shoulder brushes mine, and I glance down to find her looking at me.

Her eyes linger, searching, and my gaze dips to her mouth—soft, full, the kind of lips that make a man wonder what they'd taste like if he just leaned in a little more. I swallow, my hand lifting almost on its own, fingers brushing the side of her face. Her skin is warm beneath my palm, delicate in a way that makes me want to hold her there forever.

Too soon? The thought slides in, uninvited. I should pull back, give her space—but she doesn't move away, and the air between us feels charged, like we're teetering on the edge of something neither of us is ready to name.

Then a drop of rain splashes against my cheek, trailing down like a reminder that the world still exists outside this moment. I glance up at the darkening sky, then back at her.

The easy softness in her expression has shifted, replaced by something tighter. Worry flickers in her eyes, just enough to make me lower my hand, not because I want to, but because I want her to feel safe.

A gust of wind sweeps across the hill, rattling the branches above us and tugging at her hair. I catch the faint scent of rain in the air, sharp and earthy, just as Ivy pulls her phone from her sweater pocket. Her brows knit together as she taps the screen, the glow lighting her worried face.

"Gray..." Her voice is tight. She turns the phone toward me, the radar app showing a thick red line of storms headed straight toward Dallas. "This is bad. Like...really bad."

Before I can answer, another gust whips past, colder this time, making her flinch. I step off the tailgate and stand in front of her, my hands settling firmly on her shoulders. "Hey." I wait until her eyes meet mine. "We're okay. I've driven through storms like this before."

She shakes her head. "You don't understand—I hate storms. I mean, hate them."

"It's ok," I say softly. "I'm here. You're not alone in this, Ivy. I'll get you back to your apartment before it even hits, alright?"

Her breath comes out in a shaky rush, but she nods. I give her shoulders one last squeeze before stepping in closer.

"C'mon," I murmur, sliding my hands to her waist. I lift her down from the tailgate, her shoes hitting the gravel softly. My hand finds hers without even thinking, and I don't let go as I walk her around to the passenger side.

I open the door and wait until she's settled in, seatbelt clicked, before closing it gently and circling around to my side.

When I climb in, the cab is warm from her presence, the air thick with rain and electricity. I start the engine, resting one hand on the wheel and the other palm-up on the console between us—close enough that if she wants it, it's hers.

She does take it, slipping her fingers into mine like it's the most natural thing in the world...until the first flash of lightning streaks across the sky and she drops my hand with a breathless, "Two hands on the wheel, Gray."

I bite back a smile. "Yes, ma'am."

The truth is this storm isn't half as bad as it looks on her radar app. I've driven through worse. But I've got precious cargo tonight—someone who hates storms and trusts me to get her home safe. And that trust? I'm not taking it lightly.

The rain starts in light, uneven taps on the windshield, the wipers sweeping them away as we head toward the city lights. The wind pushes against the truck, but I keep it steady, thinking about the story in Mark where Jesus calmed the storm with just a few words. If I could, I'd do the same for her right now—not just the one in the sky, but the one in her chest.

"Almost there," I say, glancing at her. Her shoulders loosen a little, and she nods, watching the road like it's the only thing keeping the storm from catching us.

By the time we pull into her complex, the rain has eased into a mist. The wind's still tossing the trees, but it's lost the bite it had earlier.

I park in front of her building, already reaching for my door handle. She gives me a look like she might argue, but I'm not giving her the chance. I'm out of the truck and around to her side in seconds, opening her door and offering my hand.

"You don't have to—"

"Yeah, I do." My voice leaves no room for debate.

She slips her hand into mine, and I walk her up the path. She pulls out her phone, glancing at her radar app. "Huh. It's already moved north. Guess it wasn't that bad."

"Maybe not," I say, though I'm not about to admit I knew that the whole time. Bad or not, she deserved to feel safe.

At her door, she pauses, her hand still warm in mine. "Thanks for...you know, everything tonight. For not making me feel silly."

"You could never be silly to me."

Her lips twitch into a smile, and she glances down at

our joined hands like she's thinking about letting go—but doesn't. For a beat, neither of us moves. The rain softens to a whisper against the awning, and she finally looks back up at me, eyes shining in that way that makes my chest feel too small.

Then, before I can process it, she leans in and presses a soft kiss to my cheek.

It's over too quickly, the brush of her lips lingering in my mind as she steps back—but still, she doesn't open the door right away. She lingers there, her back against it, like maybe she's not ready for the night to end either.

"Goodnight, Gray."

"Night, Ivy."

Only then does she slip inside, the door clicking shut between us. I just stand there in the quiet hallway, one hand braced over the spot her lips touched, staring at the closed door like I'm trying to memorize the moment.

If I had any doubts before tonight, they're gone now. I'm in trouble—good, beautiful trouble.

Chapter 11
Gray

This week has flown by.

After my date with Ivy on Wednesday night—overlook, tailgate, storm clouds—I haven't been able to shake the image of rain in her hair, how we almost kissed.

Thursday was back to real life. I spent the morning finalizing the set list for Sunday—three songs I know the band will nail, two that'll stretch us just enough to keep things fresh. Later that night I went to The Well with a few friends for trivia night. We lost by two points, thanks to a ridiculous "Who invented the waffle iron?" question I still say was a setup. Didn't matter though—it felt good to laugh until my sides hurt.

And now it's Friday morning.

The sun's breaking over the rooftops, and my truck smells faintly of coffee from the thermos in the cup holder. I've had this breakfast penciled in since the moment we planned it, and it's been the one thing on my calendar I've been counting down to all week.

Truth is, I don't think it's the pancakes I'm looking forward to.

I pull up to Ivy's apartment but before I can even put the truck in park, she's already skipping down the steps, hair catching the sunlight, smile easy and unguarded.

I step out and lean against the passenger side door, arms crossed loosely as I watch her make her way toward me. She's got that kind of energy that makes the rest of the street feel dull in comparison.

"Hey, you," I say when she's close enough, my voice soft but certain—the way I always say it to her now.

Her eyes light up like she's been waiting to hear it.

I reach into my back pocket and pull out the single flower I picked up on the way over. Nothing fancy—just a small, pale daisy—but it's perfect for her. "For you," I murmur, tucking it gently behind her ear.

A blush blooms across her cheeks, and she looks down for half a second before meeting my gaze again. "Thank you," she says, almost shy.

I grin, pulling open the passenger door. "Anytime."

She climbs in, still smiling, still a little pink in the face, and I make sure she's settled before shutting the door and heading around to my side.

We pull up to the diner, the neon sign flickering above us. The parking lot is mostly empty with only a couple of trucks, an old Buick, and us.

She eyes the diner as I park, her head tilting. "This looks...sketchy. Are you sure it's open?"

I grin. "Sketchy? This place is a local treasure."

She glances at the nearly empty parking lot. "Then where is everybody?"

"They're missing out," I say, cutting the engine. "Don't worry, the food's worth it. I promise."

Her lips twitch like she's not entirely convinced. "This is how people end up in true crime podcasts."

"Fair," I say, offering my hand to help her down. "But at least you'll go out on the best pancakes of your life."

We walk inside, greeted by the smell of maple syrup and coffee that's probably been burning for hours. It's classic, with checkered floors, vinyl booths, and a chalkboard menu with the specials half-erased. I've been coming here for years; it's my favorite place.

We slide into a booth by the window, the vinyl squeaking slightly beneath us. The waitress comes over, pad and pen at the ready. "What can I get ya?"

"I'll take a black coffee," I tell her. "And she'll have a vanilla latte with oat milk."

Ivy's brows lift, clearly surprised.

Before she can say anything, the waitress interrupts with a deadpan tone. "Sir, we don't have lattes. Just plain coffee."

I freeze, caught mid-smile. "Oh. Uh...right."

Ivy starts giggling, shaking her head. "I'll just do coffee with cream and sugar."

The waitress scribbles it down, not missing a beat. "Anything to eat?"

"Two stacks of blueberry pancakes," I say confidently, "each with a side of bacon and scrambled eggs."

Ivy's eyes narrow, but she's smiling. "You just ordered for me."

I hand the menus back to the waitress, who disappears

with a wink. I turn back to Ivy, resting my arms on the table. "Is that a problem?"

She laughs softly. "No. I guess not."

"I told you. Breakfast connoisseur."

She laughs, shaking her head. "I'm starting to believe it."

I'm feeling good, like I got this. But then she looks down at her hands, her lips twitching.

"Just one thing..." she starts, her voice soft.

My brow furrows. "Yeah?"

Her eyes lift to mine, a glimmer of apology in them. "I'm actually allergic to blueberries."

I freeze. My hands instinctively pull back from the table. My mind races, how did I not know that? I just ordered her a plate full of something she can't even eat.

"Oh, man...I'm so sorry. I—"

Her face cracks, the apology melting away, replaced with a grin that spreads slow and wide. "I'm kidding," she says, her voice breaking on a laugh. "Bad joke. I'm sorry."

It takes a second for the words to land, but when they do, I can't help it. I laugh. Hard. The kind that actually doubles me over, my shoulders shaking with relief and disbelief.

She giggles too, her hands covering her mouth. "I'm sorry!" she says again, barely catching her breath. "Your face...I couldn't help it."

I wipe a tear from the corner of my eye. "That was evil. Actually evil."

She reaches across the table, her fingers grazing mine. "But you remember my coffee order."

I take her hand, squeeze it just slightly. "That I do."

And for a moment, I forget about control. About playing it safe. About everything I'm trying to keep from spinning out of my hands.

Right now, it's just her. And that's enough.

The waitress returns balancing two steaming mugs and a small plate piled with creamers. She sets them down with a nod before disappearing toward the kitchen.

Ivy reaches for a sugar packet from the holder between us, tearing it open with a flick of her wrist.

I wrap my hands around my cup, letting the heat soak in. "So...have you always lived in Dallas?"

She shakes her head, pouring cream into her coffee until it turns a warm caramel color. "Nope. I grew up in Ashen Mills—a little town about thirty miles east of here."

"Ashen Mills," I repeat, tasting the name. "Sounds small."

Her mouth curves. "Small enough that everyone knows everyone."

I grin. "And you liked that?"

Her eyes soften, a hint of nostalgia slipping into her smile as she stirs her coffee. "I did. I mean, I didn't always appreciate it when I was younger, but...I miss it now. The quiet, the way neighbors looked out for each other, the little traditions that never changed."

She glances up at me, almost shy. "One day, I think I'd like to settle down back there. Start fresh, maybe raise a family."

Something in my chest tightens at the thought—an image of her in a sundress, laughter spilling across a front porch, sunlight catching in her hair.

I nod toward her. "Does your family still live there?"

She smiles over the rim of her mug. "Yeah. My parents still live in the same house I grew up in. My older sister, Sarah, is just a few streets over. And then there are all my cousins...way too many to count."

Her eyes soften, and there's a little laugh in her voice.

"Holidays are always hectic—people crammed into every corner of the house, kids running everywhere—but it's cozy. The kind of chaos you don't want to escape from."

"That sounds wonderful," I say, meaning it.

Her smile lingers as she stirs cream into her coffee. "What about you? Do you have a big family?"

I shake my head. "No. It was just me and my mom." I keep it vague, not ready to unpack more than that yet.

Before she can press further, the waitress returns with our plates, sliding hers in front of her and mine in front of me. The smell of fresh pancakes and bacon fills the air.

I pick up my fork but glance at her again. "Okay, my turn. What's one thing most people don't know about you?"

Her eyebrows lift. "That's a dangerous question."

I grin. "I like dangerous questions."

She taps her fork against the edge of her plate, pretending to think. "Most people don't know...that I once won a pie-eating contest at the Ashen Mills Fall Festival."

I almost choke on my coffee. "Wait—what?"

Her laugh bubbles out, warm and unguarded. "Pumpkin pie. No hands allowed. I still can't look at one without remembering it."

"That's...actually impressive." I lean forward. "And slightly terrifying."

"Your turn," she says, pointing her fork at me. "One thing most people don't know about you."

I think for a second, then lean back casually. "Most people don't know...I'm a dad."

Her fork freezes midair, eyes going wide. "You're a— wait, what?"

I can't hold back the grin. "Cat dad," I clarify, drawing the words out.

She exhales a laugh, shaking her head. "Gray, you cannot pause like that. I almost dropped my fork."

"That's the fun part," I say, smirking. "His name's Goliath. He's enormous. Thinks he runs the place. Honestly...he's probably right."

Her eyes sparkle. "I need to meet him someday."

"He would love you," I say.

She smirks, then tilts her head. "Okay, my turn. What's something you've always wanted to do but haven't yet?"

I think about it, swirling the coffee in my cup. "Hmm...play an outdoor set in the middle of nowhere. Like—stars overhead, fireflies, just a few people who actually care about the music."

Her smile softens. "That sounds perfect."

"What about you?" I ask, leaning in. "Biggest thing on your list?"

She stirs her coffee, eyes dropping to the table. "Honestly? I want to restore an old house. Not for a flip. Just...to live in. Something with creaky floors and history in the walls. Maybe back in Ashen Mills."

I picture it—her barefoot in some sunny old kitchen, laughter echoing down the hall. "Yeah," I murmur, "I can see that."

We linger over the last bites, talking about everything and nothing, but the clock on the wall doesn't care. Ivy sighs, setting down her fork. "I really should get to work."

"Or," I offer, leaning back with a grin, "you could just call in and let me kidnap you for the rest of the day."

She laughs, shaking her head. "Tempting, but I can't. I have deadlines."

I tilt my head, pretending to consider. "Okay. Then maybe tomorrow morning you can sneak away for something more fun?"

Her brows lift. "Fun like what?"

"Rehearsal. At church," I say. "Nothing fancy—just me, the worship team, and a whole lot of coffee."

She hesitates, the corner of her lip catching between her teeth. "I don't know…"

I lean in, voice dropping just a bit. "Come on, Ivy. You'll get a front row seat to the music before anyone else hears it."

Her smile curves slow. "Fine. I'll come."

On the drive back, she slips her hand into mine, her fingers fitting like they've been there all along. I keep my palm resting against hers on the console, letting my thumb brush over the top of her hand. When I do, I catch the way goosebumps chase up her arm. Not from the A/C—no, this is something else entirely. And I can't stop doing it, just to see her pretend she's not affected.

We pull up outside her apartment, but neither of us moves right away. "Thanks for breakfast," she says softly, still holding my hand.

"Thanks for letting me watch you put sugar in your coffee like you were defusing a bomb," I tease, grinning.

She rolls her eyes but grins back, finally letting go. "See you tomorrow?"

I nod, holding her gaze. "Bright and early. And Ivy?"

"Yeah?"

"You look really good in my morning."

She laughs, then leans in to kiss my cheek—quick, warm, and over far too soon. "See you tomorrow, Gray."

She hesitates for a heartbeat in the open doorway, like she might say something else, but instead she smiles and slips inside. I sit there a moment longer, my hand going to the spot where her lips touched, and all I can think is, I'm in trouble.

Chapter 12
Ivy

The church feels almost unfamiliar without Sunday's energy.

For one, it's a lot quieter. It's also less polished. The echoes aren't of people shuffling into their seats, but of guitar strums from rehearsal and the faint echo of someone testing a mic. It feels almost...intimate. Like I'm peeking behind the curtain of something top secret.

Gray invited me to stop by rehearsal, but the second I stepped into the lobby, nerves hit me like a wall. This isn't a service. There are no crowds to disappear into. No rows of people to blend into the background. Just, him. His people. His job.

And I don't want to mess it up. Walking into his world and meeting his colleagues.

I clutch my tote bag a little tighter as I wander past the welcome desk. The lights are dimmed and there's a soft hum of conversation coming from the sanctuary, peppered with the occasional burst of laughter.

I peek through the side door.

Gray is up front, talking to a man with a headset. He's

wearing a plain black tee and jeans with a guitar slung over his shoulder like it's another limb on his body. He doesn't see me yet. But I sure do see him.

He's completely in his element. Confident and focused, not performing, but more like leading. His fingers brush over the strings as he talks, absentmindedly plucking out quiet chords that hum through the speakers. I watch his hands, the way they move like they're sure of every note.

I hesitate, gripping the door handle, half-thinking I should turn around before I interrupt whatever this is. But before I can fully talk myself out of it, I push the door open and step inside.

The music softens and his eyes flick up, catching mine instantly. His whole face brightens, that familiar grin spreading across his lips.

"Hey you!" His voice instantly warms me. "You made it."

I shrug, trying not to sound too eager. "Figured I'd drop in and get a little behind the scenes look."

He laughs and waves me up to the stage. "This is the team. Everyone—this is Ivy."

A chorus of smiles and waves greets me. One guy near the back adjusts the lights and gives me a polite nod and a few introduce themselves. There's an easy energy in the room, like they've been doing this together for years. Like it's home for them.

"You can sit anywhere," Gray says. "We're just running through the setlist for tomorrow."

I nod and try to look casual as I step off the stage and slide into a seat a few rows back. The music swells, their voices blending into harmonies that feel like they're warming the empty spaces.

That's when I hear it.

A faint, frustrated sigh drifts above the music. I glance at the woman sitting in front of me, hunched over her laptop, shoulders tight, lips pressed together like she's seconds from snapping the laptop shut.

"Why won't this work?" she mutters, tapping sharply at the trackpad. "The background just...won't layer right. And now the whole thing looks blurry."

I shift in my seat, fidgeting with my hands in my lap. Something in me itches to help, but I hesitate. Maybe she doesn't want a stranger jumping in. Maybe I'll just embarrass her.

Another groan escapes her, this one louder, frustration echoing in the mostly empty room. A couple of heads turn before quickly going back to their own conversations.

I lean forward slightly, curiosity winning. From here, I can see enough of her screen to know exactly what's wrong. Image resolution. Too low. Easy fix.

My fingers tap against my knee. I can help. I should help.

Finally, I set my hands down with a sigh. "Um...sorry, I don't mean to eavesdrop," I say, leaning a little toward her with a tentative smile. "But I couldn't help noticing your screen. It looks like your image resolution might be too low —that's probably why it's coming out blurry."

She looks up, startled. "Wait...you know how to work this program?"

I nod, my nerves fading a little. "Yeah. I actually do graphic design for a living." My voice softens, but I gesture toward her laptop. "Do you mind if I take a look?"

Relief flashes across her face so quickly it almost makes me laugh. "Please. Be my guest."

Within seconds I'm beside her, adjusting image ratios

and shifting the layout. She watches, eyes widening. "How are you doing that so fast?"

I grin, clicking through layers. "I spend way too much time with Canva. And caffeine helps."

Gray's voice cuts in from behind me. "You're amazing."

I glance over my shoulder, surprised to see him there.

"She just saved me two hours of stress," the woman says. "Greg should hire her."

Gray smirks, crossing his arms. "I may have to put in a good word."

I feel my cheeks flush, but I don't look away. There's a softness in his gaze that lingers just a second too long before he clears his throat and looks back at the stage.

"You fit in here more than you realize," he says quietly.

I raise a brow. "Because I can fix a blurry file?"

He shakes his head, eyes locked on mine. "Because you show up with your whole heart. That matters more."

I look down, trying to hide my smile. "Thanks for inviting me."

"Thanks for coming."

Just then, a voice calls from the stage.

"Hey Gray, you still doing that sketch with the youth team Sunday?" It's a guy with messy hair, thick glasses framing kind eyes, flipping through a script.

Gray laughs, glancing back. "Yes sir!" Then he leans toward me. "That's Micah. Youth pastor. Good guy."

I glance toward the stage as Micah jokes with the crew on stage. He's clearly respected but doesn't take himself too seriously. Plus, he's apparently good with kids. Harper would eat that dynamic alive.

I make a mental note.

Gray stands, stretching slightly. "We're grabbing lunch after this, want to come with?"

I blink, surprised. "With all of you?"

He grins, nodding toward the group. "Yeah. It's kind of a post-rehearsal thing, nothing glamorous. Mostly good food and a lot of inside jokes."

I glance around at the stage where some are still packing up instruments, others are huddled around the tech booth laughing about something. They fit together like puzzle pieces, each one knowing exactly where they belong.

I want that.

I clear my throat, trying not to sound too eager. "Yeah. I'd love to."

His smile widens, and he nods toward the group. "I know you'll like them."

We gather in the lobby, the chatter bouncing off the walls as people grab their jackets and make plans for who's riding with who. Gray throws his arm around an older guy with dark hair and a deep laugh, introducing me with a casual ease that makes my nerves settle.

"Hey Greg, this is Ivy," he says, patting the guy on the back. "She basically saved the graphics for this week's bulletin."

The guy turns to me, his grin stretching wide. "You're the one who made Paige stop griping under her breath for a whole five minutes? I'm impressed."

I laugh. "I try."

Gray chuckles, then turns his full attention to me. "Ride with me."

"Of course."

We all head outside, the summer air brushing over my skin as we spill into the parking lot. Laughter and light-hearted banter echo around us as people pile into cars. I slide into the passenger seat of Gray's truck, the familiarity settling over me in a way I wasn't expecting.

The burger joint is only ten minutes away from the church. We walk in and the waitress greets them like it's routine. Like she knows them, which I guess she probably does.

We all cram into two long booths, elbows bumping, knees pressed together. Gray slides in beside me and I'm sandwiched between him and the girl named Paige who tells me all about how she accidentally erased half the graphic earlier that afternoon.

"Accidentally?" Gray teases, leaning back and stretching his arm along the back of the booth.

She rolls her eyes. "Yes, accidentally. You think I enjoy the thrill of being behind schedule every week?"

"Wouldn't surprise me," he fires back, and the whole table laughs.

I can't help but smile as I watch them. It's easy, familiar. It reminds me of my family back in Ashen Mills. I listen to them talk, tease and poke fun at each other. Every now and then, I catch Gray glancing at me, like he's making sure I'm still here. Still part of it.

I feel his hand slide under the table, gently brushing mine. It's not obvious, not a grand gesture, just the smallest connection. And I'm grateful for it.

The waitress takes our orders, it's chaotic, but she doesn't seem to mind.

Gray leans in, voice low. "You doing alright?"

I nod, meeting his eyes. "Better than alright."

He holds my gaze for just a second too long, and I'm pretty sure I'm not imagining the way his fingers brush mine again, lingering just slightly before he pulls away.

And somehow, in this tiny diner, crammed into a booth with a dozen new faces, I don't just feel like I'm blending into his world.

I feel like I'm a part of it.

The drive back to the church is quieter than the ride to the diner. My hands rest in my lap, fingers fiddling with the frayed edge of my tote bag as Gray keeps one hand on the wheel, the other resting casually on the center console.

I replay the afternoon in my head—the way his friends laughed, how easily they pulled me in, how Gray's hand brushed mine more times than I could count. It's different. Different from anything I've ever known.

We pull into the church parking lot and Gray shifts the truck into park but doesn't turn off the engine. His fingers drum lightly on the steering wheel, and I can feel the weight of his gaze settle on me.

"You good?" he asks softly.

I nod. "More than good."

His smile is gentle, just a tilt of his lips, but it reaches his eyes. "I'm glad you came."

I glance down at my hands, twisting my fingers together. "Me too."

There's a pause that stretches between us. I feel it like a current, buzzing just under my skin.

I swallow, my eyes flickering to his mouth for just a second before darting back to his eyes. His gaze doesn't waver, and for a heartbeat, I think he might lean in to kiss me.

My breath catches. My pulse pounds. I don't move.

But neither does he.

He clears his throat, glancing forward. "I should...I should let you get home."

Disappointment floods my chest before I can shove it back down. I nod quickly, fumbling for the door handle. "Yeah, of course. I've got some work to get done anyway."

I step out of the truck, the hot air stinging my skin like a wake-up call. I feel foolish, like I misread something. But before I can spiral, I hear his voice growing closer.

"Ivy, wait up."

When we reach the driver's side of my car, he hesitates, then turns to face me fully. "Thanks for today," he says softly, his eyes holding mine. "For coming to rehearsal and meeting my friends."

I nod, but the lump in my throat makes it hard to speak. Instead, I open my arms for the hug I so desperately need, and he steps into them without a second of hesitation.

His arms wrap around me in a warm, grounding embrace. One hand presses gently to my back, the other brushes my hair. I melt into him before I even realize it, the stress of the awkward truck moment, the questions I haven't found words for slowly fall away.

Just for a second, nothing else matters.

Neither of us moves.

It's the kind of hug that feels like it's trying to say something more, like maybe if we hold on long enough, we won't have to say goodbye this time.

But eventually, we do.

He pulls back just an inch, eyes scanning mine like he's memorizing the moment. "Drive safe, okay?"

I nod again, this time barely whispering, "You too."

I slip into the driver's seat, close the door gently, and he waits there until I pull away.

Why has he not kissed me yet? Am I overthinking this relationship?

My mind spins, thoughts colliding as I pull onto the highway.

He likes me...right? Like, likes me, likes me?

Or is this just a friendship? Maybe that's what this is. Coffee and late-night drives and lingering glances that I'm reading way too much into. No, that can't be it.

I chew on my bottom lip, eyes locked on the road as I drive home. I've never felt like this so fast before. Like I'm walking a line between something real and something imagined. And the not-knowing twists my stomach.

But more than that...the not-kissing.

In my past relationships, everything progressed faster. A couple of dates, and then suddenly, it's late nights and tangled sheets. Gray doesn't move like that. He's careful and intentional.

And I'm starting to realize I don't know what to do with that.

I pull into my apartment complex and turn off the engine, hands still gripping the wheel.

Do Christians even kiss?

I shake my head, laughing softly at myself. Of course they do. I think. Right?

I sigh, finally reaching for my keys. As I step out and lock the door behind me and for a moment, I swear I can still feel the brush of his hand, the warmth of his gaze.

But I'm not sure if this is going anywhere...or if I'm just hoping it is.

Chapter 13
Ivy

Getting Harper to agree to come to church was easier than I expected.

"I mean, I don't have anything else going on," she'd said, scrolling through her phone. "And if there's brunch afterward, count me in."

Classic Harper. Casual agreement, emotional firewall firmly in place. But I'll take it.

Olivia, on the other hand, was more hesitant.

"I've got plans," she said quickly, eyes flicking away.

I didn't press. Even though I'm pretty sure her plans involve avoiding emotional vulnerability and binge-watching true crime, but I get it, so I don't push.

We pull into the church parking lot, the sunlight catching the building just right, and I pause, taking it in. Harper glances over at me.

"You, okay?"

"Yeah," I say, smiling. "Just, glad you're here."

She gasps. "Ivy, you're glowing. Either it's love or the bad coffee. I'm betting love."

I roll my eyes. "Let's go."

Inside, the church is already buzzing with activity—volunteers setting up signs, fresh coffee being poured into cups of tired guests. It's warm, welcoming, and now oh so familiar even though this is only my second time at church.

We are walking down the main hallway when a door down the back hallway opens and Gray steps through with his guitar in hand, earbuds tucked around his neck. His eyes find mine instantly and that familiar spark lights up his face like it always does when he sees me. My stomach does that little flip it's started doing whenever he's near.

"Hey you," he says, voice warm as he pulls me in for a quick side-hug. I have grown to love the way he says those words in greeting. "I was hoping I'd catch you before service."

"Well, looks like you got lucky," I smile, my heart doing cartwheels. "Oh!" I turn slightly. "Gray, this is Harper. Harper, this is Gray."

He shifts his attention to her, offering a handshake. "Nice to finally meet you. Ivy told me all about you and Olivia."

Harper raises a brow. "Hopefully she left out the embarrassing stuff."

Gray grins. "Nothing but glowing reviews. She's lucky to have you."

Harper smirks. "She is."

Gray laughs, then turns back to me, that soft focus settling behind his eyes again.

"Hey, do you have plans after service?" he asks casually. But there's a hopeful edge to it, like he's already bracing for me to say no.

Before I can answer, Harper jumps in. "Yep! We're going to brunch, then to look at plants. I'm pretty sure my last succulent died of loneliness. Time to replace him."

Gray's eyebrows lift slightly. "You're going plant shopping?"

Harper nods. "Yep! And maybe grab some new pots if I'm feeling ambitious." She turns to me with a grin. "You still good with that, right?"

"Of course," I say, glancing back at Gray. His expression flickers, just for a second. A small hesitation. I catch the way his jaw tenses, how his hand slides into his back pocket like he's holding something back. "Would you like to join us?"

There's a pause, and I swear I can see him weighing his options. He opens his mouth slightly, then shuts it. Finally, he clears his throat. "No, it's okay. Y'all have your girl time." His smile is polite, almost too practiced.

My heart dips, just a bit. I don't want him to feel left out, but Harper's already looping her arm through mine, clearly ready to go find our seats and move on with our morning.

"Maybe I'll see you later?" I offer.

His eyes brighten slightly, his smile softening around the edges. "Yeah? You promise?"

I nod. "Promise."

His grin grows, and he gives my hand a quick squeeze before stepping back. "I'll hold you to that."

I watch him disappear through the door, his silhouette slipping into the shadows of the hallway. When he's gone, I swear I can still feel the warmth of his hand pressed against mine.

As soon as the door closes behind him, Harper nudges me. "He's even cuter than I remember."

I shake my head, laughing. "You're a menace."

She sips her coffee, unbothered. "You're welcome."

We're passing by the Children's ministry area, almost to

the sanctuary doors when we hear raised voices near the corner of the check-in area.

"I don't want to!"

Harper and I both pause and turn just in time to see a little boy, probably five or six, tear around the corner, tears streaming down his face.

Harper's eyes widen. "That's one of my students from last year."

Before I can respond, she's already moving.

Harper drops to her knees without hesitation and he runs straight into her arms like she's the only safe place in the world.

"Hey, buddy," she says gently. "What's going on?"

He clutches her like he's been lost for hours. "I—I didn't know where my dad went."

"He just walked you to your room, right?" she soothes, rubbing his back. "It's okay. You're okay."

Micah approaches from the opposite hallway, cautious but concerned. "Hey, is he with you?"

Harper stands, one hand still on the boy's shoulder. "He's one of my students, I teach Kindergarten at the local elementary school."

He furrows his brow. "Okay, but you can't just take him out of the room. I didn't see a name tag on you. We have policies for a reason."

"I didn't take him," Harper says, defensive now. "He ran to me. And I'm not trying to sneak him out, I'm trying to help."

Micah crosses his arms, skeptical. "I get that, but without a background check on file, you can't just..."

"I have a background check," she snaps. "It's literally required to work in the school system."

He raises an eyebrow. "And I'm just supposed to take your word on that?"

I try not to laugh. Harper's jaw drops, offended in that Harper way that's a perfect mix of sass and disbelief.

"You seriously think I'm lying about being a teacher?" she asks.

He doesn't answer. Just shrugs one shoulder.

Luckily the classroom volunteer appears, calling for the boy, who now seems perfectly content with a cup of animal crackers and a sticker.

Harper exhales, tension still riding high, but she turns back to Micah.

"Fine. Where do I go to fill out your precious background check?"

He nods to a computer station by the door. "There. It only takes a minute."

Harper marches over to the computer station by the classroom check-in desk, muttering something under her breath about red tape and overly suspicious church staff. I follow a few steps behind, but it's Micah who really watches her.

And I mean watches her.

Not in a creepy way, just casually, yet with unmistakable focus. Like he's taking mental notes. Harper's hips sway slightly as she types, her fingers jabbing at the keys like each click is making a point. Her bright red hair catches the light, wild and fierce, a perfect match for the fire in her eyes. Her jaw is tight. She's not letting this go.

Leave it to Harper to prove a point and submit to a background check out of spite.

She hits the final key like a mic drop, turns sharply, and looks directly at Micah.

"See you next weekend."

She says it with such conviction, I almost want to applaud.

He doesn't flinch. "We'll contact you if it's approved."

Harper halts mid-stride and swirls back toward him, stomping up until she's standing a little too close. She's small next to him, Micah towers over her, taller than I realized, with messy brown hair that somehow still looks intentional and a calm, steady presence that feels like the exact opposite of her storm.

He looks down at her, expression unreadable behind his thick frames, like nothing she says could rattle him. And for a beat, it's like the air shifts between them—like even their differences can't stop whatever is happening here.

"It will be approved," she says flatly.

They stare at each other for a half-second too long, and I swear, the tension in the air could be bottled.

Then, without another word, she turns on her heel and heads toward me.

As we walk toward the sanctuary, I glance back just in time to catch it—Micah's mouth tugging into the tiniest smirk. The kind you try to fight off but lose to anyway.

I mouth a quick, "Sorry."

He shakes his head with a mix of exasperation and amusement, then disappears back toward the children's hallway.

I lean closer to Harper and whisper, "I think he's like... the man in charge of the entire kids' area."

She blinks. "Figures. Control issues."

I snort.

"Sorry," she says as we slip into the hallway toward the main doors. "Didn't mean to cause a scene."

I shrug, smiling. "You know, for all your dramatics, I think you just signed yourself up to serve."

Harper doesn't respond right away, but the way her expression softens just a little tells me she's happy about it.

We push open the sanctuary doors just as the final worship song begins.

The lights are low, the atmosphere thick with reverence. Music swells from the stage, the rich harmonies are a slow build of instruments layered beneath a single voice that I'd know anywhere.

We squeeze into two open seats, basically the only ones open, nearly in the front row. I hesitate for a split second because I've never sat this close to any stage, and something about being here, this close to him, makes me nervous.

I glance up and find him in the center of it all. Guitar strapped across his chest, eyes closed, his hand lifted toward Heaven like it's second nature. His brow is furrowed, not with effort but with focus, like the rest of the world has fallen away and it's just him and God.

And I can't look away.

There's something so humbling about it—watching him worship like that. Not performing. Not trying. Just... pouring out his true feelings.

The lyrics are from a song I've never heard before—another original, maybe? The words reach into places I haven't let myself name. About being fully known and still loved. About not needing to earn love to be worthy of it.

Something cracks open in my chest.

It's not a tear, not a breakdown. Just this sudden, gentle ache.

Like someone just whispered: *this is for you.*

The song builds one final time—Gray's voice rising, steady and sure, like a prayer he's already lived through. And when the last note fades, the room is still, hearts full.

Everyone begins to sit.

Everyone but me.

I'm frozen in place, the weight of the lyrics still pressing down on me.

I glance toward the stage and find him already watching me.

Gray meets my gaze and gives the tiniest wave, his lips curved into a soft smile like he knows. Like somehow, he knows exactly how I am feeling.

My heart stumbles.

I wave back without meaning to, and it hits me how visible I am right now, how obviously wrecked I must look.

Harper gently tugs my sleeve. I blink, glancing around to realize I'm the only one still standing.

My cheeks flush hot as I quickly plop down into my seat.

Harper leans in, voice low but warm. "What was that?"

I nod, breathless. "Just...got caught up for a second."

She smiles like she gets it.

"Oh Ivy, you've got it bad," she smirks. "I am so here for this."

But maybe it's not just Gray I've got it bad for. Maybe it's this thing called the Holy Spirit that people keep talking about.

Chapter 14
Ivy

We end up back at Harper's place, her tiny apartment on the third floor of a brick building that smells faintly of fresh paint and laundry detergent. The sun filters through gauzy curtains, casting warm stripes of light across the hardwood floor. Harper kicks off her shoes the second we walk in, adding to the pile of shoes in her front entryway.

"Okay, brunch was a ten out of ten," she declares, flinging her purse onto the nearest chair with a dramatic sigh, "but I am desperate for caffeine. I used all my energy deciding between that fiddle leaf fig and my new cactus."

"You really made that poor cashier hold both for like twenty minutes," I tease, slipping off my own shoes and curling up on her couch. "I'm surprised he didn't charge you a plant indecision fee."

She waves me off. "Art requires time. You want a coffee?"

"Sure," I say, leaning back and letting the comfort of the afternoon settle over me.

The smell of fresh coffee wafts from her Keurig, and she

pops open a cabinet to rummage for snacks. "Olivia should be here soon. I texted her."

I glance at my phone, surprised. "You convinced her to come over?"

"Yes, she's coming to hang out but insisted we don't bring up the church thing." Harper's voice is muffled behind the pantry door. "But I'm working on it."

I laugh. "That doesn't surprise me."

Olivia hasn't been very thrilled by me going to church, and now Harper. It's strange how against it she is. Part of me wants to press her and find out why, but I have a feeling I should give her some space.

Harper reappears with a bag of chips and two mugs of coffee, handing me one before plopping down beside me. "I still can't believe how intense that guy was. Micah, right?" She rolls her eyes. "I swear, he looked at me like I was about to steal that kid and run off to Canada."

I choke on my coffee. "To be fair, you did kind of bull-doze him."

She shrugs, clearly unbothered. "Someone has to keep those power-tripping volunteers in check."

I laugh, but there's an edge of truth to her words. Harper's good at deflecting, turning moments of tension into humor. But I saw her face when she walked away from Micah. The way she squared her shoulders, determined to prove him wrong.

There's a sharp knock at the door before I can dig deeper.

Harper pops up, swinging it open to reveal Olivia, wearing slacks and a fancy blouse as if she just got off work. "Hello," she greets, her voice softer than usual.

"Look who actually showed up," Harper teases, stepping aside to let her in.

Olivia rolls her eyes, slipping her purse off her shoulder and hangs it on the hook next to the door. "You guilted me into it. It's too early in the day for your relentless optimism."

"Too bad. I'm fueled up on caffeine and I have chips." Harper grins, shaking the bag in Olivia's direction. "Want some?"

Olivia hesitates, then sighs. "I guess." She settles onto the armchair across from us, folding her legs beneath her.

We make small talk for a while, dipping into light topics like work, weekend plans, Harper's latest dating horror story and how bored she is during the summer months. It's comfortable and familiar, it's what we do. But there's an energy humming beneath it, a thread of anticipation I can't quite shake.

Finally, Harper leans back, stretching her arms above her head. "Sooo... I signed up for the kids' ministry at church."

Olivia's eyebrows shoot up. "Seriously?"

"Yep." Harper pops a chip in her mouth, chewing thoughtfully. "You should come with me next Sunday. Check it out."

Olivia's expression falters, eyes flicking to me as if I might save her. "Church isn't my thing."

Harper waves her off. "Come on. You sat through those lame events they threw on stage back in college. This is way better."

"It's not the same."

"Actually, it kind of is." Harper's grin is wide and unyielding. "There's music, people talking and people sitting to listen. And you might get to see me wrangle five-year-olds, which is basically free entertainment."

"I know what it is." Olivia fidgets, her hands clasping together tightly. "I just, I'm not really ready for that, okay?"

The room goes quiet for a beat, tension stretching thin between us.

Harper's smile fades slightly, her tone softening. "You don't have to be ready. You just have to show up."

Olivia's eyes drop to the floor, her jaw set. "I appreciate it, Harp, but I'm good. Really."

Harper opens her mouth to say something, probably to push just a little harder, but I cut in. "It's okay," I say gently, glancing at Harper before looking back at Olivia. "We can take it slow. It doesn't have to be this huge thing."

Olivia looks up, relief softening her features. "Thanks, Ivy."

Harper leans back, arms crossed but not pushing any further. "Fine. But I'm not giving up."

Olivia rolls her eyes. "I would expect nothing less."

The tension eases, and the conversation shifts back to safer topics. But I can feel the ripple it left behind, a hint of something raw and unspoken lingering just beneath the surface.

And I know Harper isn't done trying.

Not by a long shot.

I curl deeper into my blankets, laptop balanced on my knees, the soft glow of my bedside lamp the only light in the room. The video call window fills my screen, and just like that, it feels like Gray is here with me. He's sprawled on his couch, guitar across his chest, fingers strumming easy chords that hum faintly through my speakers.

It shouldn't feel so intimate—just a call, just a Sunday

night after church—but it does. Maybe it's the way the lamplight beside him softens his features, or how relaxed he looks, like I'm seeing him in a version of himself reserved for when the world isn't watching.

I tuck my knees closer to my chest, the blanket wrapped around me like armor. My hair is piled in a messy top knot that's probably falling apart, but from the way his eyes flick toward the screen every so often, I wonder if he notices. And if he does...what does he see?

He asked earlier how Harper liked church—like it mattered to him. Like he was paying attention to not just me, but to the people I love. I told him she'd survived it, which in Harper terms means she probably didn't hate it. But the way he smiled when I said she signed up to serve...it stirred something warm in my chest. Something I don't want to name yet.

Now the room is quiet, except for him—his guitar, his humming, his presence filling the silence in a way that makes it feel anything but empty. My laptop screen glows, framing him in a rectangle of light, and I realize with a little jolt of truth: this is the best part of my day.

The steady strum from his guitar slows until it fades into silence, and I watch as he closes a little notebook resting on the arm of his couch. He tries to move casually, but my curiosity sparks instantly.

"What are you writing?" I ask, propping my chin into my palm.

He hesitates, lips quirking. "Just lyrics. Nothing finished. Nothing for public ears yet."

Lyrics. The word makes something flutter in my chest. He says it so offhand, but I can tell it matters to him. It matters a lot.

I smile before I can stop myself. "What inspires you?"

His eyes lift to the camera, and even though it's just pixels and light, the weight of his gaze makes my stomach dip. He drums his fingers against the guitar like he's stalling, then finally says, "Moments, mostly. Things I feel but can't really explain any other way."

"Moments?" I tilt my head, urging him on.

He shifts, leaning forward, like the conversation suddenly got heavier. "Like...the other day. When we almost kissed."

My breath catches. My blanket feels too warm, my skin prickling under his words. Of course I remember. My heart has replayed that moment on an endless loop.

He doesn't look away, doesn't soften the edges of what he's admitting. "I haven't stopped thinking about it," he says, voice lower now, like it's a secret meant only for me. "The way you looked up at me...I knew you felt it too. But I didn't want to push. Not if it meant scaring you off."

Something inside me flips. The way he says it makes it hard to breathe. Because he's right. I did feel it. I do.

I open my mouth, but words stall, tangled somewhere between my throat and my heart. My silence should feel awkward, but it doesn't. It's charged. Alive. Like he can hear the unspoken yes pulsing through me.

Then he says my name—soft, steady, reverent, "Ivy."

The sound of it from his lips sends a shiver through me.

"I wanted to kiss you so bad."

I blink, stunned by how direct he is, my heart thudding like it's trying to escape my chest. And before I can talk myself out of it, I whisper the truth that's been lodged in my chest since that night. "I really wanted you to kiss me."

The silence stretches, but it isn't heavy. It thrums between us, like the aftertaste of a song you don't want to end.

Then Gray leans closer to the camera, elbows on his knees. His voice is steady, but I catch the flicker of a smile tugging at the corner of his mouth. "Movie night at my place tomorrow?"

The question sends a rush of warmth through me, stronger than I expect. He says it so casually, but there's nothing casual about how much my heart jumps.

"Yes," I say before my brain can second-guess. My cheeks heat, but I don't care. "I'd like that."

His grin spreads slow and wide, and my pulse skips at how boyish and genuine it looks. "Good. I'll text you the address."

"Finally. I get to see this mysterious apartment of yours. And meet the infamous Goliath." I tease to cover the flutter in my chest.

He chuckles, leaning back on the couch. "Brace yourself. He doesn't share affection easily. But don't worry—I warned him you're special."

My heart stutters at that, and I duck under my blanket to hide my smile. "I'll bring popcorn."

"Perfect," he says. Then his voice softens, dipping lower, almost like he's talking to himself. "Fair warning, though…"

I narrow my eyes, suspicious. "About what?"

"I don't think I'm gonna sleep tonight."

The way he says it—firm, almost playful—sends a shiver down my spine. "Why? Too much coffee?"

He shakes his head, grin sharpening into something that steals my breath. "No. I'll be too busy planning how I'm going to kiss you tomorrow."

My entire face burns. I cover it with my hand, laughing in disbelief. "Gray…"

He smirks, unbothered. "Something sweet. Slow. Classic. Unless you've got suggestions?"

I sputter out the only comeback I can manage. "J-just... try not to miss."

His laugh rolls through the phone, warm and full. "Wouldn't dream of it."

"Goodnight Gray."

"Sweet dreams, Ivy."

The screen goes black, and I just sit there staring at my own faint reflection. My cheeks are warm, my lips curved into a smile I can't wipe away no matter how hard I try.

I sink deeper into the blankets, pulling them up over my chin like they might muffle the way my heart is still thundering. I've never had a guy say things like that to me—so direct, so sure. Like he isn't afraid of the weight in his words. Like he already knows what tomorrow means.

I should be nervous. And I am. But it's the kind of nerves that feel like standing at the top of a rollercoaster, breath caught in your throat, knowing the drop is coming and you want it.

I roll onto my back, staring at the ceiling, replaying his grin, the casual promise in his voice: *I'll be too busy planning how I'm going to kiss you tomorrow.*

It echoes in my chest, soft and impossible to ignore.

Tomorrow, Gray isn't just going to kiss me. Tomorrow, I think he might change everything.

Chapter 15
Gray

I hear the knock before Goliath does, but the second I stand, the big lug is already trotting to the door like he owns the place. I open it, and there she is—hair loose around her shoulders, casual shorts, soft t-shirt. Beautiful in a way that knocks me back every single time.

"Hey you," I say, leaning on the doorframe even though my heart just tripped over itself.

Her eyes immediately drop to the large cat rubbing himself against her ankles. "And this must be the man in charge." she says, crouching to scratch behind his ears.

"That's Goliath," I say, grinning. "Big personality, bigger ego. Don't let him fool you—he'll trade loyalty for a handful of treats."

She laughs, the sound filling up the doorway. "He's perfect."

"Don't tell him that. He's already full of himself."

I'd cleaned this place top to bottom. Floors mopped, counters wiped, even dusted the bookshelf—which I hadn't touched since I moved in. Not because I thought she'd notice, but because I knew she would.

Sure enough, the second Ivy steps inside, her eyes drift around the apartment like she's cataloguing it all. She doesn't say anything, but the way her hand trails across the spines of my books makes my chest tighten. She pauses at the window, looking out at the Dallas skyline glowing against the dusk.

"Not bad," she says, turning back to me with a smile that could knock the air right out of my lungs. "So what movie are we watching?"

"A cheesy rom-com, of course. My guilty pleasure." I wink, reminding her of the confession I'd made on one of our dates.

Her laugh softens the air between us, warm and teasing.

"Can I get you something to drink?" I ask, heading toward the kitchen before she can answer.

"Sure, what do you have?"

I open the fridge, and my stomach sinks. Right—spending three hours scrubbing grout apparently made me forget something important.

I scratch the back of my neck and turn back to her. "Don't hate me...but all I have is tap water and I don't have snacks. Half a bag of stale chips, maybe?"

"Crap, I forgot the popcorn." She gasps dramatically, shooting up from the couch. "You can't watch a movie without snacks!"

Before I can reply, her hand finds my arm, tugging me toward the door with a playful grin. "Come on. Convenience store. Down the street. I'm not letting you ruin rom-com night."

And just like that, she's pulling me out the door, laughter bubbling on her lips, and all I can think is—yeah, I'd clean the whole place again if it meant this.

I hook both hands through the thin plastic handles, two bags full of popcorn, chocolate, gummy worms, gummy bears, and chips. Ivy insists it's "bare minimum movie survival gear," her words, not mine.

We stop at the doors, rain pounding so hard it looks like the street's dissolving.

"I don't think it's going to let up anytime soon," I say, glancing from the radar on my phone to the downpour just outside the convenience store doors.

Ivy peers at my phone, a green blob glows across Dallas. She exhales. "Green's fine. Red's the scary one."

Her voice is light, but I catch the flicker of relief in her eyes.

I tilt my head, watching her.

"It's now or never," Ivy says, and there's something daring in her voice that makes me smile.

I reach for her hand. She doesn't hesitate. Her fingers slide between mine like they've always belonged there.

"One, two..."

The second I say three, we burst out the door of the convince store and into the storm, running full speed down the sidewalk, hand in hand. The rain is ice cold, soaking through my shirt in seconds. It stings against my skin, drips into my collar, and weighs down my jeans. Water sloshes in my shoes as puddles splash beneath us.

But none of it matters.

I glance at Ivy and almost lose my footing. Her hair is plastered to her face, her eyes squinting through the rain, but her smile makes everything else disappear. She kicks at a puddle, laughing as she runs, and it hits me so hard I forget to breathe.

I'm completely gone for this girl.

My apartment is just ahead when I spot headlights rounding the corner too fast.

"Ivy, wait!"

I yank her arm, and she stumbles into my chest as a car barrels past, missing her by inches. The horn blares. Water sprays up from the tires. My arms lock around her without thinking, holding her tight.

She tilts her face up, breath caught, eyes wide like she's standing at the edge of something she's only dreamed of. Her chest rises and falls against mine, quick and unsteady, each inhale pulling me closer without a word.

Rain pours down around us in sheets, but I barely feel it. I'm too lost in her. The droplets running down her cheeks, the way her lashes cling together, the soft tremble of her bottom lip—I could memorize every detail and still crave more.

My hand lifts before I can stop it, brushing wet strands of hair from her face. My fingers linger at her cheek, stroking once, slow and careful.

And then I kiss her.

No second thoughts. No time to think. Just the undeniable pull that's been building for weeks, demanding to break free.

I'd spent last night wide awake, picturing this moment— imagining it like a perfect scene in a movie. I thought I'd know how it would go, how she'd taste, how she'd melt into me.

But this?

This is better.

It's messy and breathless, wild in a way no script could ever capture. Rain clings to her lips, cool at first—but then her mouth parts under mine, warm and soft, sending fire straight through me. Her hand fists in my soaked shirt, tugging me closer, like she's been waiting for this just as long.

And in that instant, we're the only two people in the world. No thunder, no headlights from the street, no storm —just us, tangled together in a kiss that feels like both a beginning and a promise.

Heat and adrenaline. Longing and relief. Her taste, sweet and real.

When I finally pull back, I'm gasping, forehead pressed to hers, water dripping between us. She's just as breathless, lips parted, eyes shining like she can't believe this either.

And all I can think is: I'll spend the rest of my life chasing this feeling if she'll let me.

The storm begins to lighten, the rain softening into mist. She looks up at me, blinking, her eyes impossibly blue.

And that smile, the one that tugs at the corner of her mouth, it eases every doubt I didn't know I had.

Then, without warning, a car flies by, hitting a puddle just right.

A tidal wave of freezing water drenches us both.

"Oh my Godsh-shhh!" Ivy yells, half laughing, half squealing.

"Godsh-shhh?" I ask, grinning.

"I was going to say oh my God, but then I remembered what I read on the Bible app the other day...about how, once you're a Christian, you kind of just want to stop doing things that don't please Him. Like saying His name in vain. It just slipped out, but then I caught it, and..."

She's rambling. And it's adorable.

I can't stop smiling. I stare down at her, proud, amused, and something else I can't quite name.

Man. This girl. Lord, thank You for putting her in my life.

I brush another strand of hair from her cheek, my thumb grazing the edge of her jaw.

"Ivy," I say quietly, "you almost just got hit by a car."

"Gray," she breathes, "you finally kissed me."

We both start laughing, standing in the middle of the street, soaked, shivering, and somehow completely warm.

We get back to my apartment, soaked to the bone, rain still dripping from our hair and clothes.

But honestly? That's the least of my problems.

I kissed Ivy. Finally.

I close the door behind us, the sound echoing in the quiet room. We just stand there, staring at each other, water pooling on the floor beneath us.

"I, um..." Ivy starts, glancing down at her soaking wet clothes.

"You can shower and borrow some of my clothes if you'd like," I say before I can think better of it.

Her eyebrows lift. "Oh, um..."

Right. That might've sounded, not great. Like now that I've kissed her, I'm suggesting she undress in my apartment. That's not what I meant.

"I can take you home instead," I add quickly, trying to reassure her. "If you'd be more comfortable."

But she just smiles, small and sincere. "I was kind of

looking forward to our movie night. I mean, we did survive a natural disaster for those snacks." She gestures toward the bag still clutched in my hand. "You don't mind if I borrow something dry?"

"No, Ivy. I don't mind."

She follows me into my room, and I dig out a pair of sweatpants and a T-shirt from my drawer. Nothing fancy. Nothing remotely girly.

I motion toward the bathroom. "Shower's full of men's products, but use whatever you need. I'll grab you a towel."

I set everything on the counter and start to step out, but her voice stops me.

"What about you?"

I freeze.

Does she mean? No. She doesn't. Of course she doesn't.

"Ivy," I say slowly, "I don't think that's a good idea."

Her face turns beet red. "Oh my Godsh-shhh! Dang it! No, that's not what I meant!" She hides her face in her hands. "I just meant you're soaked too, and maybe you'd want to shower first. Not...not with me. Definitely not with me."

She's rambling again, and somehow it makes her even more endearing.

I run a hand through my wet hair, suddenly way too aware of how small this bathroom is.

"Ladies first," I say, stepping toward the door. "I'll be out here. Just...holler if you need anything."

I shut the door before I can say anything dumber.

Out in the kitchen, I unpack the snacks while Goliath stares at me from the back of sofa. Candy, chips, cookies, soda. Everything we'd risked our lives, and dry clothes, for.

The water runs on the other side of the door, a low hum through the quiet apartment.

I shiver. Both from the cold and from the thought of Ivy in my shower.

The old me, before faith really meant something, probably wouldn't have walked away back there. Especially not after a kiss like that.

But now?

Now I know better.

I take a deep breath and say a silent prayer.

Lord, keep my heart focused on You. Help me honor Ivy. Help me be the kind of man You're calling me to be.

I busy myself tidying the counter, replaying the kiss in my mind over and over. The way she looked at me. The feel of her hand in mine. Her lips still linger in my thoughts, like the moment was etched onto my skin.

The water shuts off, and a few minutes later, the bathroom door creaks open.

I look up—and freeze.

She's padding barefoot across my living room, swallowed up in my sweats and T-shirt. The hem nearly brushes her knees, the sleeves loose enough to slip past her elbows. Her damp hair is pulled back, strands curling against her flushed cheeks.

And it hits me.

She doesn't look like a guest. She doesn't look out of place. She looks like she belongs here. Like this apartment was waiting for her to soften it.

My chest tightens, a strange mix of wonder and want. I've lived here for years, but suddenly the space feels different—warmer, fuller, alive. She's only been here an hour, and yet she's already turned my place into something that feels like ours.

"Careful," I murmur, trying for lightness but failing, because my voice dips low, rough with everything I can't quite hide. "You don't even know what you're doing to me right now."

"I'm pretty comfy." She twirls in front of me.

She glances up, eyebrows raised, and I give her a half-smile, shaking my head.

"I've never seen anyone make my clothes look so good. Or make my place feel this much like home."

There's something about seeing her in my clothes that short-circuits my brain a little.

Lord help me.

Because if this is what forever might look like...

I wouldn't mind at all.

"Of course you do!" Ivy yells at the TV, her voice muffled slightly by the gummy worms she's crammed into her mouth.

On screen, the female lead has just confessed her love to the clueless guy she's been best friends with for years. Ivy is completely hooked—eyes wide, body leaning forward like she's part of the scene. I can't believe she's never seen this one.

I've seen it at least a dozen times. It's one of those comfort movies that is predictable and heartwarming, with a slightly cheesy but perfectly satisfying ending. A bookstore meet-cute. A misunderstanding. A grand gesture in the rain. Classic stuff. I've always been a sucker for movies like this, though I wouldn't admit that to just anyone.

But while Ivy's focused on the screen, I've been focused on her.

The way her expressions shift with every scene—how she grins at the banter, bites her lip during the tension, clutches the blanket during the dramatic moments. She's wrapped up in one of my throw blankets, oversized and soft, pulled up to her chin. My sweatpants and T-shirt still drown her petite frame, and she's curled into the couch like she belongs there.

We started the movie with a safe stretch of space between us, like two bookends on the same couch. But somewhere along the way, we drifted closer. Now my arm rests behind her, draped along the back of the cushions. I've been debating for the last twenty minutes whether to lower it, to let it settle around her shoulders, but I don't want to make a move she's not ready for.

Then it happens.

"Oh my gosh, finally!" Ivy says as the couple on screen finally shares a kiss. She tosses the half-empty gummy worm bag onto the coffee table and leans back with a satisfied sigh.

Right into me.

Her shoulder brushes mine. Then her head rests gently in the crook of my arm. My heart skips.

I take the opportunity and ease my arm down, wrapping it around her like it was meant to be there all along.

She doesn't flinch. Doesn't pull away.

She just melts into me.

And I swear, I could stay like this forever.

There's a peace in it. A closeness that's more than just physical. Her presence calms something restless in me. I've never felt so aware of someone else's breathing, or the warmth of their skin through a borrowed T-shirt.

We stay like that as the final scenes roll out—laughter, reconciliation, the happy ending Ivy was rooting for.

When the credits appear, she turns to look up at me.

There's a single tear trailing down her cheek. I reach up and brush it away with my thumb, gently.

I know exactly what she's feeling. That ache. That hope. That impossible longing for a love that feels written into your story before you ever saw it coming.

"It was just a movie," I say softly, even though we both know it was more than that.

She searches my face, and then her gaze drifts to my mouth.

"You can kiss me again if you want," she whispers.

And I don't hesitate.

I take her face in my hands and press my lips to hers, not with the calm intensity of the first kiss, but with something deeper—something messier. Frantic, searching, like I need her to know how much she's starting to mean to me.

She gasps softly against my mouth, and then we're both lost in it. Moving, adjusting, falling into the kiss like it's the only thing that makes sense.

"I like kissing you," I murmur between kisses.

"I like—" she starts, but I catch her mouth before the words can finish. Her laugh is breathless against my lips. "Kissing you too."

That undoes me. I kiss her harder, both hands sliding up to frame her face, fingers threading into her hair, holding her like I can't get close enough. She shifts without hesitation, straddling my lap, and my chest pounds with every move she makes against me.

Her arms loop tight around my neck, her fingers tugging at my hair, and the kiss turns wild—messy, consuming. I grip her back, her waist, anywhere I can anchor her to me, not to take anything from her, but because I need to feel her everywhere.

The kiss turns reckless, messy, too good. And I forget

everything but the taste of her, the warmth of her mouth, the way she clings to me like she never wants to let go.

Then the heat shifts and I feel it, the pull toward something I can't let happen. Not like this.

"Ivy—" I murmur against her lips, but she kisses me again, and I almost give in. Almost.

With a groan that costs me everything, I tear my mouth from hers, pressing my forehead to hers, forcing my breathing to steady. My hands are still cradling her face, holding her like she might break if I let go.

Her wide eyes search mine, lips swollen, chest rising and falling in time with mine.

I swallow, voice low, rough. "If we don't stop now..." I pause, tightening my grip on her just slightly. "I won't be able to."

Silence settles between us. Ivy nods, then lays her head on my chest, and I pull the blanket around both of us. My hand moves slowly across her back, just tracing. She relaxes completely in my arms.

Later, I walk her to her car, headlights casting long beams across the quiet parking lot. She glances back at me, smile tugging at the corners of her mouth, and I wonder how I'm supposed to let her drive away after this.

I lean against the hood of my truck long after her taillights disappear, heart still racing, lips still tingling.

I'd joked last night that I wouldn't be able to sleep, imagining how I would kiss her for the first time.

Turns out, it was nothing like I imagined.

It was better. So much better.

Chapter 16
Ivy

My kitchen table looks less like a place for meals and more like a war zone of sticky notes, empty coffee mugs, and open sketch pads. Two different clients are blowing up my inbox —one wants their logo in "a softer shade of teal", and another can't decide if their bakery font should be whimsical or professional. Spoiler: it can be both.

I rub my temples, push my blue light glasses up the bridge of my nose, and lean closer to my laptop. Three tabs open with design programs, two with stock photo sites, one with Pinterest, and exactly zero with food delivery, though I'm regretting that now.

"This is what freedom looks like," I mutter under my breath, half convincing myself. I traded in the office job for this—clients from all over, projects that make my brain stretch, and the ability to work in sweatpants without anyone judging me. Well...unless you count Harper, who swears I'm a workaholic now, or Olivia, who says I look "too happy" to be as swamped as I claim.

They're both right.

Because somewhere between revising website banners

and re-coloring Instagram templates, I've developed this ridiculous new crutch: Gray.

And okay, maybe I've replayed that kiss in my head more than once this week. Or a hundred times.

It's been a week since that night at his apartment—since the rain, the movie, and the way his lips felt against mine like he'd been holding back for years. We haven't kissed again, mostly because we haven't seen each other in person. Life got in the way—work deadlines, friends and other obligations pulling us in opposite directions.

But even with the distance, the tension hasn't faded. It lingers in every late-night call, every playful text that stretches longer than it should, every pause where neither of us wants to hang up.

My mind blanks. The creative spark that's usually quick to light stays frustratingly still.

I close my laptop with a sigh, lean back in my chair, and stare at the ceiling. My to-do list is long, but what I really want is something simple.

I want to hear his voice.

Before I can overthink it, I grab my phone, thumb hovering over his name.

I rub my temples and glance at the screen. I had promised to call Gray at some point today. My thumb hovers for just a second before I hit his contact and press the call button.

"Please distract me from hex codes and deadlines," I whisper as it rings.

And then...nothing.

It rings.

And rings.

And rings.

No answer.

I stare at the screen for a beat too long, the silence on the other end somehow louder than I expected. A little knot tightens in my chest and fills with, well, disappointment. Like a balloon losing air slowly.

I set the phone on my nightstand and decide this is a sign that I need to focus on work.

Just start somewhere, I tell myself.

I open my laptop again, click into the file, and begin fiddling with fonts, adjusting spacing. Nothing feels right. Every letter feels stiff, every color too dull. I drag the text box three pixels to the left, then three pixels back, then delete the whole thing with a groan.

Frustrated, I snatch up my phone and fire off a message to the group chat with Harper and Olivia.

IVY

Someone tell me why my brain refuses to cooperate with typography tonight.

HARPER

Because you were up too late overthinking a certain worship-band boy 😌

OLIVIA

Or because fonts are evil. Pick Arial and go to bed.

IVY

Arial?? That's a crime. You're both banned.

HARPER

Not banned. Just honest. Also: did you eat dinner?

IVY

Popcorn counts.

The back-and-forth makes me smile, but it doesn't fix the blank page staring me down. With a sigh, I set the phone aside, determined to at least try again.

I shift another headline across the page. Change the font. Delete it. Start over.

Still nothing.

Then—buzz.

My phone lights up with Gray's name, and suddenly every pixel on my screen blurs out of focus.

My heart jumps before I even register it, and suddenly that knot in my chest loosens just a little.

I answer on the first ring, nearly spilling my tea in my rush to tap the green button.

"Hello!" I practically yell, breathless.

His soft chuckle comes through the line, warm and slow. "Hey you."

Oh, his voice. How it instantly wraps around me like a hug I didn't know I needed. I swear, I could sit here all night just listening to him talk. He could read me the back of a cereal box and I'd probably swoon.

"Sorry I missed your call," he says, his tone low and a little sheepish. "Just got back from a run and hopped in the shower."

Gray. In the shower.

Images I have no business imagining flash through my mind: water gliding over tanned skin, dark tattoos slick and gleaming beneath the spray.

I sit up straighter, as if good posture will somehow purify my thoughts.

We've known each other for, what, four weeks? That doesn't exactly give me a license to picture him in the shower.

Or to wonder if those tattoos on his arms continue across his chest, his back...

Oh no. Nope. Brain, stop.

This is not helpful behavior.

"You there?" he asks, teasing creeping into his voice.

Ugh. Get it together, Ivy.

"Yep! Yep, I'm here. Sorry, I was buried in work."

"Oh man, I'm interrupting," he says. "Should I let you get back to bossing fonts around?"

I laugh into my pillow, he already knows me so well. "Please don't. I've been staring at the same project for an hour and it's starting to feel personal."

"Stuck?"

"Majorly. I've redone this thing three times and it still looks...blah. I want it to be simple but still make people stop scrolling and care."

He hums, like he's really considering it. "Okay, give me the rundown. What are you trying to say with it?"

I flop onto my back, staring at the ceiling. "That this brand isn't just another cookie-cutter startup. They want to feel approachable, welcoming, creative but trustworthy. Like...you'd hire them and also want to grab coffee with them."

"That's oddly specific," he teases, and I can hear the smile in his voice.

"Welcome to branding," I mutter.

"Well," he says slowly, "sounds like you already know the heart of it. You just need to design from that. Forget the trends. Just...show people what you just told me."

I pause, letting his words sink in. Not just because they're good advice, but because it's him. Gentle. Steady. Like he's not just pointing me in the right direction but sitting here with me in it.

"You make it sound easy," I whisper.

"I think it's just easy for me to believe in you," he replies, like it's the simplest truth in the world.

Something warm unfurls in my chest. "Careful. You're dangerously close to becoming my official design assistant."

He chuckles. "Do I get paid in coffee or kisses?"

My breath catches. I should laugh it off. I should tease him back. But instead I whisper, softer than I mean to, "Kisses. Definitely kisses."

There's a heartbeat of silence, then his voice drops low, rougher now. "Good. Because that's the only currency I'm interested in from you."

And there it is. Full swoon. Someone call NASA because I am no longer tethered to the earth.

We drift into lighter conversation after that, letting the seriousness fade.

"So, weirdest injury you've ever had?" Gray asks.

I grin. "That's easy. Middle school, gym class. I tried to jump rope with three people at once, tripped, and sprained my wrist. The nurse gave me a bag of ice and told me I was talented."

He laughs, low and warm. "Talented at what? Falling?"

"Apparently."

"Okay, my turn," he says. "I once broke a toe playing air guitar."

I choke on a laugh. "Air guitar? You mean imaginary strings?"

"Yes, ma'am. Rocked too hard, miscalculated the jump, and met the coffee table with my foot." He shakes his head, laughing. "The ER basically told me there's nothing you can do for a broken toe except tape it and walk it off."

"Wow. So heroic."

"Exactly," he says, smirking. "Really adds to the rock star image."

The conversation slides into music, then food, then into that hazy territory of pure silliness.

"I once ate a bowl of SpaghettiOs with crushed Doritos on top," he admits proudly, "and called it dinner."

"That's not dinner, that's a crime against humanity."

"Oh yeah? What's your culinary confession?"

I hesitate, then groan. "Pickles and peanut butter. Straight from the jars."

There's silence for a beat. Then he makes a gagging noise so dramatic I bury my face in the pillow.

"Separate jars!" I yell. "Not together!"

"Oh, well, that makes it totally normal then," he says, voice dripping with sarcasm.

We debate whether cereal counts as a meal and then move on to ranking fast food fries.

"Waffle fries are superior," Gray insists.

"Wrong. Curly fries win every time," I shoot back.

"No way. You only like them because they look fun."

"Exactly! Food should be fun. Who decided fries had to be boring?"

We're still bickering, both laughing too much to take it seriously. Somewhere between waffle fries and curly fries, between laughter and the easy rhythm we've fallen into, the words tumble out before I can stop them.

"Okay, but if my boyfriend doesn't agree with me, then..."

I freeze. The word hangs there, heavy, impossible to snatch back.

Silence.

My stomach plummets. "Oh no. Oh my gosh. I didn't mean to—I wasn't trying to label us. I don't even know why

I said that, I wasn't trying to overstep or assume anything, I just..."

"Ivy."

His voice is quiet. Calm.

"Yeah?"

"Your boyfriend. I like the sound of that."

I freeze. "You...do?"

He laughs and the sound of it makes my toes curl. "Yeah, I really do. I mean, I've kinda been walking around all week acting like I was yours anyway. Guess it would be nice to make it official."

I bite my lip to keep from smiling so wide it hurts. "So... boyfriend and girlfriend?"

"Unless you want to go steady with someone else," he teases. "But I gotta tell you, I make a pretty great boyfriend. I'm available 24/7 for pep talks and bad days. I'd write you a song—might even sing it if you asked. I bring flowers just because. And my hugs? Elite. My snuggles? Even better."

My heart does this ridiculous flip, and for a second, I forget how to breathe. He can't possibly mean all that. But oh, how I wish he did.

"I'll take my chances," I whisper, somehow managing to find my voice.

"You sure?" he grins, playing it up. "This is a big commitment. I may also flood your inbox with voice memos and bad jokes."

"Sounds like heaven," I murmur, pulse racing, and before I can stop myself, I add, "I wouldn't mind more of those snuggles. And for the record...I really like flowers."

There's a pause. A warm, comfortable silence that says maybe he's just as undone as I am.

Then suddenly, I sit up a little straighter. "Oh my gosh —I know what to do!"

Gray chuckles. "For the graphics?"

"Yes! It just clicked. Like fully, completely. I can picture it now."

"I knew you'd get there," he says, his voice full of pride —and maybe a little reluctance. "I'm glad I could be of some inspiration to my girlfriend."

I smile. "I should probably hang up and get to work before I lose the spark."

"Agreed," he says, but there's a playful pout in his tone. "Go, be brilliant. But I'm taking full credit for the design."

"You're ridiculous."

"Ridiculously supportive," he quips. "Now go. Before I distract you again with more of my impressive boyfriend energy."

I bite my lip, heart too full. "Goodnight, boyfriend."

"Goodnight, girlfriend. Knock those graphics out. I'm already proud of you."

Chapter 17
Ivy

The sun slices through my curtains like it's got something to prove, landing right in my eyes. I groan, squinting as I sit up in bed, disoriented. My laptop is still perched on the edge of the mattress, surrounded by open notebooks filled with sketches, messy doodles, and bursts of half-legible inspiration.

And then I remember last night.

The phone call.

The way Gray made me laugh, made my heart feel like it finally had somewhere to land. The way he listened—really listened. And that slip of the word boyfriend? The way he didn't flinch, didn't run, but embraced it with warmth and gentle confidence? It unraveled something tight in my chest.

That's what sparked it.

That's what gave me the vision for the graphics.

This idea that maybe that's how God loves too—not demanding perfection first, not asking you to clean up your mess before you're welcome. Just...meeting you where you are. Like Gray did with me. No pressure. Just presence.

And once that clicked, it was like creativity exploded out of me.

I worked until nearly one a.m., designing visuals that felt honest and full of grace. I wanted people to look at the graphics and feel the same thing I felt on the phone with him, seen, safe and invited.

I glance at the clock.

10:15 a.m.

Whoa. I haven't slept in this late on a weekday since...well, ever. I jolt upright, panic flaring until I remember—I work for myself. No meetings. No deadlines. Just the lingering scent of inspiration and the ache of staying up past midnight chasing it.

I grab my phone on the way to the kitchen, still yawning, still very much in the sweatshirt and joggers I wore yesterday. My hair's in a crooked bun that's probably defying gravity.

That's when I see the texts.

GRAY

Good morning, girlfriend

GRAY

Assuming you're still asleep. I've got something for you. Let me know when you're up and I'll bring it over.

GRAY

Still sleeping?

GRAY

Trying not to overthink our convo from last night. Hope I didn't scare you off.

GRAY

Ivy...

GRAY

Okay. I'm on my way over.

Wait. What?

A knock sounds at the door.

My silly smile at his rambling texts vanishes in an instant. I glance down at myself, total chaos gremlin mode. I shuffle to the door anyway, nerves sparking all over, and pull it open.

There he is.

Gray, in all his gloriously handsome, slightly-out-of-breath glory, holding something behind his back. His brows knit together the second he sees me.

"Hey, Ivy, I—"

I don't let him finish. I step forward and wrap my arms around him.

His body stills for a second, then melts into mine like he's been waiting for this exact hug all morning. I bury my face in his chest, not even caring that I probably smell like sleep and bad breath.

When I pull back, I can't help the awkward laugh that bubbles up.

"Okay, I need to warn you. This is yesterday's sweatshirt, I haven't brushed my teeth, and I look like I've been hit by a tornado."

Gray opens his mouth, then closes it again. His gaze softens as he takes a step back, eyes trailing over me.

Then he says,. "Is it weird that I think you're even more beautiful like this?"

My breath catches. "Like this?"

He nods, his voice a little rough around the edges. "Yeah. I like seeing you unfiltered. It suits you."

I laugh, both flattered and flustered. "That's definitely

the nicest way anyone's ever described bedhead and bad breath."

He grins. "I mean it."

I blink. "Gray..."

He runs a hand through his hair, shoulders tense. His voice rushes out in pieces.

"I'm sorry. I should've waited. This was probably too much. I just—I woke up and couldn't stop thinking about last night. Then I overthought everything, and by the time I drove over here I was convincing myself this was stupid, that you'd think I was..."

"Gray." I step closer, gentle but firm. "Breathe."

His chest rises like he's holding it all in, so I reach for his wrist and press my thumb lightly against the inside, the way you'd ground someone. "In," I whisper. "With me."

He inhales shakily. His eyes finally meet mine.

"And out."

We do it again. Once. Twice. Until some of the storm in him quiets.

"That's better," I say softly, not letting go. "Now show me what you've been hiding."

His jaw flexes, but the panic loosens enough for a small smile. Slowly, he brings his hand forward. The bouquet is messy, beautiful—pink blooms wrapped in brown paper. My heart stumbles.

And then I see the note taped across the front, his handwriting uneven like he scribbled it before he could lose his nerve.

IVY, I DARE YOU TO BE MY GIRLFRIEND.

My eyes fly to his, and for a second, all I can think is how this all started with a dare. A silly moment, a held hand, a stranger. And now here he is, daring me again—but this time, to be his.

"I know," he says quickly, scratching the back of his neck. "We technically made it official over the phone last night, but I was planning on asking you this way in a few days. I had it all in my head—flowers, the right moment, maybe even a cheesy line or two. But then I woke up and couldn't wait. So...here I am. Making it in-person official. That is, if you still want to say yes."

I don't even try to hold back the smile that takes over my face. "I will accept your dare."

His shoulders drop like he's been carrying weight all morning, relief softening every line of him. A grin tugs slow and steady at his mouth.

When he opens his mouth like he's about to tumble into another ramble, I press my hand to his chest, right over the wild rhythm beneath.

"Easy, heartbeat," I whisper. "You're spiraling again, and it's adorable, but unnecessary."

His breath evens, one beat, then another, until I can feel the change under my palm—the frantic race slowing into something calmer, steadier. His eyes meet mine, and this time there's no panic, just warmth flickering there.

"That's better," I say softly, giving him the faintest smile.

"Yeah," he exhales, voice quieter now. "That's better."

I step back just enough to gesture toward the kitchen. "So...do you want some coffee?"

"Only if I get to sit across from you and memorize every detail of how you look in that sweatshirt," he says, calmer now but no less intense. His grin curves, and he leans just a little closer. "Because honestly, it might've ruined me for anything else."

Gray stands by the door a few hours later, keys in one hand, his other resting on the doorknob like he's unsure whether to turn it. His body tilts toward me, like he's half-ready to go, half-hoping I'll stop him.

I bite the inside of my cheek.

Neither of us says anything for a moment. The silence stretches, but not in a bad way. Like we're both listening to something invisible.

Finally, he glances at me. "Okay," he says, softly. "I should go."

I nod, but I don't move. "Yeah. Of course."

But I don't want him to. I want him to stay. To sit back down, to hold my hand across the table again, to say that it's too early to leave something this good.

He rubs the back of his neck, looking suddenly unsure of himself. "Unless...you need help with anything else? Graphics? Planning your groceries for the week? A coffee refill?"

I laugh under my breath. "I think I've got it covered."

He nods again, slower this time. "Right. Okay."

He turns the knob, cracks the door just a few inches but doesn't step through. His shoulders rise with a breath he doesn't fully release, then he glances over at me with a lopsided smile.

"I'm really glad I came," he says.

My voice comes out softer than I intended. "Me too."

He takes a small step forward, then stops again. His

hand brushes mine, just barely. "You make it really hard to leave, Ivy."

My heart thuds once, hard and fast.

He leans in like he's about to kiss me. Just a little. Just enough for me to feel the possibility crackling between us.

Then he pauses, grin tilting crooked. "You know...I think I'm going to cash in on those kisses you owe me."

Before I can breathe, his hand slides gently to the side of my face, thumb brushing my cheek, and his lips find mine. Once. Twice. Slow, lingering, like he's memorizing the shape of me.

When he finally pulls back, his forehead rests against mine, his breath unsteady. "Dangerous," he whispers, voice low and rough. "You make it way too hard to walk away."

My heart trips over itself. "Then don't."

He laughs under his breath, pulling back reluctantly. "I really do have to go before I'm late to rehearsal."

I pout, half teasing, half very real. "Fine. Go be responsible."

He glances back at me, that grin still tugging his mouth. "Don't worry. I'll make it up to you next time. Double the payment. Maybe triple."

I swallow, somehow managing to smile. "Have a good day, Gray."

He exhales through a grin, backing out the door. "'You too, girlfriend."

And just like that, he's gone.

I lock the door and lean my back against it, staring at the spot where he stood just moments ago. My apartment is still filled with the warmth he left behind—the smell of his cologne lingering in the air, the half-full mug on the table, the silence that somehow hums with his absence.

I let out a slow breath, my hand drifting to my lips like I need to remind myself not to grin too hard.

He brought flowers. Wrapped in brown paper, a messy little note scrawled in his handwriting. I will cherish this moment forever.

I'd never seen a bouquet of pink flowers look so beautiful. So personal. I put them in a vase while I waited for our coffee to brew, and slipped his note on my desk, they look stunning on my kitchen counter.

I tuck my legs underneath me and open my laptop, scooting it closer until the soft glow of the screen lights up my face. My next project deadline is looming, and I want to give the final files one more look before I send them off.

The logo sits bold at the top of the page: a fresh, modern design for a local coffee shop. I hover the cursor over the image I chose—a soft palette of sage green and cream, paired with a hand-drawn illustration of a steaming mug. It isn't flashy. But it feels warm and inviting.

I click through the rest of the mockups: menus, social media templates, even a quirky little loyalty card with tiny coffee beans to stamp. It's clean. Polished. Professional.

And for the first time all day, I exhale. This isn't just pixels on a screen—it's someone's dream, and I get to help bring it to life.

I select the files, attach them to an email, and hit send.

A quiet thrill runs through me. I did it.

The sound of the whoosh as the email leaves my outbox feels final. I sink back into the couch and sip the now-cold coffee beside me. It's gross, but I don't care.

Because the project is done. I put the flowers in a vase. And there's a boy who makes me feel like maybe I'm not so hard to love after all.

I lean back into the couch and let my gaze wander to the

flowers again. They're a little uneven, a little wild, like they were picked with more heart than coordination. Which makes them perfect.

Just like this morning.

It started with coffee, of course. I was still half-asleep and somehow poured creamer into both mugs before I remembered—Gray takes his black. I started apologizing, but he just took a sip, smiled, and said, "Tastes like dessert. I'm not mad."

Then he poured us both a second cup.

And when my stomach rumbled loud enough to echo off the walls, I'd winced, embarrassed. "I, um, don't really have anything to eat. Only cereal."

He grinned like it was the best news he'd heard all day.

Ten minutes later, we were side by side on my couch, knees brushing, two mismatched bowls of Cinnamon Toast Crunch in our hands. Mine was in a soup bowl. His was in a Christmas mug with a chipped handle. We didn't care.

It was easy. Effortless.

We talked between bites about everything and nothing. I asked him if he was from Dallas and he shrugged, like the answer still surprised him.

"Colorado, originally," he said, tilting his spoon through the milk. "I ended up here after a tour with a band I used to be in."

"A band?"

"Metal," he added with a grin, like he already knew how ridiculous it might sound to me. "I was the lead vocalist. Screamed a lot, wore way too much black. It was a whole vibe."

I laughed so hard I nearly choked. "Please tell me there are pictures."

He groaned but couldn't hide his smile. "Unfortunately,

yes. And believe it or not, Micah can play guitar. Him and my buddy Chris will drag me out sometimes to play at random bars. We mix in Christian stuff here and there—it's not everyone's cup of tea, but it's fun. Keeps the glory days alive without the bad eyeliner."

He told me Dallas was supposed to be a stop, not a destination. But something about the city and the warmth, the people, the second chances—made him stay. "It just... felt like home."

Then, softer, he mentioned his mom. Said he only sees her once a year, by choice. And when I opened my mouth to ask more, he just shook his head.

"It's okay," he said gently, like he knew I was curious but didn't want to make it heavy. "I've got good boundaries now. God's been kind in that."

He didn't mention his dad. Not once. But I noticed.

And I didn't push.

He stayed on my couch like it was the most natural thing in the world. He laughed at my dumb jokes, held my gaze like he saw everything I was still afraid to show.

It was nothing big.

But it felt like everything.

Chapter 18
Ivy

The past two weeks have slipped by in a blur. Somehow, it's already August—which means Harper is back to work at the school. My phone buzzes less now without her constant texts about being bored or asking if we want to hit the mall "just to browse."

Gray and I have only grown closer. We've carved out time for movie nights, late walks around the park with iced coffees in hand, and even a disastrous attempt at cooking dinner together that ended in takeout and laughter on the kitchen floor. Some evenings it's as simple as me tucked under his arm on the couch, listening to him strum his guitar while I pretend to read.

And in the middle of it all, something in me has shifted. I've gone to church every Sunday without fail. Every morning, I open my Bible before the day can swallow me whole. Half the time I don't fully understand what I'm reading, but modern apps and devotionals fill in the gaps—and when they don't, I've got a boyfriend who somehow never tires of my endless questions about faith.

Now, I'm back at my desk, the glow of my laptop screen

still lingering after a Zoom call that ended with polite good-byes and awkward waves. I sink into my chair, the silence of my apartment pressing in after thirty minutes of forced smiles and professionalism.

This is it—my biggest gig yet. A new client who could actually put my name on the map if I don't screw it up. But now that the adrenaline from smiling through the meeting has worn off, the weight of their feedback lands like a brick in my chest.

The first round of design edits flashes on my screen, bleeding in more red than I'd like.

I scroll through the notes slowly: adjust the spacing here, change the color scheme there, try a more modern font. None of it is awful. In fact, most of it makes sense. But all I see is critique. Not of the design—of me.

I drag my hands down my face and blow out a breath. This is supposed to be the one thing I'm good at, the place where I don't feel like a fraud. But right now, all I hear are the whispers of self-doubt clawing their way to the surface.

Maybe they made a mistake asking me.

My phone buzzes from the edge of the desk. I reach for it, half-hoping it's Gray, but it's just Harper lighting up our group chat.

HARPER

Picnic after church on Sunday. You're both coming.

OLIVIA

Nope.

I smirk, typing back.

IVY

Did you even think about it?

OLIVIA

I did. For a full ten seconds.

HARPER

I'm picking you up. Wear something cute.

OLIVIA

Wear something cute to go stand outside and swat flies? Hard pass.

HARPER

Yes, Olivia. God forbid you look cute while eating potato salad.

OLIVIA

I'm not going. Y'all have fun.

HARPER

You know what Liv, I didn't want to have to do this but here we go. I dare you to come to the church picnic with us tomorrow.

I chuckle, shaking my head. I glance at my phone, equal parts horrified and impressed. That was genius. Can't believe I didn't think of that myself—it is Olivia's turn for a dare, after all.

Harper's relentless optimism is a force of nature, and Olivia's stubbornness is the only thing I know strong enough to withstand it. But now? This is going to be good.

For the past three Sundays, Harper's been coming with me to church. She jumped straight into serving in the children's ministry—and she loves it, even if she won't stop grumbling about how "bossy" Micah is. And truthfully, I'm proud of her. She is now practically running the kids' area with the kind of energy that only Harper could pull off.

There's just one issue. Harper doesn't just serve during one service hour, she volunteers for both. Every Sunday, she's wrangling preschoolers through snack time and crafts, wiping runny noses, and keeping the peace when someone inevitably tries to steal the red crayon.

"Don't you want to sit in for service?" I asked her last Sunday before we parted ways.

Harper waved me off with a grin. "Oh, I'll watch it online later. And honestly, I kind of like it better that way. I can fast-forward through announcements and pause for snack breaks."

I'd just rolled my eyes. "That's not the same."

"Sure it is, I still get the message, I'm just not crammed into a seat with a hundred other people."

But I can't help but feel like she's missing out. There is something different about being in service, about feeling the music shake the walls, seeing hands lift in worship, hearing voices blend together like they are all reaching for the same hope. I've grown to love it.

I'd even caught Micah giving her an impressed nod last Sunday when she managed to single-handedly calm a room of sugar-hyped seven-year-olds with nothing but a whisper and a bag of Goldfish crackers. She claimed it was the snacks. I think it's something else.

But as much as I love seeing Harper get involved, there's this quiet ache every time I look at that empty spot beside me. Then there's Olivia.

I tried asking her once—if she'd ever consider coming with me. Just once. She laughed it off, saying, "You and Harper are enough. You don't need me."

But she's wrong.

I want her there. More than I can explain. It's not just about filling a seat; it's about experiencing this thing that's started to feel important to me and to Harper.

And sometimes, I catch myself daydreaming—three of us side by side, flipping through our Bibles, laughing too loud during prayer time because Harper can't stop cracking jokes, Olivia sighing dramatically but staying because she secretly loves it.

But that's just a daydream. For now, anyway.

My phone pings, pulling me from my thoughts.

GRAY

Ice cream later?

My heart does a weird little flip.

IVY

Absolutely. Time?

GRAY

I'll pick you up at 7.

I stare at the screen for a second longer than necessary, biting back a smile before setting the phone down. I lean back in my chair, staring at the mess of design edits sprawled across my laptop.

I can fix them. I know I can. But that nagging voice in the back of my mind whispers: *They only hired you because they couldn't find anyone else.*

I shake off the thought, straightening up and clicking back into my work. I don't have time for doubt. I have designs to fix and an ice cream date with Gray to get ready for.

The bell above the door jingles as we step into the ice cream shop. The place is straight out of a movie—black-and-white checkered floors, red vinyl barstools lined up against a shiny counter, and walls plastered with retro posters of sundaes that probably have enough sugar to knock out a linebacker.

Gray grins, nodding toward the chalkboard menu stretched across the wall. "Pick your poison."

I squint up at the board, eyes scanning the options. "There are, like...a hundred flavors. How do you ever choose?"

"It's a talent," he says, stepping up to the counter like he owns the place. He taps his fingers on the glass, inspecting the tubs of brightly colored ice cream. "I've pretty much tried them all."

I raise an eyebrow. "All of them?"

"Yep." He points to a tub of something violently blue with swirls of pink. "That one tastes like bubblegum, regret, and poor life choices."

I laugh, shaking my head. "Good to know."

The girl behind the counter steps up, her hands already wrapped in plastic gloves. "What can I get for y'all?"

Gray doesn't even hesitate. "I'll do a scoop of the Java Chip and a scoop of Rocky Road in a waffle cone."

She nods, scooping out the flavors with practiced ease before turning to me.

I glance back up at the board. "Uh...Salted Caramel Pretzel in a cup, please."

Gray turns to me with mock judgment written all over his face. "A cup? Really?"

"What?" I lift a brow. "Cones are messy."

He leans in a little, eyes gleaming. "That's the point. Where's the fun if you're not at risk of having ice cream all over your face?"

I smirk. "You say that like it wouldn't be a total disaster."

He shrugs, voice low and playful. "Disaster, maybe. But kind of adorable. I mean, I wouldn't mind helping you clean it up."

My face goes beet red.

Gray runs a hand through his hair, eyes wide. "Okay—yikes. That was...I didn't mean—wow. That sounded way less inappropriate in my head."

I burst out laughing, and he groans, burying his face in his hands. "Can we pretend I said something way cooler than that?"

"Not a chance," I say through my giggles. "That one's going in the vault."

"On second thought, I'll take a cone."

The girl nods, hiding a smile as she turns to scoop.

Gray glances at me sideways, clearly trying not to laugh. "Changing your mind, huh?"

I cross my arms. "Just living on the edge."

Gray grins like he's just won something. "Knew you'd come around."

We slide into a booth near the window, the setting sun pouring in like a spotlight on this weirdly perfect little moment.

I take my first bite—sweet and salty with the perfect crunch of pretzel—and let out a small sigh. "Okay, this is actually amazing."

"Told you," Gray says around a bite of his own cone. "I don't mess around when it comes to ice cream."

Time slips by as we eat and laugh and share bites across the table. I'm halfway through my cone when I catch Gray watching me with the biggest smile on his face.

"What?" I ask, self-conscious all of a sudden.

He leans in slightly, voice soft. "You've got some right here." He taps the tip of my nose with his finger, swiping away a smudge of ice cream. Then, before I can process it, he licks his finger, grinning like he's fully aware he's messing with my head and enjoying every second.

"Told you I wouldn't mind helping you clean it up," he says with a wink.

I practically melt into the vinyl seat.

I'm about to respond when I hear a crash from the front of the shop. We both turn just in time to see a kid, no older than six, staring in horror at his ice cream splattered across the checkered floor. His mouth is open, eyes wide, like he hasn't quite processed the tragedy yet.

The woman behind the counter looks torn between sympathy and horror. "Oh, honey..." she starts, but the kid's lower lip is already trembling.

Before I can react, Gray's already on his feet, heading toward the counter. He leans down, dropping to a squat in front of the kid, his expression softening.

"Hey, buddy," he says gently. "That's a real bummer."

The kid sniffles, nodding slowly. "It was my favorite..."

Gray glances at the sad splatter of mint chocolate chip smeared across the tile and nods solemnly. "Yeah, that's the good stuff." He looks up at the woman behind the counter. "Can I get another scoop? On me."

Her eyes widen, and she nods quickly, already scooping out a fresh mound of mint chocolate chip. The kid stares at

Gray like he just grew a cape and flew in from a comic book.

"Thank you," the boy whispers, cradling the cone like it's the most precious thing in the world.

Gray pats him on the back, standing up and walking back over to me, wiping his hands on his jeans. He slips back into the booth like it was nothing, like he didn't just make that kid's entire day.

I'm staring at him, my cone paused mid-air. "That was really nice of you."

He shrugs, taking a bite of Rocky Road. "It's just ice cream."

"No," I say, shaking my head. "It's not."

Gray glances up at me, his eyes meeting mine. For a second, the lightness fades, replaced by something deeper. "I guess you're right."

The silence lingers between us, warm and comfortable, until I finally clear my throat. "So, you do this often? Save the day in random ice cream shops?"

He laughs, breaking the tension. "Only on Wednesdays."

He catches me watching and raises an eyebrow. "What? Do I have ice cream on my face now?"

I shake my head, grinning. "No. Just, you're really committed to that cone."

He glances at it. "You can't mess around with ice cream. It's a race against time."

I laugh. "Is that so?"

"Absolutely."

I snort. "Didn't realize I was eating with such a pro."

He leans in slightly, voice playful. "Stick with me. I'll teach you a few things."

My stomach flips. "You're something else."

He tilts his head. "Something good?"

My breath catches. "Maybe."

His eyes drop to my lips for a second and I feel heat rise up my neck. Then he leans back, casual, but his eyes never leave mine.

"You wanna know something?" he asks.

"That depends," I say, narrowing my eyes. "Is it embarrassing?"

He shrugs. "Maybe."

"Now you have to tell me."

He grins. "First time I saw you. New Orleans."

The memory hits like a wave—the dare, his hand in mine, the way the noise of the street melted away.

"I remember thinking," he says slowly, almost like the words cost him something, "that you were the boldest, most unforgettable girl I'd ever seen."

My mouth opens, but no words come.

"You walked up like you belonged next to me," he adds, softer now. "Like you'd always been there."

I blink, stunned. "Gray..."

He gives me a half-smile, like he's embarrassed he said too much. "I didn't expect you to stay in my head after that. But you did."

For a moment, I forget about the ice cream in my hand, the shop around us, everything. I can only hear the sound of my heart hammering in my chest.

"I didn't think I'd see you again," I whisper.

"Me either," he says, his voice a low hum. "I'm glad we were wrong."

I glance down, trying to breathe past the ache in my chest. "You surprise me."

His smile turns playful again. "Good. I like keeping you on your toes."

Just then, I realize my ice cream cone is melting fast, dripping down the side like a sticky waterfall. "Dang it," I mutter, twisting the cone and trying to catch it with frantic licks. "This thing is out of control."

Gray laughs. "Here, let me help."

Before I can protest, he gently pulls my hand toward him, my fingers still wrapped around the cone, and leans in. I watch, stunned, as his tongue sweeps along the side of the cone, cleaning up the caramel drips like it's the most casual thing in the world.

My breath catches. I don't move. Can't move.

He glances up through his lashes, a grin tugging at his lips. "Crisis averted."

My jaw drops. "Gray!"

He smirks, unbothered. "What? It was a matter of public safety."

My face goes red, heat rushing to my cheeks. "You're ridiculous."

He shrugs, letting go of my wrist with a wink. "Maybe. But you're still here."

Chapter 19
Ivy

My phone buzzes across the desk: **Unknown Caller.**

Normally, that's an automatic decline. Straight to voice-mail, no guilt. But something about it makes me hesitate. A little nudge in my chest, quiet but insistent, telling me to pick up.

"Hello, this is Ivy Taylor," I answer, my voice catching just slightly.

"Hi Ivy! This is Greg with New Chapter Church—how are you today?"

"Oh! Hi, Greg. I'm doing great," I say, though my thumb is already digging at my cuticle, wondering why one of the church's pastors is calling me out of the blue.

He clears his throat. "So, here's the thing—we've had a huge growth in attendance the past few months, and the pastors decided last week to put together a special Prayer and Worship night. It's in two weeks, and we'd love to make it something meaningful for the community. We're a little behind on graphics and Gray mentioned you do freelance design work, and I know you helped Paige a few weeks ago with some design work which was very helpful."

I sit up straighter, heat rushing to my cheeks at the mention of Gray's name.

Greg continues, his tone hopeful. "We can offer a small stipend for your time."

For a second, I forget how to breathe. I left the security of corporate life for the uncertainty of freelancing, but the idea of something steady here, in a place I'm beginning to love, doesn't feel random. It feels like a door opening.

My pen is already in my hand before I realize it.

"Yes," I say, the word tumbling out faster than I expect. "I'd love to help. What exactly do you need?"

Greg laughs, the kind of warm chuckle that makes the whole thing feel less intimidating. "We'll need a few social media graphics, a couple of flyers, and—if it's possible—a backdrop for a photo booth."

I scribble the words in my notebook, underlining backdrop twice, ideas already starting to swirl.

"That all sounds doable," I say, chewing lightly on the end of my pen. "Deadline?"

"If we could have everything finalized a week from now, that would be incredible. And Ivy, there's something else." He pauses. "There's a part-time position opening on the creative team. Paid, flexible hours. This could be a good way to see if it's something you'd like to apply for."

"I'd definitely be interested," I say, my voice softer this time.

"Great. I'll email you the details so you have everything in writing."

"Perfect. Thanks so much for thinking of me, Greg."

We hang up, and before the call has even fully disconnected, I'm already swiping to Gray's contact. My hands tremble with something that feels an awful lot like joy.

He picks up on the second ring. "Hey, you. Miss me already?"

I grin, pressing the phone tight to my ear. "Always. But you're not going to believe the call I just got..."

The weekend rolls around faster than I expect, and I find myself crammed into the passenger seat of Harper's Jeep, Olivia reluctantly perched in the back.

"This is my hostage face," Olivia mutters, arms crossed over her chest.

Harper flicks her eyes to the rearview mirror, unbothered. "You're gonna have fun. You might even smile. Don't fight it."

Olivia snorts. "We'll see."

The church picnic is already in full swing by the time we arrive. Tables are set up under massive oak trees, kids are chasing each other around, and there's a smell of barbecue lingering in the air.

"Wow," I say, stepping out of the Jeep and taking it all in. "They go all out."

Harper grins. "Welcome to the South. We don't do anything halfway."

We weave through clusters of people, waving at familiar faces. Harper immediately zeroes in on the kids' area, her eyes lighting up as she spots a crafts table. "I'm going to check that out. If I'm not back in ten, send a search party."

I laugh. "Good luck."

Olivia glances around, clearly out of her element. "Do they serve wine at these things?"

"Pretty sure it's sweet tea, but I saw a sign for apple cider back there."

She sighs. "Figures."

We find a spot near the edge of the crowd, far enough from the main cluster of picnic tables to feel like our own little space, but close enough to hear the hum of laughter and conversation. I shake out the blanket we brought and smooth it over the grass.

"Having fun yet?" I ask, nudging Olivia with my shoulder.

She shrugs, but there's less tension in her shoulders than I expected. "It's not the worst."

"I'll take it."

I glance around, scanning the sea of faces. My eyes catch on Gray across the field, standing near a grill and laughing with a group of guys I don't recognize. He's got a pair of sunglasses perched on his head, his hair a little messy, sleeves rolled up casually. He looks happy.

"Think he'll come over?" Olivia asks, following my gaze.

I flush, snapping my attention back to her. "I don't know."

But before I can overthink anything, a group of girls nearby giggles loudly, pulling my attention. They're huddled around the dessert table, one sipping apple cider, another scrolling through her phone with sparkly pink nails.

One of them leans in, voice just loud enough to carry. "I'm telling you, Gray only dates girls who can quote Scripture and sing in harmony."

They all laugh, glancing over at where Gray is talking with a group of guys, that easy smile on his face, his hands tucked into his back pockets like he's never been unsure of anything.

My stomach twists.

Because that? That is so not me.

I don't know Scripture by heart. I get lost flipping through the Old Testament. And the only harmony I've ever mastered is humming off-key in the car. I've never been in a Bible study, never sung into a mic, never belonged in that kind of world.

The laughter from the girls floats on the breeze, but I hear it like it's directed at me. Like they know I don't fit here. Not with them. Not with him.

I turn to Olivia, forcing a lightness I don't feel. "You wanna go grab something to eat?"

She nods, standing up and brushing the dust off her jeans. I follow her, head held high, pretending I didn't hear what I just heard.

But as I walk away, I can't help but wonder.

Is that true?

Would he only date someone who fits that perfect image?

The kind of girl who grew up in church—Sunday school ribbons, vacation Bible school crafts, youth group lock-ins. The kind of girl who can quote Scripture without even blinking, who sings harmonies effortlessly during worship, who never once thought about sneaking into a party or questioning if God was really there.

The kind of girl who doesn't have to wrestle with her past, who doesn't carry mistakes like shadows that creep in at night. The kind of girl who looks put-together and polished, faith on display like a pressed dress and a polished smile.

I picture her—whoever she is—and I shrink in comparison. Because I'm not that girl. I never have been.

I want to believe the answer is no. That Gray wouldn't

box love into that mold, wouldn't only want someone who checks all the "perfect Christian" boxes.

But that tiny seed of doubt is already planted.

And it's starting to grow, winding its way around every part of me that wonders if I'll ever be enough.

I take the cup of apple cider Olivia hands me and follow her through the maze of picnic tables and lawn chairs, the hum of laughter and conversation swirling around us. She stops at the dessert table, already eyeing a plate of brownies.

"You good?" she asks, one eyebrow raised as she shoves a napkin into her purse.

"Yeah, I just…" I glance around, searching for an exit. "I think I need some space. You okay here?"

Olivia waves me off, already reaching for a cookie. "I'll survive. There's plenty of snacks to keep me busy."

I slip away from the main crowd. My feet take me toward the edge of the picnic area where the trees grow thicker, stretching up like a canopy above. The noise dulls to a soft hum, and I sink down onto the grass beneath the shade, letting the coolness seep into my legs.

I take a sip of apple cider, warm and sweet, but I barely taste it.

Gray only dates girls who can quote Scripture and sing in harmony.

The words echo in my mind, looping around my thoughts until I feel them like pinpricks. I know I shouldn't let it get to me—gossip and whispers from girls who probably don't even know him like I do. But still…

I tug at a blade of grass, running it through my fingers until it snaps. Quote Scripture and sing in harmony.

I can't do either.

Not well, anyway. I think back to every church service I've attended, I'm just starting to figure this out.

What if I'm not enough?

I shake off the thought, tossing the blade of grass aside and wiping my palms on my jeans. I'm being ridiculous.

But I can't shake the whisper that maybe I'm not his kind of girl.

I hear footsteps before I see him. The crunch of gravel and a soft whistle that's just slightly off-key. My heart stumbles over itself, and I glance up to find Gray standing a few feet away, hands shoved into his pockets, a grin spreading across his face.

"Found you," he says, tilting his head.

I smile, scooting over just enough to make space. "You were looking?"

"Always." He doesn't hesitate. Just drops down beside me on the grass, stretching his long legs out and leaning back on his palms. He glances around the quiet patch of green. "Escaping the madness?"

I nod, staring down at my cup of cider. "Just, getting some air."

"Smart." He lets out a slow breath, eyes drifting to the sky. "I've been running around for the last hour. Almost got roped into face-painting. I barely dodged it."

I laugh, shaking my head. "You'd make a terrible face-painter."

He gasps. "I would be excellent. My stick figures are practically museum-worthy."

I roll my eyes, but I'm smiling now.

He glances over at me, eyes softening. "You okay? You seem...I don't know. Somewhere else."

I force a little smile, tracing the rim of my cup. "Just thinking."

"About?"

I hesitate. The words taste silly on my tongue, but they press anyway. "Do you...ever feel like you should be with someone who's more..." I bite my lip. "Put-together? Like one of those perfect church girls who has all the verses memorized and sings in the choir and never misses a Bible study?"

Gray's brows knit, his whole body shifting toward me. "Where's that coming from?"

I shrug, eyes glued to the cider in my hands. "I overheard some girls talking. About you. About the kind of person you'd actually date." My throat tightens. "And it wasn't...me."

He exhales slowly, like he's catching his temper before it sparks. "Ivy, you really think I'd let some gossip define what I want?"

"I don't know," I admit, my voice small. "It just...got in my head."

Gray's jaw ticks, but his eyes soften as they find mine. "I don't have a checklist," he says firmly. "But if I did? You'd be on it. Every single time."

The world stills for a beat. My cheeks heat, the cider cooling between my palms.

"You don't have to be someone else," he adds, quieter now, leaning closer. "I want you—mess, questions, imperfections, all of it. That's what I like."

My heart stutters, caught between disbelief and hope.

Before I can form words, Harper's voice slices through the trees, loud and unapologetic.

"There you two are!" She's practically jogging over, waving her arms like she's directing traffic. "I need help. Both of you. Now."

Gray raises an eyebrow, glancing at me. "You think she's serious?"

"She's always serious," I laugh. "We should probably go before she drags us."

Gray groans but stands, brushing off his jeans. "I was just getting comfortable."

"Well, duty calls," I say, tilting my head toward the chaos.

He sighs dramatically, but when he offers me his hand to help me up, I take it. His fingers are warm and steady, and for a moment, I forget about those whispers. I forget about everything.

We make our way back to the picnic tables, Harper waiting with her hands on her hips. "Finally! There's a three-legged race starting and we need more teams. Get ready."

Gray laughs, glancing at me. "You up for it?"

I nod, my heart still fluttering from the quiet moment under the trees. "As long as you don't trip me."

"No promises," he grins.

Chapter 20
Gray

Harper doesn't give anyone time to think before she's tossing a strip of neon orange fabric at us. "Here. You're paired up. Get to it."

I glance down at it, then up at Ivy. "Wait, now? We don't get to practice or—"

"Nope," she chirps, already moving on like she's running the church Olympics.

I look at Ivy, raising a brow. "You ever done one of these before?"

She laughs. "Not since like...middle school. And I think I fell three times."

"Perfect," I grin. "We're setting the bar nice and low."

She crouches down to tie the strip around our ankles—my left to her right—but fumbles with the knot. I kneel beside her, gently nudging her hand. "Here, I got it." My fingers graze hers as I pull the fabric snug, double-knotting it for good measure.

"There," I say, standing and testing the tension. "We're locked in."

Ivy scans the field and nudges my arm. "Look."

I follow her gaze—and sure enough, Harper is already paired up with Micah.

My eyebrows shoot up. "Well, well. Look who's making friends."

Micah's saying something to Harper, all smug confidence. She rolls her eyes, arms crossed, but there's the faintest smile playing on her lips.

I let out a low whistle. "Should we be worried?"

Ivy snorts. "I'm worried for him."

Up front, the announcer waves everyone toward the starting line. We shuffle forward, awkwardly tied, and I reach for her waist to help us balance.

"You ready for this?" I ask, my voice low so only she hears.

She glances up, eyes catching the sunlight. "As ready as I'll ever be."

The whistle rises.

"On your marks...get set...go!"

And all at once—chaos.

We take off at the whistle, but Ivy's half a beat behind me, and we lurch forward in a tangle of limbs. She stumbles, and my arm shoots out instinctively, wrapping around her before she face plants into the grass.

"Easy there," I say, laughing as I steady her. "Left, then right. Got it?"

"Got it."

We try again. Left, right. Left, right. It's awkward at first —she's laughing, and I'm trying not to trip over my own feet —but eventually, we find a rhythm. Not a graceful one, but it works.

Just ahead, I spot Harper and Micah—bickering loudly.

"Lean left!" Micah yells.

"I am leaning left!" Harper fires back.

I chuckle. "They're gonna take each other out."

"Should we help them?" Ivy asks between laughs.

I glance at her, grinning. "Nah. It's more fun to watch."

We're gaining ground, steps syncing better than I thought possible. I keep one hand firm at her waist, guiding her gently whenever the grass gets uneven. She glances up at me, and for a second, I forget we're racing anyone at all.

"You're good at this," she says, sounding genuinely surprised.

I smirk. "Years of being forced into church picnics. You pick up a few things."

She laughs, and something about the way she looks at me—light in her eyes, wind in her hair—makes it hard to focus on anything else. The moment stretches longer than it should, her hand on my arm, mine still on her waist.

We round the last bend, Harper and Micah still ahead —barely. He's practically dragging her now, and she's laughing so hard she can't run straight.

"You call this running?" Micah teases.

"Would you stop yanking me around like a Labrador?" Harper snaps, but there's no heat in it—just laughter.

I point ahead. "Finish line's right there!"

We hit the finish line just seconds before Harper and Micah go crashing past us, collapsing into the grass like a pile of limbs and laughter.

I stop, breath coming hard, and realize Ivy hasn't let go. My hand's still on her waist—gripping my forearm like she doesn't want to let go either.

"Not bad, Ivy," I manage, voice a little rough from the run—and from something else entirely.

She looks up at me with that grin that does something dangerous to my chest. "Not bad yourself."

We're still tied together. Still close. I can feel the heat

radiating off her, the way her chest rises and falls, breath syncing with mine. For a second, I forget there's anyone else on the field.

I let my gaze linger, just taking her in—the flush in her cheeks, the curve of her smile. She's beautiful. More than that, she's herself. Not some polished version of faith people gossip about, but the girl who makes me want to prove every doubt in her head wrong.

And then I notice it—a small smear of grass on her cheek.

I lift my hand slowly, brushing my thumb across her skin. Gentle. Careful. Reverent.

"You've got grass on your face," I murmur, though really I just want an excuse to touch her.

She stills, breath catching. So does mine.

I shouldn't—not here, not now, not in front of half the church. We've kissed plenty, but always in private, away from curious eyes. I know Ivy worries she's not "enough" of a Christian girl, and part of me wants to protect her from every sideways glance.

But another part—the stronger part—wants to silence every whisper in her mind. Wants her to know she's exactly who I want.

So I lean in. Her eyes widen, lips parting just slightly. We're a breath apart, the picnic chatter fading until it feels like just us.

And then...

"Okay, for the record," Harper groans from behind us, dragging us both back to earth, "that was not my fault."

I pull back, just barely, my thumb slipping from Ivy's cheek. But I don't look away. Can't. The space between us still feels charged.

Harper's still sprawled in the grass, fanning herself

dramatically. "If Micah had better coordination, we would've crushed you two."

Micah laughs, brushing off his jeans. "If you hadn't tackled me mid-run, maybe we wouldn't have somersaulted into the finish line."

"Details," Harper mutters, waving him off.

I lean toward Ivy again, just enough that only she can hear me. "Raincheck on that kiss," I murmur, letting my thumb brush her hand. "But fair warning, the second we're alone, I'm cashing in."

Her breath catches, and I smile, low and sure.

Before she can answer, Harper groans again. "Micah! You literally tripped me."

"I did not," Micah fires back, brushing himself off. "Your coordination is just trash."

I chuckle, finally dropping my hand, though the heat of her lingers against my palm.

She steps back just slightly, cheeks flushed, but there's a smile tugging at her lips. "I guess we won."

I meet her gaze, softer now. Steady. "Yeah. I guess we did."

By the time the last of the tables are cleared from the church lawn, the sun has already dipped low, painting the horizon in streaks of orange and gold. The August heat hasn't given up yet, but in the evenings you can almost believe fall is on its way, and the lingering scent of cinnamon-spiced cider follows us as we lug everything back inside the fellowship hall.

I balance a cooler against my hip, pushing the door open with my shoulder while Ivy trails behind me, arms full of folded blankets. Olivia carries a half-empty jug of cider like it's gold, and Micah shuffles through with a stack of folding chairs. Harper follows close, cinching a trash bag tight as if it personally offended her.

"Don't drop that," she warns Micah, eyeing the wobbling tower of chairs in his arms.

Micah arches a brow. "Relax, Harper. I've got it."

"Famous last words," she mutters, brushing past him to set her garbage bag down.

Ivy leans against the counter, tucking a stray piece of hair behind her ear as she smiles at Olivia. "They're definitely going to fall for each other."

Olivia grins, lowering her voice just enough for me to catch it. "Oh, for sure. You can practically feel the tension."

I snort, dropping the cooler onto the linoleum floor. "Tension? That's not chemistry—that's a disaster waiting to happen."

Ivy's eyes light with mischief as she looks at me. "Or... it's the start of something."

"They argue about everything," I say flatly, gesturing toward Harper, who is now lecturing Micah about how he stacked the chairs against the wall. "That's not love. That's war."

Olivia smirks, stacking her empty cups neatly. "Sometimes those are the same thing."

Ivy laughs, her shoulders shaking as she tries to stifle the sound.

Harper must hear, because she spins around, eyes narrowing suspiciously. "What are y'all doing just standing there? Some of us are actually working."

Ivy lifts a folded blanket with mock innocence. "I'm working."

Olivia raises the cider jug like evidence in court. "Me too."

Harper doesn't look convinced. "Then quit whispering and help so we can all go home before it gets dark."

Micah walks by with that infuriatingly calm grin, clearly enjoying himself. "Bossy much?"

Harper whips around, glaring at him. "I'm not bossy—I'm efficient."

"Sure," he says, dragging out the word. "That's what all the bossy people say."

Ivy and Olivia erupt into quiet laughter again, and I have to turn away, hiding my grin behind the cooler lid I'm pretending to adjust.

By the time the last cooler is stowed and the trash bags tied, the fellowship hall looks almost normal again. Harper and Micah are still arguing over the "right" way to stack chairs, Olivia is leaning against the counter sipping what's left of the cider, and Ivy's laughter lingers in my ears like the last note of a song.

She's riding back with the girls, and I know once she slips into Harper's car, the chance will be gone.

So when she starts to say her goodbyes, I don't think—I just move.

"Ivy," I call softly, catching her wrist before she makes it to the door. The others are distracted—Harper mid-lecture, Olivia texting, Micah pretending not to roll his eyes. Perfect.

I tug her just around the corner of the hallway, out of sight but still close enough to hear the muffled chatter behind us. She blinks up at me, surprised, a question on her lips.

I answer it without words.

"Raincheck," I murmur, voice low, before I dip my head and kiss her.

Her hands clutch at the front of my hoodie, pulling me closer, and I cradle the back of her neck, deepening it just enough before I force myself to pull back.

Her cheeks are pink, lips parted, eyes shining in a way that nearly undoes me.

I rest my forehead against hers, catching my breath. "Worth the wait."

She laughs, soft and breathless, brushing her thumb over my jaw. "You're ridiculous."

"Maybe," I grin, pressing a quick kiss to her temple before letting her go, "but I'm also right."

From down the hall, Harper's voice cuts through. "Ivy! Let's go before Micah tries to reorganize the entire storage closet!"

Ivy squeezes my hand one last time before slipping away, her smile still lingering as she disappears around the corner.

I lean against the wall, grinning like an idiot, fully aware I'll be teased later—but not caring one bit.

I stay there in the hallway, back against the wall, trying to catch my breath. My chest still feels tight, not from carrying tables or hauling cider jugs, but from her. Always her.

The sound of my heartbeat finally starts to slow when footsteps echo down the hall. I straighten, too late.

Micah rounds the corner, a stack of folded tablecloths in his arms. He squints at me. "Why are you breathing like you just ran a mile?"

Heat creeps up the back of my neck. I clear my throat and shift against the wall. "Just...working hard."

"Uh-huh." He sets the tablecloths down on a chair, not breaking eye contact. "Or maybe it's because you snuck over here with Ivy."

I try not to laugh, running a hand over my face. "You're imagining things."

Micah smirks, leaning against the opposite wall, arms crossed now. "I'm imagining you looking like a man who just got away with something."

I raise a brow, refusing to take the bait. "Shouldn't you be double-checking Harper's cleanup system instead of checking my pulse?"

That gets the reaction I expect—Micah groans, muttering something under his breath about Harper being impossible. But I catch the faintest hint of a smile tugging at his mouth before he grabs the tablecloths again and stalks off toward the storage closet.

I shake my head, still grinning, still not quite steady on my feet.

Chapter 21
Ivy

We're at Gray's apartment again, the glow of his TV the only light in the room. A second movie plays half-forgotten in the background, but I couldn't tell you what's happening on the screen.

Because I'm curled into Gray's chest, his arm draped around me, his fingers tracing slow, absent-minded lines along my back like he's memorizing the shape of me.

The movie we actually meant to watch ended ages ago, credits rolling into silence. But we didn't move. We stayed right here, long after the screen went dark.

I shift slightly, lifting my head from his chest with quiet reluctance. I have an early morning tomorrow, and as much as I don't want to move, reality's already creeping in.

Gray blinks at me with those soft, sleepy eyes, his hair adorably tousled, his expression mirroring my own.

"So..." he murmurs, voice low and rough with exhaustion, "I guess this means you're not staying forever?"

"Tempting. But I think my landlord might notice." I joke, laughing under my breath.

He grins and shifts just enough to prop himself up on one elbow, his hand still resting gently at my waist.

I glance down at the oversized hoodie I borrowed, smoothing a wrinkle that doesn't really matter. "So...are you ready for tomorrow night?"

Gray's eyes flick to mine, steady and calm. "Yeah. More than ready."

"What songs did you end up picking?" I ask, curious.

His whole expression brightens, like this is the part he's been waiting for. "We're starting with Living Hope—it always sets the tone. Then Run to the Father—I feel like people need that reminder. And..." He pauses, a little grin tugging at his mouth. "We're debuting something new. A song I wrote."

I sit up straighter. "Seriously?"

He nods, the grin softening into something more thoughtful. "It's been on my heart for months. I just...I can't wait to see how Jesus uses it. The whole night—it's not about us. It's about what He's going to do in that room."

The conviction in his voice sends a shiver through me. I love this part of him—the way he talks about faith like it's not just belief.

"Sounds like it's going to be powerful," I say quietly.

He shrugs.. "That's the prayer. That people walk out changed."

For a while we just sit there in the hush of his apartment, the TV screen dark, the air between us steady. My head rests against his shoulder, and I can hear the even rhythm of his breathing.

Finally, I stand. "I've got an early morning, I should get home."

He groans and leans back against the couch, arms

stretched over his head. "You make goodbyes feel like punishment."

I laugh softly as I slip on my shoes, heart still thudding in my chest from everything we just said—and everything we didn't have to.

But as I grab my keys and head for the door, his voice stops me.

"Wait, Ivy."

I turn, brows lifting. "Yeah?"

He stands, running a hand through his hair like he's a little nervous. "There's something I've been wanting to do. If you're okay with it."

I step a little closer, curiosity blooming in my chest. "What is it?"

He looks me straight in the eyes. "I'd like to pray over us. Our relationship. Just...ask God to be in it. Would that be okay?"

Emotion rises in my throat so fast I can barely speak.

I nod. "Yeah. I'd like that."

He takes both of my hands in his, and we stand there in the soft glow of the kitchen light, hearts wide open.

Gray closes his eyes and exhales, then begins quietly, his voice low and tender.

"God, thank You for Ivy. For the way You brought her into my life. I don't take that lightly. I ask that You'd guide us as we grow closer—to You and to each other. Help us to love well. To honor You with every step we take. And to be brave, even when it's scary. Thank You for this—whatever this turns out to be. We trust You with it."

By the time he finishes, my eyes are wet.

He squeezes my hands gently. "Amen."

"Amen," I whisper back.

For a moment, we just stay there. Quiet and full.

And when I finally do walk out the door, my heart feels steadier than it has in a long time.

The car is quiet.

No music. No distractions. Just the low hum of the engine and the steady rhythm of the wipers brushing away the last traces of rain from the windshield.

But inside me? It's anything but quiet.

I press my lips together, still feeling the ghost of his kiss. Or, more accurately—kisses. Plural. Repeated. Unapologetic.

Somewhere between the movie credits, I lost count. And honestly? I didn't want to keep track.

Because each one felt like something new being unlocked. Like he wasn't just kissing me—he was choosing me.

And then he prayed over our relationship.

My heart hasn't stopped racing since.

His prayer loops through my mind like a song lyric I can't shake, warm and anchoring, wrapping around all the uncertainty I've carried for so long.

I pull into the lot outside my building and cut the engine. The night air is cool when I step out, but I barely notice it. Gray's hoodie still clings to me, oversized and soft. It smells like him—clean and warm, something I can't name but already crave.

Inside my apartment, everything feels quieter than usual. Maybe it's the contrast. Or maybe it's just that I've grown used to the way his presence fills a space.

I walk toward my bedroom and change into pajamas, but I pull his hoodie back on before climbing into bed. It's soft and oversized, hanging off my shoulders like it belongs there. The fabric carries the faintest trace of him, and it wraps around me like a memory I don't want to let go of.

I climb into bed and pull the covers tight, my body sinking into the mattress, my mind still floating somewhere in the warmth of his arms.

Every kiss.

Every glance.

The way his voice softened when he told me he didn't want something temporary.

The way he looked at me like he meant every word.

My eyes start to close before I even realize I'm drifting.

The hum of the night settles around me, soft and steady. But something stirs deeper—something I can't quite explain. Like my heart isn't ready to let go of this day just yet.

So I open my eyes again, barely a sliver, and whisper into the stillness.

"Hi... God."

It feels strange. Vulnerable. Like cracking open a door I've always kept shut.

But I keep going.

"I don't really know how to do this. But I think... I think I just want to say thank you."

My throat tightens, but I don't stop.

"For him. For today. For this feeling I can't name but don't want to let go of. I don't know what comes next. I'm still scared sometimes. But if You're in this...if You're writing this story...please don't stop."

A breath escapes me.

"Amen."

And just before sleep claims me, peace slips into the room.

Like maybe, just maybe, He heard me.

My fingers brush across my lips, still tingling from last night.

It's been nearly twenty-four hours, but my heart hasn't caught up yet. I've been floating all day, that giddy post-kiss glow still clinging to me like Gray's t-shirt—soft, oversized, and impossible to shake.

I'm thankful I work from home. No coworkers to raise eyebrows at the smile that's been plastered on my face since sunrise. No one to question why I keep pausing in the middle of tasks just to relive every detail—his hands, his words.

I finish up a client call, give my final feedback on a design file, and close my laptop with a sigh of contentment. Technically, I should change for the worship night at church.

But I can't bring myself to take off Gray's hoodie. It's a reminder of the warmth I've stepped into, not just with Gray, but with God.

But tonight is important and I need to look presentable.

So I slip out of my pajamas and trade them for my church's volunteer T-shirt—a soft, navy cotton with "Here to Serve" printed across the chest in bold white letters. I tuck it loosely into a pair of jeans and then stand barefoot for a moment in front of the bathroom mirror, hair a little wild from the day.

I run a brush through it, touch up the waves with my curling wand, and swipe on some mascara and blush. A little more put-together for a night that deserves the intention.

As I lean closer to the mirror to apply a light coat of gloss, my phone buzzes on the counter.

GRAY

Almost at sound check. Not gonna lie…
feeling a little nervous. New song + packed
house = mildly sweating 😅

I smile, fingers still resting on the gloss tube.

IVY

I can't wait to hear the song, Gray. You
wrote it for the Lord—and He's going to
use it.

GRAY

You trying to preach to me through text
right now?

IVY

Maybe I am • •

GRAY

Okay well then…"Blessed is the man
whose girlfriend reminds him to calm down
and not sweat through his shirt."- Psalms-
ish

A laugh bubbles out of me before I can stop it. I shake my head, trying to steady the eyeliner I'm now attempting to apply.

IVY

That is not Scripture 😂

GRAY

It's the Message translation. Very niche.

IVY

You're ridiculous. But seriously, you've got this.

GRAY

I know. That's probably why I feel better already.

My lips curve into a quiet smile as I set my phone down.

He's nervous, but he's still him.

And somehow, that combination only makes me like him more.

I swipe on a layer of gloss, run my fingers through my curls one last time, and step back from the mirror. My reflection looks calm enough, but my stomach's a different story. I signed up to help with check-in—smiles, directions, welcoming people as they arrive. Simple enough. Except nothing about this feels simple.

I'm still figuring all of this out. The verses I've been reading, the conversations I've had with Gray—they make sense, and I like what I'm learning. But part of me wonders if I'm just pretending. Smiling, nodding, acting like I belong when half the time I'm still unsure.

That thought lingers for only a second before something steadier brushes over me. A peace I can't explain. Almost like an invitation. So I do what I've seen Gray do a hundred times—I pray.

Lord, help me be faithful tonight. Give me joy as I welcome every person who walks through those doors. Help me make them feel seen, wanted, like they belong here. Let this night be beautiful. Let it be real. Fill my cup, Father.

And if there's something You want to show me...open my eyes.

I breathe out and for the first time all evening, I actually feel ready.

I look at the time, realizing I'm running a little behind.

I grab my sneakers, slipping them on quickly, and toss my denim jacket over my shoulders.

Then I head out the door, ready for whatever God has planned tonight—because something tells me, it's going to be more than just good music and pretty lights.

By the time I pull into the church parking lot, I'm five minutes late. I park quickly and rush toward the entrance, my heart pounding from more than just nerves.

When I step into the lobby, I freeze.

There, glowing across the entryway, are the photo backdrops I designed. They stretch higher than I imagined, vibrant and alive, splashed with watercolor skies and threaded with golden light. "He is Worthy." "Night of Praise." Words I typed on my laptop in the quiet of my bedroom now stand like banners, welcoming the whole church.

It doesn't even look like my work anymore. It looks holy.

My throat tightens, tears stinging at the corners of my eyes.

Can God really use my designs in a way that will bring tears to the eye?

I've heard the pastor say it before—how God takes the gifts He's placed in us and turns them back into worship.

But I never thought it could be true for me. Not with my mess. Not with my fractured faith and all the doubts I still wrestle with.

Yet here it is. My design skills. My restless late-night edits. My obsession with color and fonts. All of it, offered up to Him—and somehow turned into glory.

Not because it's perfect. Not because I am.

But because He can breathe purpose into anything.

The thought rushes over me, so heavy and so tender I can't hold it back. I press a hand to my chest, trying to steady the rise and fall, and whisper, barely audible over the hum of people gathering, "Thank You, Lord. Thank You for letting me be part of this."

Then I head toward the volunteers, weaving through the buzz of last-minute prep and warm greetings. I find my spot at the welcome table just as the doors open and the first wave of guests filters in.

Tonight isn't about me.

But it feels good to be doing more than just attending this space, but also contributing.

And the joy of it—the honor of it—feels even better than last night's kiss.

Well, almost.

The lobby is buzzing with energy. Volunteers offering warm smiles, worship music playing softly in the background and guests filing in with coffee cups in hand and anticipation in their eyes.

There's something different about tonight.

People keep arriving, arms outstretched for hugs, voices rising in laughter, but my focus stays steady. I'm not sure if I'm doing this the "right" way, but I want to. I want people to feel welcome, even if all I can give is a smile and a little bit of nervous energy.

When the last wave of guests moves into the sanctuary, I finally take a breath, glancing at my phone to see text.

HARPER

Front row. Left side.

I glance at the clock. It's time.

I weave through the side hallway and slip into the back of the main auditorium just as the house lights dim and the band steps into place.

The sanctuary is packed. A sea of raised hands and warm lighting fills the space.

I weave my way down the row, murmuring apologies as I pass a few people. When I finally spot Harper, I start to slide into the empty seat beside her—only to freeze.

Because Olivia is sitting on her other side.

My mouth parts in shock. She must have snuck in while I was busy at the welcome table, because I definitely would've noticed her. For a second, all I can do is stare, my heart thudding with something between disbelief and delight.

Then I drop into the seat between them, grinning so wide it almost hurts. "Liv, you're here?"

She gives me a half-smile, almost shy, and something warm blooms in my chest. I make a mental note right then: I have to ask Harper later how in the world she managed to talk her into coming.

And then it begins.

The first notes ring out, clear and steady. Gray's voice

joins with the music and the room seems to sing in unison. It's the new song. His song. The one he was nervous about. The one he wrote.

The lyrics hit like truth wrapped in melody. Lines about surrender, about trust, about a God who stays. The harmonies rise and fall like a tide, and I feel the weight of everything—every doubt, every fear, every unanswered prayer—melting away.

> *You brought people I didn't pray for*
> *Showed me love I didn't earn*
> *You turned strangers into anchors*
> *And used every scar to help me learn*

Harper's already on her feet, arms lifted, eyes closed, moving with the rhythm like it's in her bones. Joy radiates from her.

Olivia stands still, but I glance at her just in time to see a single tear slip down her cheek.

And something about that undoes me.

It's not just the music. It's not even just Gray.

It's all of it.

My friends beside me. The presence of God thick in the room. The feeling that somehow, I'm exactly where I'm supposed to be. That God is using me, surrounding me, inviting me deeper.

I press a hand to my chest, heart full, and whisper a quiet thank You. For the music. For the moment. For the unexpected ways He weaves things together.

Gray sings the final chorus, his voice rising with the congregation, and I close my eyes because I want to feel it.

Chapter 22
Gray

You met me there, in the middle of the mess
With arms wide open, You gave me rest
You didn't wait for me to get it all right
You found me in the dark and brought me to light
You're the God who stays, the God who cares
I didn't find You...
You met me there

"You met me there, in the middle of the mess..."

The final chorus lifts, voices swelling until the sound fills every corner of the sanctuary. Hundreds singing like they actually believe it. Like they've lived it. I pour everything into the words, my chest tight with gratitude that this room is alive with praise—not because of me, not because of us on stage, but because of Him.

The last chord rings out, reverberating against the rafters. Slowly, the room hushes, like everyone is collectively holding their breath for what comes next.

Pastor Jack steps forward, mic in hand, his voice warm but steady. "Friends, we've sung of His mercy. Now let's pause, open our hands, and pray. You don't have to have the right words. You don't even have to speak them out loud. Just offer Him whatever you've been carrying."

I set my guitar back on its stand and bow my head. The lights dim, leaving only a soft glow over the stage. From where I stand, I see a sea of bowed heads, lifted hands, some kneeling right there on the floor. People whispering prayers. Others silent but undone.

I whisper my own prayer under my breath.

Lord, let this night be more than music. Let it soften hearts. Break chains. Draw someone closer to You who didn't even expect it when they walked in.

I lift my head, scanning the crowd almost without meaning to. That's when I spot them—Harper and Olivia on each side, Ivy in the middle.

Harper is swaying to the music, her smile wide and unrestrained, like she can't keep the joy from spilling out of her.

Olivia, on the other side, looks restless. Her head is dipped, but her eyes aren't closed—they flick nervously from side to side, her hands fumbling together as if she doesn't know what to do with them.

And then there's Ivy.

Right in the center, framed by her friends, she steals the air from my lungs. Head bowed, eyes shut tight, her lips move faintly with whispered prayer. Her palms are open like she's offering all of herself. She looks...present. Seeking. Nothing—and no one—has ever stolen my heart faster than the picture of her, praying like she means it.

Something in me shifts. I've seen her bold and teasing, I've seen her unsure and hesitant. But this—this quiet reverence—it undoes me. Nerves skitter in my chest, because suddenly the stakes feel higher. She's not just here because of me. She's here...maybe because God is tugging on her heart.

And I don't want to get in the way of that.

I exhale slowly, palms pressed together. *Okay, Lord. She's Yours before she's ever mine. Help me remember that. Help me love her in a way that leads her closer to You, not to me.*

The worship team shifts into a softer melody, instrumental, underscoring the prayers rising in the room. A man in the front drops to his knees. A woman a few rows back wipes at her face. The Spirit is thick here. Tangible.

Jack steps back and gives me a nod. My throat tightens, but I reach for the mic anyway.

"Church," I begin, "we just sang about a God who meets us right in the middle of the mess. And maybe for you, that's not just lyrics—it's your life. Maybe you walked in here carrying more than anyone knows. Fear. Doubt. Guilt. A weight you don't think you can lay down."

I pause, scanning the faces lit dimly by stage lights.

Nerves prickle under my skin. Because leading worship was never supposed to be about who was in the crowd. But tonight, seeing her there, it reminds me—this isn't just a setlist. This is a chance for God to move in ways I'll never fully see.

I grip the mic a little tighter. "Here's the good news. You don't have to fix yourself up before God will listen. You don't have to have perfect words. You can just open your hands and say, 'Here I am.' That's enough. He's enough."

A hush settles again. A few hands lift. Someone sniffles in the third row.

"Let's pray," I say, closing my eyes. "Father, thank You for meeting us right where we are. For not waiting until we had it all together, but loving us in the middle of our weakness. I pray for every person in this room—that they would feel Your presence, Your peace, Your forgiveness. That chains would break tonight. That hearts would soften. That someone who walked in far from You would leave knowing You've been chasing them all along. In Jesus' name, amen."

When I open my eyes, the sanctuary is thick with quiet reverence. People praying aloud. Some whispering. Others just...still. And the band plays gently behind it all, underscoring the holy weight of the moment.

The night carries on like that—waves of worship rising and falling. Voices lifted in songs that echo through the rafters, prayer after prayer offered up, some with tears, some with laughter, some with nothing but silence.

Every chorus feels heavier than the one before, but not in a burdensome way—in a way that settles deep into your bones. A room full of people meeting with God, unpolished and unhurried.

By the time the last note fades, it feels like hours have passed and only minutes at the same time. My throat is raw, my heart wrung out, and yet—there's a peace here. A fullness.

Nights like this remind me why we do it. Why it matters.

We step off stage, but my heart's still somewhere between the last chord and Heaven.

The crowd hasn't moved. No one's ready for it to end. Voices rise in waves—some singing, some praying, some just standing still with tears on their cheeks and hands lifted like they're reaching for something more.

And they are.

Because tonight wasn't about lights or lyrics or anything we rehearsed.

It was about Him.

God showed up. In the cracks. In the silence. In the voices that refused to stop singing even after the music did.

Micah claps a hand to my back as we head down the side hallway. "You were on fire tonight, man."

I shake my head, still dazed. "We all were. That was..."

"Holy," one of the vocalists says softly behind us. "It felt holy."

Yeah. That's exactly it.

Not perfect. Not polished. But holy.

Like Heaven cracked open just enough to let us breathe something real.

I'm still gripping my guitar, my hands not quite steady, when I glance down the side hallway.

And that's when I see her.

Ivy.

Standing just beyond the edge of the crowd, like she's not sure if she belongs in it or apart from it. Her eyes are rimmed red, cheeks streaked with mascara, like she's been crying for a while and forgot to care.

And something in me breaks wide open.

I don't hesitate.

I hand my guitar off to someone, don't even check who, and start weaving through the chaos. People are still praying, still crying, still clinging to the holy weight in the air.

But all I see is her.

She looks up right as I reach her, and before I can think better of it, I wrap her up in my arms. I lift her off the ground for just a second, spinning her once before setting her down slowly.

Her arms are still around my shoulders when I pull back just enough to see her face.

"Did you feel that?" I whisper, breathless.

She nods, eyes glassy. "Yeah. I felt it."

And I know she doesn't just mean the music.

I pull back, just enough to see her face, and my breath catches.

Tears have carved soft trails down her cheeks, catching in the glow of the hallway lights. And without thinking, I lift my sleeve and gently wipe them away.

She doesn't flinch.

Doesn't apologize or laugh it off.

She just closes her eyes and lets me be there with her. The real her.

And for a second, I forget every voice, every sound, every person around us.

When her eyes open again, they're full of something unspoken.

She parts her lips.

Then stops.

Whatever it is, she tucks it away with a small, shaky nod.

And I get it.

Some things don't need to be said, yet.

Some things need room to bloom slowly.

And if it's with her, I'll wait as long as it takes.

And somehow, that silence means more than any words ever could.

Because I see it.

In her eyes. In her steady breath. In the way she doesn't try to hide the emotion streaking across her face.

She's not running from it. Not pretending it didn't hit her just as hard.

And I think, I know, we're standing in something sacred right now.

Not because it's neat or tidy or easy.

But because it's honest. And because God's in it.

Layer by layer, moment by moment, He's building something here. Something I never saw coming but now can't imagine letting go.

And with Ivy right in front of me, still holding on, I don't want to.

I look at her and it nearly undoes me.

The way she lets me see all of it. The side of her no one else gets.

"Ivy..." My voice comes out lower than I meant, thick with something I don't have words for. "Do you even realize what you're doing to me?"

Her breath catches.

We're not alone. Not even close. The room hums with movement—volunteers winding down, families reuniting, music still threading through the air.

She doesn't say anything.

She doesn't need to.

Her silence is full of trust, full of yes.

So I lean in, giving her space to pull away, to change her mind. One breath. Two. Three.

She stays still.

So I kiss her.

Right there, in the middle of the crowd and the noise and the holy hush still hanging in the air.

It's not fireworks or fanfare.

It's better.

It's steady. Certain. Like a promise even when no words are spoken.

When we pull back, she rests her forehead against mine, and I don't think I've ever felt more aware of my heartbeat—or hers.

We're both smiling.

Soft. Wrecked. Changed.

"Everything about tonight..." I whisper, my voice barely audible between us, "feels like a beginning."

She nods, her thumb brushing gently over mine, and in that simple touch, I feel the echo of every unsaid prayer she's still learning how to speak.

She may not have the words yet.

But I see it.

I feel it.

And I'll wait—because I know who's writing this story now.

And He's not done with us.

Not even close.

After the final hugs are exchanged, the night exhales into quiet.

Everyone heads their separate ways.

Ivy hugged me goodbye, her eyes still soft from worship, then left with Harper and Olivia—off to grab milkshakes.

She promised she'd text me later. And I believe her.

But still, when I walk into my quiet apartment and flip on the hallway light, the silence hits harder than I expect.

The high from earlier still hums under my skin—like

I'm carrying the echoes of worship, the weight of every lyric, every lifted hand. But now?

Now it just feels like noise with nowhere to go.

I toss my keys on the counter, peel off my sweatshirt, and stand there, staring into the stillness that is both too quiet yet too loud.

I turn on music. Then turn it off. Walk to the window. Shut the blinds. All while Goliath watches me with curious eyes.

My thoughts drift to Ivy—her laugh, those streaks of mascara, the way she looked like she was about to hand me her whole heart.

But she didn't. And now she's gone, and I'm here.

And I hate how much that unsettles me.

Not because I don't trust her. Not because I think anything's wrong.

But because some twisted part of me wishes I could've just asked her to come home with me instead.

Just to stay.

Just to sit on my couch and talk about the night until we both crashed.

Not even to talk about us. Just to be near her. Just to let the night keep going a little longer.

But I know that would've been about me.

About my comfort. My fear of being alone. My need to hold things together.

Control.

Always control.

I shower, hoping the hot water will clear my head. It doesn't.

I lie in bed, staring at the ceiling.

Toss. Turn.

This isn't just restlessness. This is conviction.

I flip onto my back with a groan.

God, I know what this is. It's You. You're calling me out.

I sit up, breathing hard, the tension in my chest thick and aching.

Then I slide off the bed and kneel beside it, resting my elbows on the mattress.

My voice is low. Honest. Tired.

"God...I don't want to carry this anymore."

My voice cracks. The weight of everything I've tried to control presses down like bricks.

"I keep trying to manage it all—her feelings, my fear, the pace, the outcome. I say I want to honor You, and I do. But I've been holding the pen like it's mine to write with."

Silence stretches, but it's not empty.

"I trust You. Help me live like I do."

I stay there for a while. No script. No rehearsed prayer. Just presence.

When I finally stand and crawl back into bed, my phone buzzes on the nightstand.

Ivy's name is on my screen.

My chest tightens—not from control this time, but surrender.

This isn't coincidence. It's grace.

A gentle reminder that I'm seen.

That He's still writing.

Chapter 23
Ivy

I should be asleep.

The worship night ended hours ago. My makeup is long gone, my hair's a mess, and my feet still ache from standing —but I can't stop replaying everything in my mind.

The music. The message. The moment Gray kissed me in front of everyone.

I trace my fingers over my lips, still feeling the ghost of it.

I tuck the blanket tighter around my shoulders and sit up in bed, the glow of the streetlight outside casting faint patterns across my ceiling.

I should feel whole right now. Joyful. At peace.

And I do. Kind of.

But also—I don't.

Because the truth is, I wasn't completely honest with Gray tonight. Even when we talked on the phone earlier.

He looked so alive after worship. He ran to me like I was part of it. Like he wanted to share that mountaintop moment with me.

And I let him believe I felt it too.

I did feel something. Absolutely.

But not in the way he probably thinks.

It wasn't just the music or the message or the packed sanctuary.

It was that song. His song.

The way the lyrics spoke directly to parts of me I didn't know were still bleeding. The line about not having to earn your place with God. About Him having arms wide open, giving me rest, not waiting till I had it all together. It hit me like a wave.

I nearly told him that.

Nearly said, "I felt like that song was written for me. Like it was peeling something open that I've kept hidden for a long time."

But I didn't.

Because saying that felt too...intimate.

Too much.

Like if I admitted it, I'd be crossing a line from interested in God to all in.

And I don't know if I'm ready to be all in yet.

What if I say too much and disappoint Gray?

What if I open up and it changes the way he sees me?

What if he finds out I'm still half-lost and doesn't want to stick around to help me find the rest?

I roll over and grab my phone, thumb hovering over his name.

I type: **I wish I had said more tonight.**

Then delete it.

I try again: **Your song, it made me feel something I didn't know I needed to feel.**

Delete.

Eventually I decide not to send anything at all.

I turn my phone on silent, plug it into the charger, and curl deeper into the blankets. The quiet hum of the night fills my room, but in my head, it's not silence at all. It's Gray's voice, his lyrics, wrapping around me like a melody that refuses to let go.

I close my eyes, my lips tugging into a small smile, and let the sound of him linger in the dark like a prayer I didn't know I needed. My chest feels warm, heavy and light all at once.

And with his song echoing in my memory, I finally drift toward sleep.

I tug at the hem of my blouse for the third time before stepping through the glass doors of the church office. My stomach knots the way it always does before interviews—except this doesn't even feel like an interview. At least, not in the traditional sense.

The prayer and worship night graphics had been my "trial run." A way to dip my toe in, see if I fit. And apparently, I did—because when Pastor Greg emailed to set up this meeting, he said they wanted to talk "next steps."

Still, my thoughts spiral: What if I misunderstood? What if this is just a polite thank-you and a smile? What if they realize I'm not the "church girl" they're expecting?

I balance my portfolio in one hand, swipe a clammy palm across my jeans, and whisper under my breath, "Okay, Lord. If this is from You, open the door. If it's not, shut it tight."

The receptionist waves me back to the conference room, where Pastor Greg and Emily—the communications director—are already seated with coffees in hand.

"Thanks for coming, Ivy," Pastor Greg says, his smile wide and steady. "We'll get right to it."

I freeze halfway into my chair. That's fast.

Emily slides a folder across the table toward me. "We don't want to waste your time with formality. We loved your work, and the truth is—we want you on our team. Part-time, flexible hours. And the first big project?" She grins, almost conspiratorial. "Christmas Eve service."

My jaw drops. "Christmas? But it's August."

Emily laughs. "Exactly. The timeline leaves room for edits, printing, and promotion. We've learned the hard way that Christmas can't be rushed."

Her words blur for a moment as I stare at the folder in front of me. *Lord...is this really happening?*

I prayed before I walked in—asking Him to open the right doors. And here I am, with one wide open in front of me.

My chest tightens, but not with fear this time. With awe.

Okay...wow. So, uh...You really are using me, huh? Even with my random design skills? Like, fonts and colors and obsessing over Photoshop layers at 2 a.m.. That's...actually something You can use?

That doesn't even sound real. But here it is. A church job. My work up on display. Not because I'm "good enough," but because You decided it mattered. Because somehow You think I matter.

That's wild, God. Really wild.

I press my hand against the folder, swallowing the lump

in my throat, and whisper a silent thank You before looking back up with a shaky smile.

For a second, the room blurs. My mind races ahead to colors, fonts, Christmas lights, giant banners with Scripture woven through them. Ideas spill faster than I can catch them. It feels too big and too good, and for a heartbeat, I forget where I am.

"So," Pastor Greg's voice breaks through my thoughts, warm and steady, "are you in?"

My head jerks up, cheeks heating. "Yes. Yes, absolutely. I'm in."

His smile deepens, and he gestures for the team to gather closer. "Let's pray over Ivy and this new role."

We bow our heads, and his voice carries with a gentleness that makes my eyes sting.

"Father, we thank You for Ivy. Thank You for the creativity You've placed in her, the eye for beauty, the heart for excellence, the desire to serve. We believe You don't waste any gift, Lord, and tonight we set her apart for the work You've called her to do here. Use her talents to glorify Your name. Give her peace when deadlines feel heavy, fresh ideas when inspiration runs dry, and joy in the process. May every design she creates point people back to You, the true Artist. Surround her with encouragement and remind her she's not doing this alone. We pray protection, provision, and blessing over this next season. In Jesus's name, amen."

By the time they lift their heads, I can hardly sit still. My chair scrapes back, and I promise to follow up soon, but my feet are already light as air.

I all but skip out of the meeting, folder hugged to my chest, giddy grin stretched wide.

I slip into the driver's seat of my car, still clutching my

tote bag against my chest. My hands are shaking a little, enough that I have to take a few deep breaths before I even think about turning the ignition.

I'm on the team.

The words replay in my mind, over and over, like they're caught on a loop. I press my palms against my cheeks, feeling the warmth there. The adrenaline is still coursing through my veins, leaving me wide-eyed and practically buzzing.

"Did that really just happen?" I whisper to myself, staring out the windshield at the buildings in the distance. The sky is a pale, soft blue, dotted with clouds that look like they were painted there.

I pinch my arm, yelping a little when I do. But it's real. This is real.

I sink back against the headrest, covering my mouth as a laugh slips out. How did I get here? Two months ago, I didn't even know this church existed. Now, I'm designing their Christmas Eve service. Getting paid for it. Actually getting paid to do what I love.

I pull my phone from my bag and scroll to Gray's contact. My fingers hover over the screen for a second, and then I type out a quick message:

IVY

Are we still on for dinner tonight?

I stare at the screen, my heart doing a familiar flip as the three little dots pop up almost immediately.

GRAY

Of course. How did your meeting go?

I bite my lip, a grin spreading across my face. My fingers hover for just a second before I decide to keep him guessing.

IVY

You'll see.

The dots pop up again, pausing, disappearing, and then finally:

GRAY

So that's how it's gonna be, huh? Keeping secrets?

IVY

Maybe just one 😌 See you at 7?

GRAY

Wouldn't miss it.

I drop my phone into the cup holder, my hands gripping the steering wheel as I take another deep breath. My whole body feels lighter, like I'm floating. Like maybe this is what it feels like when things start falling into place—not in some big, cinematic way, but in the quiet, ordinary steps that add up to something extraordinary.

I glance in the rearview mirror one last time, the church framed against the sky. The building looks the same as it did when I pulled in earlier—red brick, clean lines, nothing flashy. But it feels different now, like it's part of my story instead of just a backdrop to someone else's.

As I back out of the lot and ease onto the main road, the smile on my face softens into something steadier. I don't know what this new path is going to look like. I don't even know if I'm fully ready for it.

But maybe that's the point.

Maybe faith isn't about having every answer lined up before you move forward. Maybe it's about taking the next step anyway, shaky and unsure, trusting that God will meet you where your courage runs out.

The thought makes my chest ache in the best way—like hope is stretching wide inside me, making room for something new. I roll down the window, letting the late-summer breeze tangle through my hair, and whisper into the quiet hum of the road,

"Okay, Lord. I'm in."

Chapter 24
Ivy

The knock on my door is gentle but solid, and I don't think I've ever moved faster to answer it. When I pull it open, Gray is standing there, a bouquet of flowers in one hand—another messy, beautiful mix of pinks and whites—and that familiar grin softening his expression.

"Hey you," he says, his voice low and warm.

I giggle, stepping aside to let him in. "Gray, I still have flowers from last time in a vase on the kitchen counter."

He shrugs, stepping through the door and wrapping his arms around me in that full-hearted hug he does that makes the world fall quiet. His lips brush the top of my head as he murmurs, "I remember. But I told you—I'm your boyfriend now. It's kind of my job to bring you flowers. Get used to it."

I smile against his chest, my heart doing that little flip it always seems to do around him.

He smells like his typical mix of leather and vanilla. His hands slide gently over my back, not rushing, just there. I close my eyes, resting my head against his chest.

"I could stay here forever," I murmur against his shoulder, the words slipping out before I can catch them.

Gray chuckles softly, his chest rumbling beneath my cheek. "Not gonna lie, I wouldn't mind that."

I pull back just slightly, my hands still resting on his sides as I look up at him. His eyes search mine, a question there, but he just smiles. "So...how'd the meeting go?"

I shift back, walking toward the kitchen and tossing him a casual glance over my shoulder. "Well...they want me to work on the Christmas designs. But there is something else."

Gray's brows pull together as he follows me into the kitchen. "What do you mean?"

I turn to face him, leaning against the counter, trying, and failing, to hide the grin tugging at my lips. "They offered me a job."

He stares at me, waiting for me to say more. When I don't, he tilts his head. "Like...an actual job?"

I nod, biting my bottom lip. "Part-time for now, but yeah. It's real. I'm officially on the team."

The words are barely out of my mouth before he's across the room, his arms around me, lifting me right off the floor. I squeal, clutching his shoulders as he spins me around, his laugh warm and unrestrained. "You did it!"

I can't stop laughing, my head tipping back as he spins us one more time before setting me down. His hands are still on my waist, his smile still wide and genuine. "I knew they'd see it. I knew it."

I shrug, but I'm beaming. "I wasn't sure at first...but when they offered, it just felt...right."

Gray's eyes soften as he takes a step back, still smiling. "I'm so proud of you, Ivy."

Then he pauses, like he's remembering something, and reaches into his jacket pocket. "I have something for you."

He pulls out a small box with a little gold bow that's slightly crumpled, and holds it out.

My heart flutters. "Gray, what..."

"Open it."

I lift the lid and find a delicate gold bracelet inside. A tiny cross charm glints in the light, and as I turn it gently in my fingers, I notice the small engraving inside — 1 Corinthians 13:13.

I trace the numbers with my thumb, swallowing hard. "What verse is this?"

Gray's smile softens, his voice low and full of meaning. "And now these three remain: faith, hope, and love. But the greatest of these is love."

Tears fill my eyes. "It's beautiful."

"I wanted you to have a reminder," he says quietly, taking the bracelet from my hand and fastening it around my wrist. "Of how much faith I have in you. How much hope I have in our future. And how much...love I have for you."

His fingers brush my skin, lingering just long enough to make my heart skip.

"I love you Ivy," he adds.

My breath catches, and the words tumble out, soft but certain. "I love you too, Gray. I think... I've been falling for you since that first dare."

His grin softens into something deeper, something that makes my knees feel unsteady. He leans in, just enough for his forehead to brush mine, and for a heartbeat, we stay like that, wrapped in the weight of what we've just said.

Then I clear my throat, turning back to the stove, my heart still racing. "Well... we can officially celebrate with mediocre pasta and day-old breadsticks."

Gray chuckles, leaning against the counter. "Sounds perfect to me."

The words settle in my chest as I turn back to the stove, where the pot of pasta is still simmering. I grab the spoon and give it a quick stir.

I grin, sprinkling a bit of parmesan over the pot and turning off the burner. "You say that now. Just wait until you're actually eating it."

He reaches over, grabbing a piece of bread from the counter and taking a bite. "I'm not too worried."

"Famous last words," I tease, ladling the pasta onto two plates and setting them on the coffee table.

We sit cross-legged on my living room floor, plates balanced on the coffee table between us. He swears it's the best thing he's ever eaten, which is either wildly flattering or proof that the man doesn't cook.

Music plays low from my phone. The overhead lights are off. Just the warm flicker of a single lamp in the corner, casting a soft glow over the room. He reaches for another breadstick, and I take the opportunity to study him—the curve of his smile, the way his lashes frame his eyes when he looks down.

"Okay, seriously," Gray says, pointing his fork at me. "What did you put in this?"

I laugh, twirling my fork through the last bit of spaghetti. "Um...garlic? Salt? A touch of desperation?"

He raises an eyebrow, chewing thoughtfully. "If desperation tastes like this, I'm concerned for your mental state."

I snort, covering my mouth with my hand. "I guess I'm just that good."

Gray's eyes soften, his smile turning genuine. "You are."

Heat creeps up my neck, and I glance down at my plate. "It's just pasta."

"And I'm just a guy," he says, nudging me with his shoulder. "Sometimes simple things are the best things."

I pause, my fork halfway to my mouth as I let the words settle, nestling into the spaces between us.

He catches my eye, his smile turning a little sheepish. "That was deep, huh?"

I chuckle, taking a sip of my water. "Yeah. Very hallmark-movie of you."

Gray leans back against the couch, stretching his legs out. "What can I say? I'm full of surprises."

"Oh yeah?" I challenge, raising an eyebrow. "Name one thing that would surprise me."

He tilts his head, considering. "I know how to juggle."

I burst out laughing. "No you do not."

Gray shrugs. "I do. Two years ago, one of the kids in the youth group begged me to learn. So, I did."

I cross my arms, skeptical. "Prove it."

He raises his hands like he's surrendering. "I'm not juggling marinara-covered meatballs in your living room."

I laugh again, the sound echoing off the walls of my tiny apartment. "Fine, I guess I'll just have to take your word for it."

"You will." He grins, leaning back and stretching his arms out along the back of the couch, fingertips brushing my shoulder. "Okay, your turn. What's something that would surprise me?"

I hesitate, biting my lip. "Hmm...I can play the ukulele."

Gray's eyebrows shoot up. "Are you serious?"

I nod, laughing. "I bought it at a garage sale in college and taught myself how to play. I only know, like, five songs, but still."

He's grinning now, eyes bright with disbelief. "Okay, I need proof. Please tell me you still have it."

I look toward my bedroom door, then back at him. "I do...it's probably a little out of tune."

"I don't care." His grin widens. "Please? I've got to see this."

I roll my eyes, but his excitement is contagious. I get up, disappearing into my room and digging through my closet until I find the faded blue case. When I come back out, Gray is sitting up straighter, his hands clasped like he's about to witness a miracle.

"Here it is," I say, plopping back down on the floor. I unzip the case and pull out the tiny instrument, brushing the strings with my fingers.

Gray's smile stretches even wider. "This is amazing."

"Don't get too excited," I warn, plucking a few strings and wincing at the tinny sound. "Like I said, I only know a few songs. And they're...well, kinda ridiculous."

"Now I'm even more excited," he laughs, settling back. "Play me something ridiculous."

I roll my eyes but settle the uke on my lap. After a quick tune, I strum the first few chords of a silly, half-written song I made up back in college. It's ridiculous and embarrassing and full of nonsensical rhymes, but Gray is absolutely loving it, leaning back with his hands behind his head, laughing like he hasn't laughed in years.

When I finally stop, he claps loudly, even whistles. "You have been holding out on me, Ivy."

I groan, shoving the uke back in its case. "You weren't supposed to like that."

"Oh, but I did." He reaches over, brushing his fingers along mine. "You surprise me."

I pause, the weight of his touch sending sparks up my arm. "Good surprise?"

He nods, his smile softening. "The best kind."

My heart stumbles over itself, and I glance down at my plate, cheeks warming. "Well...now you know my secret talent."

Gray chuckles. "I think I need to start digging for more."

"Good luck with that," I tease, nudging his shoulder.

Gray leans in just slightly, his voice going soft. "I think I'm up for the challenge."

I laugh, the sound catching in my throat as he inches just a little bit closer, eyes locked on mine. For a moment, the air shifts—something heavier, deeper settling between us. I feel it, that electric hum that's been threading through every moment we share lately.

He pulls back, but the feeling lingers, stretching out like a thin thread, unbreakable. I clear my throat, glancing back at my plate, but my heart is nowhere near calm.

We've been doing this more lately.

Spending time. Talking about real things. Laughing until it hurts.

And kissing.

A lot of kissing.

The closeness between us hums in the air like static. Every brush of his hand, every glance across the table, it's like my body remembers how it felt to kiss him in the rain. How safe it felt. How electric. How seen.

And the longer we sit here tonight, the harder it is to pretend that I don't want more of that. More of him.

I set my empty plate aside, and he does the same. When he leans back against the couch, I follow, scooting close until his arm wraps around my shoulder. I curl into his side like it's the most natural thing in the world.

His fingers trail slowly down my arm.

I turn to face him, heart pounding. Our faces are inches apart.

Then less than inches.

I kiss him.

Soft. Sweet. Until it's not.

He deepens it, one hand cradling my jaw, the other sliding to my waist. I melt into him, letting my fingers roam under the hem of his shirt. He's warm. Solid. Familiar in a way that startles me.

My hand starts to tug his shirt upward, just enough to lift the fabric—

But he stops me.

Gently, firmly, he takes my wrist and pulls back, just enough to break the kiss. His breathing is heavy. So is mine.

And in the quiet that follows, a flicker of something sharp twists inside me. Rejection. It sneaks in fast, before I can talk myself out of it. Before I can remember who he is and what he stands for.

Because every other guy in my past? They never said no. They never even hesitated. And some dark, bruised part of me whispers that maybe Gray's hesitation means I'm not enough. Not pure enough. Not worthy enough.

I force myself to meet his eyes, searching for anger or disappointment—some confirmation of the lie curling in my chest. But all I see is restraint. Respect. A war inside him that has nothing to do with me and everything to do with God.

Still, the ache lingers. I swallow hard, pressing my free hand against my thigh to ground myself. Why does no feel like failure? Why does being honored feel so close to being unwanted?

I sit back, suddenly aware of what I was doing. "I...I'm sorry. I didn't mean..."

He reaches for my hand, lacing our fingers together.

"Ivy," he says softly, "you have nothing to apologize for."

I nod, but the heat in my cheeks says otherwise.

"It's just..." I trail off. "This is usually the point where things go further. Where guys expect more. And I just assumed..."

He brushes a strand of hair from my face, his thumb resting briefly against my cheek. "You shouldn't feel like you have to take your clothes off to feel loved."

My throat tightens.

"A man of God," he continues, "won't need you to take your clothes off to see your beauty. He won't make you guess his intentions. He'll pray for you—without you asking. And he'll never ask you to compromise."

I stare at him, my heart absolutely wrecked in the best way.

"But you've..." I swallow. "I mean, you've been with someone before, right?"

He nods slowly. "Yeah. I wasn't always following Jesus. But now? Now I'm saving myself for marriage. Not because I don't want to—I do." He gives a low laugh. "So badly. But I know it's important to God. And to me."

I exhale, relief and longing all tangled together.

"Ivy," he says, cupping my face in both hands, "you have no idea how badly I want to. But I want to honor you more than I want to indulge in a moment."

I blink back sudden tears.

"Okay," I whisper.

He presses his forehead to mine. "We're not going to rush this. Love doesn't have to prove itself in heat. Sometimes the most powerful thing you can do...is wait."

I nod again, eyes stinging.

Then, as if on cue, a loud crack splits the silence. The lamp flickers—and dies.

A blown bulb.

I shriek. He jumps.

And just like that, we're both laughing, tangled in a ridiculous heap of limbs and nerves on my living room floor.

"I'm pretty sure that was God telling us to cool it," I say between giggles.

Gray grins, rolling onto his back. "Honestly? Can't even be mad about it."

Chapter 25
Gray

I push off the floor, stretching my arms overhead until my back gives a quiet crack. Ivy's already on her feet, gathering our plates, and I trail her into the kitchen. The room falls into that soft, lingering silence as if the night is winding down but doesn't quite want to end.

She moves toward the sink, reaching for the faucet, but I step in before she can turn it on. My hand brushes over hers. "Uh-uh," I say with a grin. "You cook, I clean. House rules."

She lifts a brow at me. "House rules? This isn't even your house."

I laugh and nudge her aside with my hip. "Doesn't matter. Rules are rules."

I roll up my sleeves, water already running, and reach for the sponge. The ink on my arms catches the light, and for a second I wonder if she's watching. When I glance her way, sure enough—she's leaning back against the counter, arms crossed, studying me like I just turned into a science project.

I shake my head, trying not to smile as I rinse each plate.

Old habit, really—scrub, rinse, rack. Stack the cups upside down. Shake off the water so they dry faster. It's the kind of muscle memory you don't forget when you've spent years living alone. Or when doing the dishes was the one thing that made you feel useful during the messiest parts of life.

"You do this often?" she asks, voice laced with curiosity.

I look over my shoulder, catching the surprise on her face. "You act like you've never seen a guy do dishes before."

She smirks. "Not one who actually knows what he's doing."

I grab a towel and dry my hands, trying to play it cool. "Guess I'm full of surprises today."

"You know," Ivy says, her voice light but laced with something bolder, "a guy who can juggle and do dishes might just be the most attractive thing I've ever seen."

I laugh, the sound echoing off her tiny kitchen walls. "If I'd known dish soap was the key to winning you over, I would've started scrubbing on day one."

She rolls her eyes, but the grin she's wearing tells me I hit the mark. I can't help it—teasing her feels effortless.

"Just saying," I add, drying the last plate and sliding it onto the rack. "You haven't even seen my full repertoire. I can fold a fitted sheet."

She snorts. "No way."

I place a hand over my heart, as serious as I can manage. "Swear on my life."

She shakes her head, laughing. It's soft, real, and tugs something loose in my chest.

"I'm not sure I believe you," she says.

I dry my hands on the towel and toss it onto the counter, then turn toward her. "Guess you'll just have to find out."

Our eyes lock. Something shifts—subtle but sure.

The air gets thicker. Quieter.

I step closer, slow but certain, until she's right in front of me. My hands find her waist, and I pull her in, letting my arms wrap around her like I've been waiting to do it all night.

She melts into me, her cheek resting against my chest, and I close my eyes for a second, breathing her in.

No words.

Just her heartbeat against mine, the warmth of her skin through my shirt, and the quiet hum of something sacred settling between us.

And I think—not for the first time—how easy it was to fall in love with this girl.

"I'm proud of you, you know that?" I murmur into her hair, my voice quieter than I mean it to be.

She tilts her head, eyes meeting mine. "For what?"

I look at her—really look—and there's too much I could say. Too much she doesn't even realize she's carrying with strength and grace.

"For everything," I say softly. "For this new job. For stepping into this whole new world like you were made for it. For showing up—fully, bravely, even when it's hard." I shake my head a little, the weight of it catching in my throat. "Just...I'm proud of you."

Her smile makes my chest ache in the best way. She whispers a simple thank you, and it hits deeper than she knows.

I brush my thumb along her cheek, letting the softness of her skin slow my thoughts. I should go. I know I should go.

"I should leave before I change my mind," I say, though I don't move.

My hand slips from her cheek to her shoulder, trailing

down the line of her back. When I reach her waist, I pause. Just for a second. Just long enough to feel the pull between us tighten.

My eyes flick to hers—searching, asking.

She doesn't move.

So I let my hand drift a little lower, fingers grazing the curve of her hip. The contact sends a jolt through me, not just of want but of awareness—of how close we are to crossing lines I've worked so hard to honor.

I feel it in her breath, the way it catches.

I feel it in my body, how badly I want to stay right here.

I want her, but more than that, I want her to know she's safe. That I'll choose restraint when it matters.

So I let my hand move again—up, not down—sliding back to the space between her shoulder blades, pressing my palm there like I'm grounding us both.

I lower my forehead to hers, eyes closed, trying to breathe past the ache.

"You have no idea how hard it is to leave," I whisper.

Her hands fist in my shirt, tugging me closer. Her voice is quiet, tentative. "You don't have to."

The words hit me like a wave.

And for half a second, I think about staying.

But I can't. Not if I want to do this right.

I pull back, just enough to meet her eyes. My voice is rough, barely controlled. "Yeah, I do."

I run my thumb along her spine, slow and steady. "Because if I don't, Ivy... I won't be able to stop."

The words are out before I can stop them—raw, honest, unguarded.

And I see it on her face. The way her eyes drop to my mouth.

My hand tightens reflexively on her back, my heart

hammering like it's fighting against every ounce of self-control I've got left.

For a split second, I almost cave.

But I don't.

I close my eyes, forcing myself to breathe, to remember who I am now. Who I want to be for her.

And then, slowly, I let her go.

My hands fall to my sides like they're protesting the decision, and I take a step back, putting space between us I don't actually want.

Her eyes are wide, uncertain. And the ache that hits me in that moment is sharp—like walking away from something I've spent years hoping to find.

"I have to go," I say, but it comes out hoarse. Like I'm trying to convince myself.

She nods, but her silence says everything. She doesn't want me to go either.

I rake a hand through my hair, hesitating at the door. Every part of me is pulling in two directions—toward her warmth, her trust, her lips still tinged with goodbye...and toward the promise I made to do this the right way.

I glance back, meeting her eyes one last time, my voice softer now. "But if you only knew how much I didn't want to walk away."

Her voice is barely a whisper. "I know."

I reach for the doorknob, fingers tightening around it, but my heart won't let me go just yet. I turn back, needing her to hear this. "If you need anything, anything, you call me. I'll be there."

She nods, her eyes shining. "I will. And Gray?" She hesitates, cheeks flushing pink as the words spill out, shaky but sure. "I love you."

That's all it takes. I cross the space between us one last

time, cupping her face like I need to memorize it, and kiss her—desperate, tender, full of everything I'm feeling.

"I love you too, Ivy," I murmur against her lips, my voice thick.

I linger, forehead resting against hers for a beat longer, then force myself to step back before I ruin what we're building by risking it all.

"I'll see you soon," I whisper, and then the door clicks shut behind me.

And the moment it does, the silence hits like a wall.

I reach my truck and stand here for a beat, staring at the night sky, hands in my pockets, trying to breathe around the ache in my chest.

I didn't stay.

Not because I didn't want to.

But because I did.

Because I want her for more than a moment.

And that's what makes walking away the hardest choice I've ever made...and the most important one too.

The coffee shop smells like cinnamon and roasted beans—comfort baked into the air. I spot Jack right away in the back corner booth, same place as always, sipping on what's probably his second cup of black coffee.

His head lifts when I walk in. "Hey, stranger."

I slide into the booth across from him, shrugging off the cool morning air. "Hey, old man."

Jack smirks. "Still clinging to that insult, huh? Pretty sure I've earned 'wise' by now."

"Wise men don't wear socks with sandals," I mutter, eyeing his feet.

He barks a laugh. "You came in with attitude today. What's up?"

I shrug, leaning my elbows on the table. "Didn't sleep much."

"Something on your mind?"

I stare down at my coffee. "Yeah. Ivy."

Jack raises an eyebrow but doesn't say anything, which is how I know he's listening.

"She's...incredible," I say slowly, like I'm trying the words out. "She's kind and bold and real in a way I didn't know I needed. I told her I loved her last night, but..."

Jack's smile is soft but knowing. "But?"

I let out a breath. "Last night we were at her apartment. Nothing happened—nothing we'd regret. But it got...close. Like, too close."

Jack's expression doesn't change, but I can tell he's taking that in.

"I stopped it," I add quickly. "I told her I'm waiting until marriage. Even told her I haven't always, but I am now."

"And how'd she take it?"

"Better than I expected."

Jack nods slowly. "So what's the problem?"

"I'm proud of us. I am. But it scared me, Jack. Because it wouldn't have taken much for things to go the other way."

Now Jack's expression hardens—not unkindly, but like he's shifting into mentor mode.

"Gray," he says carefully, "you shouldn't be spending time alone at her apartment."

My brows furrow. "What? You think I shouldn't hang out with her?"

"I think you're playing with fire. You're a man. You just said how close it got. Next time? You might not stop."

I bristle, sitting back in the booth. "You don't get it. We love each other. We're careful. I'm not gonna throw the whole relationship in the trash just because of one close call."

"I'm not telling you to throw it away," Jack says, calm but firm. "I'm telling you to protect it."

I don't answer. Not right away.

He leans in a little. "You think boundaries are about restriction. But they're not. They're about vision. You've got a vision for this relationship, right? For something holy and real and built to last?"

"Of course I do."

"Then act like it. Set yourselves up to win. That doesn't happen by accident."

I stare out the window, jaw clenched.

Jack lets the silence sit for a beat before adding, "Look. You don't have to decide right now. Just...pray about it."

I sigh, dragging a hand down my face. "Yeah. Okay."

Jack softens again, tapping his fingers on his mug. "I know it feels like you're being told to walk away from something good, but that's not it. You're just being invited to guard it differently."

I nod slowly. "It just feels...extreme."

"Gray, so is temptation."

He's right, and I hate that he's right.

But maybe I needed to hear it.

I let out a breath, quieter this time. "I'll pray about it."

Jack gives me a small nod. "Good. And in the meantime, remember this—any relationship built on honoring God doesn't lose momentum when you slow the physical down. It gains depth."

That sticks with me.

And as I leave the coffee shop, I realize I've been thinking about how not to lose Ivy...but maybe it's time to think about how to protect what we're building—even if that means saying no before things ever get too far again.

Chapter 26
Ivy

The hallway hums with energy—volunteers bustling back and forth, parents ushering children to classrooms, and the soft strum of a guitar drifting from the sanctuary. I lean against the welcome desk, a cup of warm coffee in my hand, my eyes flicking to the front doors every few seconds.

Harper spots me from across the hallway, clipboard tucked under her arm as she weaves her way through the crowd. Her ponytail bounces with every step, her expression curious. "Is she not here yet?"

I shake my head, glancing at the clock on the wall. Two minutes until service starts.

Harper rolls her eyes. "You know she's gonna slide in at the very last second. Probably with that ridiculous oversized purse and a latte that's more sugar than coffee."

I laugh, despite the knot of worry tightening in my stomach. "I know. But still..."

Harper nudges me with her shoulder. "She'll be here." Her voice is confident, almost dismissive, like it's obvious. Like there's no other option. "You need me to stick around?"

I shake my head. "You've got kids' ministry today, right?"

She raises the clipboard like it's a trophy. "You bet. Got my clipboard. Got my schedule. Got a plan for world domination via craft time."

I snort. "You're ridiculous."

"And you love me," she sings, throwing a wave over her shoulder as she heads toward the children's wing.

I turn back toward the door, chewing on the inside of my cheek. People shuffle in, brushing past me with nods and murmured greetings. I watch each face, searching for Olivia's sharp eyes and skeptical smile.

One minute to go.

I swallow hard, the knot in my stomach growing tighter. Maybe it was too much to ask. Maybe last week at worship night was a fluke, and she...

The door swings open, and there she is.

Olivia steps through the threshold, cheeks flushed from the brisk morning air, hair a bit tousled like she hurried to get here. She spots me instantly, her eyes narrowing in playful accusation. "Are you waiting on me?"

I grin, holding out her coffee. "You're late."

She shrugs, snatching the cup from my hand. "I'm here, aren't I?"

"Barely." I laugh, relief flooding my chest. "Ready to head in?"

She hesitates, glancing over my shoulder toward the sanctuary doors. "Do we have to sit near the front?"

I shake my head. "Not if you don't want to."

Olivia lets out a breath. "Good. Because last time, that pastor made so much eye contact I thought he was reading my mind."

I laugh, looping my arm through hers. "Come on, I promise I won't let him call you out."

She snorts, but she follows, her pace matching mine. We slip into the sanctuary just as the music swells, the soft strum of guitar blending with the hum of voices.

I find us a spot a few rows back, not too close but not hidden, either. Olivia settles beside me, her hands wrapped around her cup like it's a lifeline. I can see her scanning the room, eyes darting over the rows of people, the raised hands, the soft sway of bodies moving with the music.

I lean over, my voice soft. "You ok?"

Olivia's eyes stay forward, but she nods. "Yeah…just still getting used to it."

"That's okay." I squeeze her arm. "Just…let it happen."

She glances at me, her gaze softening. "You make it sound so easy."

I smile. "It's not."

She doesn't say anything else, but she stays. And for now, that's enough.

The last song ends with a lingering chord, voices still humming the final note. I glance over at Olivia—her eyes are still forward, her hands gripping her coffee cup like it's the only thing tethering her to this moment.

Pastor Jack's voice echoes in my mind, still steady and warm even though he's stepped off the stage. He'd talked about friendships today—not just casual, surface ones, but the ones that sharpen you, steady you, and point you back to Jesus when you're tempted to drift. "God never meant for us to do faith alone," he'd said, pacing slowly, eyes sweeping over the crowd. "The people you walk with shape the path you'll take. Choose friends who remind you of God's truth, not just your feelings. Choose the ones who pray with you when life caves in and celebrate with you when joy overflows."

Even as he listed those qualities, I knew I was sitting beside one friend who didn't seem like she wanted anything to do with God, and had another who was giving every spare moment she had to church—even if it meant skipping the message. Both of them mattered to me. Both of them are part of my story. And in the middle of it, I couldn't help wondering where I fit in. Was I the friend pointing them to God—or the one who needed pointing?

He'd closed the message with a challenge: "Think about the people God's placed in your life. Don't take it lightly. Friendships aren't accidents. They're assignments." The word assignment had stuck with me, heavy in my chest. Could it be that Harper and Olivia weren't just random girls I'd been dared into road trips and late-night snacks with—but women God had woven into my life for something more?

When the lights brighten and people start filing out of the sanctuary, I give her arm a gentle nudge. "Want to go grab Harper? She's only serving for first hour today."

Olivia blinks, like she's just snapped back to reality. "Yeah. Sure."

We weave through the crowd, dodging volunteers and families gathering in little huddles, until we reach the kids' wing. I spot Harper almost instantly—talking with parents, telling them how sweet their kids are and wishing them a great day.

Her ponytail is coming loose, and her sweater has a small smear of glitter across the sleeve. She spots us and waves dramatically.

"Hey!" she calls out, her voice bright and breathless. "You guys found me at the perfect time. I just finished liberating the playroom from a glitter invasion. I think I'll be washing sparkles out of my hair for a week."

Olivia raises an eyebrow. "You look like you had a run-in with a craft store."

Harper laughs, brushing off her sweater. "Don't judge me. The kids wanted sparkly flowers, and who am I to deny them artistic expression?"

We follow her to the volunteer break room, where she drops off her clipboard and grabs a bottle of water. She takes a long sip, leaning against the wall and sighing like she's just finished a marathon.

"So, how was the service?" she asks, glancing between us.

Olivia shrugs. "Not terrible."

Harper raises an eyebrow. "That's practically a glowing review coming from you."

I laugh, nudging Olivia's shoulder. "Baby steps."

Harper nods approvingly, twisting the cap back on her water. "You coming back next week?"

Olivia hesitates, her eyes flicking to me before she responds. "I...I think so."

"That's all you have to do," I say, smiling. "Just keep coming back."

Olivia sips her coffee, her gaze flicking around the hallway. "Hey...I didn't see Gray up there today."

I shake my head. "He's out of town for the weekend. A Christian music camp for teens."

"Oh, wow, that's impressive" Olivia nods, taking that in. But Harper's eyes light up like someone just handed her a golden ticket.

"Wait, so that means..." Harper claps her hands together. "We can go to brunch!"

I raise an eyebrow, chuckling. "We can go to brunch even when Gray is here."

Harper rolls her eyes dramatically. "Um, yeah, okay. Like it doesn't take all his strength to not spend time with you." She grins like she just delivered the punchline of the year.

I open my mouth to argue, but nothing comes out. A flush creeps up my cheeks instead. "That's not true."

Harper just raises both eyebrows. "Sure. Keep telling yourself that."

Olivia chuckles into her coffee cup, and I stare at my feet for a moment, biting back the smile that's threatening to break free. I think back to the dinners, the long drives, the countless hours spent talking and just being together.

I mean, she's not wrong.

But still...

Am I spending too much time with him? The question rolls through me, a thread of uncertainty tugging at the corners of my thoughts. It's not like I'm dropping everything to be with him. I still work. I still see my friends. I'm still... me.

Right?

Harper doesn't notice the pause in my thoughts. She's already halfway out the door, calling back to us. "Come on, I'm starving! And I'm making it a rule—if Gray's not here, we're getting double mimosas."

Olivia snorts. "Deal."

I follow them out, shaking off the unease. But the question lingers.

Am I losing myself in him?

Or worse...am I losing pieces of who I'm supposed to be?

We pull into the parking lot of Sunny Side, the local brunch spot in Downtown Dallas with creaky floors and endless coffee refills. Harper practically bounces out of the car, her ponytail swinging as she bounds up the steps and pushes open the door.

Olivia and I exchange glances, her eyebrow quirked. "Is she always this excited for food?"

"Only when there's syrup involved." I laugh, holding the door open for her.

Inside, the place is bustling—mugs clinking, plates clattering, the smell of bacon and fresh waffles filling the air. We find a booth near the back, tucked away from the main traffic. Harper slides in first, pulling a menu toward her.

"Okay, hear me out," she says, her eyes sparkling with mischief. "We order one of everything and just split it. That way, we don't have to choose."

Olivia snorts. "That sounds both excessive and genius."

"Thank you," Harper says, flipping the menu dramatically. "I pride myself on my excessive genius."

I settle in beside her, resting my elbows on the table. "I don't know if I can eat that much. You forget I'm not wrangling toddlers all morning."

Harper waves me off. "That just means you have more room for waffles."

When the waitress comes by, we order a spread that's borderline ridiculous—pancakes, waffles, French toast, and a side of bacon that Harper insists is absolutely necessary for balance.

As soon as the waitress walks away, Harper turns to Olivia. "Okay, spill. What did you really think of service today?"

Olivia shrugs, stirring her coffee absentmindedly. "It was fine. I mean...I don't know." She pauses, her spoon clinking against the ceramic edge. "I just don't get it yet."

Harper props her elbows on the table, leaning in. "Get what?"

"This whole faith thing. I see you guys diving in, and I just...I don't feel it. I don't want to fake it just to fit in." Her voice is quiet, almost apologetic.

I lean back, watching her. "No one's asking you to fake anything, Liv."

She nods, her gaze dropping to her coffee cup. "I know. It's just...it's like I'm waiting for something to click, and it never does. I want to believe—I do. But I also don't want to pretend."

Harper reaches over, grabbing a sugar packet and tearing it open. "I think everyone feels like that sometimes." She empties the sugar into her coffee, stirring it slowly. "Honestly? I've been around church my whole life and I still don't get everything. That's kinda the point, right? You're not supposed to have it all figured out."

Olivia glances up, her eyes softening. "Do you ever feel like you're faking it?"

Harper laughs, the sound sudden and loud enough to draw a glance from the booth behind us. "Me? Oh, all the time. But that's what clipboards are for."

Olivia blinks. "Clipboards?"

Harper nods, tapping the table. "When I don't know what I'm doing, I just write random things on my clipboard. Pretend I've got it all handled. Eventually, I do." She shrugs.

"Fake it till you make it. Or, you know…until you get glitter bombed by a bunch of three-year-olds."

I snort, shaking my head. "You hide behind structure."

Harper doesn't flinch. "I hide behind a lot of things."

The confession hangs between us, fragile and real. It's the first time I've ever heard her say it out loud. Olivia's gaze flickers between us, her expression softening.

"Maybe I need a clipboard," Olivia mutters, half to herself.

Harper laughs, handing her a sugar packet. "Here, start with this. Sugar's the foundation of all good plans."

Olivia actually laughs—like, really laughs. The sound is light and unburdened, and it makes me realize how much I've missed it.

The waitress brings our food, and the table is quickly covered with plates of breakfast perfection. Harper immediately starts cutting into the waffles, piling strawberries and whipped cream onto her plate.

We dig in, the conversation lightening with every bite. Harper's retelling stories of her morning, complete with dramatic reenactments, and Olivia actually seems…relaxed.

But through it all, I can't stop the little voice in my head —the one that's replaying Harper's comment back at the church: *It takes all of his strength to not spend time with you.*

My fork hovers over my plate, my mind running circles around the thought.

Harper nudges me with her elbow, her mouth half-full of syrupy waffle. "Are you ok? You look like you're having an existential crisis over pancakes."

I laugh, the sound lighter than I feel. "Just…thinking."

Harper rolls her eyes. "You think too much."

I shrug, picking at my food. "Yeah. Maybe."

But even as the conversation swirls back into jokes and sarcasm, I can't shake it. That question. That lingering thread of doubt.

Am I giving too much of myself away?

Or...am I finally giving it to the right person?

Chapter 27
Gray

The van smelled like old french fries, sweaty teenagers, and half-used Axe body spray, but I swear I could've ridden another hundred miles if it meant keeping that buzz from the weekend a little longer.

Music camp for teens wasn't exactly my idea of a relaxing getaway, but somewhere between the late-night worship sets and those cracked-open conversations with kids who reminded me way too much of myself—I remembered why I said yes in the first place.

Because Jesus shows up when you least expect it.

And because every time I lead worship in a room full of kids with chipped armor and stubborn hearts, I remember the night He showed up for me.

Still, four days without Ivy felt like four weeks. I don't know when she became my soft place to land, but I'm not fighting it.

I'd texted her the second I got into town, and when she said "Come over," I didn't even go home first.

Her apartment complex comes into view, and my foot

taps the brake like I'm trying to slow time, like I need a second to breathe before I see her.

But I don't slow down.

Not really.

I park. Climb out. Heart thudding louder with each step toward her door.

She opens it before I can even knock, like she's been standing there waiting, and maybe she has. She's wearing my oversized sweatshirt, the one I let her borrow after our first kiss in the rain and she has yet to give it back. Her smile spans from ear to ear and the sight of her wrecks me.

"You're back," she says, voice warm and sweet and way too much for a guy who hasn't kissed her in four days.

I can't help it—I pull her into my arms without a word.

She melts into me, like she always does. Arms winding around my back like they never want to let go. And I don't want them to. Not for a second.

"Missed you," I murmur, my face buried in her hair. The scent of vanilla and floral fills my lungs, and I feel myself exhale for the first time all day.

"Me too," she whispers against my shoulder.

I lean back, just enough to see her face—those bright eyes, that faint pink rising in her cheeks, the curve of her mouth like she's trying not to smile too wide.

And then...I don't wait.

I kiss her.

Not soft and slow, not this time. It's deep, drawn-out, four days of missing her pressed into a single breath. Her fingers twist into my shirt, and I feel the ache rise in my chest—the ache of wanting her close and not knowing how to be near without unraveling a little.

She kisses me back like she's been waiting for this exact

moment. Like the past four days built up a hunger that only now is being met.

But even as the intensity climbs, there's still that thread of care—of reverence. I cradle her face in my hands, thumbs brushing her jaw as I pull back just an inch, trying to catch my breath.

She's breathless too, blinking up at me like I just knocked the wind out of her in the best way.

Her voice is barely a whisper. "Hi."

I laugh, resting my forehead against hers. "Hey you."

A beat of silence. And then she tugs my hand, cheeks flushed. "Come in. I made cookies."

I raise a brow, still recovering. "You baked? For me?"

"Don't get used to it," she teases, already pulling me inside.

"Oh, I will," I say, following her inside. "This is how it starts, you know. Next thing you know, we're married and you're packing my lunch."

She snorts. "You wish."

Yeah, I do.

Her apartment is warm, cozy in that lived-in way. Soft lighting. A blanket tossed across the couch. Two mugs on the coffee table and a plate of cookies that actually look edible.

We settle in, side by side. Closer than we need to be, but still not close enough.

I grab a cookie, break off a piece, and pop it into my mouth. "Okay, these are dangerously good. I was not expecting that."

She glares at me. "Rude."

I shrug, smiling around the bite. "Just being honest."

The conversation flows easy—catching up, talking about the camp, laughing over something Harper said in the group chat. But my mind is already starting to drift. Not away from her—just deeper. Past the surface.

Because underneath the jokes and cookies and comfort of this couch...I know there's something I need to tell her.

Something I haven't said out loud in a long time.

Something that changed everything.

And maybe it's time she knew.

Ivy's laughter fades as she curls her legs under her, one hand wrapped around her mug, the other tugging the sleeve of my hoodie down past her knuckles.

She looks up at me like she sees something deeper.

And maybe she does.

"You've been quiet. What's on your mind?" She asks.

I stare at the coffee table for a second, the edge of my boot tapping a silent rhythm against the rug. "You really wanna know?"

Her head tilts just slightly. "Gray. I wouldn't ask if I didn't."

I nod, my fingers dragging across my thigh. "I wasn't always...this. The guy you know. The one who plays guitar and talks about grace like I didn't used to drown in everything opposite of it."

She doesn't move. Doesn't flinch. Just watches me, steady and open.

I clear my throat. "I never knew my dad. Not even a photo. My mom...she was around, but not really. Alcohol always came first. Some nights I made my own dinner, put myself to bed, figured out how to be invisible. Most nights, she didn't even notice."

Ivy's hand shifts like she wants to reach for me, but she waits. Lets me talk.

"I got good at disappearing. Good at pretending I didn't care. Fell in with the wrong crowd—guys who wore the same numb look I had. We didn't talk about much. Just music. And eventually...the band."

A soft breath escapes me. "We thought we were gonna make it. Toured through the southeast—nothing big. Dive bars, low-rent venues. Some towns I don't even remember. The others...I try not to."

I glance at her, and her eyes haven't left mine.

"They partied hard," I continue. "Drugs, alcohol, all of it. For a while, I stayed sober. Told myself I was different. Told myself I was in control. Not wanting to be anything like my mom. But eventually I caved."

A pause.

"Then we hit Dallas."

I don't realize how hard I'm gripping the edge of the cushion until my knuckles ache. "It was our last stop. Everything had gone wrong—equipment issues, fights in the van, our lead guitarist threatening to quit mid-set. And something just...snapped. I couldn't fake being okay anymore. I drank more than I ever had and got high on...I don't even remember what, actually. I woke up on the steps of a church downtown with vomit on my shirt and the worst headache of my life."

I laugh, but there's no humor in it. "I thought I was hallucinating when a guy sat down next to me. Turns out, his name was Jack."

Ivy's brows lift slightly. "Pastor Jack?"

I nod. "Yeah. He didn't ask what I'd done. Didn't ask if I deserved help. Just looked at me and said, 'You look like someone who's trying to outrun something big. Want to come inside?'"

I breathe in slowly. "He meant the church. I didn't go that first time. But he gave me his number. Told me he'd be there next Sunday. And the one after that."

A beat passes.

"I went. Three weeks later. Still hungover. Still angry. But I went. And for the first time, I didn't feel invisible. I didn't feel like I had to prove anything. The worship...the message...it cracked something open in me."

I feel Ivy's hand slide over mine now.

"I didn't give my life to Jesus that day. Took a few more Sundays. A few more breakdowns. But when I finally said yes...it wasn't because I had my life together. It was because I didn't. And He still wanted me anyway."

I close my eyes. "That wrecked me."

Ivy squeezes my hand, and I look at her again.

She's crying. Silent tears. No dramatics. Just emotion—real and raw.

"You're not him anymore," she whispers.

"No," I say quietly. "But he still lives in my head sometimes. And I'm scared if I'm not careful, he could come back."

Her thumb brushes mine, slow and grounding.

"He won't," she whispers. "Because you're not fighting alone anymore. Not against your past. Not against the lies in your head. You have Him now. And you have me." She swallows, her tears catching in her throat. "I know what it's like to hear that voice that says you'll never be enough. But I've seen what grace can do. And Gray, that grace is all over you."

And I want to believe that.

I really do.

We're still sitting close. Too close.

Her fingers are laced with mine, her other hand resting lightly against my leg. And maybe it's the quiet. Or the safety. Or the way she looked at me when I told her everything. But suddenly the distance between us feels like it's shrinking without either of us moving.

I glance at her lips.

Then away.

Then back again.

And I can feel it—that pull.

The one that starts in my chest and burns its way down.

She leans her head against my shoulder, and I exhale slowly, trying to steady my pulse. But the scent of her, the softness of her body tucked against mine—it's all too much and not enough at the same time.

"I missed you," she whispers.

I swallow hard. "I missed you too."

She turns just enough to look up at me, her hand still in mine. The space between us collapses inch by inch. One of my hands slides around her waist without thinking, pulling her just a little closer. Her hand rests against my chest now, over my heart. I know she feels it—how fast it's pounding.

She tilts her face up.

I should move.

I don't.

My nose brushes hers, and her breath catches.

"Ivy..." Her name is a warning. A prayer. A plea.

But I don't pull back.

Neither does she.

When I kiss her, it's soft at first. Careful. Like we're both waiting for the other to stop.

But we don't.

My hand finds her waist, then slides up her back, pulling her closer until I can feel every breath, every tremble. I shift, guiding her gently back against the couch, my body moving over hers until I'm hovering—barely touching, but everywhere at once.

Her breath catches.

So does mine.

I brace myself with one hand beside her head, the other drifting lower, fingertips slipping just beneath the hem of her shirt—only an inch, maybe two. Her skin is warm, soft, and my thumb grazes the curve of her waist like it's something sacred. Because it is.

Her hands find my back again, tugging at my shirt, fingers brushing my spine, and for a second...I almost forget.

Almost surrender.

I press a kiss to the corner of her mouth, then another just beneath her jaw. She arches ever so slightly, and something primal stirs inside me, something I've spent years laying at the feet of Jesus.

And I want to.

I really want to.

But I can't.

Not like this. Not now.

I force myself to still, breathing hard, forehead resting against hers.

"Ivy..." My voice is raw. "I can't. We can't."

I pull back suddenly, my forehead resting against hers, both of us breathing hard.

"I want to. You have no idea how much."

She nods, her eyes searching mine. "I know. I'm sorry."

"Don't be sorry." I cup her cheek gently. "You didn't do anything wrong. I just—" I trail off, shaking my head. "I need to tell you something."

She pulls back just enough to really look at me, brow creased. "What is it?"

I sit up straighter, raking a hand through my hair. "Before I left for the camp, I met up with Jack. We talked about you. About us. I told him what happened last time... and how proud I was that we stopped."

She nods slowly, unsure where this is going.

"But he said something I haven't been able to shake," I continue. "He said we shouldn't be alone like this. That next time we might not stop. That...maybe it's not about self-control. Maybe it's about wisdom."

Her face tightens slightly. "So...what are you saying?"

I blow out a breath. "I'm saying I didn't like it at first. I got mad, actually. Told him I could handle it."

"And now?"

I look at her, really look at her. "Now I think he might be right."

The silence stretches.

And then, Ivy exhales, her shoulders relaxing just a little. "I've been feeling it too," she says. "That edge. Like we're always a few seconds away from crossing a line we can't uncross."

I nod, heart heavy but sure. "Then maybe we make a choice. Not because we have to. But because we want to honor what God's doing here. In us."

She studies me, then slowly, she reaches for my hand again.

"Okay," she whispers. "Let's choose that."

And something about that simple agreement steadies me.

This isn't the end of something.

It's the beginning.

A boundary drawn not from fear, but from trust.

From faith.

From love.

It's quiet again.

Not awkward quiet. Not the kind that's full of unspoken tension or words left unsaid.

Just...peaceful.

Ivy leans her head on my shoulder, her hand still in mine, and we sit there like that—still and steady—for a long time. The earlier heat between us has cooled into something deeper. Weightier. Like the decision we made just now solidified something that was already being written underneath the surface.

Still, the moment is delicate. Fragile in its holiness. And I know if I stay here too long, the clarity I feel right now might start to blur.

I turn slightly, brushing my lips against her temple. "I should go."

She doesn't argue.

She just nods and looks up at me with eyes that are somehow both soft and fierce—like she knows the cost of this kind of love and is still willing to pay it.

I stand, stretching slightly, and she walks me to the door, the weight of our promise following every step.

Her fingers graze mine as I reach for the handle. "Thanks for telling me everything tonight."

I look at her, heart full. "Thanks for listening."

She gives me a small smile that says she gets it, all of it. "Text me when you get home?"

"I will."

And then I pause, one hand on the doorknob, the other reaching for her waist one last time. I press my forehead to hers, not kissing her—just breathing her in, letting this closeness anchor what we just decided.

"I care about you so much," I whisper.

She nods slowly. "I know."

"I want this to last, Ivy."

"So do I."

"I love you Ivy."

"Love you too."

I take a steadying breath, then let go.

The door clicks shut behind me, sprint down the stairs until the night air hits my face, crisp and quiet. My truck's parked under the streetlight, and as I climb in, I don't feel regret.

I feel reverence.

This isn't a story driven by impulse. It's one built on choice.

And tonight, we chose something better.

Even if it's harder.

Even if it aches a little.

Because maybe that's what love really is—doing what's right not because you have to...but because they're worth it.

Because He is.

Because we are.

Chapter 28
Gray

It's been seven days since Ivy and I looked each other in the eye and agreed—we couldn't be alone in her apartment anymore. Or mine. Not if we wanted to keep our promises to God.

I told her it was the right choice. And I meant it. Still do.

But tonight, sitting here in my quiet living room with the TV off and the silence pressing in, I can't help wishing she were curled up beside me. No expectations. No lines crossed. Just her head on my shoulder, her laugh breaking up the dark.

I grip the edge of the couch cushion and shake my head. Who am I kidding? That's exactly how it starts. A little closeness. A little comfort. And before I know it, I'm pushing the line I swore I'd never cross.

So instead of calling her, I pray.

Lord, give me strength when everything in me wants to take the easy way. Teach me that honoring You means trusting You...even with this ache.

I lean back, staring at the ceiling. My chest feels tight,

like I'm holding my breath even though I'm not. This is harder than I thought it would be. Not because I don't want purity. But because I've never wanted someone the way I want her.

I rub a hand over my face, dragging it down like I could scrape the ache away. The silence presses in harder, mocking me. My apartment's too clean, too quiet, like it's waiting for me to finally admit I hate being here alone.

I can practically see Ivy stretched out on the couch across from me, her feet tucked beneath her, hair falling across her shoulder as she smiles at something on TV. She'd probably roll her eyes at whatever documentary I picked, then end up loving it halfway through. I can almost hear her laugh—soft and surprised.

The thought guts me. Because I don't just want to kiss her. I don't just want her curled into me. I want her here. Shoes by the door. Coffee mug on the counter. Her presence filling the cracks in this place that always feels like it's missing something.

I push off the couch, pacing. One step, two. My pulse thuds louder than my footsteps. Don't think about it. Don't dwell on it. But the more I tell myself that, the louder the ache becomes.

I stop at the window, looking out at the streetlights painting the parking lot in dull yellow. Cars come and go, couples disappearing inside their apartments, lights flicking on in warm squares across the building. And here I am, stuck in the dark, wishing I could have what they have without the guilt clawing at me.

My chest tightens again. I drop onto the edge of the couch, elbows on my knees, and press the heels of my hands against my eyes. *God, I don't know if I'm strong enough for this.*

The silence doesn't answer back.

My gaze snags on the guitar leaning in the corner, like it's waiting for me. I cross the room and pull it into my lap, fingers curling over the neck like they remember what to do even when my head doesn't. The first strum vibrates through me, grounding me.

I start with something aimless—just chords, nothing that means anything. But before I know it, the melody that spills out is the one that's been haunting me for weeks. The one I can't seem to finish.

Her melody.

I close my eyes, letting the notes rise and fall. Soft at first, then steadier, clearer. It feels like prayer and temptation tangled into one. Words hover on my tongue, half-formed lines I've scribbled in notebooks and napkins. I sing them under my breath, quiet, almost afraid to let them out.

Every step, every prayer, every night I wondered
If I was enough, if I'd lose my way
But You were the grace I didn't know I'd needed
You stayed, you stayed

My voice cracks, and I let the words die. The ache in my chest sharpens, too much, too close. Because it's Ivy. Every line. Every note. She's in all of it, even the spaces between the chords. And I don't know if I can write this song without crossing lines I promised I wouldn't.

I drop my head back against the couch, guitar still in my lap, strings buzzing faintly beneath my fingertips. "Get it together, man," I mutter. But even the sound of my own voice feels hollow.

The truth is, I don't want to get it together. Not tonight. Tonight I want to give in, just once. To call her. To tell her to come over. To forget about rules and boundaries and do what my heart and body are begging for.

I swallow, shaking my head. No. That's not who I am anymore. That's not who I want to be.

But the old version of me, he's right there in the shadows of my mind, smirking like he's been waiting for this moment. He whispers that I'll never be strong enough. That sooner or later, I'll cave and ruin this relationship.

I grip the guitar tighter, knuckles white, and let the strings hum under the pressure.

"Not tonight," I whisper. "I won't let you win tonight."

The words don't make the ache disappear, but they hold me steady for a breath. Just one.

I set the guitar back in the corner and push off the couch, pacing again, slower this time. I can feel the war inside me, tugging both ways—between desire and discipline, love and lust, the old man and the new one.

Finally, I drop to my knees in the middle of the room. No music. No pretense. Just me and God in the silence.

"Help me," I pray, voice breaking. "Help me want You more than I want her. Help me love her the way You do."

The words hang heavy in the air, like they're too big for the room. My shoulders sag under the weight of them.

I stay there until my knees ache, forehead pressed to the carpet, the quiet filling with something softer—peace, maybe. Not enough to erase the ache. But enough to remind me why I'm still fighting.

I climb back to my feet, heart still restless, body still humming with the absence of her. But there's a steadiness too, faint but real. Enough to keep me standing when everything in me wants to fall.

I kill the lights and head for bed, whispering the same prayer again as I crawl under the covers.

"Help me love her the way You do"

It's only been a week, but it feels like a year.

I've checked my watch so many times I've convinced myself the second hand is broken. My leg bounces against the bench I'm sitting on, nerves wound tight as guitar strings. Every car that pulls into the lot makes my chest lurch, only to fall again when it's not hers.

I hate how much I've missed her. Or maybe I love it. Maybe this is what happens when you finally let someone in—you ache when they're gone, even if it's only for a little while.

I shove my hands in my pockets, then yank them out again. Fidget. Stretch. Pace a step, sit back down. I'm ridiculous. I know it. And I don't even care.

Then, finally, I see her car turn in. My heart kicks so hard I swear it echoes in my ears. Before she's even in park, I'm already moving. Practically jogging, which is not my style, but I couldn't hold myself back if I tried.

She opens the door and barely gets one foot out before I'm there. "Hey..." she starts, but I scoop her up like she weighs nothing and spin her once, twice, her laughter spilling into the air.

"Gray!" she squeals between giggles, hands clutching at my shoulders. People are watching, I know they are, but I couldn't care less. She's here. She's in my arms. And I feel alive again.

When I finally set her down, her cheeks are pink, her eyes wide with that sparkle that ruins me every time. I don't even give her a chance to catch her breath. My hands frame her face, my thumbs brushing her cheeks, and I press my mouth to hers—firm, sure, like I've been waiting all my life for this exact moment.

The kiss isn't long, but it's enough to steal the air from both of us. When I pull back, I rest my forehead against hers, breathing her in.

"I've missed you," I whisper, the words coming out rougher than I meant. My chest tightens, because it's the truth, simple and raw. "So much."

Her smile curves soft and sweet, her fingers curling in the collar of my shirt like she's afraid to let go. "I missed you too."

She looks like fall—at least, as much as fall exists in Texas. A lightweight purple sweater hangs loose against her frame, her black leggings tucked into sneakers, and her hair is braided over one shoulder in a way that makes it impossible for me not to stare. If the air had fully committed to the season, it would've been perfect. But this is Texas: seventy degrees in the shade, eighty if you walk ten steps too far. Still, with the sun hitting her just right, she could've walked straight out of a September postcard.

Ivy's hand slips into mine as we leave the parking lot and wander down the path toward the park. The late afternoon light spills golden through the trees, shadows stretching long across the grass. Families are spread out on blankets, kids running wild, the sound of a basketball hitting pavement somewhere in the distance.

It should feel ordinary. But with Ivy beside me, nothing does.

"Feels good to finally see you," she says, brushing her shoulder against mine.

I huff a laugh, tightening my grip on her hand. "Good? I

thought I was gonna lose my mind. I checked my phone so many times I'm surprised it didn't file a restraining order."

She giggles, the sound bubbling up easy, and my chest loosens in a way it hasn't all week. I swear I'd walk this path forever if it meant hearing her laugh like that again.

We stroll in comfortable silence for a while. Every so often, I catch myself looking at her instead of the trail, soaking her in—the way the breeze lifts strands of her hair, the way her eyes light up when she glances at me like I'm more than I deserve.

I'm not paying attention, too caught up in Ivy, and my shoulder slams against someone else's. Hard.

"Sorry, man," I mutter automatically.

The guy looks to be mid-thirties, ball cap shoved low, sunglasses hooked on his shirt. He freezes, eyes narrowing as they lock onto mine. "Grayson?"

The name cuts through me like a blade. My stomach drops, chest locking up tight. I haven't heard that name—not like that—in years.

Ivy's hand stiffens in mine. She looks between us, confusion flickering in her eyes.

The guy grins, like he can't believe it. "Man, I'll be— Grayson Bennett. I thought that was you." He laughs, shaking his head. "Haven't seen you since Austin. What was it, that dive bar off Main? You were..."

"Wrong guy," I snap, sharper than I mean to. My pulse hammers in my ears, hot and bitter. "You've got me mixed up with someone else."

The man's smile falters. He squints, taking a half step closer. "Nah. It's you. Grayson. You used to play with..."

"I said you've got the wrong guy." The words come out low, clipped. My jaw's tight enough to crack.

For a second, the guy hesitates, like he's about to push

back. But then his shoulders lift in a shrug. "If you say so." He gives Ivy a polite nod, then keeps walking, disappearing into the crowd.

The air feels heavier now, the golden light dimmed. My hand is clammy around Ivy's, my whole body buzzing with adrenaline.

We walk a few more steps in silence before she speaks, her voice cautious. "Gray...who was that?"

I keep my eyes fixed ahead, jaw grinding. "Nobody."

"Gray." She tugs gently on my hand, slowing us down until I have to look at her. Her eyes are searching, soft but steady. "He knew you. He called you..." She hesitates, then says it quietly. "Grayson."

The name makes me flinch all over again.

I drag a hand through my hair, exhaling hard. I don't want this right now. Not here, not when all I wanted was to hold her hand and forget the rest of the world existed.

"I told you not to call me that," I mutter, more to the ground than to her.

Her brows knit together. "You said it once, but...you never told me why. And now..." She pauses, worry slipping into her voice. "Gray, what's going on?"

I stop walking, pressing the heels of my hands into my eyes for a second before dropping them to my sides. The words knot in my throat. How do I explain that the name feels like a chain? That it drags me back into a life I've spent years trying to bury?

"It's nothing," I say finally, the lie bitter on my tongue. "Just...part of the past. Leave it there."

Ivy slows, tugging gently on my arm. "Gray..."

The way she says my name undoes me. I blow out a sharp breath and nod toward an empty bench beneath a sprawling oak. "Come on. Let's sit."

We walk the few steps in silence. My pulse hasn't slowed since that guy said my name, and my palms are slick. I sit down, elbows on my knees, staring at the ground. Ivy lowers herself beside me, close but not pressing, like she's giving me the choice to speak.

After a long moment, I glance at her. The worry in her eyes twists me up worse than the memory ever could. I sigh, dragging a hand through my hair. "I'm sorry. I shouldn't have snapped like that. You didn't deserve it."

Her expression softens. "I just...want to understand. That man knew you."

"Yeah," I admit, my throat tight. "He did. And that's the problem."

She tilts her head, waiting.

I rub my hands together, the motion restless. "Grayson is my full name. Always has been. But it's not who I am anymore. When I finally moved to Dallas—when I finally gave my life to Jesus—I left Grayson behind. Started going by Gray."

She doesn't interrupt, just nods like she's listening with every piece of herself.

I swallow hard, pushing the words out before they can choke me. "That guy back there...he wasn't some old friend. He was one of my dealers. Back when I was with the band, we spent a couple months in Austin during a tour break. Three months, give or take. And in those three months, I saw him more than I should've ever seen anybody."

Her lips part slightly, but she doesn't speak. I keep going.

"I wasn't strung out the way the rest of the guys were," I say quickly, almost defensively. "But I wasn't innocent either. I drank too much. Smoked too much. Got high when I wanted to forget who I was for a night. And Grayson..." I shake my head, jaw tightening. "Grayson was the guy who made those calls. Who went looking for numb instead of healing. Who couldn't say no."

The silence stretches heavy between us. My pulse hammers as I wait for the disgust, the judgment, the step back that says she finally sees what I've always known—I'm not good enough for her.

Instead, Ivy's hand slips over mine. Gentle. Steady. Her thumb brushes across my skin, anchoring me. "And Gray?" she asks softly.

I blink at her. "Yeah?"

She tilts her head. "If Grayson was the one running to numb, then who's Gray?"

Something loosens in my chest. I look down at our joined hands, her fingers small against mine. "Gray is the man who walked into a church hungover and furious and still heard God calling his name. The man who finally stopped running."

Her eyes shimmer, but it's not pity I see there. It's pride. Maybe even admiration.

I let out a breath that shakes on the way out. "I switched to Gray because I needed the reminder. Needed to hear something different when people said my name. Something that didn't drag me back to the boy I was. I guess it was my way of drawing a line in the sand—past on one side, new life on the other."

She squeezes my hand tighter. "Gray fits you," she whispers. "Not because you're hiding, but because you're new. And I love that you chose to live in that truth."

Her words hit deeper than I expect. I swallow hard, blinking up at the trees overhead, because if I look at her too long I might lose it completely.

"That guy back there..." I shake my head. "He's a ghost

from a world I don't want to touch again. And the way he said my name—Grayson—it felt like he was pulling me backward. Like he wanted me to wear it again."

"But you don't," Ivy says firmly. "You're not that man anymore."

I finally meet her gaze, and everything else falls away. No ghosts. No chains. Just her eyes steady on mine, reminding me of who I am now.

A slow breath fills my lungs, steadier than before. "No. I'm not."

She leans her head against my shoulder, and I let myself rest there too. The park hums around us—kids laughing, a dog barking, the scrape of skateboard wheels on concrete— but for once, the noise doesn't press in. It fades. Because with her here, with her hand in mine, the past feels a little farther away.

I press a kiss to the top of her hair, whispering the truth I couldn't have said an hour ago. "I'm Gray. And I'm not going back."

Chapter 29
Ivy

It's been two weeks since I've been truly alone with Gray.

Sure, we've hung out—almost daily, actually. But always with friends. Always in public. Always with that invisible line drawn between us like a boundary we both agreed to.

I hate it.

And I get it.

I really do.

We made a choice. A good one. A necessary one. The right one.

But it doesn't make it easier.

Not when I'm sitting next to him in the church café, watching the way he laughs with Micah like he doesn't have a single care in the world. Not when his hand brushes mine by accident during group prayer, and I feel the tremor in both of us when we pull away. Not when he walks me to my car at night, keeps his hands shoved in his pockets, and says goodnight with his eyes instead of his lips.

And when he does kiss me, it feels less like temptation and more like a promise. Like he's telling me with his restraint that I'm worth waiting for, worth honoring, worth every boundary we've drawn together.

It's like we're holding our breath in slow motion.

And I don't know how long we can stay in this limbo without bursting.

I want to ask him—what happens next? Where do we go from here?

Because if the only way to be closer is through marriage...and I'm not ready for that yet, then what? How do we grow when we've drawn a line in the sand and put everything physical on the other side of it?

In every past relationship, getting closer meant more physical touch. That was the rhythm. The unspoken rule. Holding hands. Kissing longer. Staying the night. It was how we marked progress, how we felt seen, wanted, chosen.

But maybe that was the problem.

Because now that I think about it, really think about it, those relationships never grew in the ways that actually mattered. The closeness was surface-level. Temporary. A substitute for something deeper we never really built.

And maybe that lack of real love, the kind that protects and honors and actually knows the other person— maybe that's why the intimacy always felt a little bit hollow. A little bit like chasing something that kept slipping away.

So now, with Gray...it's different. Slower. Harder. Yet better.

And I don't know how to do this.

But I think maybe...that's the point?

I press the brakes a little too hard pulling into the church parking lot, exhaling as I shift into park. A few cars are already lined up near the front entrance, all staff and volunteers on a Thursday morning. I grab my sketchbook and laptop from the passenger seat, trying to shake the restless energy buzzing in my chest.

It's just a meeting. No big deal.

But I know better.

Because Gray's probably inside with rehearsing.

And we won't be alone.

And somehow, that still doesn't make it easier.

I climb the front steps slowly, the chill of the September wind nipping at my cheeks. Inside, the warmth of the building hits instantly.

I paste on a smile, the one I reserve for being "fine," and push through the door.

Let's do this.

The meeting goes well.

Better than well.

The team loved the final Christmas Eve designs, and for the first time in weeks, I feel like I can actually breathe. Like maybe I'm doing something right.

I walk out of the conference room clutching my empty coffee cup like it's some kind of trophy. The hallway is quieter now, most people already headed out or lingering in small groups near the exit.

And then I see him.

Leaning against the wall in the lobby, hands in his pockets, head tipped slightly like he's been waiting. When his eyes catch mine, that crooked smile breaks across his face and my heart does that ridiculous flip thing it always does around him.

"You survived," he says, voice low and warm.

I laugh, nodding. "Barely."

He steps forward and opens the door for me, holding it wide as I step into the sharp morning air. The wind bites at my cheeks, but I'm not cold. Not with him standing beside me.

"Wanna grab breakfast?" he asks.

I start to smile but hesitate. The words have been sitting in my chest all morning, and I know if I don't say them now, I'll lose the nerve.

"Actually..." I pause, turning toward him. "Can I ask you something first?"

His brows pull together, instantly attentive. "Of course."

I tuck a strand of hair behind my ear, heart thudding. "What does it mean to be saved?"

Gray's face softens, and he doesn't answer right away. He just looks at me like he knows this moment is heavier than it sounds. Finally, he exhales, his voice low and steady.

"Being saved doesn't mean you've got your life cleaned up and polished. It's not about praying the perfect prayer or checking every box at church. It's...realizing you can't save yourself. That no amount of good deeds or pretending will fix the mess inside."

He laces his fingers in mine as we walk down the steps toward our cars. "And then it's trusting that Jesus already did what you couldn't. That when He died and rose again, He carried every mistake, every failure, every sin—yours, mine, all of it. Being saved is saying, 'I can't do this, but You can. I'm Yours.'"

He pauses, eyes searching mine. "It's surrender. But it's also freedom. Because the second you belong to Him, you don't have to keep carrying the weight of proving yourself. You're already loved. Already forgiven. Already His."

I swallow hard, throat tight. His words are simple, but they press into all the questions I've been holding close since Olivia's offhand comments weeks ago—*it's like I'm waiting for something to click, and it never does. I want to believe—I do. But I also don't want to pretend.*

Gray must see the storm in my face, because he pulls me in for a hug. "It doesn't mean you won't wrestle. Or fall. Or wonder if you're doing it right. It just means you've trusted the only One who can carry you through it. That's what it means to be saved."

I'm trying to make sense of the way those words tug at something deep inside me.

"But how?" I whisper. "How do you just...know you're saved?"

His eyes don't waver. "You stop trying to fix yourself. You stop pretending you can carry it all. And you trust that He already has. You give Him your mess, your sin, your heart—and you let Him make you new. You ask Jesus to be a part of your life...you surrender and give your life to Him."

Let Him make you new.

The phrase presses into me like a gentle hand to the heart.

"Surrender," I murmur, more to myself than to him.

Gray nods. "Exactly. That's the whole point."

The silence between us stretches. Full of things I'm still figuring out how to say. Full of truth I'm still learning how to believe.

Then he smiles again, gentle and familiar. "Now...how about some pancakes?"

I let out a breath, the corner of my mouth lifting. "Yeah. I'd like that."

The little diner Gray takes me to is the same one we've been coming to for weeks now. Tucked away on the edge of downtown, its neon sign flickers slightly, casting a warm glow against the early morning haze. Maple & Main. It's become our place—the kind of spot where the waitress knows our order before we even sit down and the smell of fresh coffee feels like home.

Gray holds the door open for me, nodding to the hostess as we walk inside. "Morning, Deborah," he calls out.

She waves back with a grin. "Y'all want your usual booth?"

Gray glances at me, his hand brushing the small of my back. "Usual booth?" he asks with a smile.

I nod, smiling back. "You know I'm a creature of habit."

"Hey, I'm not complaining."

We slide into the booth by the window, the same one we always do. The cushions are worn and the table wobbles just a little if you lean on it too hard, but it's perfect. Our little corner of the world.

Deborah appears almost instantly, pad in hand. "The usual?" she asks with a wink.

Gray nods. "Full stack for me, short stack with strawberries for her. Black coffee, cream and sugar."

She scribbles it down, snapping her gum. "Comin' right up."

I lean back in the booth. "You know my order by heart now?"

Gray leans forward, stretching his arm out along the

back of the booth, his eyes locked on mine. "I remember everything you say, actually."

I blush, ducking my head slightly. "That's dangerous."

His grin is slow and deliberate. "Guess I like a little danger."

I can't help but laugh, the tension slipping away. This is easy. Being with him like this. I find myself sinking back into the booth, my body relaxing in a way I didn't know it needed.

Our waitress brings the coffee, setting it down gently, and we both thank her. Gray picks up his cup, blowing on it before taking a sip. His eyes flick back to me, and there's that familiar spark of curiosity.

"So," he starts, setting his cup down, "I've told you about my messy past. What about you? What was Ivy like before New Orleans?"

I take a sip of my latte, letting the warmth settle my nerves. "Oh, not nearly as exciting as yours, I'm afraid."

He arches a brow. "I find that hard to believe."

I shrug. "Born and raised here in Texas. I grew up in the same house my whole life, did the whole school thing, went to college, then got into graphic design. Pretty standard, really."

Gray leans back, watching me carefully. "No wild streak? Not even a little?"

I laugh, shaking my head. "Not unless you count binge-reading romance novels under my covers with a flashlight."

He chuckles, stretching his arms across the back of the booth. "You don't fool me, Ivy. I think there's a little rebel in there somewhere."

I pause, my fingers tracing the rim of my mug. "Maybe," I admit, glancing out the window. "But nothing...crazy."

I'm not sure why, but I feel the urge to tell him. To open

up about things I've kept buried. My fingers tap nervously against the edge of the table, and the words slip out before I can catch them.

"I wasn't always...good at relationships."

Gray's expression softens, his gaze steady. "Yeah?"

I nod, taking another sip of my drink. "I got really good at pretending everything was fine. Like, really good. But...sometimes things weren't."

Gray doesn't interrupt. He just waits, quiet and patient, like he knows if he gives me space, the truth will come.

I swirl the liquid in my mug, watching it chase itself in circles. "I used to think love meant giving everything. Even when it cost me."

My throat tightens, but I keep going.

"I let guys use me. Not always in obvious ways, but...in ways that chipped at who I was. I'd say yes when I wanted to say no. I'd push down my feelings because theirs always seemed more important. I let their needs, their wants, their approval define everything."

I finally glance up at him. "I thought if I could just be easy. Low-maintenance. Chill. Then maybe they'd stay."

Gray's jaw tightens—not in anger at me, but in the way someone clenches when they're holding something back. Like it physically hurts him to hear this.

"I didn't know I was allowed to say no," I whisper. "Not if I wanted to be loved."

He shifts forward, elbows on the table, eyes locked on mine. But this time, his voice is low. Grounded. Almost fierce.

"You were." He doesn't stop there. "You are."

His jaw tightens, and I can see it—whatever he's about to say is coming from deep inside him. Not rehearsed. Not softened.

"I don't care who made you believe love had to hurt, or that your 'yes' was the only way to keep a man. They were wrong. And they didn't deserve you."

I forget to breathe.

His voice drops even lower, rough with conviction. "If a man isn't strong enough to honor your no, he's not strong enough to deserve your yes."

I swallow hard, my eyes stinging.

He leans closer, gaze unwavering. "I would rather wait a lifetime than take something from you that isn't freely given. Because love—real love—never demands. It protects. It covers. It reflects Christ."

My heart stutters.

"And Ivy...I want to love you like that."

A lump rises in my throat, unexpected and sharp.

Gray's hand moves across the table, palm up. No pressure. Just a silent offer.

I slip my fingers into his, and his grip is warm and sure.

"I know better now," I say, my voice quieter. "But sometimes I still feel like...if I don't give enough, I'll lose everything."

Gray shakes his head, eyes fierce with something like promise. "Real love doesn't ask you to shrink yourself, Ivy. It doesn't make you smaller. It shows up. It honors. It waits."

I squeeze his hand, and for the first time in a long time, I believe him.

The waitress returns with our food, setting the plates down with a polite smile. The clink of silverware and warmth of fresh breakfast gives the moment a needed breath.

Gray barely waits for her to leave before he digs in, cutting into his pancakes with the kind of enthusiasm that makes me laugh. I dig into mine too, letting the warmth of the syrup and strawberries settle me back into the moment.

He picks up his fork, glancing at me as he stabs a piece of egg. "Well," he says lightly, "that got deep real fast."

I let out a soft laugh, grateful for the small release of pressure. "Yeah. Sorry. I didn't mean to..."

"Don't apologize." His voice is gentle but firm. "I'm glad you told me."

We eat in silence for a few moments, the kind of silence that doesn't ask to be filled. And then Gray sets his fork down and leans back, studying me in that quiet, intentional way he always does when he's about to say something that matters.

He drags his fingers along the rim of his mug, then looks up, eyes steady on mine. "Can I ask you something?"

I nod, suddenly aware of the way my heart starts to race.

Gray leans in, resting his elbows on the table, eyes never leaving mine. "Where do you see this going?"

My mind blanks.

I open my mouth to answer, but nothing comes out. Not because I don't want to—but because I do. So badly. And that terrifies me.

Where do I see this going?

With him? I see everything. A life. A future. A love that doesn't vanish when things get hard.

But I don't say that.

"Umm..." I fumble, cheeks flushing. "I...I don't know."

His lips tug at the corners like he wants to smile but holds it back. He nods gently, like he's giving me space instead of pressure.

"I'll go first then," he says, voice dropping to that soft, gravelly tone that always makes me melt. "I see us growing closer...a lot closer."

My breath hitches.

"I love you, Ivy," he says. "Fast. Hard. In a way that doesn't make sense but feels more right than anything I've ever known."

"I want more than this," he continues, eyes locked on mine. "Not just the good dates and late-night phone calls. I want the lifetime. I want to be the one who brings you coffee on a slow Monday morning. The one who fights with you over stupid stuff and then laughs about it five minutes later. I want all of it. With you."

My throat tightens.

Then he adds, softer, a little breathless, "You know, I have to admit...it's taking everything in me not to get on one knee right now."

My stomach drops.

His eyes widen slightly, like the words slipped past his guard. "Oh boy," he mutters, running a hand over the back of his neck. "I didn't mean...that's not..." He exhales, shaking his head. "What I meant is...I know we're not there yet. I do. But, Ivy..." His gaze finds mine again, steady this time. "You're my person. I don't need more time to figure it out. I already know."

My heart is racing as I try to process his words.

"But," he adds with a crooked grin, "if that freaks you out, you can totally pretend I didn't say any of that. Blame it on the coffee and sleep deprivation."

I laugh, but it's weak, shaky. My pulse is thunder in my ears.

"It doesn't freak me out," I say, though my voice is thin.

He tilts his head, studying me. "Are you sure?"

I nod too fast. "Yeah. I just..." I glance away, eyes catching on the napkin I've been shredding in my lap. "I think I just need to catch up."

Gray is quiet for a moment. I feel the shift coming before he speaks again.

His gaze sharpens, earnest and unblinking. "So, about what you asked me earlier...are you ready for that? To actually make that decision? To be saved?" His words tumble out in a rush, like he's been holding them back for weeks and can't anymore.

My chest tightens.

He leans forward, elbows braced on his knees, voice low but urgent. "Because Ivy, it's everything. It's the whole point. You don't have to wait until you've caught up or figured it all out. You can say yes to Jesus right now, tonight, and nothing will ever be the same again."

The intensity in his eyes makes it hard to breathe. I open my mouth, but nothing comes out.

"And..." He hesitates for half a beat, then presses on. "Have you thought about getting baptized?"

The questions land like stones being thrown at my chest.

I don't even think. "No."

His eyebrows lift, surprised. "No?"

"I'm not ready," I say quickly. "I just...I don't know. It's a big deal."

He leans back slightly, his brows pulling together. "But you've been coming to church. Reading your Bible. Hanging out with me. You believe in Jesus, right?"

"I do," I whisper. "I think I do."

"Then what's stopping you?"

His voice is gentle—but it still feels like pressure. Like I'm failing some invisible test.

"I don't know," I say, but that's not true. I do know. I just don't want to admit it. Not yet.

I feel the weight of his gaze, and suddenly I can't breathe.

"You don't have to be perfect to be baptized," he adds. "That's kind of the whole point."

I look down at our joined hands, his thumb still brushing over mine. I know he means well. I know this is Gray—steadfast, sincere, full of conviction.

But suddenly, it all feels like too much.

I pull my hand back slowly, folding it into my lap. "I just need more time."

The silence that falls between us isn't cold—but it isn't comfortable either.

Gray nods, eyes flicking to his coffee. "Okay. I get it."

But I wonder if he really does.

Because there's a flicker of something in his expression. Not disappointment exactly. More like...fear. Like maybe I'm slipping away.

He's been here before—I can feel it.

"I'm not trying to push," he says quietly. "I've just...I've done that before. Expected too much. And it didn't end well."

My chest aches. "I know." Even though it's partly a lie.

He meets my eyes again, and something softens there. "I just want you to know you're safe here. With me. No matter how long it takes."

I nod, blinking fast. "Thank you."

The silence between us this time is gentler. Like maybe we're both trying to find the edges of each other's wounds—and learning not to press too hard.

Chapter 30
Gray

The silence in my truck is deafening.

I can still feel the way she hugged me goodnight—quick, stiff, her eyes darting anywhere but mine. No lingering smile. No soft moment at the car door like usual. Just a polite "thanks for tonight" before she slid inside and shut the door a little too fast.

And I knew. Right then, I knew I'd blown it.

I'd let all the things I wanted for her come tumbling out like a flood I couldn't hold back. Word vomit. That's what it was. My zeal drowning out her pace, my urgency silencing the quiet way God's been working in her heart.

I took control.

Before I even turn the key, I bow my head for just a second, hands resting on the steering wheel. *Lord, help me see her heart the way You do. Help me not get in the way of whatever You're doing. Please...guide me.*

I've got the windows cracked, hoping the cool air will knock some sense into me, but all it's doing is making my knuckles tighter around the steering wheel.

What just happened?

I replay the breakfast conversation over and over—every word, every breath. The way Ivy's voice faltered when I brought up baptism. The way her smile didn't quite reach her eyes when I told her I she was my person. The way she slowly pulled her hand out of mine, like she didn't even realize she was doing it.

I meant every word I said. I don't regret telling her how I feel.

But I pushed. I pushed.

And I felt it—the moment she started to retreat.

I thump my head back against the seat at a red light, exhaling hard. "Come on, man," I mutter. "You promised yourself you wouldn't do this again."

But here I am. Same pattern. Different girl.

I blink, and suddenly I'm not in my truck anymore. I'm back in that cramped apartment two years ago. Sitting across from Claire, my last girlfriend. She had her arms crossed, eyes glossy with tears.

"You don't get it, Gray," she said, voice trembling. "I'm trying, but it's like I'm always behind. You expect me to be perfect. To believe as hard as you do. To want everything you want—right now."

I remember sitting there, stunned. Thinking I was helping her. Guiding her. But all I was doing was pushing her toward a version of faith that looked like mine—but wasn't hers.

She walked out two weeks later. And I told myself I wouldn't be that guy again.

But this morning...I felt it happening all over again. The urgency. The fear. The need to seal something before it slipped away.

I grip the wheel tighter, jaw clenched. "I can't lose her," I whisper.

The light turns green, but I pull over instead. Park along the curb and stare at my phone for a second before dialing the one person I know will call me out and still love me after.

Jack.

Voicemail.

"Of course," I mumble, scrubbing a hand down my face. "Of course you're preaching or off saving the world."

I hesitate a beat, then scroll to the next name that matters.

Micah.

I hit call before I can talk myself out of it.

It rings once. Twice. Then—

"Gray?"

Relief punches through me.

"Hey, you free?" My voice cracks in a way I hate. "I...kinda need someone to talk to. Like, now."

There's a pause, then Micah says, "Yeah, man. You okay?"

I exhale, pinching the bridge of my nose. "Not really."

"I'm at the church. Come by."

I nod like he can see me. "On my way."

I hang up and toss my phone onto the passenger seat, heart pounding.

Because the thought I can't shake is the one I've been too afraid to say out loud: what if she doesn't choose Him?

What if Ivy never gets there? What if all my prayers, all my waiting, still end with her walking away—from Jesus? And from me?

The questions circle like vultures, heavy and relentless. I grip the steering wheel until my hands ache.

For the first time in a long time, I feel like I'm this close to messing up something good.

And I'm not about to let fear and old habits take Ivy away from me.

The church hallway is quiet, yet it feels too loud with my head being this full. I find Micah in his office, hunched over a clipboard with crayon doodles on the edge.

He looks up, and the grin that spreads across his face is equal parts relief and welcome. "There you are. I was starting to wonder if you'd actually show up."

I manage a half-smile, though it feels thin.

Micah pushes the clipboard aside and nods toward the chair across from him. "Sit down, man. Whatever's eating you, we'll figure it out."

I sit, elbows on my knees, trying to find the words. "I messed up, man. With Ivy."

Micah doesn't flinch. "How bad are we talking?"

"I don't know. Breakfast started fine, but then I told her I have been thinking about our future. That she's my person. Basically almost proposed over pancakes."

Micah lets out a low whistle. "Wow. You really swung for the fences."

"She didn't say no," I add quickly. "But she didn't really say anything either. And then I brought up baptism."

His eyebrows shoot up. "Bold move."

"She's been going to church, reading her Bible, having conversations about God. It didn't feel that crazy to ask."

Micah's brows knit, his voice gentler than his expression. "Gray...has she even given her life to Christ yet?"

My mouth opens, but nothing comes out. My silence is its own answer.

Micah exhales, leaning back in his chair, arms folded. "Bro, baptism isn't the first step. Salvation is. Surrendering her heart to Jesus has to come before any outward symbol. Otherwise it's just getting wet."

I drag a hand down my face, heat creeping up my neck. He's right, and I hate that he's right.

"And what'd she say?" Micah asks finally.

"She shut it down. Flat-out no. Wouldn't even consider it."

There's a long pause.

"And that bothered you."

I nod, jaw tight. "It wrecked me."

Micah doesn't speak right away. When he does, his voice is low. Careful. "Gray, you know I love you. But man...sometimes you hold people to a standard they haven't even agreed to yet."

I bristle, straightening. "I just want her to grow. To see what life could be like when it's centered on something real."

"I get that," Micah says. "But let me ask you something, and I need you to really hear this, is your hope that she falls more in love with Jesus...or more in line with you?"

I blink. "What's the difference?"

Micah's tone sharpens. "The difference is control. You don't mean to, but you want to control the pace. Her faith. The outcome. Maybe even her."

The words hit harder than I want to admit.

"I'm not trying to control her," I say, defensively. "I just —I've been through this before. I don't want to watch someone drift because I didn't speak up."

Micah exhales slowly. "And maybe you did need to say

something. But Gray, you can't push her over the finish line. That's not how faith works. And it's not how love works, either."

I look away, throat tight.

"Just...give her time," Micah says more gently. "And trust that the God who saved you is more than capable of doing the same for her. Without you forcing His hand."

I stand, a little too quickly. "Yeah. Thanks, man. I appreciate it."

Micah watches me for a beat. "You don't sound like you believe it."

"I'll think about it."

"That's all I'm asking."

I turn to leave, my pulse pounding. "I've got rehearsal."

"Gray."

I pause.

Micah's voice is calm, but firm. "Don't let fear talk louder than grace. You've come too far for that."

I nod once, tight, and head down the hall.

But the weight of it doesn't lift.

If anything, it presses harder.

Because what if Micah's right?

And worse—what if I can't stop myself from proving him wrong?

The notes should feel like they belong—stacked perfectly, flowing seamlessly, like a river running smooth and sure. But today? Everything is jagged and offbeat.

I run my hands through my hair, gripping the ends a

little too tight as I watch the team try to pull it together. Caleb is a half-second behind on the drums. The harmonies are tripping over each other, flat in one spot, sharp in another. My teeth clench.

"All right, hold up!" I snap, louder than I intended. Everyone stops, instruments trailing off into an awkward silence. A few of them exchange glances, uncertain. "We're losing the rhythm, guys. Drums, you're coming in late. Keys—you've got to hold that note for another count before you transition. And, Molly..." I look back, her eyes wide. "You're rushing the verse. Slow it down. Let it breathe."

Her cheeks flush, and she nods quickly, adjusting the mic stand even though it doesn't need adjusting. My stomach twists, but I press on. "Let's run it from the top."

The guitarist, Chris, clears his throat. "We've been running it from the top for the last thirty minutes, Gray."

I swallow hard, jaw locked tight. "And we're going to keep running it until we get it right."

An uneasy tension ripples through the room. Usually, rehearsal is light, even fun. But right now, it feels like a pressure cooker ready to blow. I grip the edge of the music stand, knuckles white. I know I'm pushing. I know I'm making it tense. But I can't stop.

"Again," I bark out, nodding to Caleb. He hesitates before tapping the sticks together to count us off.

We get four bars in before the harmony slips. Molly misses her cue, her voice faltering on the word grace.

My hands slam down on the music stand. The crash echoes through the sanctuary. "Stop!"

Silence. Thick and heavy. No one meets my eyes.

I rub my hands over my face again, fingers pressing into my temples. "Five-minute break. We'll...we'll try again." I don't wait for their responses. I turn and shove open the side door, the cool hallway air hitting me like a slap.

The door swings shut behind me, muffling the whispers I can already hear starting up. I pace the narrow corridor, hands on my hips, breath coming in shallow bursts. I press my back against the wall, sinking down until I'm sitting on the floor, knees pulled up.

What is wrong with me?

This isn't me. I'm not the guy who slams music stands or snaps at Molly for singing too fast. But it's like something is clawing at my insides—this relentless need for everything to be perfect. To go smoothly. To be in control.

But it's not just about rehearsal, and I know it.

My hands rub over my face again. Lord, I don't want to be that person. Not again.

The hallway is silent except for the distant hum of fluorescent lights and the soft echo of someone's footsteps. I don't look up until they stop right in front of me.

"You good?"

I glance up to see Luke—one of the worship leaders and probably the most patient guy I know. He's holding two cups of coffee, one stretched out toward me.

I stare at it for a second before accepting. "Thanks."

He leans against the opposite wall, crossing his arms. "You want to talk about it?"

I blow out a breath, the coffee steaming in my hands. "Not really."

Luke nods, taking a sip of his drink. "You're kind of ripping people apart in there."

I cringe. "I know."

"Not like you."

I sigh, my shoulders sagging. "I don't know what's wrong with me, man."

Luke doesn't rush me, just lets the silence stretch. Finally, I look up. "I guess...I'm just trying too hard to make everything perfect."

He raises an eyebrow. "Everything? Or something specific?"

I stare down at my coffee, the ripples on the surface stilling as my hands stop shaking. "It's just...Ivy. Things are getting real. Fast."

Luke nods, his eyes softening. "And that's a bad thing?"

"No, it's just...I don't want to mess it up. I've messed it up before. Tried to force things. Tried to control what wasn't mine to control."

Luke watches me for a long moment. "You're talking about Claire."

I stiffen at the name, but nod. "Yeah. I just—I don't want to be that guy again. The one who tries to take the reins when it's God's job to lead. But it's hard...when you care this much."

He leans his head back against the wall, closing his eyes. "That's the thing about faith, man. You don't lead. You follow."

I let that sink in. It feels heavy and light all at once, like a weight I didn't realize I was carrying just got lifted, even if just a little.

After a beat, Luke pushes off the wall, stretching his back. "You good to go back in?"

I nod, standing slowly. "Yeah. I'm good."

He claps me on the back. "Just don't bite anyone's head off, alright?"

A small laugh escapes me, and I shake my head. "I'll try my best."

We step back through the door, and I take a deep

breath, hoping—praying—that this time, I can let go. Just a little.

Chapter 31
Ivy

The sanctuary is packed today—families filtering in, friends greeting each other with side hugs and wide smiles. I slip into my usual spot, Harper and Olivia trailing behind me. Harper's grumbling under her breath, practically ripping the lid off her to-go coffee.

"Are you okay?" I ask, glancing at her as I settle into my seat.

Harper rolls her eyes, taking an aggressive sip of her coffee. "I'm fine. Except Micah thinks I'm going to burn out and made me take this weekend off from the kids' ministry." She scoffs. "I told him I'm fine, but he just gave me that 'I know best because I'm the youth pastor' look."

I bite back a grin. "Maybe he's just looking out for you."

"He's looking out for his control issues is what he's doing," she huffs, crossing her arms.

Olivia snorts. "Maybe you actually do need a break."

Harper glares at her. "You sound just like him."

I hide my smile behind my hand. "Well, I'm glad you're finally joining us for a service in person."

She softens just a little. "Yeah, yeah. I guess it's good to actually hear the message for once."

I glance toward the stage where the band is setting up, adjusting mics and tuning guitars. My heart does a tiny flip when Gray steps up, his hand running along the edge of his guitar. But there's something off. His movements are sharp, his eyes a little too focused.

"Everything ok?" Olivia asks, nudging me.

I blink, tearing my eyes away. "Yeah. Why?"

"You're staring."

Harper smirks. "I think that's just her new normal now."

I nudge her back, trying to laugh it off. "Shut up."

The music starts, and Gray's voice cuts through the noise, clear and steady. But there's a hardness to it. A tension I don't recognize. I watch his hands move along the guitar strings, the way his jaw tenses when the drummer misses a beat.

Something's wrong.

"Wow," Harper whispers, leaning in. "He's really intense today."

I nod, unable to tear my eyes away. "Yeah. He is."

The songs flow one into the other, but Gray doesn't settle. Normally, he's so composed, so full of grace. But today, he looks like he's holding something together by sheer willpower.

Olivia nudges me. "You should probably check on him after."

"Yeah," I say softly, my eyes flicking back to the stage. "I think I will."

Harper scoffs, tossing her hair over her shoulder. "I still say brunch is the priority."

I chuckle, shaking my head. "You and your waffles."

"What? I'm not ashamed," she says, folding her arms. "But seriously, you should check on him. He looks...I don't know. Kinda...off."

I nod, chewing on the inside of my cheek. "I know. I see it too."

Harper raises an eyebrow. "Guess we're skipping waffles."

"Not on my account," I protest, but Harper waves it off.

"It's fine. You go do your check-in thing, and we'll catch up after."

I smile, touched by her willingness to sacrifice her brunch ritual. "You're the best."

Harper shrugs. "I know."

The final chord fades, and the sanctuary settles into that familiar hum of post-service chatter. People rise from their seats, stretching, hugging, moving toward the lobby. Harper and Olivia are already halfway to the doors, talking about where to eat, but I'm distracted—my eyes searching the stage for Gray.

He's wrapping cords, talking to someone on the tech team, but even from here, I can see the tension still wound tight in his shoulders. Olivia's words echo in my mind. *You should probably check on him after.*

I take a step forward, weaving through clusters of people. He doesn't see me yet, and I'm halfway up the side aisle when a voice calls out.

"Ivy!"

I turn, coming face to face with a blonde I've seen

around before. She's always at the events—serving at the food tables, setting up chairs, organizing things with the kind of confidence that makes you think she's been doing it forever. Her smile is bright, a little too perfect, and she loops her arm through mine before I can process what's happening.

"Hey!" she chirps, squeezing my arm like we're old friends. "I just wanted to tell you how proud I am of you."

I blink, caught off guard. "Proud?"

"Yeah!" Her smile widens. "You've been around so much more lately. I keep seeing you at events, helping out with graphics, even coming to rehearsals. It's inspiring."

"Oh." I smile, though it feels a little stiff. "Thank you."

"I mean, it's really good for Gray, you know?" she continues, voice dropping slightly like we're sharing a secret. "He deserves someone strong in faith after everything he's been through."

My heart stutters. "What do you mean?"

Her eyebrows lift, a little too knowingly, as if I should already be in on the gossip. "Oh, you know...his past. What happened with Claire."

I freeze. "Claire?"

Her eyes widen just slightly—fake surprise, the kind people use when they've said too much but don't actually regret it. "Oh...I just assumed he'd mentioned her."

I shake my head slowly, my voice coming out softer than I intended. "No. He hasn't."

She hesitates for half a beat, then shrugs like it's nothing, though the glint in her eyes says she's enjoying this. "Well, I'm sure he will eventually. Just...it was a lot. I'm just glad he's found someone who's firm in their faith. He deserves that after everything."

The words land sharp, like a compliment with a hook in it.

I try to keep my expression neutral, but my mind is spinning. *Who is Claire?*

I want to ask her, but she's already breezing on, oblivious—or maybe not—to the thousand questions burning a hole in my heart.

"Anyway," she chirps, her voice too bright, patting my arm like we're girlfriends swapping secrets. "I'm really happy for you two. You're exactly what he needs."

The emphasis lingers, heavy with judgment, as if she's the authority on what Gray does and doesn't deserve.

I nod numbly as she waves and disappears back into the crowd, leaving me frozen in the aisle, her words echoing in my ears.

What happened with Claire? Who is she? Why hasn't he mentioned her?

Strong in faith. Grounded.

Is that how he sees me? Is that what he thinks I am? Or worse...is that what he needs me to be?

I turn back toward the stage, searching for him, but he's gone. The tech team is coiling cables, chatting quietly as they pack up. I scan the side aisles, catching glimpses of familiar faces, but not him.

I weave through the aisles, nodding politely at people I pass, my heart thumping harder with each step. He has to be here somewhere. My feet carry me instinctively to the backstage entrance, where I hesitate just long enough to collect myself before pushing the door open.

The sound of metal strings being plucked echoes softly down the hallway. I follow the noise until I find him in one of the side rooms—guitar on his knee, fingers brushing across the frets absently. His jaw is clenched, brows knitted together, like he's wrestling with something invisible.

He doesn't notice me at first. He's muttering under his breath, barely audible but thick with frustration. His hand slides up the neck of the guitar, fingers pressing down hard enough to make it squeal off-key. He curses under his breath and starts again.

"Gray?"

His head snaps up, eyes sharp with surprise before they soften. "Hey...didn't expect you back here."

I take a hesitant step forward. "I was looking for you. You disappeared pretty quick after service."

He nods, setting the guitar down against the wall. "Yeah. Just needed a minute."

I move closer, crossing my arms to keep my hands from shaking. "You alright?"

He forces a smile, one that doesn't quite reach his eyes. "Yeah, I'm fine."

But I don't believe him. The tension in his shoulders, the way his jaw ticks—everything about him looks wound tight.

"You don't seem fine." My voice comes out softer than I expect, but steadier too. "Did something happen?"

Gray shrugs, eyes darting away. "Just a long day."

"Gray..." I try again, the knot in my chest pulling tighter. "You've been off since before service. Talk to me."

His hands rake through his hair, a frustrated sigh slipping past his lips. "It's nothing, Ivy. Really."

The deflection stings, and for a moment I almost let it drop. Almost. But the echo of that woman's words won't stop rattling in my mind, and the longer he shuts me out, the louder they get.

I bite the inside of my cheek, warring with myself. I

shouldn't. I shouldn't. But the question burns through anyway.

"Who's Claire?"

The silence that follows is deafening.

The air between us shifts—sharpens. His expression goes blank for a second too long. His hands drop from the guitar, fingers curling into fists at his sides.

He blinks, his jaw tightening. "What did you say?"

I swallow, the knot in my throat growing tighter. "Claire. I...I ran into someone who mentioned her. Said she was part of your past."

Gray's eyes harden, and he takes a measured breath, running a hand through his hair. "Who told you that?"

I shake my head, trying to catch my breath. "Just someone I've seen around. I don't even know her name. She said she was proud of me for being strong in my faith. Said... said you deserved someone like that after...after Claire."

His jaw flexes, the muscle ticking with the pressure. He looks away, staring hard at the wall, his chest rising and falling in slow, controlled breaths.

"Gray..." I step closer, my voice softening. "Who was she?"

He doesn't answer right away. His eyes stay fixed on the wall, his fists unclenching slowly. "It's not important," he finally says, his voice low and clipped.

My heart twists. "It is if it's bothering you."

He sighs, running both hands through his hair now, gripping the back of his neck as if the tension there is the only thing keeping him upright. "Look...I don't want to talk about it. Not right now."

"But..."

He turns to me, eyes shadowed with something I can't quite name. Regret? Pain? "Not right now, Ivy."

His voice is gentle but firm, the kind that leaves no room for argument. I swallow back my questions, nodding even though it leaves a thousand loose threads dangling between us.

"Okay," I whisper.

He exhales, shoulders sagging slightly. "I just...I need a minute. Alright?"

I nod again, feeling a sting of hurt I can't explain. He steps back, hands still gripping the back of his neck, and leans against the wall, staring at the ceiling like he's searching for answers.

I linger for a second longer, waiting for him to look at me, to say something that will make it better. But he doesn't. He just stands there, eyes closed, breathing deeply like he's trying to regain control.

Finally, I turn, slipping back out into the hallway, my heart heavier than when I walked in.

Who is Claire?

Why won't he tell me?

And more importantly...what kind of woman did he love before me?

The line rings twice before Harper picks up, her voice bright and teasing. "Changed your mind already, huh?"

I can't help but laugh, though it feels forced. "Guess I'm in the mood for waffles after all."

"Good," she chirps. "We're at Rosie's. You want us to wait for you?"

"I'll be there in ten." I hang up, taking a deep breath

before starting my car. I try to push Gray and Claire out of my mind, but her name lingers like a shadow, creeping into every thought.

The drive to Rosie's Diner is short, and I pull into the gravel lot to find Harper and Olivia already settled at a corner booth, cups of coffee steaming in front of them. Harper waves me over, her expression warm and inviting. I muster up a smile and head inside, the bell above the door jingling as I enter.

"Look who decided to join us," Harper announces as I slide into the booth across from her.

"Couldn't miss out on those waffles," I reply, forcing a grin.

Olivia nudges the extra mug of coffee toward me. "Figured you'd want one."

"Thanks." I take a sip, the warmth settling my nerves just a bit.

Harper wastes no time, diving into her menu with a kind of intensity that only she can manage. "I'm thinking blueberry pancakes this time. What about you guys?"

I shrug. "Waffles, I guess."

Olivia just nods, her eyes flicking between me and Harper.

"So," Harper says, folding her menu and setting it aside. "Did you get to talk to Gray? Is he ok?"

My hand stills on my coffee mug. I swallow, trying to sound casual. "Oh, he...uh, he had plans with the worship team. I didn't want to bother him."

Olivia glances over her menu, eyes sharp. "Did you two get into a fight?"

"No!" I rush to say, my voice a little too high. I clear my throat. "No, everything's fine. He's just...busy."

They exchange a look I can't quite decipher. Harper leans back, crossing her arms. "Well, if you say so."

I force a smile and change the subject. "So, what were you guys talking about before I got here?"

Harper and Olivia glance at each other, almost like they're deciding who's going to speak first. Finally, Olivia sighs, setting her menu down. "We were actually talking about church...and faith."

My eyebrows lift. "Oh?"

Olivia hesitates, her fingers fidgeting with the edge of her napkin. "I don't know...I've been thinking about it a lot. You and Harper seem so at home there. Like you belong. I just...don't feel that way."

"I wouldn't say it's easy." I say.

Olivia's gaze sharpens, turning back to me. "But it is for you. I mean...you didn't even go to church a few months ago. Now you're practically a regular."

The words sting more than I expect. "I mean...yeah. I guess."

Olivia leans forward, voice dropping. "How? How did you just...change like that? Because I've been trying, Ivy. I really have. And it just...I don't feel what you feel. I don't understand it the way you do."

I blink, completely caught off guard. "I...I don't know. It's not like it happened overnight."

"Didn't it?" she asks, her voice sharper than I'm used to. "You go to one service, then you're going every Sunday. You're volunteering, doing graphics, dating the worship leader..."

Harper's eyes widen. "Olivia..."

Olivia's shoulders sag. "I'm sorry. I don't mean it like that. I just...I don't get it." Her voice cracks a little, and she looks down at her coffee, fingers tapping the side of the mug. "I wish I could feel what you and Harper feel. But I don't. And I don't want to fake it just to fit in."

I feel the weight of her words settle between us. For a long moment, none of us speak.

But I can still feel it—those questions lingering in the air, unspoken but heavy.

And suddenly, it's too much.

The weight of the last twenty-four hours presses down like a dam finally breaking.

I drop my menu.

"I can't do this," I whisper.

Harper and Olivia both look up, startled.

My throat tightens as heat burns behind my eyes. "I don't have the answers either, okay? I'm not some spiritual expert. I don't even know what I'm doing half the time."

"Ivy..." Harper reaches for me, but I shake my head.

"No. I need to say this." The tears fall now, hot and fast, and I don't even try to stop them. "I feel like I'm being pulled in every direction—by God, by Gray, by all of it. And I want to believe I'm doing the right thing, but I'm scared. I'm so scared."

Olivia stares, eyes wide. "You...are?"

I nod, breath shaking. "Gray wants so much from me. He says all these beautiful things and talks about forever and faith and baptism and I'm just..." I press the heel of my hand to my chest. "I'm still trying to figure out if I even believe in all this."

Harper's voice is gentle. "Of course you do..."

"No," I cut in, wiping my cheeks with the back of my hand. "I mean really believe. Not just showing up at church or volunteering or smiling through Bible studies. I want to know God. I want to feel like I'm not faking it either. But I don't know how."

The table is silent.

I feel my shoulders shaking, chest caving inward. Olivia's confession cracked something open in me—but it wasn't her fault. It was already splintering.

"I'm trying," I whisper, barely able to speak. "But what if I'm not enough? Not for Gray. Not for God. Not even for me."

There's a long beat of silence, broken only by the soft clink of silverware from a nearby table.

Then Harper slides out of the booth and sits next to me, pulling me into her arms. "You don't have to be enough," she murmurs, her voice steady but tender. "That's the whole point of the gospel. None of us are enough on our own. That's why Jesus came. God knew we could never fix ourselves or earn our way to Him, so He did what we couldn't. He sent His Son to take every failure, every not-enough place, and nail it to the cross.

She squeezes me tighter, resting her cheek against my temple. "You don't have to prove yourself, Ivy. Not to me. Not to Gray. Not even to God. Because in Christ, you already are enough. You're already loved."

I nod against her shoulder, but the ache doesn't go away.

Because I'm not sure I believe it yet.

And I don't know how to say that without breaking again.

Chapter 32
Ivy

The drive home is quiet.

Not the kind of quiet that soothes—but the kind that stretches. Long. Still. Heavy with everything I didn't say, and everything I did.

I keep one hand on the wheel, the other curled in my lap, fingers still trembling. I feel wrung out—like I left pieces of myself back in that diner booth. Like my faith cracked open in front of the people I love most.

And maybe that's not a bad thing.

Maybe it needed to crack for something real to take root.

I glance out the window as I turn down the road toward my apartment. The sun's low in the sky now, golden light casting long shadows across the pavement. The world feels still. Waiting.

Like maybe I'm on the edge of something.

Not a breakdown.

A breakthrough.

Because for all the messiness of today—Gray's silence, Olivia's questions, my own unraveling—I can't shake the feeling that God is still here. That He saw it all. Heard every word. Collected every tear.

Maybe he's not disappointed in me.

Maybe He's drawing me closer.

I remember Gray telling me once that God doesn't wait for us to have it all together—He meets us right in the middle of the mess. Or maybe it was that verse Pastor Jack preached on last month: "The Lord is close to the broken-hearted and saves those who are crushed in spirit."

Either way, the truth presses in now, quiet and steady. Maybe this unraveling isn't failure. Maybe it's the thread He's tugging on to draw me into His arms.

I pull into the parking lot, shifting the car into park but not moving. I sit there for a moment, breathing in the quiet. The chaos of the morning feels far away now. Like something I lived through, not something I'm still drowning in.

I want to meet God in the silence. I want to ask Him what to do with everything I'm feeling.

And this time...I want to mean it.

The apartment is too still, the silence settling like dust in the corners of the room. I sit on the edge of my couch, fingers laced together, my knuckles white with tension.

I've never done this before. Not like this.

Prayer always felt...distant. Like I was sending words into the void, hoping they might stick somewhere on the way up. But today...

Today, I want them to stick.

I draw in a breath, shaky and unsteady. "Okay," I whisper, glancing around the empty room. My voice feels too loud in the stillness, but I push forward anyway. "Um...hi, God."

I fold my hands tighter, knuckles pressing against each

other. "I don't really know how to do this—talking to You. But...I'm going to try."

The silence stretches, but I keep going.

"I don't want to fake this. I don't want to just show up at church or read the Bible because it makes Gray proud of me. I want it to be real. I want You to be real to me."

My throat tightens. "And I guess that means I have to be honest. I don't feel like I measure up. I never have. But Gray keeps saying it's not about being enough—it's about what Jesus already did. That You sent Him because I couldn't fix myself. Because I can't save myself."

The words scrape out of me, raw and halting. "So...if that's true, I don't want to keep pretending I've got it all together. I don't. I need what He did for me. I need forgiveness. I need...Him."

I close my eyes, hands falling into my lap. "I don't want this to just be another Ivy-tries-to-fit-in moment. I want it to be surrender. I want You to take this heart of mine and make it Yours. Not because of Gray. Not because of Harper or Olivia. But because Jesus gave His life for me. Because He's worth it."

A tear slips down my cheek as the last words tumble out, small and trembling. "So here I am, Lord. Please forgive me. Please make me new. Help my unbelief."

The silence stretches long and deep, and for a moment, I wonder if I'm doing it wrong. If maybe I'm not good enough at this to get an answer.

But then my phone rings.

My eyes snap open, the sound cutting through the room like a blade. I scramble to find it on the coffee table, the screen lighting up with Gray's name. His picture flashes up —a candid shot I took of him laughing at something I said over coffee a few weeks back.

My thumb hovers over the screen.

It would be easy. So easy to answer and let him talk me down from the ledge. He's good at that—at making me feel seen. Safe.

But...

I let out a slow breath, my thumb moving away from the screen. I watch it ring until the call drops off and the room is silent once more.

I set the phone down carefully, my hands still shaking. For some reason, the quiet feels heavier now. Like it's pressing down on me.

My eyes drift back to my hands, fingers still locked together. It feels strange, but I don't let go. I take a deep breath, and before I can stop myself, the words spill out.

"God...if You're real...if You really hear me...can You just...fill me with something real? A peace that's not pretend? Not something I'm trying to make happen, but something that only You can do."

My voice wavers, but I press on. "I don't want to just do this because it makes Gray happy. I want it to be for me. For You. I want it to be...real."

The room is still. My breath is loud in my ears, and I'm not sure what I'm expecting—some sign, maybe? A whisper? A warmth that floods the room?

But there's just...silence.

And yet, it doesn't feel empty.

I sit there for a long moment, letting the quiet stretch out around me, feeling it wrap itself around my shoulders like a blanket. My chest loosens, the tension slipping away bit by bit.

Maybe this is what peace feels like.

I draw in a breath, deeper than I've taken in a while, and the words come before I can even think to hold them back. "I think...I think I need to focus on You. Not just Gray. Not just church. Just...You and me for a bit."

The thought is startling, but it fits. Like a puzzle piece I didn't know was missing. I'm always running from one thing to the next—trying to prove I belong, trying to fit. But maybe...maybe belonging isn't about fitting. Maybe it's about being held.

I stand slowly, the motion feeling deliberate. I head to the bookshelf by the window where I stacked the books I picked up from the church gift shop weeks ago. My fingers brush over the soft leather binding of the Bible I bought on a whim—along with the pastel highlighters, sticky notes and pens. Beside it is the small devotional I'd picked up. The title reads *Grace Upon Grace*.

I hesitate for just a second, then grab them both and head back to the couch. I settle in, tucking my legs beneath me, the Bible heavy in my lap. I trace the letters on the cover before flipping it open, thumbing through pages until I land on a verse I remember from Sunday service.

"But he said to me, 'My grace is sufficient for you, for my power is made perfect in weakness.' Therefore I will boast all the more gladly of my weaknesses, so that the power of Christ may rest upon me." — 2 Corinthians 12:9

My breath catches. My power is made perfect in weakness.

I let the words soak in for a moment before setting the Bible aside and opening the devotional. I crack the spine, flipping to the first page.

Day 1: Grace Upon Grace

God's grace isn't earned. It isn't something you deserve. It's something you receive because He loves you. It's not about perfection. It's not about performance. It's about trust. It's about resting in the knowledge that He's already done the work for you.

My eyes blur with tears, and I blink rapidly, sniffling against the wave of emotion rising up. It's not about performance.

It feels like a whisper straight to my soul.

I press my hand to my chest, swallowing back the lump in my throat. "Okay," I whisper, voice cracking. "Okay, God. I'm listening."

I put my phone on do not disturb and spend the next half hour reading through the devotional, marking down thoughts in the margins, circling verses that feel like they're meant for me. Not earned. Not deserved. Just given.

It's a concept I'm not used to. I've spent my whole life earning—approval, love, validation. But this? This just... exists. Freely.

By the time I'm finished, there's a softness in my chest. A crack in the armor I've been holding up. Maybe it's small, but it's there.

I lean back against the cushions, Bible and devotional still in my lap, and close my eyes. "Thank you," I whisper, the words slipping out without thought. "For meeting me here. I'm going to try...to meet You here too."

The sky outside fades into a soft wash of lavender and gold, the sun beginning its slow descent behind the buildings. The apartment is quiet, still, but it doesn't feel empty anymore. Not in the same way it did earlier.

I wrap a blanket around my shoulders, letting the weight of the day settle over me. Not the heavy, soul-crushing kind—but something lighter.

I don't know everything yet. I'm still full of questions. Still scared. Still unsure of what's next.

But for the first time in a long time, I'm not trying to fix it all myself. I'm not trying to be the version of Ivy that fits what someone else needs.

I'm just...here.

Me and God.

And somehow, that feels like enough for tonight.

I reach for my phone again, not to check for missed calls or scroll aimlessly, but to open the notes app. My fingers hover over the screen for a second, then I type slowly, deliberately.

Things I'm learning:

- **Faith doesn't have to look perfect.**
- **Grace is free. I don't have to earn it.**
- **It's okay to take a step back so I can take a step forward.**

I stare at the words for a moment, then lock the screen and set the phone aside.

There's still a conversation waiting for me.

With Gray.

And I know it won't be easy. I know I'll probably cry,

and he might look at me like I'm breaking something beautiful—but I'm not doing it to break us.

I'm doing it to make room for something deeper. Something real.

I'm choosing to believe that if this love between us is rooted in something holy, it will hold. Even if I have to loosen my grip for a while.

Even if it hurts.

I press my forehead to my knees, whisper one last prayer into the quiet.

"Give me the strength to follow You. Even if it means letting go."

Chapter 33
Gray

I wake up with the taste of regret heavy on my tongue. My eyes blink open to the muted light filtering through the blinds, and I roll over, squinting at the clock. 7:12 a.m.

It feels like I barely slept.

The memories of yesterday replay on a loop—my harsh tone, the clipped words I threw at Ivy backstage. Her face, startled and unsure, flickers across my mind like a bad dream. I run my hands over my face, groaning as I sit up and plant my feet on the cold hardwood floor.

I haven't been that guy in years. The one who lashes out without thinking. The one whose words cut before he can reel them back.

I reach for my phone on the nightstand, flipping it over. My thumb hovers over the screen, and I tap it awake.

Nothing.

Not a single text. Not a missed call.

I swipe through my call log. Four calls. The first rang, the rest went straight to voicemail. I left her a message after the first two, but it was awkward and jumbled—an apology tangled up with excuses. I don't even remember what I said. Probably just more rambling.

A knot tightens in my stomach, and I push off the bed, pacing my room. My hands find my hair, fingers knotting through the strands in frustration. Why couldn't I just talk to her?

The truth is, she didn't deserve any of it. Not my mood. Not my sharp words. Not the way I brushed her off like she didn't matter.

I feel the familiar sting of guilt clawing its way up my chest, suffocating and thick. This is what I used to be. Angry. Reactive. I thought I'd left that behind. Thought I'd buried it deep enough that it couldn't surface again.

But one bad day, and I snapped.

GRAY

You free today?

I send the text and toss the phone onto the bed, pacing the room again. My hands feel restless, fingertips drumming against my thighs as I walk. What if she's mad? What if I crossed a line I can't come back from?

What if I ruined everything?

My phone vibrates in my hand, the screen lighting up with her name. My heart does this weird lurch, and I fumble to unlock it.

IVY

Can I come over? We need to talk.

My heart drops straight to my stomach, the words blurring for a second before I can even process them.

We need to talk.

I sit down hard on the edge of the bed, my breath

coming quicker than it should. I've heard those words before. I know what they mean.

I type back, fingers fumbling slightly.

GRAY

Of course. I'm here. Whenever you want.

I stare at the screen, waiting for those three dots to appear. They don't. The screen stays still. Silent.

I exhale, head hanging low as I rub my palms together. I can't lose this. I can't lose her. Not because of my own mistakes. Not because I let old demons crawl back to the surface.

I close my eyes, pressing my palms together. It's not a graceful prayer. It's barely a whisper. But it's real.

"God, help me fix this. Help me make it right."

I pace the length of my living room, back and forth, hands rubbing together like I can burn off the tension pooling in my chest. I straightened up the apartment twice—fluffed the couch pillows, wiped down the counters, even ran a quick vacuum across the floor. Not that Ivy would care, but I needed something to do with my hands.

Her text still flashes in my mind: *We need to talk.*

I can't shake the feeling that it's bad news. That she's going to walk in, sit down across from me, and tell me she can't do this anymore. That my mess, my baggage, my brokenness, is too much.

I hear a soft knock on the door, and my heart lurches. I pause, inhaling deeply before making my way over. My hand hesitates on the knob for half a second before I twist it open.

She stands there, eyes a little softer than I expected, but her shoulders are tense, one hand gripping the strap of her bag like it's her lifeline.

"Hey," she says quietly.

"Hey you." My voice is rougher than I intend. I step back, holding the door wider. "Come in."

She steps inside, and I close the door behind her, the click of the lock sounding too loud in the stillness. I watch as she scans the room, her gaze lingering on the freshly arranged pillows. Her lips quirk up just slightly, and I clear my throat.

"Can I...do you want something to drink? Water? Coffee?" I'm rambling, and I can't seem to stop. "I have tea...somewhere."

She shakes her head, slipping her bag off her shoulder and setting it by the door. "No, I'm good."

"Okay."

A beat of silence stretches between us, and I swear I can hear the ticking of the clock in the hallway. This is the first time we've been alone together in weeks.

I can't take it any longer. "I'm sorry," I blurt out, the words tumbling out before I can stop them. "About yesterday. Backstage. I was a jerk. I shouldn't have snapped at you. I shouldn't have..."

"Gray, It's fine." She cuts me off gently, her eyes meeting mine. My shoulders sag with relief, but she steps forward, crossing her arms lightly. "I'm not here to talk about that."

My brows knit together. "You're not?"

She shakes her head, taking another step closer. I catch the faintest scent of her perfume—that perfect blend of florals I've grown to crave. It's like a punch to the chest, a reminder of how much I've missed her.

"I'm not here to talk about yesterday," she repeats, her voice firmer. "I'm here because...I need to tell you something."

My heart kicks up a notch, but I nod, waiting. She's so close now, just a foot of space between us, and I resist the urge to reach for her.

She takes a deep breath. "I prayed yesterday."

The words hang between us, fragile and full. My heart stutters, and I try to catch my breath. "You did?"

She nods, her gaze never leaving mine. "For the first time. Like...really, actually prayed." Her hands twist together in front of her, and I watch her fingers fumble, knuckles going white. "I was sitting in my apartment, and everything just...crashed in on me. I realized I've been trying to fit into this mold I didn't understand. I realized..." She pauses, blinking rapidly. "I realized I didn't want to just fit in anymore. I want to belong."

My throat tightens, and I take a step forward, my hands slipping into my pockets to keep from reaching for her. "Ivy...that's..." I can't find the words.

But she's not done. Her gaze flickers to the floor, then back up to me, fire and uncertainty battling in her eyes. "I prayed for peace. I prayed to...to feel something real. And it was there, Gray. It was real."

I can barely breathe. "That's amazing," I whisper, my voice barely a rasp.

Her lips curve into the softest smile, the kind that's almost a secret. "I don't know what I'm doing. I don't even know where to start."

For a moment, neither of us speaks. We just stand there,

the distance between us charged and humming. Finally, I clear my throat. "Do you...do you want to sit?"

She nods, and I guide her to the couch, sitting beside her but keeping a few inches of space between us. My hands rest on my knees, fingers laced together, and I steal a glance at her.

"You have no idea how grateful I am to see you choosing Him."

Her eyes shimmer, but she blinks quickly, nodding. "Thank you."

There's silence again, but it's comfortable this time.

Finally, I speak, the words coming out softer than I intend. "I was scared, you know. When I didn't hear back from you."

She looks up, surprised. "You were?"

I nod, swallowing hard. "I thought I'd messed everything up. I thought..." I pause, forcing the words out. "I thought I lost you."

I can't help it—I reach for her. My hand instinctively moves toward hers, fingers stretching out like they might catch the slipping threads of this moment. But before I make contact, she shifts back. Not dramatically. Not harshly. But enough.

Enough to make my hand freeze in midair before I awkwardly pull it back.

My chest tightens. I feel the shift, like a thread snapping in the middle of a long stretch. Panic surges up my throat, clawing its way into my words.

"Ivy," I blurt, leaning forward, voice already trembling. "If this is about yesterday...about what happened backstage. I swear to you, it's not who I am anymore. I don't want to be that guy. I don't want to push you away."

Her eyes flick up to mine, soft but guarded. I keep

talking because I can't stop. "And if you need to know...
about Claire, I'll tell you. I will. I just...I didn't want to
dump that on you. I didn't want you to think...to think that
I'm still holding on to that, because I'm not."

Ivy blinks, her expression almost stunned. I can feel my
hands shaking. I press them to my thighs to still them, but it
doesn't work. My breath is ragged, and I don't even care if
she sees.

"I'm not trying to make you something you're not," I say,
voice cracking on the last word. "I don't want to lose you. I...
I can't lose you."

Her eyes glisten, and she looks away, pressing her lips
together. I feel like I'm free-falling, scrambling for something to hold on to, but there's nothing but air. Nothing but
the fragile silence between us.

"Ivy?" My voice is barely above a whisper now.

Her eyes flick back to mine, and I catch it—just a flicker
of pain. She scoots forward, bridging the gap, her hand
reaching out to brush a tear from my cheek. I hadn't even
realized I was crying. Her touch is soft, grounding, and it
nearly breaks me.

She leans in, wrapping her arms around me, and I fold
into it, clutching her like she might disappear. Her chin
rests on my shoulder, her hands gentle against my back.

"I'm not leaving you," she whispers, and my breath
shudders out in relief. "But..."

My arms tense. "But?"

She pulls back just enough to look me in the eyes. Her
hands stay on my shoulders, her gaze steady. "I need space,
Gray."

I swallow hard, the words hitting like a punch. "Space?"

Her nod is slow, deliberate. "I need to figure out...all of
this. What I believe. What I want. What I'm actually ready

for." She pauses, her eyes glassy but determined. "I don't want to pretend, not for you, not for anyone."

I open my mouth, but nothing comes out. My mind scrambles for the right thing to say, the thing that will fix this. But there's nothing. There's just the truth of her words, hanging heavy between us.

"I don't want to hold you back," she whispers, her voice barely audible. "And I don't want to fake faith just to fit into your world. You deserve more than that."

My hands find hers again, clasping tightly. "I don't want more, Ivy. I just want you."

Her eyes well with tears, and she gently pulls her hands free from mine, pressing them to her chest like she's holding herself together. "I want to want that too," she says, her voice cracking. "But right now...I just don't know."

A tear slips down her cheek, and I reach to brush it away, but she stands, wrapping her arms around herself instead. The space between us feels like a canyon, and I can do nothing but watch her.

"I need to find out who I am with God before I can figure out who I am with you," she says, her voice stronger this time.

My throat burns. My hands feel empty. "And you think you can't do that...with me?"

She hesitates, then shakes her head slowly. "I think I have to do it alone."

Her words cut deeper than I expect, and I flinch back, nodding even though everything inside me is screaming. "Okay," I choke out. "If that's what you need."

She bites her bottom lip, her eyes searching mine. "I'm sorry."

"Don't be." I force a smile, even though it feels like my

chest is caving in. "You do what you need to do. I'll still be here."

Her breath catches, and for a second, I think she might change her mind. But she doesn't. Instead, she nods, her shoulders pulling back like she's fortifying herself. "Thank you," she whispers.

I manage a nod, even though everything in me wants to reach for her, pull her back, hold on. But I let her go.

I watch as she picks up her bag, slinging it over her shoulder. She pauses at the door, turning back one last time. "Bye, Gray."

My jaw clenches, but I force the words out. "Bye, Ivy."

And then she's gone.

The door clicks shut behind her, and the silence settles back in. Heavy. Unyielding.

I stand there for a long time, staring at the door like she might walk back in. But she doesn't.

And I don't move.

Chapter 34
Gray
2 Months Later

I adjust the strap of my guitar, the leather soft and familiar against my shoulder. The sanctuary hums with the usual Sunday morning buzz—people shuffling to their seats, conversations drifting like whispers through the aisles. This should feel normal, routine. But it doesn't. Everything feels different now.

Eight weeks.

It's been eight weeks since she sat on my couch and told me she needed space. Eight weeks since I watched her walk out my front door, shoulders stiff, her chin tilted up in that stubborn way she does when she's trying not to cry.

Eight weeks of nothing but occasional texts and stolen glances at church.

And I'm starving for more.

I step up to the stage, the overhead lights flickering on, casting long shadows across the rows of chairs. My fingers flex over the strings instinctively, plucking out a few notes before the rest of the band joins in. But my eyes? They scan the room.

The first chord strikes, vibrating through my chest.

Worship has always been my anchor—a place to lose myself and find myself all at once. But today, I'm distracted. My gaze sweeps the crowd, almost on its own accord, landing where it always does.

Third row. Left side.

She's there.

Ivy sits between Harper and Olivia, her head bowed slightly as the music begins to swell. Harper's animated as always, clapping along, red hair bouncing with every beat. Olivia, stiff and reserved, wraps her arms around her middle, like she's bracing herself against the vulnerability of the moment.

But Ivy...

She stands still, eyes closed, lips moving just slightly with the words of the song. It's like she's absorbing it—really taking it in. Something stirs in my chest, a mixture of pride and longing I'm not quite prepared for.

We move through the first song, then the second, and each time I glance back, she's still there, eyes closed, swaying just a little with the rhythm. A prayer tumbles unbidden through my mind.

Keep her close, God. Keep her seeking.

It's not much, the little I've had of her these past weeks. A few texts. Pictures of her food. Once, she sent me a photo of her Bible open on her lap with a caption that just said: Trying. Another time it was her journal, pen resting across the page, the words blurred except for one line circled three times: Trust Him more.

Most days it's nothing more than a simple "Good morning" or a check-in before bed. Sometimes she sends me a verse that struck her, no explanation attached. Other times it's just a photo of her coffee mug with the words thinking of you.

It's minimal. Fragmented. And yet, every piece feels like a breadcrumb, proof that she's still there—even if she's holding more back than she used to.

And I've let her. I've almost forced myself to. Let her set the pace, steer the conversation, decide how much or how little to share. The last thing I want is to push too hard and make her feel like she has to choose between me and God. If this break was about her growing closer to Him, then I have to believe He's working in her even when I can't see it.

But it doesn't make the silence easier.

Every unread space between her words feels like a canyon I want to bridge. Every time I stop myself from asking for more, it feels like swallowing back a piece of my heart.

Still, I'll wait. I'll keep waiting. Because if the choice is between pushing her away or letting her find Him on her own, then I'd rather live in the ache than lose her altogether.

I glance back at her one more time, catching her eye as she looks up. She offers me a small smile, and I can't help but smile back. For a moment, the world feels like it's tilting back into place.

Service ends with the usual hum of chatter and the slow shuffle of people stretching and making their way to the exit. I pack up my guitar, slip the strap off my shoulder, and place it back in its case. The rest of the team is lingering, but I'm restless. I wave off a few invitations to lunch, mumbling something about needing to get home.

The parking lot is still dotted with cars, families

lingering to chat, friends making plans for brunch. I unlock my truck, tossing my guitar case in the back before climbing into the driver's seat.

My phone pings just as I'm about to start the engine. I pull it out, half-expecting another spam email. But it's not.

IVY

Great message today. Worship was beautiful.

I stare at the screen for a while, thumb hovering over the keyboard. I type out three different replies before erasing each one. Finally, I settle on something simple.

GRAY

You have no idea what that means to me.

My finger hovers over the send button for just a second too long. I hit send and watch the little message bubble disappear.

And then I just sit there, staring at the screen. I shouldn't get my hopes up. It's been eight weeks of this—flashes of hope, whispers of connection, but always just out of reach.

But she's still here. I have to keep telling myself this.

I lean back against the headrest, closing my eyes for a moment.

Every text. Every random snapshot of her day.

They're not much, but to me they're everything—little lifelines that carry me from one week to the next. Reminders that even with the distance, I'm not forgotten. That she's still tethered to me in some small way... and for now, that's enough.

You have no idea what that means to me.

She has no idea at all.

I walk up to Pastor Jack's office fifteen minutes early, nerves coiling in my stomach like I'm walking into something heavier than I can carry. I've been here more times than I can count—sat on that cracked leather couch across from him when I was still figuring out how to breathe again. Jack's been my anchor since the day he found me slumped on the steps outside this church, hungover on regret and barely holding it together. I didn't know what I was looking for back then. But Jack saw through the mess, sat down beside me, and stayed long enough for me to believe I was worth something more.

But today feels different. He's going to want updates. And I'm going to have to admit the one thing I've been avoiding: I'm not handling this well.

His assistant waves me back without even looking up from her computer. I weave through the narrow hallway, stopping just outside his door where his name is printed in gold letters: Jack E. Willis, Senior Pastor.

I knock lightly and hear his voice boom from the other side. "Come in!"

I step inside and immediately feel the warmth of his grin. Jack's sitting behind his desk, glasses perched low on his nose, a Bible open in front of him and a mug of coffee that's definitely more cream than anything else.

"Gray!" he says, standing to shake my hand. His grip is firm as always. "Good to see you, son."

"You too," I say, settling into the worn leather chair across from him.

Jack eases back into his seat, eyeing me carefully. "You look better than the last time you sat there."

"Low bar," I mutter with a half-smile.

He chuckles. "Still progress."

He gives me space to speak first—he always does. I glance toward the window, the light slanting in through the blinds like it's trying to warm something deep in my chest. Finally, I say, "It's been eight weeks."

Jack nods slowly. "Since she asked for space?"

"Yeah." I let out a breath, scrubbing a hand over my face. "We still talk. Still see each other from a distance. It's not like we're strangers, but...it's different now. We're friends. Just friends."

"And how's that going?"

I laugh, but there's no humor in it. "Harder than I thought. Not because I don't want to support her—I do. I really do. But I was planning our future, Jack. I was already halfway down the aisle in my head, thinking about rings and forever. And now I'm sitting here trying to act like I don't care that she doesn't text back right away or that I haven't kissed her in two months."

Jack doesn't flinch. He just nods, arms resting on the desk, patient as ever. "Sounds like you're grieving something."

"Yeah," I admit. "I guess I am."

A silence settles over the room before Jack leans in slightly. "Gray, can I ask you something?"

"Of course."

"Why do you think this is so hard for you? The friendship part."

I stare at the floor. "Because it's not what I want."

"But she's what you want."

I nod. "Yes."

Jack lets that sit for a beat. "So what do you do when the thing you want the most doesn't look the way you pictured it?"

I don't have an answer.

He leans back. "Son, you've always had a strong pull toward fixing things. Taking control. It's one of your best traits, but it's also one of the things that gets you in trouble. Especially when it comes to love."

"I'm not trying to control her..."

"I know," he interrupts. "But I think you've been trying to control the outcome. The timing. Maybe even her pace with God."

I shift in my seat, uncomfortable with how closely he's hitting the mark.

"You don't mean to," Jack continues. "But when you love someone like that, it's easy to start believing it's your job to hold it all together. To make sure she doesn't drift.

"But listen, Gray—leading her toward Christ, toward purity, that will be your calling when you're her husband. Not now. Right now, she doesn't need you trying to manage her faith like it's yours to control. Because it's not. You can't force her into a relationship with Jesus. You're not responsible for her salvation. What you can do is pray without ceasing. Be steady. Be ready to answer her questions when she asks. And trust that the same God who got ahold of you is more than capable of reaching her too."

My jaw tightens. "What if she never comes back?"

"What if she does?" he counters, then softens. "Gray, you said it yourself—you were thinking about marriage. That kind of love is rooted in patience, not pressure. And I know this feels like a step back, but sometimes God has to do work in the stillness. And Ivy...she's worth waiting for, isn't she?"

I nod, throat tight. "She's worth everything."

"Then let her grow. Let her seek. Let God speak into the spaces you can't reach." He leans forward, his tone firm but kind. "And in the meantime, you keep living. Keep serving. Keep trusting. Don't waste this season trying to rush past it. When the worry creeps in—because it will—turn it into prayer. Every time you're tempted to wonder if she'll make it back to you, bring her before the Lord instead. Pray for her faith more than you pray for your future together. That's where your energy belongs right now."

I look down at my hands. "It's just hard to breathe sometimes. Like I'm holding it all in, waiting for her to come back."

"Then breathe on purpose," Jack says. "Not because you're holding space for her, but because you're trusting the God who loves you both more than you ever could."

The words hit hard—true and tender and exactly what I didn't want to hear but needed to.

Jack stands, moving around the desk and placing a hand on my shoulder. "You've come so far, Gray. Don't let this season define you. Let it refine you."

I nod, holding back the emotion welling in my chest.

"Let's pray," he says simply.

We bow our heads, and his voice settles into the quiet.

"Father, we come to You as sons who need Your wisdom. I lift up Ivy to You right now—her heart, her questions, her search for truth. Meet her where she is, Lord. Draw her close in ways no one else can. Let Your Word come alive for her, not because of Gray, not because of anyone else, but because she sees You for who You are. And I lift up Gray. Thank You for the love You've planted in him—for his desire to honor You, even when it hurts. Teach him patience. Teach him how to hold loosely what he loves most, knowing You hold it tighter still. When fear whispers that he's losing her, remind him that she was never his to keep—she's Yours to redeem. Give him strength to wait well, faith to pray without ceasing, and peace that passes understanding when the longing feels too heavy. And Lord, remind him that Your plans are good, even in the waiting. We trust You with Ivy. We trust You with Gray. We trust You with the story You're writing."

When we finish, I open my eyes and exhale.

"Thanks, Jack."

He smiles. "Anytime. Keep walking forward, even if it's slow. And when you feel like you're losing your grip—remember, you're not the one holding all the pieces together. God is."

I step out of his office into the bright light of afternoon, heart still heavy but steadier than before.

She's worth the wait.

Even if it breaks me a little to do it right.

I push up from the floor and glance toward the corner of the room, where my guitar leans against the wall..

For a moment, I hesitate.

Then I cross the room, pick it up, and settle back onto the couch. My fingers hover over the strings, and I let them fall into a quiet rhythm—something slow, steady. Like a heartbeat.

The song's been in the works for months, pieces of it scattered across napkins, notebooks, and the notes app on my phone. It started as a love song. Then it became a prayer. Now...it's both.

I flip open my notebook and scan the scribbled lines, some crossed out, others circled. There's one section I've rewritten half a dozen times—the chorus. It never felt finished.

But now, something in me shifts. Maybe it's the prayer. Maybe it's the release. But suddenly, the words come.

Soft at first, then stronger.

I'll wait in the quiet, no need to be sure
Of timelines or answers—I'll stand and endure
Love isn't pressure, it's patience and grace
I dare to believe... you're worth the wait.

I pause, the final line settling in. My throat tightens. I whisper it again, slower this time, letting it sink in.

I DARE TO BELIEVE...YOU'RE WORTH THE WAIT.

I scribble the line down, fingers trembling. It's not just lyrics. It's a release. A vow.

I set the notebook down and lean the guitar against the couch, wiping my eyes with the heel of my palm.

That's it.

That's the chorus.

And when the time comes—when she's ready—she'll hear the whole song. Not as a plea. Not as a fix. But as a promise.

Until then, I'll wait.

And I'll pray.

Because she's worth that.

Chapter 35
Ivy

Harper's apartment smells like spiced pumpkin and cinnamon, the kind of warm, sweet scent that clings to your sweater and makes you want to linger. A fall garland drapes across the bookshelf, little pops of orange and gold leaves catching the light. On the coffee table, a candle flickers beside a half-finished mug of cider, and a plaid blanket is thrown carelessly over the arm of the couch.

I'm curled up on the couch with a fuzzy blanket wrapped around my legs, Harper bustling in the kitchen with her chai latte concoctions while Olivia sits beside me, unusually quiet.

"You okay?" I ask gently, nudging her with my elbow.

She gives a small nod, her fingers wrapped tightly around the warm mug Harper just handed her. "Yeah. Just...been thinking a lot."

Harper flops onto the armchair across from us, sipping from her snowman mug. "About?"

Olivia's eyes shift to mine, then drop to the blanket. "About that brunch. When I said all that stuff to you."

I blink, surprised. I hadn't expected her to bring it up.

She clears her throat. "I was frustrated. At myself, mostly. But I took it out on you, and that wasn't fair. I shouldn't have questioned your faith like that."

I open my mouth to respond, but she keeps going, her voice softer now. "But...honestly? I think you needed to hear it. And I think I needed to say it. Because watching you these last few weeks—I mean really watching you—something's different."

My throat tightens. "Liv..."

"No," she shakes her head, a faint smile pulling at her lips. "Let me say this. You've always been good at adapting. At becoming who people needed you to be. But this? This doesn't feel like that. You're not trying to perform, or please anyone. You just...are. And it's beautiful, Ivy."

Harper exhales slowly, her eyes glossy. "Amen to that."

I press my mug against my chest, warmth blooming deeper than just the chai latte. "Thank you," I whisper. "I think your words were exactly what I needed, even if they hurt in the moment. They kind of...cracked something open in me."

Olivia swipes at the corner of her eye with her sleeve, then shrugs with a watery laugh. "Guess we're all a little broken."

"We are," I say, reaching over to take her hand. "But I think that's the whole point. That's where grace meets us."

She nods slowly. "Yeah...I think I'm starting to get that."

Harper leans forward, her smile playful but her tone sincere. "You should come to church tomorrow. They're doing a Thanksgiving message—'Thankful, Grateful, Blessed.' I heard it's supposed to be really good."

Olivia hesitates, then glances at me. "Okay. I'll come. But no promises on the singing."

"That's fair," Harper grins.

And just like that, something shifts between us. A new layer. A deeper thread weaving through old friendship.

Not perfect. Not polished.

But real.

Thanksgiving feels...different this year.

It's been eight weeks since I pulled away from Gray. Eight weeks since I stood in his living room and told him I needed space—not just from him, but from everything.

I never imagined it would feel like this—like breaking apart and coming back together at the same time. The first few days were unbearable. I couldn't focus. Couldn't think straight. Everything reminded me of him. Of us. I'd lie awake at night, replaying every word, every look, wondering if I made a mistake.

But I knew. Deep down, I knew. If I didn't figure out who I was in this faith journey on my own, it would always be tangled up in him. I didn't want that. I couldn't have that. If I was going to believe in God, it had to be real.

So I took a step back.

And then I took another.

I threw myself into my role at the church. I finalized the promotional graphics for the Christmas Eve service, made weekly bulletins, even helped Harper with the posters for the kids' ministry Thanksgiving party. I showed up early. Stayed late. And for the first time in my life, I wasn't just attending church.

I was part of it.

And I started praying. Really praying. Not the kind of desperate, scattered prayers I used to whisper when everything was falling apart. These were different—intentional. I'd light that cinnamon candle, open a devotional, and just sit with God. Sometimes I spoke. Sometimes I didn't. Sometimes I cried and said nothing at all.

And slowly...I began to feel something.

Not lightning. Not fireworks. Just...peace. Gentle and unexpected. Like He'd been waiting for me to get quiet enough to notice.

Verses I used to skim over started to mean something. Words like grace and mercy weren't just abstract ideas—they were personal. Real. Woven into every crack in me. And for the first time, I didn't feel like I had to earn it.

I think back to last Sunday, standing in the back of the church while the worship team played Reckless Love. I've heard it a dozen times, but something about it hit different this time.

Oh, the overwhelming, never-ending, reckless love of God.

My hands trembled as I gripped my notebook. Tears fell before I could stop them—not because I was ashamed, but because I believed it. Really believed it.

This love wasn't earned. It wasn't about performance. It was just...there.

Always had been.

And Gray—he never stopped showing up. Not in person, but in little things. A verse he was studying. A photo of his cup of coffee at sunrise. A voice memo of him playing guitar late one night. I must've replayed that one a hundred times.

He didn't push. He didn't pressure. He just...stayed.

And that made all the difference.

I still haven't called him. Not because I don't want to—but because this journey, this fragile becoming, still feels sacred. And I need to walk it alone for just a little longer.

The Thankful, Grateful, Blessed service is coming. Everyone says it'll be meaningful—warm music, stories of gratitude, and a message that speaks right into the heart of the season. Part of me wonders what I'll feel. If I'll be ready.

I don't know what I'm expecting.

But something in me is starting to hope.

Maybe...I'll be ready by then.

The church is quieter than usual when I arrive that evening. The lobby smells faintly of cinnamon and cloves from a candle flickering at the welcome desk, and the muffled sound of kids' voices drifts down the hallway where they're working on decorations for tomorrow's Thanksgiving party.

I pull my cardigan tighter around me and carry the poster tubes under one arm, walking toward the sanctuary doors. Inside, volunteers are taping construction-paper turkeys and "thankful leaves" along the walls, the kind kids scribble prayers and blessings on in shaky handwriting. Tables are being lined with butcher paper and crayons, ready for the chaos of tiny hands and sugar-high laughter.

Harper spots me from across the room and waves. "You're a literal lifesaver," she says as I hand her the posters for the gratitude wall.

"Anything for my favorite overworked children's ministry volunteer," I tease.

She rolls her eyes but grins, brushing a strand of red hair

from her face. "Seriously though, thank you. I don't know how you've managed to juggle all this and still keep showing up with that sweet, calm energy."

I laugh, shrugging. "Maybe it's the pumpkin spice latte I grabbed on the way here. Feels like liquid patience."

She snorts, then her expression softens. "You doing okay?"

I pause, fingers tracing the edge of the poster tube before I nod. "Yeah. Actually...yeah."

She studies me for a second, like she's trying to read between the lines. "You look...lighter."

"I feel lighter."

And I do. Not all the time. Not every minute. But enough that I notice.

Harper pulls me in for a quick hug. "You know I'm proud of you, right?"

"I know."

We part, and she heads off to prep the kids' area. I linger in the sanctuary, slowly walking the center aisle. A few paper leaves have fluttered down from the gratitude board up front, scattered across the floor like reminders that even blessings can be messy. I glance toward the stage—toward the spot where Gray usually stands with his guitar. My heart clenches, but it doesn't ache the way it used to. It feels more like longing laced with peace.

Tomorrow morning, people will gather here—families, students, grandparents. Some grateful, some heavy, some searching. Pastor Jack will talk about what it means to live thankful, grateful, blessed—not just as a cute slogan, but as a way of seeing God's hand in every season.

And maybe... maybe that will be the moment for me. Not waiting for some dramatic sign, but choosing to believe that even in the quiet, even in the waiting, He's here.

I exhale slowly and whisper, "I'll be ready."

The words echo in the empty sanctuary, and for the first time in a long time, I believe them.

It's almost midnight when I finally get home.

The apartment is quiet, save for the low hum of the heater kicking on. I kick off my boots by the door, shrug out of my coat, and let the silence settle around me.

I move through the space slowly, turning on the little lamp by the couch, lighting the candle I keep near my Bible. The soft glow fills the room, warm and golden, wrapping around me like a familiar hug.

I sit down cross-legged on the rug, Bible in my lap, journal nearby. My phone buzzes.

GRAY

"Do not be anxious about anything, but in every situation, by prayer and petition, with thanksgiving, present your requests to God. And the peace of God, which transcends all understanding, will guard your hearts and your minds in Christ Jesus." Philippians 4:6–7

I smile. He's been quieter lately, but the messages haven't stopped. They never stop. Each one is like a small flame. Never demanding anything from me, just...being there.

I set the phone aside without replying. Not because I don't want to. But because I need this moment to be just mine.

I flip open my journal and write the date, then sit for a long time, pen hovering. The words don't rush out like they usually do. Instead, I find myself writing slowly, thoughtfully.

The service tomorrow is about "Thankful, Grateful, Blessed." Pastor Jack even joked that it sounds like something you'd see on a Hobby Lobby sign, but he said the message would be about more than just a cute slogan. About choosing to see God's hand in every season—even the waiting ones.

So tonight, I'm trying. I pulled out this journal, and instead of overthinking what I'll wear tomorrow or whether Harper will rope me into helping with the kids again, I'm going to write down what I'm thankful for.

November 26th

Thankful—for the way God has carried me through these past weeks. For the mornings that felt heavy but somehow I still got up. For laughter with Harper when I didn't feel like laughing. For Olivia showing up even when she doesn't feel sure about church. For little reminders that I don't have to have it all figured out to be loved.

Grateful—for the Bible that sits on my nightstand now, worn from my fumbling hands, and for devotionals that help me make sense of it piece by piece. For songs that settle into the cracks of my heart

when words don't come. For quiet mornings
with coffee and highlighters, when I feel
closer to God than I ever thought I could.
Blessed—for Gray.

I almost hesitate to write that, because things are complicated. But even with the distance, he's been a steady thread. The simple "how was your day?" texts. The way he still checks in without pressing too hard. The verse he sent last week—Philippians 4:6–7.

Do not be anxious about anything, but in
every situation, by prayer and petition, with
thanksgiving, present your requests to God.

I write that down, reading it over and over. It's like I want to believe it, but my heart still stumbles.

Because the truth is? I'm anxious.

I wonder if he would even want to be with me again. Before, he was ready. More than ready. He talked about a future, about marriage, about leading me in faith and life. And I panicked. I wasn't there yet. I needed space to find Jesus for myself—not through him, not because of him. So I told him I needed a break.

Now, two months later, I wonder what's left of us. Did I hurt him too much? Did I push him too far away? Would he even want to step back into this with me...or has he decided it's safer to guard his heart?

I trace the verse again with my pen: ***Do not be anxious about anything.***

Maybe that's the whole point. To stop gripping so tightly. To stop trying to figure out if he still wants me, and instead ask if God still wants us.

Maybe it's not about rushing into answers, but learning to live in the questions with open hands.

I set the pen down and rest my palms on the page, staring at the words until they blur. My chest aches with longing, but there's something steadier underneath it too— like maybe gratitude and ache can coexist.

I bow my head, whispering into the quiet.

"Lord, You know me. You know Gray. You know the way my heart pulls toward him, even when I try to focus only on You. I don't want to idolize him. I don't want to make him the center when that belongs to You. But I also don't want to lose what we had. So if it's time—if You're saying we're ready—show me. Make it clear. And if not, help me trust Your timing. Help me release the fear that I ruined everything. Help me believe that if You want us together, nothing can undo that."

Slowly, I thumb back through the pages of my journal, tracing the scrawled prayers, the verses that once felt foreign but now feel like lifelines, the messy notes from Sunday messages, the moments I poured my heart onto the paper because I didn't know what else to do.

I pause at the very first page.

Taped to the inside cover is that small, crinkled note Gray left with the flowers months ago. His handwriting stares back at me.

I DARE YOU TO BE MY GIRLFRIEND.

The tears come before I can stop them. Big, quiet sobs

that shake my shoulders as I clutch the journal to my chest. I ache. Ache for him. For his arms around me, for the way his hugs made the world feel safe. I miss him so much it physically hurts, and I don't know how much longer I can go without that comfort.

Chapter 36
Ivy

Sunday morning hums through my apartment, the sound of worship music spilling from my phone speaker and bouncing off the walls. I've got the volume cranked just high enough to drown out my nerves, letting the lyrics anchor me as I move around the room.

The mirror reflects a girl who almost looks put together—a soft cream sweater dress that skims just above my knees, a pair of brown boots, and gold hoop earrings that Harper swore would "class up any outfit." My hair is loose except for one side pinned back, simple but enough to feel intentional. It's not glamorous, not perfect, but it feels like fall.

I smooth my hands over the knit fabric and take a steadying breath. Today is the Thanksgiving service. And I want to be ready—not just on the outside.

Then my eyes fall to the small gold bracelet lying on the dresser. I pick it up, fingers tracing the inscription I know by heart: **1 Corinthians 13:13**.

And now these three remain: faith, hope, and love. But the greatest of these is love.

Gray gave me this when I got my part time job on the church design team—when I was still figuring out who I was, what I believed, where I belonged. He said he loved me that day, but I had loved him long before he said it.

I hesitate, fingers lingering on the clasp. We're not together. Not right now. But this reminder of him, of the way he's always seen me, supported me, loved me without asking for anything in return—it feels like grace.

I fasten the bracelet around my wrist, the metal cool against my skin, and meet my own gaze in the mirror.

God, I really miss him.

The ache is so deep it steals my breath.

And I know I can't go another day without saying it. Without telling him what's been true all along.

I spot Harper's bright red hair before I even make it to the front doors. Olivia's beside her, holding two travel mugs.

"Saved you one," Olivia says as I walk up, handing me a cup with a little smile.

I blink. It hits me all at once—that's the first time I've seen her smile at church. Not her polite, go-through-the-motions kind of smile. A real one, small but genuine.

"Thanks," I say, fingers brushing hers as I take the cup. "You have no idea how much I needed this."

We fall into step together, the hum of conversation around us as people filter through the doors. It feels easy—comfortable in a way it didn't used to. I sip my coffee and let myself enjoy the moment. The warmth. Their laughter. The steady rhythm of footsteps carrying us toward the auditorium where the doors are open wide.

Harper tugs my sleeve, voice hushed. "Um...okay, this place is packed."

She's right. The rows are already full, people squeezing in where they can, coats being shrugged off and draped across laps. A few ushers stand near the back, gently guiding people toward open spaces.

One of them spots us and waves us forward. "There's room near the front."

I blink. "Like...front, front?"

"I'm not sitting that close," Olivia says, her eyes wide with a mix of horror.

Harper shrugs with a grin. "I don't think we have any other option Liv."

We weave down the aisle, the sanctuary buzzing softly with conversation, organ music drifting in the background. I catch glimpses of familiar faces—volunteers I've worked with, friends from around town, older couples dressed in their best.

And then we slip into a row, just three rows from the front.

I glance up at the stage. The worship team is gathering, adjusting microphones, tuning instruments. My breath catches when I spot his guitar resting against a stool.

Gray.

Seeing that guitar so close—knowing he'll be just a few feet away after all these weeks—makes my pulse skip, my hands tremble slightly as I smooth my dress over my knees.

It'll be the closest I've been to him since the day I told him I needed space.

And now?

Now I don't know how I'll make it through this service without my heart giving me away.

"Alright," Pastor Jack says, his voice steady but kind, "let's bring this together. We've talked about what it means to live thankful, grateful, and blessed. Not as a catchy slogan, but as a way of walking with Jesus every day."

He lifts his Bible, flipping back a few pages.

"First—thankful. Scripture says in 1 Thessalonians 5:18, 'Give thanks in all circumstances; for this is God's will for you in Christ Jesus.' Notice it doesn't say give thanks for all circumstances. Some of what you're walking through is hard. Heavy. But God's Word says that in every circumstance, there's still reason to thank Him—because He's with you in it. Thankful isn't about pretending life's perfect. It's about anchoring yourself to the One who never changes."

He pauses, letting the words settle.

"Second—grateful. That's more than polite appreciation. Colossians 3:16 tells us, 'Let the message of Christ dwell among you richly...singing to God with gratitude in your hearts.' Gratitude flows when we realize we don't deserve this grace, and yet God pours it out anyway. Grateful hearts worship. Grateful hearts see the fingerprints of God in ordinary moments—sunrises, laughter, friendships that carry us through. Gratitude shifts our focus from what's missing to what's already been given."

Pastor Jack leans forward slightly, his voice lowering.

"And third—blessed. That word gets tossed around a lot, but Jesus defined it in Matthew 5:3 when He said,

'Blessed are the poor in spirit, for theirs is the kingdom of heaven.' Being blessed isn't about possessions or perfect circumstances. It's about knowing you belong to Him. It's about peace that doesn't make sense, joy that can't be stolen, hope that reaches further than the grave. Blessed means you are held—fully, securely—in the love of God through Christ."

He closes his Bible softly. "So as we go about our week, remember this: thankful looks back and says thank You. Grateful looks around and says I see You here. And blessed looks forward and says I trust You still. That's the life Jesus invites us into. That's the posture that changes everything."

My chest tightens, the words settling heavy and gentle all at once. Thankful. Grateful. Blessed. It sounds so simple, but sitting here, it feels impossible. My past is littered with regrets, my present is full of questions, and my future feels like one big unknown.

I swallow hard, palms damp against my knees. My heart is pounding so loud I'm sure Harper and Olivia can hear it.

"If you're sitting here thinking, I still have questions... but I know it's time to come home, I want to walk you through what that looks like. You don't have to have it all figured out first. Right now, right here, you can take that step. Would you pray this prayer silently, right where you are?"

I bow my head, but it's already happening—my heart cracking wide open. Every word he says sinks deep, like he's speaking directly to the ache I've been carrying.

"Repeat after me. Just pray something like this in your heart: God, I don't understand everything, and I still have questions I can't answer. But I know this—I'm a sinner, and I've lived for other things besides You. And yet, I believe You died for my sins. I believe the cross counted for me because of Your love. I believe You rose from the dead, and You live to give life to anyone who will call on Your name.

My lips move with the words, barely a whisper. My chest feels tight, like the weight of years is pressing down and lifting all at once. I've tried so hard to be enough, to hold myself together, to pretend I didn't need saving. But right now—sitting here in this crowded room—it feels like every wall I've built is crumbling.

"I don't understand it all yet, but as best as I know how, I choose to live for You first. Today I receive the free gift of forgiveness—not because of anything I've done, but because of what You've done for me. No matter how long I've walked away or how far I've rebelled, thank You that Your grace is still enough. Thank You for adopting me as Your son or daughter, for making me Yours."

Tears slip down my cheeks as a strange peace settles over me. Steady. Like I'm finally standing still after a lifetime of chasing everything else.

"Now, with heads bowed and eyes closed...if you prayed that prayer today, if you're crossing the line of faith and choosing Jesus—here in a moment, I'm going to count to three. And when I do, I want you to raise your hand. Because something happens in us when we respond outwardly to what God is doing inwardly. It's an act of bold faith."

He pauses, voice steady but urgent.

"One—God loves you more than you can imagine. Two—you're not here by accident; He brought you here for a reason. Three—lift your hand. Right now. Don't wait. Say with your whole life, I'm coming home. God, I need You. I receive Your forgiveness."

A ripple of movement passes through the room. Jack's voice softens, filled with awe. "Yes...hands going up. Keep them raised, high and steady. What a picture of grace—people all over this room saying yes to Jesus."

I don't even think.

I lift my hand.

It shakes, but it's high. Bold. Like my soul is reaching toward heaven.

And in the stillness of that moment, I open my eyes—mostly to wipe the tears blurring my vision.

That's when I see him looking down at me.

Gray.

He's on stage, near the side, his head lifts just enough for our eyes to meet.

His gaze hits me like a wave.

And he sees it.

He sees me.

My hand, still raised. My tears. My yes to Jesus.

And his face—oh, his face. I swear I see it—one tear, sliding slow down his cheek. He doesn't wipe it away.

He just...watches me. Like the world stopped spinning and all he can do is stare.

My breath catches. My hand lowers, but it doesn't matter. Because that moment—it's etched into me.

He's not proud of me because I chose him.

He's proud because I chose Jesus.

And I've never felt more seen. More loved. More free.

Pastor Jack ends the sermon and the music begins as people around me stand to worship.

All I can feel is the warmth spreading through my chest and the truth settling deep in my bones.

This is the beginning.

And it's real.

The final song ends and the sanctuary erupts into hushed chatter and the shuffle of feet. People are hugging, laughing, wiping tears. But I can't move.

My chest is tight, like my heart is too full to contain it all. I just gave my life to Jesus.

And all I want, all I need—is to see him.

Gray.

It hits me like a tidal wave. The pull. The ache. The urgency in my chest that screams go to him. I don't know if it's the Spirit, adrenaline, or just everything inside of me that's ever loved him rising up at once, but I can't stay still.

"Ivy?" Harper touches my arm gently. "What's wrong?"

"Ivy, what are you doing?" Olivia asks, her brows pinched as I start weaving through the row of people.

"I...I have to find him," I breathe, already turning toward the side of the stage.

I ignore their voices as they call after me, the heel of my boots clicking too loud against the tile as I push through the side hallway. The backstage door is cracked, and I slip through it, the hum of post-service chatter echoing through the walls.

There they are—members of the worship team, still gathered, still glowing from the service. But no Gray.

Panic rises in my throat.

"Hey," I call breathlessly, scanning their faces. "Have you seen Gray?"

One guy—Luke, I think his name is—blinks at me, startled. "He left quick. Right after the song. Didn't even stay for the last prayer."

My heart sinks. "Do you know where he went?"

Luke just shrugs, and I don't wait for more.

I turn on my heel and sprint back toward the sanctuary, pushing through the side door into a blur of bodies. The crowd has thickened—families hugging, kids darting around legs, people moving in every direction.

I spin in a circle, breath catching in my throat.

Where is he?

And then I see him.

Across the room. Moving fast. Eyes scanning. Chest rising and falling like he just ran a mile.

Searching.

For me.

"Gray!" I call, voice trembling.

His head snaps toward me.

And everything else disappears.

He doesn't hesitate. Doesn't stop. He runs.

So do I.

I weave past a woman with a stroller, duck around a couple taking a photo, barely miss knocking a kid to the ground.

And then...

We collide in the middle of it all.

His arms wrap around me before I can say a word, pulling me into his chest like he's afraid I'll disappear if he lets go.

I clutch his shoulders, burying my face against his neck, and I don't care who sees or what they think. The tears come all over again—laughter and relief tangled together.

"I saw you," he whispers, voice rough against my ear. "I saw your hand. Ivy..."

"I couldn't wait," I whisper back. "I had to find you."

His hands frame my face, his forehead resting against mine, both of us breathless in the middle of the chaos.

"You found so much more than me tonight," he says softly.

I nod, the smile breaking through the tears. "I know. But I still needed you too."

We hold each other there, steady in the swirl around us.

And for the first time in my life, I don't feel like I'm running to catch up or running to prove I belong.

I'm just home.

Chapter 37
Gray

The drive was mostly quiet.

Ivy held my hand the whole way, her fingers laced through mine like they belonged there. Like we'd made it through something only God could've carried us through.

Now we're here. The overlook.

I've brought her here a few times before, but tonight is different. Everything's changed and the stars are truly brighter, the view deeper, and somehow, so is my heart.

The truck bed creaks as we settle into the blanket I keep in the back seat, a second one draped over our laps. Cold air nips at our cheeks, but I hardly notice. Ivy leans against me, quiet. Still.

And I don't want to be the one to break the silence, but my chest is so full I don't know if I can keep it in much longer.

She beats me to it.

"It's beautiful up here," she says softly, voice like a prayer in the quiet.

I glance down at her, the faint golden light from the

buzz of downtown Dallas reflecting in her eyes. "Not half as beautiful as what I saw tonight."

She blushes, but doesn't look away.

"Ivy...when I saw you..." My voice breaks. I clear my throat and try again. "When I saw your hand raised, I thought my heart might stop."

"I didn't mean to look up," she says, her smile small, almost shy. "I was crying and needed a tissue, and when I did...there you were."

"And there you were," I echo, my hand brushing hers. "Choosing Jesus."

She nods slowly. "I meant it. Every word of that prayer. Every tear. I meant it all."

I don't realize how tightly I've been gripping the edge of the blanket until I feel my knuckles ache. I release it and reach for her hand instead.

"I've never stopped praying for you," I whisper. "Even when you asked for space. Even when it broke me not to reach out more than I did."

Her eyes lift to mine, glassy but steady. "I know. I felt it. In the silence. In the stillness. Somehow...I still felt you."

I swallow the lump in my throat. "I didn't know how to stop loving you. And I didn't want to."

"You didn't," she says quietly. "You just loved me from a distance. And it gave me the room to finally see God for who He is—not just through your eyes, but through mine."

We fall quiet again, the sounds of the wind rustling in the trees around us.

"I've never wanted to get this part wrong," I admit. "Not with you."

Ivy leans her head on my shoulder. "So let's get it right. Together."

The stars above us are scattered like promises—some already fulfilled, others waiting to be.

Ivy shifts beside me, her voice soft but sure. "Can I ask you something?"

"Always."

She pulls the blanket a little tighter around us. "Were you really thinking about marriage? Before I asked for space?"

I pause. Not because I don't know the answer—but because the truth is heavier than I expected.

"Yeah," I say finally. "I was."

Her breath catches, and I glance at her. She's not pulling away. If anything, she's leaning in.

"I was praying about it. A lot."

She bites her lip, then looks down. "Can I tell you something?"

"Of course."

"I was scared. Not just of faith. But of you."

That stings, but I wait.

"Because you were everything I never believed I deserved. And part of me thought...if I let myself really love you, I'd ruin it."

"You could never ruin it," I say. "But I get it. I do. I've ruined things before by trying too hard to hold on. But this, what we have now, it's not something we're holding up on our own."

She nods, quiet again for a moment before speaking. "I don't want to rush anything. But I also don't want to live like I'm scared of love anymore."

A smile tugs at the corners of my mouth. "That sounds like faith to me."

"I want our foundation to be solid," she continues. "Built on Him. Not just feelings."

"Then let's build it together," I say. "Slow. Intentional. Faith-first. No pressure. Just...pursuit."

She leans into me, head resting on my chest. "Okay."

For a moment, we just sit like that, the night quiet around us, the city lights flickering below like scattered stars.

Then I shift slightly, pulling out my phone and opening my Notes app.

"What are you doing?" she asks, tilting her head to look up at me.

I smile, thumbing in a new title.

"I want to write it down," I say quietly. "So we remember. So we can come back to it when things get hard. This is our start."

And I begin to type, reading it aloud as I go.

Gray + Ivy Pursuing Jesus & Each Other:

- **Jesus first, always.**
- **We pray together before big decisions.**
- **No being alone behind closed doors.**
- **We protect physical boundaries — save sex for marriage.**
- **We pursue emotional intimacy more than physical.**
- **We go to church together and serve where we're called.**
- **We speak truth in love, even when it's hard.**
- **We encourage each other's personal walk with God.**

- **We take dating seriously — we're pursuing marriage, not just "seeing where it goes."**
- **We give each other grace when we mess up.**
- **We celebrate small wins and answered prayers.**
- **We check in regularly about boundaries and how we're doing.**
- **We ask for accountability when we need it.**
- **We choose intentional time together.**
- **We remember: Faith. Hope. Love. The greatest is love.**
- **Seek Godly counsel when needed**

I glance over at her, the screen glowing softly between us. "Anything you want to add?"

She blinks fast, a tear slipping down her cheek, and shakes her head, smiling. "No. I'd say that's everything."

Ivy's quiet voice breaks the stillness. "Gray...can I ask you one more question?"

I glance over at her, smiling. "You can ask me a million questions. We've got forever together, remember?"

She hesitates, like she's gathering courage. "The next step after giving your life to Jesus is to tell the world...with baptism, right?"

"Yes ma'am," I say, my heart already thudding, somehow sensing where this is going.

She lifts her gaze, eyes shining. "Gray...will you baptize me?"

For a second, I can't move. The weight of her words hits

me square in the chest, and I feel it—that overwhelming mix of joy, gratitude, and awe.

I stand, pacing a few steps along the gravel, the city lights below blurring as I blink back the burn in my eyes. I rake a hand through my hair, trying to catch my breath, my heart pounding like I just ran a mile.

Then I stop.

And I drop to my knees in front of her, right there by the tailgate.

Her brows knit together, concerned. "Gray?"

But I'm smiling—wide, wrecked, overwhelmed in the best way.

"Ivy," I say, voice thick with emotion. "You just asked me the greatest honor of my life. Do you know what it does to me...that you trust me with this? That I get to stand with you as you declare your faith, your future, your forever with Him? I'd move mountains for you. Baptizing you? That's the easiest yes of my life."

Her eyes fill, and I take her hands in mine, kissing her knuckles gently.

"And for the record..." I add, my grin turning crooked, trying to lighten the tears shining in both our eyes, "you're about to make me ugly cry in front of the entire city of Dallas. So thanks for that."

She laughs, the sound breaking through the emotion like sunshine.

And in that moment, I know: I am going to be getting on one knee sooner than later.

The cab of the truck is warm as we sit in the parking lot outside Ivy's apartment. It's approaching midnight, but neither of us are tired. How could we possibly sleep after what just took place?

"So...what's Thursday look like for you?" I ask, keeping the conversation flowing.

She shrugs, pulling her hair over one shoulder. "My family does Thanksgiving lunch. It's chaotic and loud and someone always ends up crying over a burnt casserole, but it's tradition."

I chuckle. "Sounds cozy."

"What about you?" she asks, twisting in her seat to face me. "What do you usually do for Thanksgiving?"

I hesitate. "Micah usually invites me to his family's thing. It's always open-door. But I told him I might just stay home this year."

Her brows knit. "Stay home?"

I nod. "Yeah. I don't know. I wasn't really in the mood for...conversations. Figured I'd finally finish that song I've been writing for months."

She stares at me, then shakes her head. "Absolutely not."

I blink. "What?"

"There is no way I'm letting you spend Thanksgiving alone," she says, a mix of sass and warmth in her voice. "Come with me. Seriously. Meet the chaos. The casserole. All of it. It's about time anyway."

My heart stutters. "You're serious?"

She bites her lip, then grins. "I am. I want you there."

It hits me harder than I expect—that small invitation, that open door. Not because of the holiday, but because she's choosing me again. Not just as a boyfriend, but as someone she wants in her world.

"I'd be honored," I say softly.

She smiles, then looks down at her lap, fidgeting with the hem of her sleeve.

"Ivy?" I say, my voice low.

She lifts her gaze.

I lean closer, my voice teasing but wrapped in something deeper. "Can I kiss you?"

Her breath catches, eyes flicking to my mouth and back again.

"Because I'm not too sure how much longer I can last without it."

Her laugh bubbles out, half joy, half disbelief, like she can't believe we're finally here. "I dare you."

That's all I need.

I close the distance, my lips finding hers in a kiss that feels like exhaling after holding my breath for weeks. It's soft at first, like I'm trying to memorize the feel of her all over again. The truth of her. The miracle that she's here.

But then she leans in. Her hands slide up my jaw, fingertips tracing the stubble there, and everything inside me unravels. The world around us blurs—the quiet night, the distant hum of traffic, the stars scattered above—until there's only this. Only her. Only us.

The kiss deepens, not rushed, but certain. Like coming home. Like finding something I thought I'd lost for good. I can feel her heart racing against mine, her breath mingling with mine, the steady rhythm of two people who've waited, ached, for this exact moment.

When we finally break apart, we're both breathless, foreheads still pressed together, laughter spilling between us like we can't contain it. Her smile is radiant, cheeks flushed, eyes shining in the dim light.

I brush a thumb across her cheek, still not quite believing. "Worth the wait," I whisper.

Her lips curve, soft and sure. "It sure was."

It's just past midnight when I step into my apartment, the door clicking softly behind me as I toe off my shoes and shrug out of my jacket.

I pull my phone from my pocket and type the words without hesitation.

GRAY

Made it home. I love you Ivy.

I stare at the message for a second longer, then hit send.

The silence wraps around me like a blanket as I move through the familiar motions—turning off lights, brushing my teeth, grabbing a clean T-shirt. My body's tired, but my heart...it's wide awake. Thrumming.

A low yowl cuts through the quiet.

Goliath hops onto the bed like he owns the place, tail flicking as if to scold me for staying out so late.

"Yeah, yeah," I mutter, tossing my jeans into the hamper. "I know it's past your bedtime."

He blinks at me, slow and unimpressed.

I sink down onto the mattress, scratching behind his ears until he purrs. "You'll never believe it, buddy," I say, grinning like a fool. "She kissed me. Well, I kissed her. But still. It happened. After two months of wondering if I'd ever get that chance again—she's mine. We're back."

Goliath stretches out, rolling onto his side like he

370

couldn't care less, and I laugh. "Don't give me that look. You're the only one who's heard me talk to the ceiling every night. You know."

The cat yawns, tucks his paws beneath him, and settles.

I lean back against the headboard, my chest still buzzing, my heart still racing. "She's worth it, Goliath. Every prayer, every mile of distance, every second of waiting. She's worth all of it."

Goliath purrs louder, like maybe he agrees—or maybe he just wants breakfast early. Either way, I can't stop smiling.

Eight weeks.

Eight weeks of ache. Of trying to be strong. Of letting go when everything in me wanted to hold on tighter. I've never fought so hard not to fight for something. But now, standing here in the stillness of my apartment, I finally understand what Jack meant. *Patience over pressure. Stillness over striving.*

It was worth every quiet night. Every unanswered prayer. Every lonely drive home after church.

Because tonight, she ran to me. She chose me—fully, freely, faithfully.

And more than that...she chose Jesus.

A laugh slips out, quiet and awestruck. I run a hand over my face and shake my head. "Thank You," I whisper into the dark. "I didn't deserve any of this. But thank You."

I slip into bed, tugging the blanket over my chest, the weight of the day finally settling around me like peace. It feels different this year, like maybe this is what Thanksgiving is really about. Thankful for the waiting. Grateful for the second chance. Blessed by the God who makes all things new.

Thursday, I'll meet her family.

Thursday, I'll walk into her world—not as the guy she's dating, but as the man who waited.

And if the moment's right...

I might just ask her dad for his blessing.

Chapter 38
Gray

The morning air is cold enough to bite, but I don't care. My palms are warm, fingers wrapped around the to-go cup from our favorite coffee shop, Royal Brew—vanilla oat milk latte. Her favorite. One of two I bought her. Because she drinks the first like it's air and always wishes she had another halfway through.

I climb the steps to her apartment, heart pounding like I'm picking her up for our first date all over again. It's ridiculous, but it's also kind of perfect. I shift the coffee to one hand and ring the doorbell.

The door opens seconds later, and there she is—glowing, and wrapped in a soft maroon sweater dress that makes my thoughts spiral in seventeen different directions.

Her smile is a little shy, like she still can't believe this is real.

"Happy Thanksgiving," I say, lifting the coffee. "For you."

She grins, reaching for it. "You're the actual best. Thank you."

"Just wait."

She tilts her head. "Wait for what?"

"You'll see." I wink, stepping back so she can grab her bag and lock the door behind her. When we get to the car, I open the passenger side and gesture inside.

She gasps, spotting the bouquet resting on the seat — deep fall oranges and creamy whites, wrapped in brown paper and tied with gold twine.

"Gray..." she breathes, touched. "I missed your flowers..."

"Oh, those aren't for you," I say, deadpan.

She blinks, confused.

"They're for your mom." I glance at her with a mischievous smirk. "You already like me. She's the one I need to win over."

She bursts out laughing, swatting my arm. "You're ridiculous."

"And charming," I add.

She lifts the bouquet to her chest, sighing with a smile. "Fine. I'll allow it."

I round the truck and slide into my seat. Before I even buckle, I reach down in the back seat and hand her the drink carrier. Inside: a second coffee, an empty to-go cup holding a mini bouquet of matching flowers, and a brown paper bag with a chocolate croissant.

Her eyes widen. "What's all this?"

"Coffee for later. I know you—you'll finish that first one before we hit the freeway and wish you had another. Problem solved." I grin. "And flowers, because of course I'm going to get you flowers, Ivy. And your favorite breakfast from your favorite coffee shop."

Her eyes fill, shining with emotion. "How are you so good at this?"

I start the engine and glance her way. "I love you. That's how."

She takes a sip, then reaches over to lace her fingers with mine.

And with her hand in mine and a heart full of anticipation, I pull away from the curb—ready for whatever this day brings.

An hour and twenty eight minutes. That's how long the GPS says it'll take to get to Ashen Mills, where her parents' live. But I wouldn't mind if it took four hours.

Ivy's legs are curled under her, coffee in hand, humming to the playlist she queued up on my phone. It's a chaotic mix of country and early 2,000's and somehow every song feels like it's underscoring the movie that is today.

"Okay," she says after a few minutes of quiet, tapping the lid of her cup. "Top three songs of all time. No skipping, no overthinking. Go."

"Easy," I say. "Oceans by Hillsong. Starting Over by Chris Stapleton. And..." I shoot her a look, grinning, "The Middle by Jimmy Eat World. Don't judge me."

Her eyebrows shoot up, and then she laughs. "Wow. That's actually...respectable. Worship song, soulful country, and peak 2000s emo? You're a mystery, Gray."

I shake my head, chuckling as I merge onto the highway. "You say that like you don't scream-sing 'The Middle' every time it comes on."

"I do not..."

"You absolutely do."

"Okay, fine," she admits. "But only because it still hits."

We've been driving for about an hour, and it's been pure magic. Ivy's sipping her second coffee—because of course she downed the first one before we even hit the highway—and singing along to some acoustic cover of an old country song like it's her personal concert. My fingers are wrapped around the steering wheel, but my heart's wrapped around her.

Every time I glance over, I'm a little more undone.

And then—I can't take it anymore.

Without a word, I ease off the highway and pull into a random parking lot.

Ivy looks at me, eyebrows knit. "Everything okay?"

I don't answer. I just put the truck in park and open my door.

"Gray?" she calls, confused.

I round the front of the truck, heart thudding. She watches me with wide eyes as I open her door.

"Gray, what..."

But I don't let her finish.

I lean in and kiss her.

Not a quick peck. Not a hesitant maybe.

A full, breath-stealing, heart-stopping kiss.

Her hand fumbles with the coffee cup before tossing it into the holder, reaching up instead to tangle in my jacket. She kisses me back like she's been waiting for this since the second she got in the car.

And maybe she has.

When I finally pull back, I tuck a piece of her hair behind her ear.

Then I grin.

"Sorry, just felt like kissing you." I say, stepping back and shutting her door like it's the most casual thing in the world.

I hear her laugh through the window as I jog back to my side.

And as I pull back onto the road, her hand finds mine again—like it always belonged there.

By the time we pull up to Ivy's childhood home in Ashen Mills, a small suburb in North Texas, the late morning sun is shining bright, casting a soft golden hue over the neighborhood.

The driveway is packed. I squeeze the truck into a tight spot behind a red minivan and glance over at Ivy. She's beaming already, eyes lit with the kind of joy that only comes from being home.

The sound of laughter and music leaks through the front door like a warm invitation.

"You ready?" she asks, smoothing down her dress.

"Nope," I say, grabbing the bouquet from the backseat, "but I'm still walking in there with you."

She glances at me, biting back a grin. "You know, I told my dad you had a tattoo. Not that you were covered in them."

I smirk, leaning closer as I hand her the flowers. "Great.

So when he starts polishing his shotgun, I'll just flex and tell him it's art appreciation."

Her laugh bubbles out, and the tension melts just a little.

She adjusts the gold bracelet on her wrist as we walk up the short path to the door. "You know I'm kinda bummed the big bouquet isn't for me." she teases, nodding toward the flowers.

"Absolutely not. These are for your mom. You already got your two coffees, a mini version, a croissant and the playlist of songs on the drive here. Don't get greedy."

She elbows me as I grin and reach for the door.

It swings open almost immediately, and we're hit with a wave of warmth—both from the heater and from the sheer volume of Ivy's family packed into every inch of the entryway.

"Aunt Icy!" A little girl calls, and I give her a sideways glance, making a mental note to ask her about that name later. Then it's just noise. Shouts, hugs, laughter, kids weaving through legs, the smell of cinnamon rolls and turkey and whatever holiday magic is bubbling in the kitchen.

Ivy's nieces and nephews tackle her before I even make it across the threshold, their squeals filling the entryway. She's laughing, arms full of kids, and I can't help but grin as I step inside with the flowers tucked under my arm.

Her mom is there in a heartbeat, eyes soft as they land on me. "Gray," she says warmly, pulling me straight into a hug before I can even hand her the bouquet.

I chuckle, holding out the flowers once she lets go. "These are for you. Figured they might last longer than another pie."

Her face lights up as she takes them, inhaling the scent.

"They're beautiful. Ivy told me you bring her flowers all the time."

Heat creeps up my neck, and I scratch the back of my head. "She might exaggerate a little."

"Mm, I don't think she does." Her mom's smile widens, a knowing kind of smile.

Before I can answer, Ivy's dad steps forward. He's taller than I expected, shoulders broad, his expression unreadable as his gaze flicks briefly to my tattoos. For a second, my stomach knots, but then his mouth breaks into a grin. He clasps my hand in a firm shake before tugging me into a quick hug.

"It's good to finally meet you," he says, voice warm but carrying the kind of weight that makes me want to stand a little straighter.

"You too, sir," I manage, grateful for the approval tucked in his tone.

The whirlwind continues as Ivy gets pulled deeper into the house, swallowed up by laughter and chatter. I follow, my pulse still quick from the introductions, and nearly collide with a woman holding the hand of a little girl.

"Oops—sorry," I say quickly.

The woman smiles, tilting her head. Her resemblance to Ivy is unmistakable. "You must be Gray. I'm Sarah—her sister." She shifts, gesturing to the little girl peeking shyly from behind her leg. "And this is Kate."

Kate's big eyes study me like she's not sure what to make of me. I crouch a little, offering a smile. "Hi, Kate. I like your bow."

Her fingers tighten around Sarah's hand, but a tiny grin tugs at her mouth.

Sarah's eyes soften. "She's not usually this shy. Guess you made an impression already."

I laugh under my breath, straightening. "Hopefully a good one."

Her smile is knowing, it makes me wonder how much Ivy's already told her. "Yeah," she says. "A good one."

And just like that, I'm folded into the chaos of Ivy's family, my heart pounding in the best possible way.

It's chaos. Absolute, beautiful chaos—voices overlapping, the smell of something sweet baking, kids darting between legs, someone shouting for more ice.

I never had a Thanksgiving like this growing up. Sure, I've experienced real holidays with Micah's family, with their kindness and traditions that made me feel welcome.

But this?

This feels different.

It feels like home.

By the time I meet everyone and we all gather in the dining room, it's a sea of folding chairs, mismatched plates, and homemade name tags scrawled in crayon. Ivy squeezes in next to me, her shoulder pressed to mine as the food makes its way to the table.

I rise slowly from my seat, Ivy's eyes flicking up to mine with a questioning smile. "Before we dig in," I say, voice steady, "if it's okay, I'd be honored to lead us in prayer."

Everyone quiets, eyes on me. I glance at Ivy—she nods, steady and encouraging.

I stand slowly and clear my throat. "Lord," I begin, voice low but firm, "thank You for this day. For this family. For joy that spills over, and for love that fills every corner of this house."

I pause, heart tightening. "Thank You for the grace that meets us where we are, for the peace You offer even in the unknown. And thank You...for Ivy, and her wonderful family."

I glance at her again, and she's already looking at me with a softness I'll never get over.

"In Jesus's name, amen."

"Amen!" echoes around the table, followed by applause, laughter, and a chorus of "Let's eat!"

And as the plates are passed, kids yell for rolls, and conversations bloom around the table, I take a moment to look around.

This isn't just Ivy's world.

It's a world I want to be part of.

The noise of the house fades into the background as I step onto the back porch, the screen door creaking behind me. The late afternoon sun hangs low, spilling gold across the yard, and the air has that November bite—just chilly enough to make me wish I'd grabbed a hoodie.

I press a hand to my stomach with a laugh. I'm so full I'm not sure I'll ever eat again. Inside, the clatter of cards hitting the kitchen table carries through the open window—everyone diving into a game, laughter and voices overlapping in a rhythm I'm still learning to keep up with.

I needed a breather. Not in a bad way—just long enough to catch up on all the love.

Because the truth is, I've never had this much. Never had a table packed shoulder-to-shoulder, never had cousins fighting over dessert, never had a family so loud and alive it spills into every corner. And standing here, watching the sky fade toward evening, it hits me how much I've yearned for this. Not just the noise, but the belonging.

I exhale slowly, letting the crisp air fill my lungs, my heart aching in the best possible way.

The door creaks again. Ivy's dad steps out, two mugs in hand.

"Figured you could use a drink," he says, offering me one. "It's decaf. Don't worry, I'm not trying to sabotage your sleep."

I laugh, accepting the cup. "Thanks, sir."

He chuckles, joining me at the railing. "You can call me David, you know. Or whatever feels right."

"David," I repeat, nodding. "Thank you—for having me today. This...all of this...means more than I can say."

He watches me for a second, like he's seeing past the words. "Ivy called us the day she met you."

That catches me off guard. "She did?"

He smiles, eyes softening. "Said she met someone different. Someone kind. She didn't give a lot of details but I could tell something shifted in her. She sounded...hopeful."

A lump catches in my throat. I stare down into my mug, blinking hard. "I didn't know she told you that."

"She's told us a lot about you, son," he says gently. "Before the break. During it."

That undoing feeling returns—chest tight, vision blurry. I grip the railing a little harder. "I've never had a family like this," I admit, my voice low and rough. "I never knew my dad. My mom...she tried, but she was battling demons of her own. It's always just kind of been me."

David nods slowly. "That's a heavy load to carry."

I nod. "And I know we haven't known each other long, but...just being here today, seeing this—what family can look like—something in me..." I pause, trying to get the words right. "One day, I want to build something like this.

And when the time's right, when God makes it clear...I hope it's with Ivy."

He studies me for a moment, not speaking right away. Then he sets his mug down and extends his hand. "You've got my blessing, Gray. Not because of what you've said, but because of the way you've waited. The way you've honored her. That tells me more than any speech ever could."

My breath catches as I shake his hand, both of us gripping tight.

"I'm not asking yet, but soon." I say, managing a shaky smile. "Not rushing anything. I just...wanted you to know my heart."

He nods, but then his expression softens even more, eyes glistening in the low light of the porch. "And now I do. But I want you to know something too."

I blink, caught off guard by the tenderness in his voice.

He clears his throat, glancing back toward the house where laughter drifts through the window. "After Ivy told us about what God was doing in her life—about how you pointed her to Him, her mom and I started going to the local church. At first, just out of curiosity. But...it changed us, Gray. It changed me. Our marriage, my heart—all of it's different now. Because you came into her life."

The weight of his words hits me like a wave. My throat tightens, emotion burning behind my eyes.

"I didn't do that," I finally manage, voice low, a little unsteady. "God did. I'm just...grateful He let me be part of it."

He smiles, gripping my shoulder. "Well, I'm grateful too. More than you know."

I nod, feeling the gravity of it all, the blessing, the impact, the promise I've made without even needing to say the words.

We stand there in quiet for a beat—two men from different worlds, joined by love for the same girl and the God who brought her home.

The door creaks open behind us, and Ivy steps onto the porch, arms wrapped around herself for warmth. Her eyes land on the two of us and she tilts her head, curious. "What are you two talking about?"

David glances at me, then back at her with a soft smile. "Just talking about how lucky Gray is," he says, giving her a wink.

Ivy blushes, stepping closer as her dad pats me on the shoulder. "You're a good man, Gray. We're glad you're here."

"Thank you, sir," I say, the words feeling heavier than they sound.

He slips back inside, leaving the door slightly ajar, and Ivy moves to lean beside me at the railing. The moment stretches, soft and full.

"I feel bad," she says softly. "Dragging you into my loud, chaotic family like this."

I turn to her, shaking my head. "Ivy... I've never wanted anything more. This chaos? This love? It's the best thing that's ever happened to me."

Her breath catches before she leans in, her forehead pressing to mine. "You really mean that?"

"Every word." I kiss her slow, savoring it, and when she pulls back she's smiling through the shimmer in her eyes.

"Best. Chaos. Ever."

I lean in, brushing my nose against hers. "I love you Ivy."

And right there, in Ashen Mills, outside of a house full of love, it feels like everything that's ever hurt in both of us is finally starting to heal.

Chapter 39
Ivy

We walk side by side through downtown Dallas, the city lights soft yet bright, the air cool but not cold—that perfect December evening in Texas where you don't need a jacket but you're glad for the excuse to stay close.

Dinner had been easy, so easy and filled with laughter and stolen glances that made my heart race even after all this time.

We'd tucked into a cozy booth at one of Gray's favorite little spots downtown.

He listened, hanging on every word as I told him how I'd finally done it—how I'd set my baptism date for just after the New Year.

"I wanted to wait until the Christmas rush was over," I'd explained, fingers tracing the rim of my glass, "so I can really take it in. So I can remember it."

Gray's eyes had softened, his hand reaching across the table to lace his fingers with mine.

"You're going to remember it, Ivy," he'd said, voice low, full of that quiet confidence I've come to love. "Because it's not just a date. It's yours. Your moment with Him."

And just like that, any lingering nerves melted away.

The rest of dinner passed in a haze of soft teasing, shared bites of dessert, and quiet looks that said more than either of us dared.

By the time we stepped out into the crisp night air, my heart felt full.

As we turn the corner, I pause in front of a shop window—the glow of neon letters spelling out: **TATTOOS & PIERCINGS** catches my eye.

I linger at the window, studying the designs, fascinated.

Gray stops with me, his hand resting lightly on my back. I glance up at him, noticing again the way his tattoos peek from beneath his shirt collar, curling up the side of his neck.

"Can you just...walk in and get a tattoo?" I ask, curiosity getting the better of me.

He laughs, that low, easy sound that always makes me smile. "Well, yeah. If they've got an open spot. If not, you make an appointment. Why?" He grins down at me, eyes dancing. "Thinking about getting one?"

I lift my chin, playful but serious. "Yeah, actually. I am."

His face lights up like a kid on Christmas morning. "Ohhh, you are speaking my love language now."

Before I can backpedal or overthink it, he grabs my hand and pulls me gently toward the door.

"Gray!" I protest, laughing, but I let him lead me inside.

The shop smells faintly of antiseptic and ink, the walls lined with bold designs, the buzz of a machine steady in the background.

Gray doesn't hesitate. He lifts our joined hands and announces—loud enough for the entire room to hear, "We're here to get our first tattoo!"

Every head turns. A guy behind the counter raises a brow.

Gray flashes that mischievous grin of his, squeezing my hand. "Well, not me obviously. This little one here."

My cheeks go up in flames. "Gray!"

He just laughs, so proud, so utterly unbothered. "What? Gotta mark the moment, babe."

I shake my head, trying to look exasperated, but I can't stop smiling.

The hum of the tattoo shop feels louder now that I'm actually in the chair. Gray leans against the wall nearby, arms crossed, watching me with that look of his—the one that's equal parts amused and head-over-heels.

Across from me, the artist, a girl about our age with lavender streaks in her hair and a half-sleeve of delicate line work, flips through sketches as we talk.

"So you're thinking something faith-related?" she asks, kind and patient, no pressure in her tone.

I nod, chewing my lip. "Yeah. At first, I thought maybe a small cross on my wrist. Or a word, like grace or redeemed."

I glance down at my arm, imagining it, but somehow, none of it feels right.

She tilts her head, offering a soft smile. "Maybe you should think about it a little longer. You want to love what you get on your skin permanently."

I pause. The noise of the shop fades.

Then I know.

I swivel in the chair, eyes locking on Gray. "Do you have a pen and paper?"

He blinks, confused, as the artist hands me a notepad and pen.

I shove it toward him. "Here. Write the word love."

He furrows his brow. "What?"

"Just...write it," I insist, heart pounding.

A beat passes, and then I see it click. That big, lopsided grin takes over his face, the one that makes my knees weak.

Without a word, he doodles the word love on the paper —his messy, familiar scrawl.

LOVE

When he hands it back, I take the pen and add my own version beneath his, small and careful.

Love

"You're getting both?" he asks, half-joking.

"Nope," I say, eyes shining. "You are too."

His grin grows. "Now that's a forever kind of dare."

The artist smiles at us, genuine and warm. "I love this," she says, taking the paper. "I'll be right back."

And as she disappears toward the back, Gray catches my hand, squeezing it gently.

"You sure about this?" he asks, voice low, sincere.

I nod, heart full. "Absolutely."

He smirks, that playful spark lighting up his eyes. "Well, that's it then. We'll be branded with each other for the rest of our lives. Can't think of anything more official than that."

I laugh, shaking my head as my cheeks flush. "Is this your version of a proposal?"

He leans in just enough to make my heart race. "Nah. When I propose, you'll know. But this? This is pretty close."

When the artist returns with the stencils, I look between her and Gray, heart thudding.

"You go first," I say, trying to sound casual, but my voice is a little too high-pitched to pull it off.

Gray grins, eyes gleaming. "Ohhh, I see how it is. Let me be the guinea pig, huh?"

I smirk, crossing my arms. "Exactly."

He slides into the chair without hesitation, shooting me a wink as the artist preps his arm.

"This one's gonna hurt the most, right?" he teases the artist with a straight face.

She snorts. "Sure, tough guy. It's tiny script. You'll survive."

But the second the needle starts buzzing and touches his skin, Gray lets out an exaggerated hiss.

"Ahhh—nope! Yep, this is it. Worst one I've ever gotten. Easily."

My eyes go wide. "Gray!"

He scrunches his face, groaning dramatically, peeking at me from the corner of his eye. "Bury me with my guitar."

"Stop!" I laugh, covering my face as my cheeks burn. "You're so mean!"

The artist pauses, shaking her head with a smile. "Don't listen to him. He's fine."

Gray relaxes, grinning like he just won a prize. "Kidding, babe. Barely feel a thing. But your face? Totally worth it."

I stick my tongue out at him, heart racing, torn between exasperation and total adoration.

And as I watch him all relaxed and confident, letting this silly, spontaneous forever mark be part of us—I know I wouldn't want to do this with anyone else.

When the artist finishes with Gray, he hops out of the chair, flexing his arm like he just conquered something heroic. "Didn't even hurt," he says with a wink, all swagger.

But as I slide into the chair, my pulse picks up now that it's my turn.

Gray moves close, crouching down so we're eye level, his hand finding mine.

"Hey you," he says softly, his gaze locking onto mine. "Eyes on me, okay? Just me."

I nod, my breath shallow.

"You've got this, Ivy. Just breathe." His thumb traces slow, steady circles over my skin. "In...and out. That's it."

The artist positions my wrist, and I feel the cool swipe of antiseptic. My heart pounds, but I can't look away from Gray.

His eyes hold me there—full of nothing but love.

"You're brave," he murmurs, so quiet only I can hear. "You're doing amazing."

The needle hums to life. I flinch as it touches my skin, but Gray tightens his grip gently, his other hand brushing a loose strand of hair from my face.

"You're doing so good," he whispers, the words wrapping around me like armor. "Almost done, sweetheart."

Every second feels like forever and no time at all. And then—the needle lifts. The artist leans back, wiping my skin gently.

Before I can even process it, Gray's hand slides to my wrist, his lips pressing a soft kiss right above the fresh ink.

His eyes find mine again, his voice thick with emotion. "Forever now, Ivy."

And in that moment—his touch, his words, his heart so wide open—I know I'll never forget this.

Christmas already feels like a blur—our first one together. We drove back to Ashen Mills, spent the weekend wrapped in family chaos and casseroles. Gray crashed on the couch, I stayed in the guest room, and in between the noise of nieces and nephews and the endless parade of food, we stole little moments that felt like ours. Sweet. Ordinary. The kind of ordinary that felt like a gift.

And honestly, Christmas Eve had been its own gift too. My designs for the service went up without a hitch—garlands of greenery, candlelight service, and a stage that felt warm and welcoming without being overdone. People kept stopping me to say how beautiful it looked, and for once, I didn't second-guess it. I just let myself be proud of the work.

Now, just a week later, it's New Year's Eve, and the scene couldn't be more different.

The low hum of music fills Micah's cozy house, laughter spilling from the kitchen where someone's trying—and failing—not to burn the queso. Someone yells for a game of charades. Someone else is handing out flimsy gold paper hats. The whole place feels alive, buzzing, like it can't wait to tip over into midnight.

I'm tucked in the corner of the couch with Harper and Olivia, legs curled beneath me, a mug of cider warm in my hands. The three of us are nestled together on a patchwork of blankets and pillows we dragged over earlier. It feels like home—even in someone else's living room.

"It's hard to believe this year's almost over," Harper says, pulling her knees up to her chest.

"I know," I say, exhaling slowly. "It flew."

Olivia stretches her arms over her head with a content sigh. "It's weird. A couple months ago I thought I was stuck, like my life was frozen in place. But now...I feel like it's finally thawing out."

Harper nudges her. "I'm proud of you, Liv."

Olivia rolls her eyes, but she's smiling. "Don't make it weird."

"No promises."

I glance at both of them, my heart full to bursting. "So...updates?"

Harper's eyes light up first. "Okay, I'll go. I'm actually kind of excited to go back to school after the holiday break. I miss my kids. I know they're five and sticky and wild, but they're mine, you know? I get to be part of their beginning."

"That's beautiful," I say honestly, already knowing she's going to be one of those teachers who changes lives.

Olivia sits up straighter. "Therapy job is still good. Hard sometimes, but good. I actually helped a kid this week process something really heavy and...I didn't freak out. I didn't freeze. I was just there. Present. That's new for me."

Harper reaches over and squeezes her arm. "That's amazing, Liv."

"And you?" Harper turns to me. "How's our little church graphics queen?"

I grin. "Busy, but happy. I'm still doing my freelance work on the side, but being part of the team at church has been... grounding. Like I finally stopped floating and planted some roots."

We fall quiet for a moment, each of us wrapped in our own thoughts as a new year waits quietly on the other side of midnight.

"So," Harper says, nudging my leg, "whose turn is it?"

I blink. "Turn for what?"

"The dare," Olivia supplies, grinning. "We're overdue."

We all pause, trying to remember. Who dared who last?

"Didn't I dare you to hold a stranger's hand in New Orleans?" Harper jokes.

"I dared you to eat a bug that one time," I say.

"And I dared Olivia to go to that church picnic," Harper adds.

We stare at each other for a beat before dissolving into laughter.

"Okay," I say, wiping a tear from my eye, "I guess we can't remember. So...let's just all dare each other something this time."

They both nod.

I go first. "I dare us to never lose faith. Even when it's easier to run."

Harper lifts her cider. "I dare us to love without pretending. No masks. No performance."

Olivia swallows, eyes glossy. "I dare us to be brave— even when it's scary."

We clink our mugs together like a promise.

And in that moment, I feel it—the warmth of friendship, the steady beat of healing, and the quiet, wild hope of a brand new year waiting to begin.

From the kitchen, someone starts the countdown.

Ten.

Nine.

Eight...

I jump to my feet before I can even think. Harper blinks up at me. "Where are you going?"

I grin, heart racing. "To find my man."

Olivia waves her hands dramatically. "Go! Run! Live your New Year's Eve movie moment!"

Seven.

Six.

Five...

I dart out of the living room, weaving through clusters of people and balloons and voices yelling over one another. My pulse thrums in my ears as I round the corner toward the hallway.

Four.

Three...

And then I see him.

Gray, standing at the other end of the crowd, head turning side to side like he's searching for someone.

For me.

Two...

His eyes lock on mine.

One.

We both move at once—shoulders brushing past friends and furniture, feet stumbling in our rush. Then suddenly, I'm in his arms, and the whole room erupts in cheers and countdown noise and confetti, but all I hear is the way he exhales when he pulls away from our kiss.

"Happy New Year," I whisper, breathless.

His hands cup my face as he looks at me like I'm his whole world. "Best one yet."

And when he kisses me again, everything else disappears.

Chapter 40
Ivy

I smooth the front of my dress, the soft white fabric light and airy, falling in graceful waves to just below my knees. The sleeveless cut and gentle scoop neckline give it an easy, sun-kissed feel, while the subtle cinch at the waist hints at my shape without trying too hard. It's simple but beautiful —breezy, feminine, timeless, and not at all what I expected to wear to a Galentine's Day party.

Harper insisted we all wear white, to go along with all of the hot pink decorations. I thought it was a little strange, but Harper gets her way when it comes to party themes, and I didn't want to be the one to ruin her aesthetic.

In the mirror, my reflection doesn't look all that different. But I feel different. Softer in the right ways and stronger in the ones that matter.

I reach for my gold earrings, the ones Olivia got me for Christmas, and smile. My girls. They've carried me through so much—through doubt and heartbreak, healing and hope. And tonight, we're celebrating our friendship.

Still, there's something about today. A feeling I can't quite explain humming beneath my skin.

My phone buzzes on the counter.

GRAY

Have fun tonight, beautiful.

Just four words, but they steal my breath a little.

I tuck the phone into my purse and do one last check in the mirror. Hair curled. Lip gloss on. Heart racing.

As I head toward the door, I whisper a quiet prayer—not for anything specific, just a soft thank you. For this faith. This hope. This love.

The walk to the coffee shop is short, barely enough time for me to overthink...but of course, I do anyway.

Harper's texts about today had been vague and Olivia hasn't responded to me.

I turn onto Knox Street, nerves fluttering low in my stomach.

I clutch my small leather purse tighter as I step inside the coffee shop, expecting the usual hum of chatter, the clink of mugs, maybe soft indie music playing through the speakers. But tonight... it's different.

It's still. Empty. The air smells faintly of espresso and cinnamon, familiar but somehow...different. I glance around, confused. There's no trace of Harper's usual party chaos. No streamers, no balloons taped to the windows, no cupcakes piled on mismatched platters.

Am I at the wrong coffee shop?

My heels click softly against the worn wooden floors as I move deeper inside, heart thudding faster now, wondering why no-one is here, not even the staff.

"Harper?" I call out, my voice swallowed by the hush.

No answer. But ahead, near the back of the shop, I spot a soft golden glow spilling from the doorway to the private room they sometimes rent out for small gatherings.

I turn the corner—and stop in my tracks.

The room is transformed. String lights drip from the ceiling like stars, their glow mirrored by the flicker of candles scattered across every surface. Rose petals in shades of deep crimson and blush pink trail along the floor, leading me forward like a path meant only for me.

And there he is.

Gray.

Standing at the far end of the room, guitar gripped in his hands, eyes locked on mine like I'm the only person in the world. His lips curve in that soft, heart-stealing smile.

Then he starts to play.

The first gentle strum echoes through the candlelight. His voice, when it comes, is soft at first, like he's singing straight to my soul.

> *Met you in the middle of a moment I didn't see coming*
> *Your hand in mine like a spark in the dark*
> *Didn't know then what You were starting*
> *But You wrote it on my heart*

I take a slow step forward, my heels soundless against the petals scattered beneath my feet. The day we met flashes in my mind—the dare, the rush of his hand in mine, the way everything else faded but him.

> *Every step, every prayer, every night I wondered*
> *If I was enough, if I'd lose my way*
> *But You were the grace I didn't know I'd needed*
> *You stayed, you stayed*

My throat tightens. Another step. His voice is stronger now, every word wrapping around me. And I see it—not just the man in front of me, but the man who waited, who chose patience, who loved without demanding anything in return.

I'll wait in the quiet, no need to be sure
Of timelines or answers—I'll stand and endure
Love isn't pressure, it's patience and grace
I dare to believe... you're worth the wait

My eyes blur with tears, but I keep moving. He watches me, like he's afraid if he blinks, he'll miss this moment.

Your laughter's been my light on the hardest days
Your searching eyes, they keep me brave
And I've learned that love's not about chasing
It's about choosing, every day

I'm almost there now. Just a few more steps. His voice wavers, just slightly, like the weight of the words is catching up to him too.

So I'll choose you in the silence, in the storm, in the fight
I'll choose you in the morning, I'll choose you every night
And when the world tells us hurry, I'll slow down and stay
'Cause I know—you're worth the wait

The final chorus begins. I stop, right in front of him, my heart pounding so hard I swear he can hear it.

I'll wait in the quiet, no need to be sure
Of timelines or answers—I'll stand and endure

Love isn't pressure, it's patience and grace
I dare to believe... you're worth the wait

He lets the last chord fade, his gaze never leaving mine. My tears fall freely now, but I'm smiling, breathless with wonder.

And in this room filled with petals, candles, and promises, I know—this is it. This is forever.

He lifts the guitar over his shoulder, setting it down then reaching for my hands. "Ivy...I'll never forget that day, eleven months ago, in New Orleans. When you grabbed my hand out of nowhere because your friends dared you to."

He let's out a quiet laugh, shaking his head.

"I had no idea who you were. But somehow...I think part of me already knew you were going to change everything."

His voice softens as he takes a step closer.

"I used to think love had to be loud to be real. Wild. All-consuming. But then you came in—soft and sure, and somehow wrecked me in all the right ways."

He draws in a breath, his expression more serious now.

"You are the calm to my storm. The answer to every prayer I didn't know how to form out loud. You've taught me what it means to love patiently...to trust God's timing, especially when it didn't make sense."

He swallows, emotion thick in his voice.

"You make me want to be better—not because you expect it, but because you believe I already am. You've seen every part of me—my broken past, my shaky in-betweens, and my redeemed present. And somehow, you've still chosen to stay."

He lets out a shaky breath and drops to one knee, the ring in his hand glinting in the soft light.

"I've already given you my heart, Ivy Taylor. Now I want to give you every part of my future. The music. The mess. The quiet mornings and the late-night prayers. The laughter and the tears. My black coffee and your overly sweet lattes. All of it—with you."

His smile is crooked, full of love.

"I dare you to marry me. I dare you to spend the rest of your life with me. I dare you to raise a family with me, grow old with me and share the gospel and spread love any chance we get."

Time stills. My breath catches.

I throw my arms around Gray, laughing through the tears. "Yes," I whisper. "Yes, a thousand times, yes."

And then, behind me, through the doorway, a flood of voices rushes in. Laughter. Cheers. Applause.

Our people.

Everyone we love is here—Harper, Olivia, my parents, Gray's friends, our church family. The ones who've walked us through the hardest and most beautiful parts of this story.

Gray rises to his feet, pulling me into his arms as the people we love pour into the room. I'm still holding his face when I feel Harper tackle me from behind in a half-hug, half-sob. "You're engaged!" she squeals, practically bouncing.

"I'm so happy for you two!" Olivia says, giving Gray a high five before hugging me like she's never letting go.

"Wait," I say, dazed. "The party...the all-white dress code...Galentine's Day?"

"You're the only one in white, babe," Harper says, wiping under her eyes. "You didn't notice that?"

Gray grins beside me. "You always steal the show anyway. We just made it official this time."

I glance down at my dress, suddenly seeing it differently

—no longer just a cute outfit I picked out for Valentines Day. Now, it's the dress I said yes in.

He leans in, his lips brushing my ear. "You look perfect."

"Do not make me cry again," I whisper.

Too late.

We don't leave the coffee shop. Instead, the night unfolds right here—warm, glowing, perfect.

Turns out Gray rented the whole place, because soon, a small team rolls in quietly with trays of food. The air fills with the scent of roasted chicken, garlic bread, and something rich and chocolatey. The long counter is lined with our favorite coffee drinks—cappuccinos, lattes, hot cocoa with little marshmallows.

The small round tables that I've sat at a hundred times before—where I've sipped coffee, sketched designs, and laughed with friends—have been transformed. Each one is topped with a cluster of candles flickering softly, their light reflecting off tiny glass vases filled with greenery, soft blush roses, and deep red blooms. It's simple. But beautiful. Effortless. Us.

I press my hand to my mouth, overwhelmed again. "Gray..."

He grins, slipping an arm around me. "I figured we'd go back to the day you crashed into my life."

"This is perfect."

Once everyone has a plate in front of them, Gray rises, reaching for my hand. "Before we eat, I want to pray."

The shop falls quiet, the glow of the lights reflecting in the windows like stars.

"Father," Gray begins, voice steady but thick with emotion, "thank You for this night. For Ivy—for her faith, her strength, her joy. For the way You've walked with us through every step. I pray You'll stay at the center of everything we build together. Let our love reflect Yours—patient, kind, enduring. Let this night remind us of Your goodness. In Jesus's name, amen."

A soft chorus of amen echoes, and Gray squeezes my hand before we sit.

The rest of the night is simple, sweet, and full of quiet magic. We eat, we laugh. The playlist Gray queued up hums through the speakers—soft acoustic love songs, a little old-school Frank Sinatra, even a few of our silly favorites.

At some point, he pulls me close, swaying with me in the middle of the coffee shop, right between the bar and the tables. His hand on my back, his breath warm against my temple, the whole world melts away.

"This night couldn't get any better," I murmur.

He smiles against my hair. "Wanna bet?"

I pull back just enough to look up at him, my heart already racing. "What did you do?"

Gray grins, reaches into his jacket pocket, and pulls out a small folded sticky note that has worn edges, he's clearly carried it around for a long time.

"I never told you about this," he says, unfolding it. The edges are soft, the ink smudged in places, but it's clearly been kept close.

He unfolds it slowly, gently, like it's sacred.

"I wrote this the morning I met you," he says. "Had no clue what was coming. I was sitting in the hotel room, asking God to take care of the woman I'd one day marry. That wherever she was, He'd keep her safe. Seen. Loved. Prepared—for me, and me for her."

My breath catches as I read the short prayer scrawled in his handwriting. It's raw, simple, beautiful.

But what undoes me completely—what wrecks me—is the way the word "her" is scratched out in every line and replaced, carefully, intentionally, with my name.

Ivy.

"You've been in this prayer since day one," he says, voice thick. "And I've prayed it every day since."

Tears spill down my cheeks. I clutch the note to my chest like it's a part of him. Because it is.

"Gray Bennett," I whisper, "how on earth am I supposed to top that?"

He grins. "You don't. Just keep holding my hand in public—it worked out pretty well last time."

Chapter 41
Gray
7 months later

The morning sun creeps over the French Quarter, casting a golden haze through the open balcony doors. I woke up before dawn, nerves humming beneath my skin—not from fear, but from anticipation.

I slip outside with my coffee and sink into the weathered wooden chair overlooking the street. New Orleans stirs below, slow and sleepy, but up here it's quiet.

I cradle the mug in my hands and breathe deep.

I open my journal, the same one I've carried for the past couple years. I flip to the back, where pages are filled with prayers I've written over time—some desperate, some grateful, some unfinished. My fingers still on the one I wrote eighteen months ago, the morning I met her.

I didn't know her name then. Didn't know that the girl who grabbed my hand on a dare would eventually grab hold of my heart in ways I never saw coming. I didn't know she'd be the one I'd wait for. The one I'd fall in love with. The one I'd pray over, wrestle for, surrender to God again and again until He brought her back in a way only He could.

And today...she becomes my wife.

I scribble one more entry, hand a little shaky with the weight of it all.

September 22nd,

Lord, today is the day. I don't know how You do it, but You always exceed anything I could ever ask for. Ivy is a gift I never saw coming but always hoped for. Help me to love her like You love. Help me lead her with gentleness and joy. Let today be full of peace, full of Your presence. I surrender this day to You. Thank You for letting me be hers.

I set the pen down, press my palms together, and let my eyes close for a moment.

Because in a few hours, she'll be walking toward me.

And I'll be standing there, heart wide open, ready to vow forever.

They tell you not to look. That the moment she walks down the aisle should be the first time you see her.

But I couldn't wait that long.

We're tucked behind the courtyard where the ceremony will take place—hidden from guests, from the whirlwind of planning and nerves. Just me, my pounding heart, and the sound of footsteps approaching from behind.

"Ivy's coming," the photographer says, quietly.

I turn to face the stone wall, swallowing hard, my palms

already sweating. I flex my fingers at my sides. Inhale. Exhale. I didn't expect to feel this undone.

"Okay, you can turn around."

I pivot slowly, not sure I'm ready for what's about to hit me.

But nothing could've prepared me anyway.

There she is.

Ivy.

Hair curled soft around her shoulders, eyes lit like the sun, lips trembling with the start of a smile. Her dress is simple and elegant, the fabric hugging her like it was sewn just for this day, just for her. Gold jewelry glints in the light, but none of it shines like she does.

And when her eyes meet mine...

I lose it.

A laugh breaks out of me, cracked and choked at the edges, and I swipe at my eyes before the tears get the better of me.

"Hey you," she whispers, stepping closer.

I take her hands in mine, lifting them to my lips before I can stop myself. "You're...you're so beautiful it's actually unfair."

She laughs, a soft breath that carries the weight of everything we've walked through. "You clean up nice too, Bennett."

"Do you have any idea," I murmur, my forehead tipping to rest against hers, "how long I've been waiting to call you mine?"

Her eyes close, a shimmer behind her lashes. "I do."

And for just a heartbeat, I lose myself in what's coming. Tonight. When it's finally just us. No more waiting. No more holding back. Just the two of us—no barriers, no distance. I can already feel the weight of her in my arms, the way her laugh will sound in the quiet, the way she'll look at me when it's only us and the world fades away. God help me, I want that moment more than I've ever wanted anything. But I'll wait, only a few more hours.

Her breath brushes my lips, snapping me back to now.

"Technically..." she whispers, a spark of mischief and heat in her tone, "I'm not yours yet."

Her gaze lifts to meet mine, full of promise and something that makes my knees a little weak. "You've still got to walk down that aisle. Say the words. Survive the reception..."

She leans in just enough to make sure I feel the weight of what comes next. "And then, Gray Bennett, I'm all yours."

She pulls back just enough to flash me that smile—the one that undoes me every single time—and then she turns, lifting the hem of her dress slightly as she heads toward the garden path where Harper and Olivia wait at the edge of the aisle.

And I swear...I almost forget how to breathe.

Every step she takes is like time slowing down. The soft sway of her dress, the breeze catching her hair, the promise in the glance she throws over her shoulder. My chest aches with it.

I drag in a breath and close my eyes for just a second, whispering a prayer deep in my heart. *God, thank You for this woman. For this day. For this love.*

When I open them, I see my mom.

Waiting off to the side of the aisle, hands clasped, looking more nervous than I feel. I hadn't known if she'd come. When I'd called—shaky voice, heart pounding—I'd half-expected the usual excuses. But she'd surprised me. She'd said yes. And now here she is.

I walk toward her, my heart pounding in a different way.

"Hey, Mom."

She looks up at me, eyes misty. "Gray, you look...you look so grown. So good."

I swallow hard. "You ready?"

She lets out a breathy little laugh. "I should be asking you that."

I offer my arm. "Walk with me?"

Her fingers tremble as she slides her hand through the crook of my elbow. "I wouldn't miss it."

We step onto the aisle together, the sunlight filtering through the trees, the garden alive with soft music and the murmur of guests. As we walk, I feel the weight of everything we've come through—the hard years, the silence, the distance. And now this.

At the front, I pause and turn to her.

"Thanks for coming, Mom."

She squeezes my arm, voice thick. "Thanks for letting me."

She takes her seat in the front row, and I move to my place at the altar, the breeze lifting my hair, the scent of wildflowers filling the air.

Jack stands at the front, Bible in hand, glasses low on his nose, just like every time we sat across his desk. Except this time...he's not mentoring me from behind a desk. He's blessing my future from behind an altar.

Micah claps me on the back as I take my place beside him, grinning. "You sure about this?" he teases.

"I've never been more sure of anything."

The music starts.

The aisle is scattered with petals as Ivy's niece Kate makes her way down, our flower girl in all her determined glory. Instead of a graceful sprinkle, she tosses them in uneven clumps, drawing a chorus of "ooohs" and "ahhhs" from the guests. By the time she reaches her mom Sarah, one of Ivy's bridesmaids, she's practically running, grinning like she's conquered the world.

Jack's expression shifts—reverent, knowing, a little misty-eyed. He's walked me through every heartbreak, every step of my faith, and now...he's standing here to witness the answer to every one of those prayers.

"Please stand."

Chairs scrape, fabric rustles, and the entire room rises, every head turning toward the end of the aisle.

And then I see her.

Her arm is looped through her father's, her steps unhurried, deliberate. It's like the whole world slows just to let me take her in. The light catches in her hair, her dress brushing softly against the floor, petals scattered unevenly beneath her shoes. And though I've seen her a thousand times, it feels like I'm seeing her for the very first time.

My chest tightens. Because she's not just the girl walking toward me. She's my future. She's the keys to the new apartment we picked out together, waiting on the counter for us to unlock. She's quiet mornings with no curfew, no boundaries to tiptoe around—just the freedom to be hers completely. She's laughter filling empty rooms, arguments about where the couch should go, whispered prayers before bed. She's every ache I've carried finally answered in flesh and bone and beauty.

I blink hard, trying to keep it together, but my eyes sting anyway.

Her gaze locks with mine, and the crowd, the music, even Jack's voice fade into nothing. It's just me and her. My heart pounding, hers steady as she draws closer.

When she finally reaches me, her father gives me her hand, and I grip it like it's the only thing keeping me upright. Because, it is.

Jack opens his Bible, his deep voice steady as he begins.

"Today isn't just a celebration," he says. "It's a covenant. Not built on perfection, but on grace. On two people who dared to believe that God's best was worth the wait."

He looks straight at me, and his voice softens.

"Gray, you once asked me how to lead someone in faith without trying to control them. And Ivy..." He glances at her, eyes twinkling. "You've answered that question better than I ever could. Today is proof of what surrender can do."

Then he smiles, flipping to a passage from Ephesians.

"'Submit to one another out of reverence for Christ... Husbands, love your wives, just as Christ loved the church and gave himself up for her.'"

He blesses our vows.

And then I say mine.

"Ivy Taylor...
I used to think love was about doing everything right. Saying the perfect thing. Being strong enough to hold someone else together.
But then you showed me it's about showing up.
Even when it's hard.
Especially when it's hard.
You taught me that grace isn't something I give, it's something I live.
I didn't know what God was doing the day I stood there in New Orleans...
But He knew.
Because He gave me you.

Dare To Hold

*I promise to keep praying for you, pursuing you, and
pointing you to Jesus every single day.
I promise to listen more than I speak, to hold your hand
when you're scared, and to celebrate every win like it's the
best day of our lives.
I promise to lead with humility, love without conditions, and
laugh at every single ridiculous thing you say because let's be
real, there'll be a lot.
You're the best yes I've ever had.
And I'll spend the rest of my life making sure you never
doubt it."*

She wipes a tear and smiles up at me, voice trembling
but sure.

*"Gray Bennett...
You weren't the plan.
You were the surprise.
The grace I didn't know I could receive.
The steady voice in the chaos.
The hand I wasn't afraid to hold.
Even when I was terrified of falling.
You loved me when I didn't feel lovable.
You prayed for me when I didn't know how.
And you never rushed me, even when it would've been easier
to walk away.
I used to think faith was about being perfect.
Now I know it's about being loved anyway.
So today, I vow to love you that same way, flawed and full of
grace.
I promise to believe in what God is doing in you and in us,
even when the road gets hard.*

*To show up, speak truth, and stay rooted in what matters
most.
And I promise to always, always choose you,
The man who dared me to believe in love and in Jesus.
You're my answered prayer, Gray.
And my forever favorite miracle."*

And when Jack says, "Gray Bennett, you may now kiss
your bride," I swear the sky gets a little brighter.

I look at her—my wife—and time slows down.

"I love you," I whisper,. My eyes lock onto hers, and I
lean in just enough that only she can hear the next part.
"And I can't wait to show you just how much...the second
we're alone.

Her breath catches, and for a beat, she just looks at me—
like I'm the only person in the world. Then that smile
breaks across her face, slow and radiant, like the sun itself
lives in her.

And that's when I kiss her—because I can't go one more
second without doing it.

Slow and tender at first, like we're both savoring the
moment we've waited so long for. Her lips are soft, warm,
familiar and new all at once. My hands find her waist,
pulling her gently closer, like I'm anchoring myself in this
single breath of forever.

Her hands slide up, fingertips threading into the back of
my hair, then resting at my neck—steadying me, claiming
me.

And in this kiss, I taste every promise we've made.
Every prayer. Every piece of the journey that brought us
here.

But then, as the cheers erupt around us and I pull back,
breathless, I can't help myself.

I grin and say, "One more for the road."

And I dip her—full swoop, like we're in a movie—and kiss her again, deeper this time, with all the joy, passion, and forever I've been holding in.

She laughs into my mouth, and the sound just wrecks me—in the best way.

We rise together, hearts pounding, and as I lace our fingers, she squeezes my hand tight.

We walk down the aisle, husband and wife, through a tunnel of cheers and camera flashes, faces full of love and sunlight, the breeze lifting the veil behind her like wings.

And I think, This is it.

This is the start of every good thing.

Chapter 42
Ivy

The courtyard glows with string lights overhead, casting everything in soft gold. Tables draped in ivory linen shimmer beneath the candlelight, and the scent of jasmine floats through the New Orleans air, sweet and heady, like the night itself is celebrating with us.

Gray's hand is still wrapped around mine, he hasn't let go since we walked back down that aisle, and I don't think I ever want him to.

The reception is small, cozy, full of everyone who matters. I spot Harper wiping tears with a napkin that's probably ruined by now. Olivia's got her phone up, recording like her life depends on it. And Micah, he's standing off to the side, smiling that knowing, quiet smile, like he's watching a prayer come true.

We're tucked together at the sweetheart table now, and I can feel him looking at me. I glance over, catch his gaze, and blush because—Lord help me—he hasn't stopped staring since the vows.

I whisper, "Stop staring," but I don't mean it.

"Never," he whispers, his thumb brushing over my knuckles.

And I swear, in this moment, I've never felt more cherished.

The clinking of glasses starts, and Harper stands on a chair, champagne flute in hand.

"Okay, okay, listen up!" she calls out, already beaming. "I'd like to make the first toast."

Everyone laughs.

She raises her glass. "To Ivy, my best friend since forever, and to Gray, who somehow managed to win over the stranger who grabbed his hand right there in New Orleans on a dare." More laughter. Gray shoots me a sideways look, grinning.

"But really," Harper continues, her voice softening, "watching you two grow together has been one of the greatest joys of my life. You're not just cute—you're faithful, intentional, and real. Ivy, I've never seen you shine like this. And Gray...thank you for loving her the way we always hoped someone would. To the happy couple!"

Olivia stands up next. "I wasn't going to say anything," she says, clearly emotional, "but I can't not. Ivy, I'm proud of you. Not just for finding love—but for finding you. And for letting us all be a part of it. You inspire me more than you know. And Gray...thanks for being patient. You're a good man. And now you're stuck with us."

Next up is Micah, Gray's best man, who grins as he taps his glass and says, "I knew this guy was in trouble the minute he came back from New Orleans and didn't talk about the music...but about a girl."

Everyone laughs again, applauding mid speech.

Micah lifts his glass. "To the ones who wait on God, to

the ones brave enough to stay when it's hard, and to the love that makes it all worth it. Cheers to Gray and Ivy."

The chatter and laughter fade as the DJ's voice comes through the speakers, warm and inviting.

"Ladies and gentlemen, if I could have your attention...it's time for the new Mr. and Mrs. Bennett's first dance."

A gentle cheer ripples through the courtyard, and the opening notes of our song float into the night air—soft, slow, and achingly familiar.

Gray rises, his hand already extended toward me, that grin I love tugging at the corner of his mouth.

"May I have this dance, Mrs. Bennett?"

My heart flips at the sound of it. "Only if you never stop calling me that," I tease, slipping my hand into his.

He pulls me close, guiding me onto the dance floor. The world blurs around us, the candles, the string lights, the faces of everyone we love—until all I can see is him.

His hand presses gently at the small of my back, guiding me as we move together, slow and easy, like we've done this a hundred times. Like we were made for it.

The music swells, and Gray leans in, his lips brushing just below my ear, his breath warm against my skin.

"You have no idea what it's taking for me not to kiss you breathless right here in front of everyone," he whispers, his voice low, sending a shiver down my spine.

I draw in a shaky breath, my fingers curling at his shoulder.

His thumb traces soft, slow circles at my waist. "Every second tonight, all I'm thinking about is how I get to make you mine."

My heart races, my pulse singing beneath his touch.

"And later," he murmurs, his lips grazing my temple,

"when it's just us...I'm going to show you exactly what that means."

I lean in, my lips barely brushing his ear as I whisper, playful but breathless, "I genuinely can't wait to find out if those tattoos are in places I haven't seen yet."

Gray freezes for half a second—then lets out a laugh, warm and unrestrained, his forehead dropping to mine like I've just undone him completely.

"Oh, they are, Ivy," he says, his grin wide and a little mischievous. "And now all I'm going to be thinking about is how fun it's gonna be showing you."

My cheeks burn, my heart soaring, and we both dissolve into quiet laughter, wrapped up in each other as the music carries us to the end of the dance.

As the music softens toward its final notes, something shifts in him. His hand moves to cradle my face, his forehead resting against mine, his breath mingling with mine as if we're sharing the same air.

His voice lowers again, this time tender, reverent. "I love you, Ivy. More than I ever thought possible. And I promise you—I'll spend the rest of my life proving it."

The world seems to still, the applause and flicker of candles a soft blur behind us.

I whisper back, tears bright in my eyes. "And I'll spend mine loving you right back."

And in that quiet, sacred beat before the world presses in again, he kisses me—slow, gentle, full of every promise wrapped inside forever.

The music picks up, something upbeat that gets half the crowd on their feet. Gray presses a kiss to my temple and lets me go reluctantly, heading toward the guys gathering by the dessert table.

I don't make it two steps before I hear it—Harper's voice, sharp but low, followed by Micah's steady, maddeningly calm one.

I glance over to see them standing off to the side near the drink station, Harper's hands on her hips, Micah looking like he's trying hard not to smile at whatever she's fuming about.

Before I can talk myself out of it, I grab Olivia's hand. "Come on. We're saving her from herself."

We weave through the crowd and reach them just as Harper's muttering, "You are impossible."

Micah crosses his arms, looking way too amused. "And yet, here you are."

I slide between them, my tone light. "Okay, okay—time out. Harper, breathe. Micah, go... refill your tea or something."

Micah gives me a nod, that signature smirk lingering on his lips, and strolls off, leaving Harper glaring at his retreating back.

Olivia raises a brow. "Do I want to know what that was about?"

"No," Harper snaps. "You don't."

I exchange a look with Olivia, and the mischief sparks before I can stop it.

"You know what, Harper?" I say, crossing my arms. "It's your turn for a dare."

Harper groans. "Ivy. No."

"Oh yes," Olivia says, grinning now.

"I dare you," I say, drawing it out, "to go dance with Micah."

Her jaw drops. "You're kidding."

I shake my head, enjoying this far too much.

"That may be even more harsh than daring me to go to church," Olivia says, laughing.

Harper looks like she's torn between fighting me and running for the hills. "You're evil, you know that?"

"Yup." I nudge her forward. "Go. One song. You've got this."

She mutters under her breath but finally squares her shoulders and heads toward Micah, who looks up just in time to see her coming—and the surprise and satisfaction that flickers across his face is all the confirmation I need.

Olivia leans close, watching them. "This is going to be so good."

I smile, heart full. "Oh, you have no idea."

Harper and Micah make their way to the edge of the dance floor, and Olivia and I stay back, watching like two nosy aunts at a family reunion.

"They're so awkward," Olivia mutters, her arms crossed, though there's a grin tugging at the corner of her mouth.

"I know," I whisper back, trying not to laugh. "Look at the way she won't even meet his eyes."

"And look at him," Olivia adds, tilting her head. "He looks like he's trying to figure out how not to step on her feet."

They move stiffly, keeping just enough distance between them that it looks less like a dance and more like a middle school slow song. I bite my lip, trying to hold back the giggles threatening to burst out.

"This is painful," Olivia says, shaking her head. "We need to look away before we make it worse."

We shift our gaze toward the candlelit tables, the twinkle lights blurring softly in the background. The music hums around us, the crowd chatting, clinking glasses, living in the moment.

After a beat, Olivia sighs. "You know what's dumb? I keep telling myself I'm fine, that I'm happy for you. And I am, really. But watching you and Gray... sometimes I wonder if I'll ever have that."

I glance at her, heart aching a little at the vulnerability in her voice. "You will. And maybe... maybe you could even start by praying about it."

She stiffens beside me. I see it happen—the way her jaw tightens, her fingers curl into her palm, the guard going up like armor.

"Liv, I didn't mean to—"

"No," she says quickly, exhaling, clearing the storm in her eyes before it spills out in words she'll regret. "You know what? Never mind. I just... I need you to show me the same grace you keep saying Gray gave you. I'm trying, okay? But I'm not ready for that, Ivy."

I go quiet, letting her speak, letting her heart open.

"I have a past with the church. I used to go every Sunday when I was a kid. And then... everything fell apart. I don't know what I believe in anymore. But you and Harper have to stop pushing me. I'm trying. I really am."

Without thinking, I pull her into a hug, tight and full of love, no words needed.

She lets me, her arms finally relaxing around me.

And that's when Harper stomps up, cheeks flushed, eyes blazing.

"We're going to the bar," she announces, grabbing

Olivia's wrist like a lifeline. "You—" she points at me, half laughing, half fuming—"are going to go dance with your husband again before I never forgive you for that stupid dare."

I hold up my hands in surrender, grinning. "Yes, ma'am."

Harper shoots me a look as she drags Olivia away, and I catch the soft grin Olivia gives me over her shoulder—one that says thanks for understanding.

And as the music rises around me again, I head back toward the man waiting for me on the dance floor, my heart full of hope.

Only...when I spot him, my heart isn't the only thing full—my lungs are full of laughter I'm trying, and failing, to hold in.

Gray stands at the edge of the dance floor, grinning like a kid at a carnival. He's somehow acquired a neon green glow stick necklace and another glow stick looped around his head like a crown. In his hands? A pretend fishing pole— okay, it's actually just one of the glow sticks he's twirling like it's a rod.

I stop in my tracks, watching as he casts his imaginary line toward me. With exaggerated concentration, he mimes reeling it in, tugging dramatically.

"Got one!" he calls, loud enough for the nearest guests to turn and grin. "It's a fighter, but she's mine!"

I play along, staggering forward like I've got no choice in the matter, giggling the whole way.

When I reach him, he tosses the glow stick "pole" aside and loops his arms around my waist, pulling me close.

"Caught the best catch of the night," he says, eyes dancing.

I shake my head, laughing, wrapping my arms around his neck. "You're ridiculous."

"And yet, you said I do."

"Best decision I ever made."

The night air in New Orleans wraps around us like a warm whisper as we slip away from the celebration. My fingers are laced through Gray's, my dress catching in the breeze as I kick off my heels and let them dangle from my hand.

I'm still laughing about something Harper said during her toast, but mostly I'm floating—because I can feel the way he's watching me. Like I'm the only thing in his world.

Like I'm his.

We reach the hotel, the soft hum of the lobby fading as Gray swipes the key card. The door clicks open, but before I can take a step inside, he sweeps me up into his arms.

A surprised laugh bubbles out. "Gray!"

He grins, that smile that always undoes me. "I believe this is tradition."

My arms loop around his neck as he carries me over the threshold, and suddenly, it's just us.

Candlelight flickers across the suite, soft and golden. Rose petals are scattered on the bed, like the room's been dressed in every love song he's ever played for me.

He sets me down slowly, gently, and my heart races as I look up at him. His eyes find mine and stay there—steady, sure, full of so much love I can barely breathe.

"So what now, husband?" I whisper, my voice trembling with joy.

Gray steps closer, his fingers brushing down my arms until he's holding my hands. "Now?" His voice dips low, playful, teasing. "Now I get to kiss my wife without a crowd watching."

My breath catches.

His lips meet mine, soft at first—then deeper, hungrier, until we're both breathless and clinging to each other like we can't get close enough.

When he finally pulls back, his forehead rests against mine, his smile soft and sure.

"I hope you know," he murmurs, "I plan on loving you like this every day for the rest of my life."

I tilt my head, that teasing spark rising. "Even when I steal the blankets?"

His laugh rumbles low. "Especially then."

Before I can say another word, he scoops me up again, carrying me toward the bed. My laughter spills out, wrapping around us like a promise.

And just before he kicks the bedroom door shut behind us, he meets my gaze—eyes warm, full of love, and just a little wicked.

"Brace yourself, Mrs. Bennett. The honeymoon starts now."

Acknowledgments

To my Lord and Savior, Jesus Christ—thank You for the convictions You placed on my heart, and for patiently waiting until I finally listened. This story is for You.

For those of you who don't know, I was previously published as a steamy romance author. But I recently made the decision to unpublish those books and step fully into this new journey as a clean romance author. Fun fact: *Dare to Hold* actually started out as a dark romance—but the Lord gently redirected me, shaping it into a beautiful love story filled with faith elements and a redemption arc. The next two books in this series will do the same, and I cannot wait for you to read them.

There are so many people I want to thank. First, to my husband—for picking up the slack around the house when I'm deep in writing mode, and for supporting me in this "fun little hobby" that I pray grows into a career one day.

To my kids—thank you for being proud of me and excited that someday you'll get to read these stories. I hope you see the changes in me, and I pray they inspire you to walk the same path with your own lives.

To my sister Ashlynn—thank you for listening to me ramble endlessly and for supporting me no matter what, even from 5,000+ miles away. It's my deepest prayer that this series touches your heart most of all.

To my friends and family—for cheering me on even when I'm terrible at texting back. Specifically, to my Home

Group ladies: I couldn't do this life without you. Thank you for keeping me on track every time I "squirrel."

To Jordan Riley—thank you for listening to my ridiculously long Marco Polos, and for sending equally long ones back. I'm so grateful our paths crossed in the author world.

To Ashley—thank you for being my accountability partner, for checking in exactly when I need it most.

To Mikayla—thank you for blowing up my manuscript in the best possible way. Here's to more projects together and cheering each other on in the writing world!

To my beta readers—you absolutely blew me away. I hope, as you read the final version of this book, you can see the ways your feedback helped me shape the first draft into this story I'm so proud of. I can't wait to work with you again on Book 2.

To the clean romance community on Bookstagram and BookTok—thank you for showing me the good side of social media, for being a place full of like-minded encouragement, and for being the best group of hype girls a writer could ask for.

And finally, to my readers—the fact that you picked up this book means the world to me. I've prayed over every page of this story, and I've prayed over you, too.

About the Author

Amber Nicole writes emotionally rich, clean romance stories filled with swoony moments, second chances, and grace. After years of writing steamy romance, Amber felt a stirring in her heart to shift directions—trading heat for heart and choosing to tell stories that honor her faith.

Now, she creates heartfelt love stories that are both tender and true, often featuring strong heroines, protective heroes, and love that grows slowly but deeply. Her debut Christian romance, Dare to Hold, invites readers into a world of redemption, intentional love, and hope that never gives up.

When she's not writing, Amber is a wife, a mom of

three, and gets to work with authors for her day job—something that inspires her daily. She lives on coffee, Jesus, and Nerds Clusters.

authorambernicole.com

instagram.com/authorambernicole

facebook.com/authorambernicole

tiktok.com/@authorambernicole

goodreads.com/authorambernicole